THE
MAGICIAN'S
WORKSHOP

Also by Christopher Hansen and J.R. Fehr

*A Pirate's Guide t' th' Grammar of Story: A Creative
Writing Curriculum*
www.piratesguidestory.com

The Magician's Workshop, Volume One
www.oceea.com

Also by J.R. Fehr

Skyblind
www.jrfehr.com

THE
MAGICIAN'S
WORKSHOP

VOLUME TWO

Christopher Hansen and J.R. Fehr

Wondertale

The Magician's Workshop, Volume Two
Copyright © 2017 by Christopher R. Hansen and J.R. Fehr
MW logo copyright © 2016 by Christopher R. Hansen
Cover copyright © 2017 by Christopher R. Hansen

Published by Wondertale, California
www.thewondertale.com
www.oceea.com

ISBN-10: 1-945353-02-3
ISBN-13: 978-1-945353-02-4

MW logo design by Sej Baur
Book design by Jennifer Hansen
Dedication page design by Everett Ranni
Copy editing by Leigh Ann Robinson

FOR

THE COLORBLIND

Table of Contents

The Islands of O'Ceea

First Watch

Region 1

Cloudy Peaks

Four Kings

Golden Vale

Region 2

Swinging Vines

Summer Breeze

The Magician's Workshop

Region 3

Crystal Lake

Sunny Rock

Region 4

Oak Falls

Region 5

The Former Region 6

Welcome back to O'Ceea

Please note that this book, *Volume Two*, begins with Chapter 23. Do not panic! This is intentional. As *The Magician's Workshop* is one long story, told in several parts, the chapter numbers continue on from one volume to the next until the end of the series. We hope this doesn't fragdaggle you too much. Enjoy!

The Dinner at Nosy's

~Layauna~

Once, I ate at Nosy's—that pantsy fancy one on the Island of the Crystal Lake—and let me tell you, it was unlike anything I've ever experienced before. Inside those walls, I felt so secure. I'm positive that if a rainstorm ever flooded O'Ceea again, that restaurant would still be floatin' on the rising waters, keepin' all us safe. It's true what they say, Nosy's really knows what we needs. It's too bad our ancestors didn't have one.

—Master Galardo is a Grain, *Commoners Worth Quoting*

Layauna is-a Wind felt her stomach churn as she rode with her grandfather, Eyan is-a Bolt, in his luxurious palanquin. Despite the comfort of the cushioned seating, she hated riding in it. It felt wrong to sit in something so big that eight men were required to carry it. *I'm perfectly able to walk.* But her grandfather insisted on using it whenever they went someplace where his reputation had to be maintained. *Which is practically everywhere.*

"Cycle rickshaws are for commoners," Grandfather Eyan had told her after she'd suggested the alternative method of travel. "You'll be a magician one day, and as such, you'll come to find it's quite important to set yourself apart. We do things like this to honor our good name as much as for our privacy."

Layauna didn't understand how that was true. *There's absolutely nothing private about riding in a palanquin. Everyone notices it*. But she had decided it was best to just get inside and not argue about it.

As soon as she had climbed into the dark, cramped wooden box, a wave of panic flooded her. *Stop it. You can't let your emotions take over. There can't be any mistakes tonight,* she had firmly told herself. Although Grandfather seemed confident there wouldn't be any problems, Layauna couldn't shake the feeling that something horrible was going to happen—that she would make happen—and so she now asked, "Are you really sure I'm ready? I mean, are you absolutely sure?"

"Your trainers have assured me you've made great progress in the last ten weeks, Dearling," Grandfather stated. "If they've assessed you correctly, there will be no problem."

What if they're wrong? Layauna felt far from ready. But she detected something in her grandfather's voice that suggested he himself believed she could do this, and that encouraged her. *It would be incredible if I actually was ready.* Her spirits rose at the thought of being able to control her projections.

But can I control them where Grandfather is taking me? "Does it really have to be at Nosy's, though?" she asked.

"We've gone over this, Layauna. This is where it happened. It's time we return."

Seven years ago. Our last holiday meal with Father.

"You want to get over that trauma, right?" he asked.

Layauna nodded. She wanted that—and more. She wanted to fix everything she'd done wrong. What had happened at Nosy's was one of those things, and she wanted to erase it from her long list of mistakes. *But my unconscious projections are still so powerful—more powerful than me.* "What if Blaze appears?"

"Then you'll have an opportunity to exercise your authority over the projections that come out of you."

He makes that sound so easy.

This was to be a special meal for their family. Mother had called a meeting because she had something important to share—in person. Layauna tried not to give in to her foolish dreams that it would be some bit of positive news about her father. She knew she should push these fantasies away, but the harder she tried, the more they lingered. *Maybe she's found him. Maybe he wants to return.* The thought of a reunion with her father gave her even more reason to work on controlling her projections.

This gathering was significant for another reason, too. Although she'd seen her mother and brother a few times a year, this would be the first time all four of them would be together in one room since her hell-dog, Blaze, bit the head off of her grandfather's projected knight three years ago. He never brought that up, but Layauna still felt tremendously guilty and was desperate to find some way to make up for it. *If I can do this, it's bound to help. I just have to survive one meal. At the fanciest restaurant. On one of the nicest islands in all of O'Ceea. Without any monsters coming out of me.* Layauna took a deep breath. *I can do this.*

. . . I don't know. Can I?

Nosy's was one of the classiest and most expensive eating establishments anywhere. Its fame came from its unrivalled ability to mix taste and smell projections with real food, and because of this, a simple meal for one person could easily exceed the number of gryns the average rower earned for laboring an entire day. Despite the cost, it seemed to Layauna that everyone—even the commoners carrying them there in the palanquin—desired the opportunity to experience these sensations, to sit among the elite, and to brag about the experience to others.

Only my Grandfather can project better, she thought, remembering that over half the items on the menu were based on projections he had created and licensed to them.

But right now they weren't being carried to just any Nosy's. This was the one located on the Island of the Crystal Lake. It was, by far, the most prestigious restaurant in the region. When Layauna was young, Grandfather Eyan had brought her and her family here four times a year. Her father wasn't ever invited, though. He only ever came to their annual Ancestors Day meal. That is, until her incident. After that, they had stopped coming here altogether.

You need to stop thinking about this, Layauna told herself. She slid open the small window on her right and stared out at the clusters of shops that surrounded the sparkling blue lake that gave this island its name. The sun had set, the Violet watch had just begun, and many of the shop owners were projecting sky lanterns outside their stores for illumination during the upcoming nightmarks.

"Grandfather?"

"Yes, Dearling."

"Is it really true that this lake has infinite Power to dissolve any projection?"

"I don't know if it's infinite, but the water has been able to dissolve everything, so far."

"And . . ." Layauna hesitated. "Is that really because of Tav?"

"That's the traditional belief, and Tavites still claim such things," Grandfather said with a sigh. "They also assert that the Staff of Light was originally a projection, and that Tav is a god and still lives—somewhere, they never say where. Legends and myths give many people comfort."

"Do you believe any of it?"

"Tav certainly was a real person, there's no doubt of that. And I do believe he was unjustly put to death under the barbaric laws commonly observed at that time. Though I suspect his death was in fact an accident. The concoctions they used for prohibitions back then were far more dangerous than those used today.

"But whether he did any of the miraculous things people have claimed . . . I don't know. If he really was able to make projections real, why hasn't anyone after him been able to figure out how to do it? Lots of people have tried—exceptionally hard. But if someone did finally manage to do it, they certainly would be a god, wouldn't they?"

"Oh, I guess so," Layauna said, then added, "but, if Tav didn't do it, then how does the lake have Power?"

"No one knows for sure. That's why it's one of the Eight Enigmas. Most theories posit that there's something unique to the structure of its water. Although water makes up virtually all of O'Ceea, there's actually a lot we don't know about it. But enough questions. We're almost there."

At this, Layauna's stomach churned. *Ah! I feel like I've got a million frogs in my gut.* She shut her eyes and tried to slow her breathing as her trainers had taught her to do. It helped, but the relief was only temporary. For as soon as she opened her eyes, she caught sight of Nosy's through the little window.

This restaurant was unique among all the touristy buildings placed along the shore of the lake. Half of the restaurant was built on land, and the other half jutted out past the waterline and over the lake. Through the clever use of projections, it appeared to be weightless and seemed to be hovering—unburdened—just above the surface of the water. *Weightless and free. I wonder if I'll ever feel like that?*

✳   ✳   ✳

Once Layauna was let out of the palanquin, Grandfather led her to the giant, platinum doors of Nosy's and waited as two men, dressed all in white, pulled them open. Layauna gasped as she followed her grandfather into the Hall of Heroes. *This is even more magnificent than I remember!* From floor to ceiling, the walls were filled with small, rounded niches. Each contained a different and incredibly detailed projected image of a famous customer. Nosy's attracted the most distinguished guests, so a tradition emerged long ago to capture projections of them enjoying their meals; thus every Nosy's had a hall like this dedicated to those who'd come before.

Layauna's eyes grew wide as she peered in at the various hollows in the wall. "Wow! This one has Magician Agatha was-a Cloud. And over there is Mage Dirkmere is-a Flash! And look! There's Mala!" Layauna couldn't believe it. She hadn't seen her best friend for over three years.

"Yes. Mala and her father, Magician Philean is-a Moss."

Her stepfather, you mean. "Oh. And look! There's Master Greydyn. I remember this projection of him from the last time I came here!"

She was nine when her mother pointed out this projection of the Master Magician. Back then, he was the only famous person she recognized. Now, after three years of training, she could identify most of the faces and could discuss at length what made each person great.

And so Layauna went from nook to nook, describing endless details about the people she saw in each. A smile formed on Grandfather's face and his eyes twinkled as he watched her. *Good! He's pleased with all I know.*

Layauna found herself captivated by the intricate details in each one. *The level of Kingdom in these projections is incredible.* It was almost like looking through little portals into different periods of time. "And look! There you are, Grandfather." She pointed to a large projection right in the center of the wall. "You look so young. Is that what you really looked like back then?"

"Indeed, I've aged a lot, haven't I? I'm surprised you could even identify me."

"It's always easy to identify a Bolt."

"That's true. You're right," he said with a confident voice.

Yes, this is going well. I might be able to survive tonight after all.

After spending a bit more time admiring the heroes, they moved on to the restaurant. At the end of the hall two more men dressed in white opened another set of gigantic doors and invited them inside.

"Magician Eyan is-a Bolt!" A short, stocky man Layauna assumed was the maître d' came running over. "What a delightful surprise! We had no idea you were coming this evening. How wonderful!"

As soon as her grandfather's name was spoken, she sensed the eyes of several diners in the restaurant turn to them. Feeling quite uncomfortable, Layauna pretended to be distracted by the numerous waterless aquariums spread throughout the room, each filled with exotic sea creature projections.

"Nice to see you again, Kent," Grandfather said. "I'd like you to meet my granddaughter, Layauna."

"A pleasure." The maître d' bowed his head respectfully. "Is it just the two of you dining this evening?"

"There will be four of us. The others will be arriving soon."

"How wonderful. Now, please give me one moment while I prepare your place." Suddenly, four identical looking women were at his side. "Please clear the promontory. One table, for four."

Layauna watched the four women cut a straight line through the center of the restaurant to its most exclusive section, the promontory. Like a balcony, it jutted out over the water and was surrounded on three sides by spherical walls of solid glass, presenting those who dined here with an unobstructed panoramic view of the lake. To make it even more exclusive, the promontory was raised two steps higher than the rest of the dining area so that it was effortless for the other guests to observe those who sat here.

There were currently four tables on the promontory, each one occupied. Layauna watched as the four women went up to the tables. After a few words she couldn't hear, the diners became visibly angry. After a few more words, they turned and looked toward her and her grandfather and the anger on their faces melted away. Now aware of who was displacing them, the four parties got up and appeared happy to be led to other, less distinguished tables.

Servants rushed in, cleaned the area, and rearranged the configuration. When they finished, a fresh table for four was all that remained.

"I'm so sorry to keep you waiting. Your place is now ready. It would be my honor if you followed me," the maître d' said, and he led them to their table.

Layauna tried her best to keep her back straight and to sit poised and confident—like she had observed the famous ladies do in the Hall of Heroes. She was fully aware that every eye in the restaurant was stealing secret glances up at them. *Why do we have to be so visible? I'd rather eat all boxed up in that awful palanquin. If anything goes wrong here, everyone will know it's me.* She looked to Grandfather and said, "I feel like we're sitting in a giant fishbowl."

"Indeed, we are the most exotic fish here."

Now more than ever, Layauna knew coming here was a bad idea. *There is a fortune of taste and smell projections stored in the kitchen. The guests are all wearing expensive designer clothes. Then there are all the projections in the Hall of Heroes . . . and Grandfather's reputation! All of that could be wiped out in an instant if I lose control and project a monster.*

"Magicians are always being observed," her grandfather continued. "That's why it's so important to learn how to maintain a graceful presence in all circumstances."

She nodded and tried to distract herself by looking out the windows at the fabulous view. In the center of the lake was a small landmass originally known as Seagull Island. There was nothing special about it, but it took on great significance back when a magician decided it would be a wonderful location to project a colorful water fountain show. Thereafter, it was known as the Island of the Brilliant Rain.

All around the island were little projected cannons that hovered a few inches above the surface of the lake, which shot colorful projected water anywhere from ten to fifty feet in the air. The cannons went off at different intervals, creating a pleasing pattern synchronized to the rhythm of various songs. It was a spectacle that had always captivated Layauna's attention when she came here as a child. Watching it again, after all these years, helped calm her. *It'll be okay. I've got nothing to worry about.*

And then she heard her mother's voice echoing through the restaurant. "We're meeting my father and daughter here."

Mom, please. You're talking too loud. As Layauna's back was to the entrance, she had to turn completely around to see them. Her mother and brother stood next to the two doormen, who were waving their hands around them. One transformed the gold necklace on Mother into a string of white pearls.

"I'm sorry, Mistress Dawyn," the doorman said. "Our guests stopped wearing gold necklaces years ago."

The other doorman completely changed all the projections her brother wore, despite his complaints. "Aw, I hate wearing stuffy clothes like this. Tunic suits are so drench."

"This is so awkward," Layauna said under her breath. "Why is the doorman re-dressing them?"

"Nosy's has a very strict dress code," Grandfather stated plainly. "You've forgotten what it's like not to have a personal tailor."

He's right, Layauna thought as she twiddled her fingers nervously on the table. The master seamstress Marmalala—whose brand of clothing was known everywhere and cost several lykes—had personally projected a shimmering blue gown on Layauna earlier that evening.

We're all about to be united—over a meal!—in the exact same place I threw up all over everything seven years ago. Layauna noticed that her grandfather was looking at her twiddling fingers with a critical eye. His gaze shot through her like a knife. She slid her hands into her lap and stared out the window.

And that's when she spotted him. Standing on the little island in the lake was none other than her two-headed hell-dog, Blaze.

Layauna's eyes grew wide with fear. *No! No! NO!* She couldn't breathe. Her worst nightmare was about to come true, and her mother and brother hadn't even sat down yet. She took in a deep breath—nice and slow—like she had been instructed to do in situations like this. Any moment now, Blaze would charge over to them, leap on top of their table, bare his bloody fangs, and tear into her family—right in front of the whole restaurant!

But he didn't move.

He just stayed on the island, surrounded by the explosions of light and color. *Maybe he likes the fountain show? Good. Just stay on the island and enjoy the pretty colors, you stupid mutt, and everything will be all right.*

*　　　*　　　*

Layauna stood up right away when her mother and brother arrived at the table, and she bowed as tradition dictated.

"It's so good to see you again," Mother said, her voice quivering with emotion. It looked like she wanted to reach out and hug Layauna.

Oh, please don't. We don't want to embarrass Grandfather. Thankfully, Mother held back and bowed instead. "I've missed you, too," Layauna replied.

They joined the table, Sorgan next to Layauna facing the lake and her mother beside her grandfather facing the dining room.

"It's been a long time since I last ate here," Mother said as she skimmed through the menu. "A lot has changed."

The family engaged in light chit-chat about their respective journeys here, to the Island of the Crystal Lake. This island was located in Region 3, between her grandfather's present home on the Island of the Summer Breeze and his ancestral home on the Island of the Oak Falls, where Layauna's mother and brother still lived.

Layauna tried to stay focused, but she kept peering out the window to keep an eye on Blaze. Although he seemed to be content where he was, she knew that could change at any moment.

"Do you all know what you're ordering?" Grandfather asked after the waiter came over and announced the specials for the evening.

"I want whatever has the most Giggle-Grease," Sorgan announced, "and Tunky is-a Crack said I had to try the Punchy-Munchies."

"Yes, let's start with a basket of mild Punchy-Munchies for the table," Grandfather ordered, "followed by one Tickle-Me-Tuna Smellwich from the children's menu—go light on the Giggle-Grease."

"Aaaaw," Sorgan moaned in disappointment. "The giggles are the only thing good about going to places like this."

"And for you, Dearling?"

"Well, I—" Both Layauna and her mother started to speak at the same time. *That's embarrassing.* "Sorry, you go ahead, Mother."

"I can't decide between the Bouquet of Beef Salad Scrambler with Particularly Pungent Pickles or the Redolent Raspberry Rainmaker. Father, what would you recommend?"

Those were two of Grandfather's creations and were listed on the "top sellers" portion of the menu.

"Both are fine options, but you can never go wrong with the Yellow Salmon Sniffler."

"Oh, yes, of course! I've forgotten how much I love that," her mother said.

Layauna didn't need to ask for advice; she knew exactly what to order. "Red Bean Whiffles with bacon syrup, please, and a glass of freshly ground and brewed pako juice."

"A most excellent choice, young mistress. The Red Bean Whiffles have recently become very popular," the waiter said. "And Magician Eyan, I must say, it's a great honor to serve you. I can't imagine how you dream up these flavor combinations, but I can tell you I've been serving them for years, and everyone absolutely loves them—myself included."

"Well, I'm touched. Truly touched," Grandfather said. "There's nothing better than knowing one's efforts have contributed to making the islands a better place. Thank you so much for sharing that with me."

So that's how you handle fans.

When the waiter left, Grandfather pulled out four pieces of namra root. The practice of eating namra before a fine meal was unique to her grandfather and his family; no one else in the restaurant would ever dream of eating such a noxious-tasting substance here.

At the sight of the root, Layauna felt her nervousness surge. It was at this point of the meal, so many years earlier, that she had projected the wrong flavor onto her piece and, after tasting it, had thrown up.

She looked out the window and was pleased to see that Blaze was still behaving. Then, without giving it much thought, she plopped the root into her mouth. She couldn't yet say she liked it, but she definitely didn't find it as disgusting as she once had.

When the waiter returned with the Punchy-Munchies, he also informed Grandfather that an important voice cube had just been delivered for him. Grandfather excused himself from the table. As soon as he was gone, Layauna turned to her brother and said, "Sorgan, you can't order Giggle-Grease in a place like this."

"Ha! I already did." Sorgan shoved a handful of Munchies into his mouth and, while chewing, added, "No, actually Grandfather ordered it for me. So it must have been fine. Ha again!"

"He just did that to avoid making a scene. Sometimes I think you must have been adopted. Why don't you ever act properly?"

"I dunno," Sorgan shrugged. "You're the one who makes unconscious projections of hell-beasts. That's not proper."

"I don't do that anymore," Layauna said.

"I hope not! It'd be embarrassing if one burst out of you here. Rawr-rawr-rawr!" Sorgan made the sound of a dog barking.

"That won't happen, okay! Now drop it."

"I bet you were the one who was really adopted. I bet your real name is Layauna is-a Butt."

"Oh, how funny. You're such a little kid."

"Wow!" Sorgan snapped back. "You've really changed. I can see it now. You're so grown up and mature in your fancy blue dress."

"Yup, I am. And you haven't changed at all," Layauna retorted.

"Children! No fighting," their mother scolded. "Sorgan's right. I don't want anything to trigger . . . well, you know."

Great, Mom's still worried about what will come out of me. Well, she should be. Outside, Blaze was now standing right at the shoreline, looking her direction. He crouched down, as if preparing to jump. *Oh, no!*

Just before he sprang into the lake, he hesitated. *Good dog.*

"So! Isn't this place amazing?" Mother asked in an attempt to lighten the mood. "I came here all the time when I was young."

"All the time? I would have hated it," Sorgan said.

Ignoring him, Mother continued, "I have so many lovely memories of things that took place in this very spot, like our last meal here—that was one of my favorites."

How could that be true? Layauna thought as she watched Blaze overcome his fear and jump into the water. She expected him to start to swim, but instead the hell-dog dissolved into nothingness the moment it touched the water. *Oh, it really does work!* Layauna had forgotten about the Power in the lake. *What was I so worried about? Grandfather must have known that this would happen!*

With Blaze gone, Layauna felt empowered to ask about something she'd often wondered about but was always too scared to bring up. "Why didn't Grandfather ever invite Father here?"

"What do you mean?" her mother answered. "He always came to our Ancestors Day meals."

"I know, but Grandfather had to invite him to holidays. I'm talking about all the other times. Why didn't he ever get invited then? I know he liked eating here."

"I suppose your grandfather didn't feel comfortable bringing a Wind into Nosy's. He has a certain reputation to uphold, after all."

"That's a dredge reason," Sorgan grumbled.

"Sorgan! Come on. You can't say stuff like that here," Layauna warned in a hushed voice.

"Why not? It's true. Grandfather doesn't even order food with projections on it. He gets the same stupid stuff everyplace he goes: A glass of some stupid-sounding wine, plain stupid black rice, and a bowl of stupid raw mushrooms. That's dredge-dredge-dredge."

Grandfather doesn't need to pay for projected flavors when he can make anything from the menu just as good. "It's better than Giggle-Grease," Layauna shot back.

As she said this, Blaze reappeared on the small island. Only this time, he was angry. Blaze ran wildly along the shore, searching for some way off that didn't involve jumping into the water.

"Stop it. This is the last time I'm going to tell you," their mother commanded.

She's right. All that this has done is cause Blaze to come back, and now he's upset. Layauna closed her eyes and took in deep breaths.

"So," her mother said after an awkward moment of silence, "how have you been, Layauna? I've heard great things about your training."

"Um. Yeah."

"Are you going to live at Grandfather's mansion after you get your Color collar?" Sorgan asked.

"Uh, I guess. I won't be there much, though. Most of the time I'll be training with a team and competing. I expect it'll be sort of the same as what I've been doing the past few years."

"Whatever. It's so cake that you get to live there!" Sorgan exclaimed. "Grandfather has so much mega stuff."

"Yeah, it's really nice. I always feel so good when I'm there."

Sorgan stopped slurping his drink—a thick, glowing green mixture called a Short-Snort—and paused, as if lost in thought. "Do you ever feel out of place? I mean . . . I always feel good when I'm there too, but I also feel . . . I don't know . . . like I don't belong there."

Of course. Grandfather's just putting up with you. To fit in you have to find some way to impress him, haven't you figured that out yet? Look at Mom. Everything she does is driven by the desire to please him. But she didn't say anything out loud. No one said anything for a long time.

All three of them knew what it felt like to not belong.

Suddenly, Blaze found a way off the island. Layauna watched as he spotted a ring of giant stones not far from the shore of his little prison and effortlessly leapt over to them.

Go back! Go! Back! Layauna commanded, but Blaze didn't obey. When the two-headed hell-dog sprang over to a second stone—one step closer to land—Layauna realized there was an entire path of them that led from the island all the way to shore. A couple dozen jumps and he would reach them.

She froze. *What do I do? What do I do!?*

Her mother, with her back to the lake, remained completely oblivious to the oncoming danger. "I almost forgot," she said cheerfully, breaking the silence. She pulled out a small brown sack and handed it to Layauna.

Layauna didn't want to look, but something about it caught her attention. "What is it?"

"It's nothing to be scared of. Look inside." The sack contained several little black boxes. "Voice cubes from your friends. They asked me to bring them to you. Everyone back on Oak Falls misses you a lot."

It had been so long since she'd seen any of her friends, and she wasn't sure if they even remembered her anymore. *But they do. They do still care about me.* As she looked at the cubes, she felt her confidence return. All at once, she knew what to do with Blaze.

With her hands hidden under the table, Layauna wiggled her fingers to project a pile of raw, bloody steaks onto a rock on the small island—just as she'd done before with the Master Magician.

To her great relief, it worked; Blaze stopped on the third stone, sniffed the air with his two ugly noses, and turned back.

Good. Go eat your steaks and leave us alone, she thought as she stared into the bag, ecstatic over all the voice cubes she saw inside. *I can't wait to listen to these!*

The Announcement

~Layauna~

*At the heart of every story is a problem. This can be all sorts of
things, and—depending on the Grand Projection—it might not
even look like a problem at all to some characters. But, whatever it
is, it always needs to be solved before the story can end, so this is
what the hero sets out to accomplish.*

> —Magician Tophious was-a Lamp, *25 Years in the Magician's
> Workshop: What I Learned About the Grand Story in Grand
> Projections*

Everything seemed to go well as the last bit of light faded
from O'Ceea. The beam of Violet went out, and the islands
passed into the darkness of first nightmark. Grandfather returned
to the table, their meal was served, and Layauna found that she
was able to eat without any frogs jumping around in her stomach.
This entire time, Blaze remained on the little island in the lake,
alternating between eating steaks and watching the fountain show.

The food truly is incredible here, Layauna thought as she
sipped her pako juice. Almost as soon as the bright blue liquid
touched her tongue, she felt her energy increase. They were all
in an agreeable mood by the time they were taking the final
bites of their meals, especially her little brother, though Layauna
suspected that was only because of the Giggle-Grease. *I don't
understand why Sorgan was complaining so much about coming.*

Look how happy he is now. He doesn't realize how privileged we are.

"I guess it's about time I explain to you all why I asked your grandfather to arrange this meeting," Mother said.

Okay. Time to find out if any of this is about Dad. Layauna tried to keep from getting excited, but it was hard. She'd waited for such a long time to hear any news about him.

"Something's happened that your grandfather and I are really excited about," her mother continued. "I've finally decided to do something I should have done a long time ago. You see, it's been quite a few years since your father left. And . . ."

As her mother spoke, Layauna noticed that Blaze had crouched low, the way he often did when he was growling. *Oh great. Please, just stay there.*

". . . well, I finally decided to take your grandfather up on his offer to return to the clan."

Return to the clan! Blaze started running in circles. *Does that mean what I think it does?* "Wait. What?" This was the last thing she'd expected. "You're a Bolt again?" Layauna asked.

Mother grinned. "That's right! We all are!"

Blaze was now running around the little island like a devil on fire. Layauna's heart raced. "We? I am too?"

"Of course," Grandfather said in a very matter-of-fact way. "It wouldn't make sense for your mother to return to the clan without her children."

"But I'm a Wind," Sorgan exclaimed. "I've always been a Wind."

Grandfather looked at Sorgan and said, "Not anymore."

I can't believe it! Layauna still had a bit of food left on her plate, but her appetite was gone. She locked her jaw to prevent herself from shouting all the things that raced through her mind. *It's not fair! They can't just make that decision for me. His name is all*

I have left of him. She caught sight of Blaze; he was racing toward them. He'd left the island and was already on the second stone!

She twiddled her fingers under the table and projected an enormous pile of raw meat on the island. But Blaze didn't care. She tried to increase the smell of the meat to lure him back, but not even one of his heads turned. He was determined to get to them. *I have to stop him, now!*

She projected a metal cage around the hell-dog. This sort of thing had never worked before, but she had to try. As she expected, Blaze snapped the metal bars to pieces and broke free. *I have to do something!* She dropped projected rocks onto the hell-dog, but they bounced off him like hail hitting armor. She projected a wall, but, of course, Blaze broke it down.

He leapt to the next stone.

Maybe I can dissolve him. She clenched her teeth and focused all her mental energy on throwing every bit of Power she could toward Blaze. But he didn't disappear. No matter how hard she strained, he didn't even flicker. He was now on the fourth stone.

"Layauna? You look white. Is everything okay?" her mother asked.

"I'm . . . I'm just . . . shocked." *What do I do? Singing has calmed him down before.* But she couldn't possibly project her dad's song right now; she was so full of turmoil that she couldn't even remember how it went. She felt like throwing up. *No, I can't let that happen again.*

She looked to Grandfather. *He must see what's going on. He thought I was ready, but I'm not. I'm clearly not.* She couldn't figure out the expression on his face as he leaned forward and said, "Dearling, trust me, this is good news. It is infinitely better to be a Bolt."

"I'm just . . ." she stammered as she saw Blaze reach the fifth stone. "I don't think I can do this."

"Of course you can. I've always seen you as a Bolt, and Bolts always come out on top."

Not me, not with this.

"Dearling," he said after a brief pause. "I see what's going on."

You do? You've seen Blaze?

"This is a serious matter," he continued. "And I fully expect you to make the right decision—I know you know what the right one is."

I do? Then, without much thought, she projected a fat little goblin on the next stepping-stone in front of Blaze. It was emerald green, wore black chainmail armor, and held a long, pointed spear. Her trainers had taught her how to project dozens of different monsters, each scary and powerful in its own way. Spear goblins had a lot of reach and were great at blocking narrow passageways, like this rock path across the lake. *Okay Blaze, if you're going to get to me, you'll have to go through my goblin guard first.*

Blaze vaulted to the sixth stone and landed right in front of the goblin. The goblin raised its spear and thrust it at Blaze a few times to keep him back. *Is anyone else seeing this?* Her mother and grandfather had their backs to the window and Sorgan's head was down. She tried to catch her grandfather's eye, but his face was turned away from her and toward the dining room. Although it was dark inside the restaurant, the lights from the Color fountain glowed brightly and illuminated the water outside. Blaze and the goblin were easy for Layauna to see. She looked around the restaurant. No one acted like anything was wrong; it appeared that no one had noticed. *So far.*

Grandfather continued, "History is filled with examples of all the great things that happen after someone takes on a better name. I know you know that."

The Bolt clan is one of the oldest and most honored in all of O'Ceea, and if I have to get a new name, Bolt is the one to have. She knew he was right. This was a common story. Her trainers had taken her to many re-projections of Grand Projections in which a character must change their name before they can become a hero.

But leaving the Wind clan still felt like it would be a betrayal to her father.

Stop it. You don't have time to worry about a stupid name. You have a much bigger problem. She watched one head of the hell-dog grab the goblin's spear in its mouth and snap it in half—*No!*—while the other head took a bite out of the goblin's neck—*No, no!* At this, the goblin slumped down to its knees, slid off the rock, and fell into the lake, where it was instantly dissolved by the crystal water. *No! No! No!*

"Now Dearling, I know this is going to be hard for you to hear, but you have to accept the truth," her grandfather said. "Your father left you. It's now time for you to leave him, too."

Without wasting a moment, Blaze thundered to the seventh stone. And the eighth. And the ninth. He was halfway to them now.

Stupid monster, leave me alone! Layauna wanted to cry out loud—so someone would hear and help—but she was sure that would only cause a panic and make things worse. Instead, she clenched her fists, and another spear goblin appeared to block Blaze. The two eyed each other suspiciously, then Blaze lunged at it. The fountain erupted in crimson, red, and violet as they battled.

Blaze made quick work of the goblin and moved on to the tenth stone. *The goblins aren't doing anything! I need a bigger barrier.* She projected a dozen dragonflies made of water. They were poorly fashioned and crude, but she didn't care about Kingdom right now. Her only focus was Power. The dragonflies swarmed around Blaze and shot tiny bursts of freezing cold water at him. But instead of dousing the hell-dog's flaming fur, as Layauna hoped, the water turned to steam.

Blaze jumped and snapped at the dragonflies. *Good. He's distracted.* Layauna projected four black warthogs with sharp, polished tusks to try to knock him into the crystal waters. *Maybe a pack of hell-hogs can stop my hell-dog. Please work. Please work.*

As she focused on the hell-hogs, Layauna suddenly realized this effort to solve her problem was risky in a different way. *People have to be seeing this.* Layauna was too scared to look around at the other diners. *Dragonflies and hell-hogs attract attention.* She hoped that everyone would just assume all her creatures were being projected for entertainment, a part of the fountain show. *They probably will, as long as Blaze doesn't get here, destroy several whispers worth of projections, and rip my grandfather's reputation to shreds.*

Layauna glanced at her brother. He hadn't noticed anything; he was busy making projections of his own. *He's upset, too.* He'd transformed the scraps of food on his plate into a battlefield, projecting little red and green knights who engaged in furious combat on and around the remaining bits of precious food that he clearly had no further desire to eat.

"Sorgan, don't play with your food," their mother said when she saw what he was doing. "This meal is expensive. Some people save for years to come here. I expect you to eat every last bite."

If Sorgan heard her, he gave no indication. Layauna felt for him and wanted to warn him, so she sent a private voice projection that said, "You should stop doing that."

"Why should I care what Mom thinks?" he projected back. "She doesn't care what we think!"

Grandfather Eyan leaned back in his seat and rolled his eyes. It was subtle, and if Layauna hadn't known him so well, she might not have noticed. *He doesn't respect Sorgan.* Even though her grandfather had never said anything against her brother, she sensed he'd always felt embarrassed by him.

Then it struck her. *Grandfather thinks he's the same as Dad!* Everything changed.

The dragonflies stopped their assault. Every single one of them turned in the air until they faced the restaurant. *No! No! No!* The hell-hogs no longer lunged at Blaze; instead, they also turned and started heading toward Nosy's, jumping over one another as they moved from stone to stone. There were many of them and their progress was slow, but they were clearly headed toward the restaurant.

Blaze did not wait for them to get out of his way. He leap-frogged over each one until he landed at the front. United together, he ushered his new army forward. They would have arrived there in a matter of moments but for two obstacles.

The first was that the stepping stones closer to shore were spaced farther apart, and thus each leap required greater effort from the beasts. The dragonflies could have been at the restaurant immediately, but they dared not advance in front of their two-headed leader. The second obstacle was the fountain. It kept shooting water into the air in unexpected places, forcing Layauna's monsters to be extra careful as they tried to avoid being hit and thus knocked into the lake.

But they'll be here soon. Layauna dug her fingernails into her hand. She longed for something she could use to puncture her heart and let all the pressure escape. She felt no love for Blaze right now, and the only time she'd ever been capable of dissolving him was after she—

A memory came back to her. *When I was with the Master Magician, he told me projections come from within us. These projections are me! The monsters are me!* As it had before, the thought unleashed a flood of emotions in Layauna. A thin veil was all that separated her from bursting into tears. *I can't break down. Not here. Not now. Magicians must maintain a graceful presence in all circumstances.*

Layauna fought to keep her feelings inside as she realized the truth of what the Master Magician had told her. *Blaze and the others, they're me. They're coming from me. Why? Think! If they're from me, why are they coming after me?* She gaped out the window as they drew closer and closer. *How can I stop them? Should I ask Grandfather for help?* She tilted her face toward him but turned away as soon as they made eye contact. *No, I can't. He brought me here to see if I can do this all by myself.*

And then she recognized something in Blaze's burning eyes. He had the look of the Crimson Blade.

Like that iconic character from *The Epics of the Cursed*, these monsters were hungry for blood. They wanted to take justice into their own hands. They would sacrifice themselves to defeat what they believed to be evil. She didn't stop to determine why they were angry, or if it was even her blood they were hungry for.

Layauna did the only thing she could think to do. She shut her eyes and imagined herself running out the front door of the restaurant. She imagined it as best as she could, trying to see as many details as possible about herself. She felt herself running down the grassy bank to the shore of the lake. She pictured herself leaping onto the stone path.

When she opened her eyes, she, to her great shock, saw it had worked. There, on a stone in the lake, stood a projected version of herself. With superhuman strength, she sprang to the next rock. *Whoa, the real me could never jump that far.*

She hurled herself onto the next rock, and stared straight at Blaze. The hell-dog snarled and snapped, but he did not attack. Instead, he waited patiently as one of the hell-hogs jumped over him and charged at her.

In a moment it was over. The projection of Layauna managed to catch the hell-hog by the tusks and—though it gored her in the shoulder—she overpowered it and threw it up at one of the dragonflies, knocking them both into a blast of violet water from the fountain. They tumbled into the lake and melted into nothingness.

Blaze watched as a second hell-hog hopped over him and lunged at her. The result was the same.

One by one, Layauna's projected self battled and defeated the monsters. But each hell-hog and dragonfly she vanquished inflicted her with wounds. By the time she caught the last dragonfly out of the air and splatted it against a rock, there was very little of her left. Her legs were torn to shreds, her face was burned and bloody, and her torso was full of so many gashes and holes that she looked like a deathwalker. She was a bludgeoned mess; if she hadn't been a projection, she would have died.

The battle caused excruciating emotional pain for the real Layauna, but she'd learned long ago how to cut herself off from these feelings. She watched herself be annihilated with the same sort of disconnection she always felt when she watched other people's projections battle in the Competitions.

When there were no other monsters left, Blaze pounced on top of her, knocking her onto her back. But it didn't matter; she knew what she needed to do. She wrapped her broken, mangled arms around the hell-dog and rolled off the rock and into the lake.

✳   ✳   ✳

Layauna snapped out of her trance as soon as the water snuffed the life out of her projections. Blaze was defeated! The projection of herself was destroyed, and she—the real she—was present again in the restaurant. Their waiter was there, standing right beside her, taking Mother's dessert order.

There was no sign of a single monster anywhere.

I . . . I can't believe that worked! I love this lake. I love it! I love it! She felt her heart flood with joy. Layauna wanted to jump up from the table and let out a victory cheer, but Nosy's was not the place for such outbursts. So she let out the breath she'd been holding and allowed a deep smile to replace the previously lifeless expression.

"What are you so happy about?" Sorgan asked when he noticed how euphoric she was.

"Dessert!" she said. "I'd like a Blood Orange Brain Buster, please." It was the most decadent item on the menu.

"Excellent," their waiter said.

Grandfather was right. I was able to keep the monsters away! He was right about me. I should never have doubted him. When the waiter was gone, Layauna spun in her seat and looked straight at her brother. "Sorgan, I know it feels wrong to change names. But Grandfather knows what's best for us."

"Maybe," Sorgan mumbled.

Layauna looked at Grandfather and smiled. "He's done nothing but take good care of us all these years. He's paid for everything we've needed. Without him, I don't know where we'd be."

"Yeah, I guess you're right."

"Grandfather, I'd be proud to become a Bolt—if you'll have me, that is."

"Of course," Grandfather said.

Layauna added, "I want things to be different."

"I do too," he agreed. "I know things have been hard, but everything ought to start getting better for you now."

Sorgan thought about that for a moment. As he took a bite of the food on his plate he said, "I guess Sorgan is-a Bolt sounds more mega than Sorgan is-a Wind."

"Without question." Grandfather smiled.

When Layauna's dessert arrived, even Grandfather couldn't refrain from taking several bites of it for himself.

✳   ✳   ✳

As they stood on the dock and waved good-bye to her mother and brother sailing away on the overnight ferry, Layauna looked up at her grandfather and said, "I . . . need to tell you something. I almost had an incident this evening."

"Oh?" Grandfather replied without breaking eye contact with the ferry.

"Blaze was coming to attack us while we ate, but I managed to destroy him."

"Really?" There was a certain lilt to his voice that made her think he wasn't surprised at all.

"Did you . . . did you know?"

"Yes. I knew," he said after a short pause. "Good work."

"But how? Your back was turned to the water the whole time."

"I've been watching you make unconscious projections for three years now, and I know the look on your face when you're about to be devoured."

Layauna sagged her shoulders. *He knew. Maybe he was helping me then.* That projection of herself had a lot more Power than she imagined she was capable of. "Oh."

"Dearling, you don't need to look so sad. You did wonderfully, as I knew you would."

"But, did you . . . I mean . . . did I do everything on my own? I thought I did."

"Yes, you were in total control. I did nothing to help you."

She found that hard to believe. "Nothing?"

"It was all you." Grandfather let out a quiet, gentle laugh. "Don't think I wasn't concerned. I was fully ready to dissolve anything that got off the lake. But you handled yourself like a true magician. You never lost your grace. I am most impressed, Layauna is-a Bolt."

She felt her confidence return under the warmth of her grandfather's smile. *Layauna is-a Bolt. I'm starting to like the sound of that.*

The Sense

~Aaro~

I got a Color! I got a Color!
Not like my brother!
I got a Color!
—Children's song

Aaro is-a Tree didn't understand why he felt compelled to get on this boat in the dark of night. He didn't have any clear reason to go where it was sailing; in fact, he'd really rather not be going there at all.

"Are you sure it's a good idea to come with me to the Festival?" asked Malroy is-a Shield. "You hate the Color Ceremony."

"I don't hate it. I hate what it does to kids," Aaro answered as he stepped off the wooden dock and onto Malroy's sailboat, a small cutter that looked to be twice as old as the two men were. To the inexperienced eye, this boat did not appear to be capable of staying afloat. But Aaro and Malroy were best friends, and Aaro knew to look beyond surface appearances with him. Masterfully crafted projections covered the hull of this otherwise pristine vessel, creating the illusion that it was worn and weathered with age. Achieving such a look and feel was a real art—one that Malroy had spent years perfecting.

"You know I won't complain," Malroy said as he untied the final line that held his boat to the dock. "I'm grateful for the company."

"Yeah, well, I figured someone should come along to keep you awake," Aaro said with a smile. "I know how much you love to take extra-long Cyan naps."

"Oh yes. Worn out old men like me—with grandsons about to stand before a puller—can always use a good long nap," Malroy said in a playful way. "But everyone knows it's really you who loves the Cyan watch."

It was true. *Cyan is such a pleasant time of day.* With almost everyone asleep and no one needing anything from him, it was an island of peace in the middle of the afternoon when he could focus on the most important things. "It's one of my favorite times to spend with Täv," Aaro said. "Maybe I should start extending it into the Blue watch, like you 'old men' so often do."

"Why not? It's a lovely perk of seniority, and you are a senior trainer now," Malroy said with a wink.

"Yes, thank you for the reminder. Fifty-three years old and still working with kids," Aaro said with a laugh. "As for this trip, have you decided how long we're going to be gone?"

"Just the first night. I don't see any reason to attend the others. But I have no idea what will happen, so I can't be sure," Malroy said as he pushed away from the dock.

"Are you nervous?"

"Of course," Malroy admitted. "I've been preparing for this for over seven years."

"I imagine he has too," Aaro said.

"Yeah. Jade will have made sure of that," Malroy said. He took the helm of his cutter, which he had fondly named *My Better Half,* and navigated out of the marina.

Aaro felt an ache in his heart whenever he left this place. The Island of the Cloudy Peaks had become more like home to him than any other place he'd ever lived. Over the past nine years, the community here had become his family. He gave one last look over his shoulder at the cozy little harbor town, which was nestled between two steep, tall mountains and set amidst a grove of ancient mango trees that were covered in snowy projections.

As he looked back, he saw that one of his students was awake. The student hummed and sang as he skipped down to the end of the dock. They were far away now, but Aaro knew exactly who it was: Yamyar is-a Ray. There was something about seeing Yamyar there, waving with both of his arms outstretched, that brought peace to Aaro.

Then a strong, squeezy feeling embraced him. He knew this sensation well. Yamyar was projecting one of his unique hugs. *Thank you. I needed that. Take care of him while I'm away.* Aaro waved back. As soon as he did, the young man leapt up into the air and yelled so loudly that his voice rang out across the water, "BYE BYE! SEE YOU SOON! BYE BYE BYE!"

"Sweet kid," Malroy said as he projected several sky lanterns around the perimeter of the boat. The orange light of the lanterns reflected off the deep indigo water and bathed the cutter in a warm, calming glow. "We could still go back and get him. You know how much he wanted to go with the others on the ferry yesterday."

"No, it was the right decision. I know he wants to see his cousin stand before the puller, but the Festival wouldn't be a good place for him," Aaro said. He turned around to face the front of the boat and look out at the dark, open ocean before them. "I suppose we can arrange for him to go and visit his relatives after the Ceremony."

They agreed to take turns keeping watch as they sailed across the sea. One took the helm while the other slept. Malroy was fond of sailing at night, so Aaro went below first. They couldn't hear the frequencies projected by the nightmarkers on the open sea, so it was impossible to know how long he slept and what nightmark they were in. He woke sometime later.

Malroy gave Aaro the helm and went into the cabin to sleep. As the boat passed the Island of the Silver Thorn, Aaro could see a faint light in the distance, coming from the glowing silvery-gold symbol of four crowns that floated above a far-off island.

Sometime later, Aaro saw the first Crimson beam of light shoot into the sky. Then, like a slow-moving wave, Crimson went up from the watchtowers of every island in sight. The first beams came from the east, and he watched the light spread to the west, signaling the end of final nightmark and announcing to everyone awake that a new day had begun.

We were dead, in darkness, when there came a glimmer of light.

*   *   *

Malroy wasn't asleep long; he came up just as the early morning sun appeared over the horizon. As its rays broke across the water, bright Red beams of light shot up into the sky from the watchtowers, replacing the Crimson lights and marking the top of the Red watch.

"Woo! I love seeing time change on the ocean!" Malroy said with wide open, expectant eyes as he chewed on a crab cake. The sky was much lighter now, and Aaro smiled when he saw that Malroy's current look of wonder had temporarily erased the creases of worry that normally framed his friend's eyes.

"So what's your plan when we get there? Are you just going to wander around until you see something that triggers the ol' mysterious 'ah-ha' button in you?"

"Maybe," Aaro answered as Malroy took back control of the helm again. "I don't know yet. As of now, there is no plan."

"Right. But you have a 'sense' that you should be there."

"It's not really a sense," Aaro said. He tried to explain the feeling that had been gnawing at him for days. "It doesn't affect any of my actual senses."

"Lingering dream projection?"

"No. It's more solid than that. And it hasn't gone away."

"Have you tried doing a soul story?" Malroy asked.

"I have, but I wasn't able to decipher it," Aaro admitted.

"Huh. And so you think this is Täv directing you?"

"I never said that."

Malroy grinned. "But you still think it."

"I wouldn't be going if I didn't suspect something. Truthfully, what I've been feeling has me puzzled. You know how I don't like it when people use Täv to justify their actions or say things like 'it was meant to be.' But, something about this feels exactly like that."

"I find it usually takes me years of hindsight before I can even hope to know if something was just another one of my foolish ideas or anything beyond myself," Malroy said. "Take my choice to leave Four Kings. That was eight years ago and I still don't know if it was wise or not."

"I have a suspicion you'll know soon."

"Anyway, whether this is Täv or just some crazy notion of yours, it's my honor to ferry you on this most secret of missions. You'll need a disguise, of course. Every spy needs one."

"No thanks," Aaro replied. "Unlike you, I've got no good reason to hide."

"Nonsense! Your Green, Cyan, and Blue are more than enough reason."

Aaro laughed. "Good thing I'm not going to be wearing my collar."

"People are still going to recognize you. Everyone knows who you are."

"They did, once. People forget."

"No one forgets a Three Color Mage, and they definitely haven't forgotten the man who declined a spot in the Workshop, forsook fame and fortune, and went off to train a motley collection of mages and void pulls. People remember that."

Aaro looked at him and said, "You know I didn't turn down a spot for that reason."

"Sure I do. I'm just messing with you. I know how much you love encouraging people to make their own projections. I'll never forget the look of delight that came over your face when you saw all those bouncing orange balls pouring out of Anastalia."

Aaro's face lit up at the memory. "Wasn't that amazing! She hadn't made a single projection in decades and then, in a heartbeat, she filled her house with them."

"You were so pleased when you saw the balls spill out her window and roll into town," Malroy said.

"Of course. Remember their Glory? You dove right into them."

Malroy grinned. "What a great day! My heart felt so light afterward."

"It was truly a wonder." Aaro would never forget watching Malroy fling himself onto the floor at the seventy-one-year-old woman's home, laughing as the marble-sized balls bounced all over him. Then he grew sober. "How long did she manage to hold on to the magic after that?"

"Not long. She was pretty sick. I don't think it was more than two weeks before she was cut off." Malroy turned his gaze to the sea.

After a long, uncomfortable silence, Aaro said, "What's bothering you?"

"I'm just thinking about Flint."

"Oh."

"Come on, let me disguise you," Malroy said abruptly.

"What?"

"I'm changing the subject. Even if you don't wear your collar, you're going to stand out, and I know how much you hate that."

"That's true." Aaro could afford a lot more, but he chose to live as a simple man. He owned an ordinary home and lived a quiet life on the Island of the Cloudy Peaks. While he appreciated the designs of elaborate clothing projections, he preferred to dress in a plain white shirt and a pair of beige pants. This was unique for a senior trainer and even more so for someone of his talent.

"People are going to be constantly hassling you to train their kids once they see you," Malroy insisted.

"I'll take the risk."

"All right, suit yourself," Malroy said with a sigh.

"I'll just tell them 'the door is always open,' like I always do."

"Hey, I think you should use that 'Color, no Color' line from that one Glimmering. 'Come to the Island of the Cloudy Peaks where all are welcome to train. Color, no Color.' Maybe the tides are turning and the next Grand Projection will finally make what you're doing fashionable," Malroy said with a laugh.

"That would be something, but I doubt that's what Greydyn has in mind. Even still, it could be a good message. Hopefully it'll encourage a few people to reconsider what Color really is," Aaro said. He began to think about all of the kids who would be named void tonight. Of all the things that pained him about the Festival of Stars, the Color Ceremony was the hardest for him. *It's too much pressure for children. How can they be themselves when their whole identity is wrapped up in obtaining a ribbon of Color?*

But it was worse than that. So much of what happened at the Color Ceremony was a deception. Aaro knew the truth about Color, and it pained him to see how many people based so much of their lives upon a lie. *So many kids are hurt every year. Please, may they one day be comforted.*

"You have that look in your eyes again," Malroy observed.

"What look?"

"The one that says you're wondering if you should have come."

"Oh," Aaro said. "I suppose I am."

"You still feel that puzzling sense?"

Aaro nodded. He was certainly stirred up by something.

"Want to try and sort it out? We could do a soul story together," Malroy offered.

"Right now?"

"Why not? There's nothing like a good soul story to get you going in the morning! That, and a swig of pako!" Malroy said with a laugh as he reached into a hidden compartment by the wheel and pulled out two bottles of the energizing drink.

Thank you for the support of this friend. Aaro began to project a story up into the sky above them. It was a new story—unique to him—and when he started, he didn't have any idea what it was about or how it would end. He simply cast the projections out of himself without thinking too much and allowed them to be whatever they would be. This was a soul story after all, not a Grand Projection. It didn't need to look good, or even make sense. It was a part of him—a little piece of his soul—that emerged in the form of a brief story.

Aaro and Malroy experienced the strange and unexpected projections that played out around them. They re-projected the story over and over and discussed it at length as they traveled through the early morning. Bit by bit, Aaro was able to grasp what this story was telling him about the state of his soul. His sense of uneasiness gradually faded away.

There was something missing in his life—*a person or a relationship, probably*—and he needed to leave Cloudy Peaks to go out and look for it. He didn't know exactly what it was. Neither did he know where or when he might find it—soul stories rarely gave that sort of clarity. But both he and Malroy believed there was enough evidence in it to indicate that he was on the right track.

When the Island of the Red Tower came into view some time later, Aaro felt confident that he'd made the right choice when he had decided to travel with Malroy. An eager excitement grew in him now, and—for the first time since he'd felt the puzzling sense—he looked forward to what this day would bring.

The Cheater

~Aaro~

Yeah, I've been known to pooze from time to time. I never gave up my clan or anything, but I used to do it a lot, back way when—before I got so famous. Some people see it as a childish waste of time, but to me, there's nothing better than becoming someone else and poozing the day away!

—Opinionator Gary is-a Heart, *How to Get What I Got and to Go Where I'm Going*

Aaro leaned against the side of his childhood friend's testing booth and nibbled on a piece of dried taro as he waited. He had positioned himself here, at the main crossroads of Granada Royce, to be available for whomever, or whatever, came his way. He still wasn't sure what he was waiting for.

In comparison, Malroy—who stood next to him all dressed up in a sophisticated projection disguise—knew exactly who he was looking for.

They'd been here for most of the afternoon, quietly observing the crowds of people shuffling around in their flamboyant outfits. Of all the islands Aaro had seen, there was none that celebrated unique fashions quite like the Island of the Red Tower.

He smiled at the creativity of the family that had just tottered by him dressed like Candy Bears, and the couple across the street who wore the same clothing as the tragic characters Nic and Nalia.

But for all that he had seen today, his mind kept returning to the ship full of poozers—that group of boys masterfully dressed like characters from *The Epics* whom he and Malroy had encountered earlier at the docks.

The captain of the ship—the one dressed like Migo the Marauder, the one Malroy knew so much about—is very talented. Help him find his way back home. Aaro's thoughts then shifted to the tall boy who had the look of burdened responsibility that often accompanied children who had been forced to grow up too soon. *He was so uncomfortable while being transformed into the Crimson Blade.* He lingered on this for a moment. Then a smile returned to Aaro's face as he pictured the delight in the youngest boy when he discovered he was being dressed up like Devos Rektor. *Why do I keep thinking about them?*

"Senior Trainer Aaro," said a lanky Orange-Violet mage whom Aaro immediately recognized as Rumingo is-a Spark. "What a pleasant surprise to see you here. Is there any way I can entice you to return to our fair home—the Island of the Swinging Vines—to give a demonstration of your spec-tac-u-lar ability? Projecting objects through walls is quite the feat. And as I have a decent budget this year, I can make it wa-wa-worth your while!"

"Trainer Rumingo, it's good to see you haven't lost your spark," Aaro replied politely. "Unfortunately, I'm going to decline. I would, however, be willing to do a training session in blindsight for your team—that is, if you're willing to bring them over to Cloudy Peaks for an early season scrimmage."

"Why, what an ex-ce-llent idea. I accept," Rumingo said. The two worked out the details. After they were finished, Rumingo glanced to the man at Aaro's right and said, "Is this handsome man your father?"

Aaro laughed and said, "No, Rumingo. Maybe you don't remember, but my father died long ago."

"Oh, that's right. I remember now. I apologize."

"I understand. You weren't very old when he was cut off," Aaro said. "This old man is Magpie is-a Boot, a friend to fools and a fool of a friend."

Although Malroy was sixty-six years old, his decrepit alter ego—Magpie—appeared to be far older. Wrinkles covered his face, he was hunched over and supported himself with a large, three-pronged cane.

"Well, Master Magpie, it's wond-der-ful to see a man your age still attending the Festival of Stars. I love it, love it. It's such a great experience for the kiddies! Really gives them a taste for fame. But, I must be away. My assistant will be in touch," Rumingo said, and then he left as quickly as he'd appeared.

"You think that was the super important meeting Täv wanted you to come here for?" Magpie chuckled.

"Absolutely . . . not," Aaro answered. "But it was nice to see Rumingo."

"He's just using you—you know that, right?"

"Of course. But it still will be nice to host him and his team for a scrimmage."

"Yuck! Pleck! Gross!" Gunthor is-a Wheel belched and spit into the bucket next to him as a nineteen-year-old left his booth in a huff because she hadn't earned a chip. Gunthor was a Yellow mage and a tester. This year, like every year, he sat in a booth and judged people's ability to make mouth-watering dessert projections. "Either of you see what you're lookin' for yet?" he asked Aaro and Malroy once there were no more people in line at his booth.

"Not yet," Aaro replied.

"Ha! No wonder. At least Malroy—"

"Magpie, Gunthor," Malroy interrupted. "I'm Magpie today."

"—at least 'Magpie' knows what he's looking for," Gunthor said. He then paused a moment to think. "Hey, wait! You're making fun of me with that name, aren't you?"

"We all know how much you like pie," Malroy said with a wink.

"And how often you eat crow, instead," Aaro added, and they both laughed.

Gunthor joined them with a hearty laugh of his own. "Now that's imagination. If you were testing, I'd give you a silver chip."

I'm so glad Gunthor hasn't lost his humor or his genuinely positive perspective on life, Aaro thought as he looked out at the street.

"Excuse me," said a middle-aged woman in an elegant dress crafted to look like it was carved of shimmering onyx. "You wouldn't happen to be Aaro is-a Tree, the Three Color Mage and Tier Two trainer?"

"I am he, yes," Aaro replied politely.

Next to the woman was a chubby, freckle-faced boy with red hair who stood a little taller than she did. He looked perfectly capable of taking care of himself, yet he clung to his mother's side in a way that indicated he hadn't been on his own much.

"What a pleasure to meet you," the woman said. "I'm Pendra is-a Twine, and this is my son, Martyn. If the gods have favored him with a Color, I'd be very interested to inquire about your services."

"Well, Martyn," Aaro said, deciding to address the boy rather than his mother, "even if no Color is pulled out of you, you'd still be welcome to train at my camp on the Island of the Cloudy Peaks. You'll find it's quite a welcoming place."

As soon as Aaro said this, Martyn tilted his head to the side and looked at his mom.

"Oh dear, no no." Pendra became anxious. "My dear Martyn requires undivided attention. A camp scenario is quite out of the picture for him. I would compensate you for your relocation to our estate."

"I appreciate the offer," Aaro said with a cheerful face, "but I'm responsible for quite a number of people. I won't leave them."

"Surely you can't mean you'd choose to stay with that team full of void pulls rather than train my sweet Martyn? He has ancestors in the Workshop, you know."

"I'm sure he's quite talented," Aaro said, then directed his gaze back to Martyn. "If you're interested in training at my camp, you have only to ask."

"Hmph. Come along, Martyn," Pendra said as she and her son left.

"There goes another missed opportunity," Gunthor said as he sucked on his pointer finger. "I don't know how you do it, Aaro. Passing up cushy jobs like that in favor of your little nothing of an island. I could never live there."

"Funny. I feel the same about living here."

Gunthor let out a deep laugh. "To each his own, I suppose."

"How can you be so sure?" Aaro asked. "You've never set foot on Cloudy Peaks."

"No reason to. You just brought me the only good thing from there," he said, holding up the finger that he was sucking on. "Nothing hits the spot quite like your Tav-a-licious apple pie."

"You can get the real thing if you come visit," Malroy said.

"Ha! Are you trying to make me fat?"

Gunthor looked like he was already very overweight, but it was only projected fat. This body mod was his signature look. The truth was he was tall and skinny—in fact, rather stringy. Moreover, he had the strange habit of intentionally wearing projected clothes that were a little too short so that they exposed his sagging gut. He said this was because he liked the way it kept kids from taking him very seriously. *But that makes no sense at all.* Aaro suspected there was something deeper going on.

"The best thing about pie is the flavors," Gunthor said. "The islands need more decent pie shops. Maybe that's why Tav wanted you to come here today. You sure you don't want me to give you a gold chip? You'd have no problem earning all the others required to join the Guild of Sweets and Savories. If you opened a pie shop here you'd be rolling in lykes in no time." Gunthor switched the finger he was sucking on to his ring finger. "Oh man, this one's great too."

"There's more to life than pie."

"I beg to differ. There's a reason people call it a little slice of the Old World. But I tell you, talent is—without a doubt—draining from the islands. Case in point, the flavors people are projecting today are terrible. I've only given out one gold chip all day. The quality seems to be getting worse every year."

"I've experienced the opposite. My students are—without a doubt—getting better," Aaro said.

"Well," Gunthor said, "it isn't hard to make improvements when you're the worst team in the region."

"What do you mean by that?" Malroy asked defensively. "Aaro's team wins all the time."

"Gunthor knows that," Aaro said.

"Oh, sure I do," Gunthor agreed with an unnecessarily loud burp, "and I also know that you could have a whole posse of magicians in the Workshop right now—sending you their sweet loyalty honorariums—if only you didn't waste so much effort on commoners."

Aaro was used to this kind of teasing. He and Gunthor were old childhood rivals. But, when they both got Colors and found themselves on the same team, they had—in time—learned to respect each other.

Malroy, however, did not have as much patience for Gunthor's sense of humor. He looked like he was about to get into an argument, but Aaro stopped it. Then, only a few heartbeats later, he noticed a sixteen-year-old boy walk by, wearing what looked like the traditional gold-and-silver vest and pants of the Shield clan.

"Hey, Magpie, look. Is that him?" Aaro motioned toward the boy.

"Where? Oh!" Malroy's eyes lit up. "Ah ha! Yes, that's him. Thanks. Okay, here I go."

"You still nervous?"

"Even more than before. This is his big day, after all."

"It's a big day for you, too," Aaro reminded him. "Now go on before he gets too far ahead."

"Yeah, go on," Gunthor said, "have fun stalking your grandson."

"We call it quality time in our family," Malroy laughed as he left them.

As they watched the old man disappear into the crowd, Gunthor leaned over to Aaro and said, "Honestly, Aaro, I can't imagine why you're pouring all your talent into void pulls."

"Well, you always were a bit short on imagination."

"That's right, go on, pick on the fat man," Gunthor said with a smile. "I may not have three Colors like you, but at least I get to live here. I mean, look at me. I sit around, tell people to project pie flavors on my fingers, and then get to determine their fate. Will they leap for joy? Or slink back to mommy and daddy in tears? And, best of all—they pay me for this. It's incredible! Here, taste what this one kid made. I gave him a gold chip for it." Gunthor extended the finger he was sucking on earlier to Aaro.

"I'm okay, thanks."

"Your loss." Gunthor shrugged and returned the finger to his mouth.

"You also have to test bad flavors, though," Aaro reminded him. "Didn't you say one tasted like it came out of a cat?"

"Oh, that was horrible. Some nutty kid from the Ray clan. It was unbelievable. Here, come on, you have to taste it," Gunthor said, extending his middle finger to Aaro.

"You kept it?"

"Absolutely. Only the best—and worst—flavors deserve to be on my fingers."

At that moment, out of the corner of his eye, Aaro noticed the group of poozers dressed like characters from *The Epics of the Cursed.*

There they are again. He felt his attention drawn to them. *But wait, something's different.* One member of the group—the tallest boy—was wearing only his threadbare. He walked with a calm, steady determination. *That's the boy who was dressed as the Crimson Blade before. He doesn't look upset, so what happened to his costume?*

"You know what, my friend?" Aaro said to Gunthor. "These poozers have me intrigued. I'm off to do some investigating. Wish me luck."

"Well, make sure to stop by before you leave. I don't want you disappearing before you give me a report—and refresh this apple pie on my finger."

*   *   *

Aaro followed close enough to listen in on the young poozers without drawing attention to himself.

"It really is quite a magical globe," said the one dressed as the iconic barbarian Migo the Marauder.

"It's totally working, Kaso. No one's questioned it once," the one dressed as Redden the Hunter insisted. "Quint still has yours. There's probably enough time left for you to test at two or three booths. Earning a few gold chips will set you up nice in case you're found void tonight."

"You're right, it probably would. Let me check out that globe," said the one in threadbare, whom they called Kaso.

"There we go, Big Brother! I'm elated that your time of rumination has brought you to a state of illumination," Migo said as he reached into a sack and pulled out a yellow testing globe. "And ho ho. Look yonder," Migo said as he pointed to a booth straight ahead. "The tumultuous temperature test awaits you. Fate has saved it for your Glory alone."

Kaso took the globe with both his hands. "Thanks," he said, and then—without warning- -he started to shake it.

Why is he doing that? Aaro wondered as the projected image of Kaso inside of the globe started to dissolve.

"But of course. You see, I always knew—wait!" Migo gasped when he saw what Kaso was doing. "Stop! Stop it!"

Kaso handed the now empty globe back with a look of satisfaction on his face.

"I can't believe you just did that," said Redden.

Kaso looked Migo in the eyes and said, "I told you I wouldn't cheat."

"Indeed, you did." Migo sounded disappointed.

"Well," Redden said, "since you clearly don't want to test, would you consider throwing me some of your warmth while I have a go at it? I'd love to have a gold chip in temperature."

"Treau, I should warn you," Kaso said to the one dressed as Redden, "we met an undercover IIRP detective earlier. I wouldn't use that globe."

"Why should that matter? We're not doing anything wrong. Quint said they're real. So, are you going to help me?"

Kaso said nothing, but he continued to walk with them.

What are these young men up to? Aaro tried to unravel the mystery.

The poozers arrived at a booth that displayed an image of

a snowflake above three vertical, squiggly lines. Three people stood ahead of them. The tester in charge of this booth was a man in his late eighties named Waelyn is-a Wick. He sat on a slab of concrete and wore a style of old-fashioned threadbare made out of whale skin that people once used for swimming. Aaro knew Waelyn from back in his competition days, when he'd been an energetic trainer, but he hardly recognized him now; the last few years had not been kind to him.

"Make me warm!" Waelyn ordered when the boy at the front of the line paid the testing fee. "I haven't been warm in twenty years."

The boy threw his arms up and an eruption of flames engulfed the old man. *Impressive.*

"I said make me warm, not broil my skin." Waelyn snapped his fingers and the fire went out. "No chips for you!" He spat the words like a curse.

"What?" shouted an opulently dressed older woman who stood beside the boy. Enraged, she held the globe in her hand and shook it, and the projected boy inside was flung about. "Burning is as good as heat."

"No it's not. Go away."

If the boy was disappointed, he didn't show it, and when he turned around, Aaro recognized him as Kai is-a Shield. *There he is again.* Aaro scanned the crowd around the booth and, sure enough, there was Malroy—or rather Magpie—observing the boy at a distance.

"Did you teach him to project fire like that?" Aaro sent his friend a voice projection. They were both skilled enough to send their voices in crowded places like this without fear of missing.

"No, it's innate. Have you seen the fire in his hand? Did it grow bigger when he did that?" Malroy projected back.

Aaro looked, but it was impossible to see. "I don't know. He's hiding the flame in his fist," Aaro responded as Kai walked away from the booth with a huge smile on his face, leaving the older woman Aaro suspected to be Jade behind to argue with Waelyn.

Poor Malroy. Aaro had never seen Jade before, and he wished he could go over to her and say something that might wake her up from the dream she was living. But as soon as he saw the stern creases on her face, he knew she wouldn't be open to his words. *I hope she won't have to experience any more pain than she already has.* But he sensed that another island-crushing storm was coming for her.

Aaro turned his eyes back to Kai, whom he now watched with intrigue. The boy broke out dancing as soon as he was away from the booth and twirled his way over to a pink-haired young woman who stood with her arms crossed. She wore an indigo jacket over a sparkling white blouse and had two curved sword projections attached to her back.

"You're such a bloomer," she said to Kai. "Who else would celebrate not earning a chip?"

"Just goes to prove I'm all flash, no substance."

"No, that's not why you're smiling," the young woman said. "What it is? Really?"

"I'm just thinking about something I once heard. 'Forget the heat, focus on the hell.'"

A tingle rippled through Aaro when Kai said this. He took a deep breath and looked over to the old man crouched across the road—who was grinning from ear to ear.

Kai remembers his grandfather's words.

"What are you talking about?" the young woman asked.

"Nothing. I'm just really happy," Kai said.

"Uh-huh." The young woman sighed.

Kai, as if suddenly realizing that his friend was unhappy, said, "Hey Snap, is it weird for you being here? I mean, I'm glad you're here to support me and everything, but you didn't have to come."

"Bud, get over yourself. I'm not here for you. I'm here for these." She held up her globe and shook it so that the handful of chips clattered inside. "I should have focused on this last year instead of on that drenchous Ceremony. You should too."

"Yeah, but . . . are you really sure you want to get into the Guild of Fashion and Design?" Kai asked.

"You got a problem with that?"

"No, not really. But . . . I don't know. It just doesn't seem right for you."

"Pfft. Are you kidding? You've seen the stuff Luge wears. The projections I create in my dreams come out dressed better than what I see around town."

In that moment, Aaro got a glimpse of the anger and bitterness that were growing in this young woman. *This is what the worship of Color does to people.* When he looked at her, he saw the same deep-rooted pain that he'd so often seen in those who hadn't yet found peace in being named common. *Another person who believes she's worthless without a Color. I hope she can find a way out of that snare someday.*

At times like this Aaro was thankful he wasn't alone. He looked over at Malroy, who, still disguised as Magpie, was approaching his grandson. *Okay, here he goes. Please help him.*

"Kai is-a Shield!" Malroy exclaimed, pretending that he'd just spotted them now.

"Master Magpie?" Kai smiled when he saw him. "What're you doing here?"

"I have a distant relative who's standing before a puller."

"Oh, that's great. I wish them well. Thanks for saying hello, especially after . . . you know, what happened a few weeks ago."

"Of course!" Malroy exclaimed. "I was more than happy to assist you. Who wouldn't love the opportunity to dissolve King King? It was the most fun this old man's had in years."

"You've got to be kidding," Snap said.

"No. It was my absolute pleasure and delight. I still don't understand how I happened to be lucky enough to be on Market Street at just the right time."

"I'm the one who ought to feel lucky," Kai said. "I'd probably still be under a prohibition if you hadn't been there to help me stop it before it did even more damage."

"Well, I'm glad it worked out for you to be here today," Malroy said.

"Kai!" Jade's voice rang out.

"I'd better go," Kai said.

"Yes, you'd better," Malroy agreed. "I wish you well today, Kai is-a Shield. Now, I might not be around next time you need help, so remember, Täv is real and is always there when we cry out to him."

"Uhhh, thanks. Yeah. Okay," Kai said.

Malroy winked at Kai and—just before Jade arrived—disappeared into the crowd.

✳   ✳   ✳

All this time the poozers had been waiting in line to be tested. Aaro turned his attention back to them and studied their every move. *They're nervous about something. Very nervous.*

When their time came, Redden the Hunter stepped forward and paid the testing fee. Waelyn then gave the same command he had given to Kai: "Make me warm!"

Redden scratched his head and said, "Do you mean, like, you want some clothes?"

"Whatever works. Just make me warm! I'm grading you on your ability to make me feel like my veins aren't collapsing."

"Um . . . can I make you feel cold?"

"I'm already frozen."

"But isn't this test for temperature in general?"

"Making people feel cold is effortless," Waelyn grumbled. "Heat me up or go away."

Redden the Hunter looked over at Kaso, who took a step away from the others.

He keeps looking at the one called Kaso. Is he asking him to cheat? I don't understand. Is there something I'm supposed to be seeing in this?

The poor poozer did his best to thaw Waelyn. He projected blankets, wrapped him in furs, and even covered his bald head with thick, fluffy hair.

Waelyn had a strange look on his face as he stared intently at Redden. Whatever it was, it wasn't the look of someone becoming warm.

What is old, cold Waelyn thinking? Aaro kept looking back and forth between Redden and Kaso.

Waelyn pressed a finger to his face and instead of saying his favorite phrase, "No chips for you!" he said, "There's something special about you, boy."

The furrow scrawled across Redden's face disappeared, and a glimmer of brightness came to his eye along with a crooked, pride-filled smile.

"Come over here with your globe. I like to congratulate boys of exceptional talent."

Redden did as he was asked, and as soon as he was within reach, Waelyn moved with unnatural speed and snatched the globe out of the boy's hand. Then something like an internal earthquake struck the other poozers. It was obvious to Aaro that all of them wanted to run. But they didn't.

Why are they standing still?

Waelyn hummed to himself as he held up the globe and gave it a close inspection. "Excellent work. The boy looks like you and the symbol appears authentic." When he held up a gold chip, all their tension fell away. "Whoever did the work on this globe deserves a gold chip," Waelyn said as he looked Redden straight in the eye. "Too bad chips aren't given out for forgery."

Waelyn raised his hand and continued, "I don't trust poozers." He pointed his finger at each of them—one by one—dissolving their projected clothing and leaving them in their threadbare.

Still, none of them moved.

"No . . . chips . . . for . . . you!" he said slowly and calmly, and with his final word they all crumpled to the ground, shivering. *Ah.* Aaro now understood. *Waelyn has been casting an ice projection on them.*

Engrossed in this drama, Aaro had not noticed that two of the poozers were no longer there. He looked around for Kaso and the little boy. *There they are.* They'd slipped away into the crowd. *Should I stay here, or follow the two who left?*

There was something mysterious about Kaso, and Aaro wanted to know why Redden kept looking to him for help. Moreover, how could he have broken free from the powerful cold Waelyn must have projected? *It crumpled all of the other poozers.* Aaro wanted to discover more, so—urged on by his curiosity and a healthy measure of faith—he followed after them.

The Offer

~Aaro~

While sponsoring a child outside your clan is a sure fire way to put some dicey-dicey into your life, you'd have to be a real Risky Ricky to sponsor an orphan. Unless, of course, the orphan is stupendously talented—like I was. My sponsor soared straight up to Tier One soon after he discovered me. Certain relationships are just meant to be.

— Chipper is-a Paste, character in the Grand Projection *The Orphan-tastic Adventures of Chipper and Charlie*

The streets were crowded, but Kaso—tall and wearing only his threadbare—was easy to spot. He and the younger boy moved speedily through the crowd and then ducked into a nearby alley. Aaro followed after them.

They hurried down a long, narrow passageway, between two brick buildings covered over with thick green vines. There was only one exit, and the boys were heading for it.

He's afraid of being pursued. He'll never stop if I call out to him, Aaro knew, and so he quickly cast a projection of himself at the far end of the passage to meet them. The projection casually entered the alley in front of them and stopped. It was an exact replica of Aaro and did not look like a projection at all. It was so realistic that it caused Kaso to skid to a stop.

"Excuse me, Master," Kaso said, "do you mind moving aside, so we can pass?"

Even while anxious, he maintains respect.

"Hello, boys. Where do you desire to go?" Aaro had his projection say.

Kaso hesitated. "To the Color Ceremony."

"Ah, then I think you're going the wrong direction."

"But isn't the stadium that way?" Kaso pointed down the alley.

"Yes, it is, up and to the left," the projection said. "But if you want to be in the Ceremony—"

"—the registration booth is back the way you came," Aaro, now directly behind Kaso, finished the sentence with his own breath.

Kaso, confused, turned and looked back.

"Please don't be startled," both Aaro and his projection said at the same time.

"What's going on, Kaso?" the young boy asked. "I'm scared."

Kaso tilted his head to the side as he examined the two versions of Aaro standing before and behind him. He was changing the angle he viewed them in order to figure out which was a projection and which was an actual person.

Clever boy. "I don't mean any harm," the real Aaro said as both he and his projection took a step backward. "I saw you just now at the temperature booth and I wanted to know who you were."

"My brother's not a cheater!" the younger boy shouted.

"I know he's not, that's why I want to learn more about him." *Am I here to help them?* Aaro still wasn't sure. "Based on the little I've seen, you came here today to test, but you've refused to cheat in order to do so. Is that correct?"

Kaso observed him and the projection without saying a word. Then, after taking a moment to collect his thoughts, he focused his attention on the real Aaro. "That's true, I did not cheat . . . My name is Kaso is-a Blank, and this is my brother, Coby. We're orphans from Region 3. I did not come here to test, only to stand before a puller so I might know whether there is Color in me or not."

"But Blanks are no longer allowed to participate in the Ceremony without a sponsor."

"Yes, and I wish I'd known that before I came all this way," Kaso said.

"And your friends? They decided to try and cheat?"

"I will not speak about them or their actions. But I assure you, I haven't cheated."

"I see no evidence that you have," Aaro agreed.

"Kaso spent all afternoon asking mages to be his sponsor," Coby blurted out. "But no one wants to help us."

The boy seeks a sponsor. Is this what you would have of me? "I'm afraid that sponsorship means much more than you might realize. To sponsor someone in Region 2 is to become responsible for them until they turn nineteen. Because of this, most mages spend tens of weeks—sometimes years—getting to know an orphan before agreeing to such a thing. The sponsor shares their clan name and becomes legally responsible should the orphan break any laws. It's quite a serious thing."

"I was told it would be unlikely," Kaso said. "But—we came all this way. I had to at least try."

He knew how difficult it would be, and yet he still refused to cheat? Who raised this boy? "What is your plan now, having not found a sponsor?"

"I'll go back to Auntie's home and try again next year."

"Is that your orphanage?" Aaro asked.

Kaso nodded.

"A good one?"

"The best!" Coby exclaimed.

"I'm glad." There were many orphanages in Region 3, but not all had a good reputation.

"You look familiar," Kaso said after a moment.

"Yes. We saw each other earlier today, while we were still on our boats, in the marina."

"Oh—yeah!" Kaso's eyes lit up. "You were the man with Mage Malroy."

"You recognized him?" That surprised Aaro. *Malroy looks nothing like himself when he's disguised as Magpie.*

"Well, no, not exactly . . . Our captain, the one dressed like Migo, told us who he was. It was Mage Malroy, wasn't it?"

"Interesting." *I'll have to remember to tell Malroy about this.* "Yes, it was. He and I are friends."

"You're friends?" Coby asked. He paused, then blurted out, "Is it true that his son cheated to get into the Workshop?"

Kaso shot his little brother a stern look. "Coby, don't ask such rude questions."

"It's okay, I don't mind," Aaro said. "Unfortunately, many believed Malroy's son, Flint, cheated because of some unusual spikes and steep drops in his scores. However, no evidence was ever found to prove he did anything illegal. Yet that didn't prevent some people from branding him a cheater."

"But if his son didn't do anything wrong, why is Mage Malroy disguised and sneaking around?" Coby prodded.

"Coby!" Kaso exclaimed.

"He said he didn't mind," Coby said to his brother. He then turned to Aaro and asked, "Do you mind?"

"No, I don't. I appreciate it when people ask honest questions, even socially thorny ones. To get the real answer you would have to ask Malroy. I'm sure he would be happy to talk with you about it. But, I do know the accusations about his son have tainted Malroy's credibility as a trainer, and it's become difficult for certain people to trust him."

"I see . . ." Kaso considered Aaro's words. "I know this is a lot to ask, but . . . do you think he might be willing to sponsor me?"

This took Aaro by surprise. *Is this desperation, or ignorance?* "You wouldn't be worried about having a man with his reputation as your sponsor?"

"If there's no proof that his son did anything wrong, then I don't need to consider what others say. From the little I saw of Mage Malroy, he seemed to be a good man. He spoke of Tav in a way that was real—like my Auntie does—and it seems to me people like that can be trusted."

Keen observation. This boy has integrity, and he sees things others don't. This meeting may very well be the reason I'm here. "Well said, young one. But I'm sorry to tell you, I am quite confident that Malroy would say no to your request."

"Oh."

The look of dejection in Kaso's eyes resonated with Aaro. He'd sponsored youths before, and would be happy to do so again, but he'd never been in the position to make an abrupt choice like this. There was a huge risk involved—not just for him, but for his whole clan. Yet there was something about Kaso that resonated with him. *Should I do this?* Aaro found the boy compelling. He held himself with certainty and steadiness. "Why are you here? Why did you come all this way?"

"To stand before a puller," Kaso answered.

"Why not wait until you're nineteen and declared an independent adult?"

Kaso took a deep breath and then shared his story. He explained his feelings after witnessing the final Glimmering, and his concern about what he sensed to be a lack of warmth in Grand Projections. Aaro, fascinated by this observation, questioned him further about it, and then asked about his life. Kaso explained how they became orphans, how they came to live with Auntie, and how they'd come here with a group of poozers. He concluded all this with, "I wouldn't be here without my Auntie's blessing. But she gave it."

Kaso's response was not what Aaro had expected. *He seems to be a genuinely good kid.* Further, he seemed to have an innate desire to bring about good for the islands, while refusing to compromise his principles. In and through this conversation, Aaro was considering what Täv might have him do. It seemed clear. *But you know how I don't like to make hasty decisions.*

It was wise to spend time with a person; time reveals who people really are. But it was the middle of the Blue watch. There was no time. *My clan stands before the puller tonight.* He needed to decide now. *Okay. I'm trusting this is a good choice. Please make things whole again if I'm mistaken.* "Young Kaso, I am willing to take you under my care—if that's something you would like."

"Wait—you?" Kaso looked confused. "I'm sorry, Master, but don't I need a mage to sponsor me?"

"Indeed."

"I don't understand."

Aaro reached into his pocket for his collar. Green, Cyan, and Blue swirled together in an intricate, mesmerizing pattern, and as soon as he pulled it out, Kaso's and Coby's eyes grew wide with surprise.

"Whoa!" Coby gasped. "I've never seen three Colors before!"

"Is that real?" Kaso asked.

"Yes."

"You're a Three Color Mage? But . . . are you really willing to sponsor me?"

"That's what I've offered."

Kaso was stunned. "You haven't even seen what I can do."

"It doesn't matter. I'm sponsoring you, not your abilities."

"But . . . what happens if I don't have a Color?"

Hmm. He seems terrified of that happening. "A sponsor agrees to be responsible for the youth until the age of nineteen, Color or not. No matter what happens, you're welcome to come to my island and remain in my care. If you aren't comfortable there, I can return you to your orphanage at any time."

"Why would you do that?"

"Because you need a sponsor," Aaro said.

"You're willing to take that kind of risk on me?" Kaso asked.

"I'm choosing you. Do you think that's a good decision, Kaso?"

Coby grinned from ear to ear and said, "It's a great one! You won't regret it!"

Aaro looked deep into Kaso's eyes. *No, I don't think I will.*

✻   ✻   ✻

By the time they exited the registration tent it was the bottom of the Blue watch. There was only a short time remaining before the testing booths shut down and everyone would begin heading to the stadium for the first night of the Color Ceremony.

Aaro held a yellow globe in his hand that was branded with the seal of the Tree clan.

"Oh wow! Kaso is-a Tree!" Coby exclaimed. "I can't believe you have a new name!" Then all of a sudden Coby stopped bouncing and asked with a big smile, "Does that mean I have a new name, too?"

"No, Coby. It's just for me so that I can stand before the puller tonight. And it's only temporary," Kaso reminded him. "This is different than adoption."

"But the name is yours for as long as you choose to stay with me," Aaro affirmed.

"I really appreciate all you've done for me," Kaso said as he looked at the little version of himself inside the glass ball that Aaro held in his hands. "But you don't need to be responsible for me beyond today. I want to make sure you understand that I'd like to return to my orphanage after this."

"I understand." Aaro paused, then said, "Will you want to go back even if you have a Color pulled?"

"Yes."

"Are you not interested in finding a trainer to prepare you?" Aaro asked.

"No. I don't feel that will be necessary," Kaso stated.

He has no doubts about his abilities. This kind of confidence was rare. It wasn't pride. Kaso hadn't once bragged about his skill. *Yet he doesn't seem to appreciate the need to be prepared.*

"Are you that certain you can get all the way to the Workshop without any training?"

"Yes. I believe I ought to be able to."

"What abilities do you have that give you such certainty?" Aaro asked.

Kaso hesitated, and before he could say anything, Coby said, "My brother's mega talented. He'll get in, no problem!"

"Come with me then," Aaro said. "I want to have you test at one booth, at least, before they close."

"Do I need to?" Kaso asked. "I didn't come here for the testing, just the Ceremony."

"There's no legal reason you need to test—many kids don't their first year," said Aaro. "But I feel it will be valuable. Moreover, the authorities from the Workshop—who run the Ceremony— like to have some idea of the abilities of the children who are going to stand before a puller."

Kaso didn't appear to like it, but he agreed. On the way, Aaro was stopped three times by people asking him to train their children. But, because they were in a hurry, he didn't have time to properly address each one.

"Wow! You're a trainer, too!" Coby exclaimed.

"Indeed, I am. I've been one—in one form or another—for

most of my life. Kaso, I want you to know that you are more than welcome to have a spot on my team, no matter what happens tonight. Though, I must inform you, the focus and purpose of my training is quite different from that of other trainers."

"I appreciate the offer," Kaso said in a way that indicated he would not accept the invitation.

Perhaps, in time, he will come to see the value in being prepared.

As they hurried through the streets, Kaso kept glancing over at Aaro. Eventually he spoke what was on his mind. "That projection you made of yourself in the alley. It was so real looking, which means you have very high Kingdom. But it didn't feel cold, like projections normally do. It was almost like it was . . ."

"Alive?"

Kaso's eyes widened. "Yeah. It had warmth—real warmth."

"Yes. Giving warmth to others is important, isn't it? That's why I'm taking you here."

When they turned the corner, Kaso saw Waelyn's temperature testing booth and stopped. "Is this a good idea? Won't he remember me, from before?"

"I'm sure he will, and I'm sure he's not going to like you testing. But he knows me, and moreover, he knows that I know the rules. I need you to stay silent the entire time, though. I will speak for you. Will you be able to obey me in this?"

"Yes, I will."

"Good," Aaro said. "I want to see what Waelyn does when you make him warm."

"Will I?" Kaso asked.

"I guess I'll see."

*　　　　*　　　　*

When they arrived at the booth, the old mage was closing up for the day. "Scram. I'm finished!"

"Oh, really? Is it closing time so soon?" Aaro asked. He knew testers weren't allowed to close up until the bells rang. *May this be a gift to him as well.*

Waelyn turned and recognized Aaro immediately. "Well, I say . . . I haven't seen you for ages." Before Aaro could respond, Waelyn exclaimed, "Hey! That's one of the cheaters. You ought to be locked up, like the rest of them."

"He is not a cheater, Waelyn. I have sponsored him. See, I'm holding his globe."

"What?! You gave him your name? You're a greater fool than even my overactive imagination could conjure. He is a cheater. You must know you're risking your reputation on a foreigner like him," Waelyn spat.

Help me to not be drawn into this fight. "It's good to see you too," Aaro said. "Please, begin the test. It is still the Blue watch. The bells have not yet rung. There is time."

"Arg. I can't understand why you Tavites risk so much on people with no future."

"Begin the test," Aaro instructed as he held out some coins.

"It's holding the islands back, you know," Waelyn grumbled. "You need to understand that, Aaro."

"Test him. Now!"

"Oh, all right." Waelyn took the coins and sat down on his large, cold concrete brick. "Make me warm, you big cheating oaf."

Kaso positioned himself in front of the old man, took a few moments to collect his thoughts, and then inhaled deeply while cupping his hands over his mouth and whistling through his nose. It was a curious style, but one that Aaro knew was used by some people in Region 3.

As Kaso whistled, a thick, wool quilt materialized all around Waelyn, covering his body. The expression on the old man's face started to shift. "A quilt, eh?" Waelyn said. "Trying to make me look like a family icon? I'm not dead yet, though."

For a time Waelyn fought to remain grumpy and distant, but the projection Kaso cast was stronger than the old man's cold resistance. The hard surfaces of his face started to soften. His eyes began to twinkle with a joy he hadn't felt in years. "Mmmm!" Waelyn leaned back and said, "Being an icon isn't so bad."

Then Kaso suddenly changed the pitch of his whistle. It was subtle, and if Aaro hadn't been paying such close attention, he might not have noticed it.

"Aw, it's fading," Waelyn whined. "Keep it going." He sat still and quiet under the quilt for a long time.

Then the bells rang, and three beams of Indigo light lit up the darkening sky.

"Oh, too late," he said as he burst up. "Enjoy another year of being a pointless poozer."

"Give him his chip, Waelyn," Aaro said.

"Why? You're the one who did it," Waelyn stated. "I should be giving you the chip."

"You know I wouldn't cheat. But if you want, I can go away and he can do it again."

The old mage hesitated and a sliver of a smile came to his mouth. *Does he want someone to make him warm again?* But then Waelyn's smile turned cold.

"I need to get going. I have better things to do. Here." Waelyn paused as he rummaged through a dusty box and pulled out a bright, silver chip. "You made me warm for a few brief heartbeats. That's something."

Interesting. Did Kaso hold back? Aaro suspected he was capable enough to earn a gold chip. *Or is Waelyn making a point?*

"Silver?!" Coby exclaimed. "He deserves a gold."

"He deserves nothing! He should be dancing around like

some stupid headless chicken, happy that he got anything at all."

Kaso clasped his hands together and bowed his head in the respectful manner of those from Region 3. Then—head still bowed—he sent a voice projection to Aaro asking, "Can I say one thing to him before I leave?"

Aaro took a deep breath. *Can I trust him?* He considered. *Yes, Waelyn should hear what Kaso wants to say.* So he projected back, "Go ahead."

Kaso raised his head and looked Waelyn straight in the eyes. "I truly hope you're able to receive warmth one day."

"Well said," Aaro projected. *Who is this Auntie who raised this orphan? I look forward to meeting her.*

When Aaro held out the globe to the elderly man, he heard him mutter something under his breath. He then looked up at Aaro and said, "Do yourself a service, Aaro. Train this boy. Take him to your forsaken island and maybe, just maybe—if he gets a Color—you might have a chance at finally becoming a Tier One trainer."

The furrow across Aaro's brow deepened and his stomach tensed. *Help me hold my tongue.*

He was tempted to defend his honor and remind this sad, cold mage how many students of his had competed in the Championships and had earned scores high enough to get into the Workshop. Or at least they would have if O'Ceeans were colorblind and all people were eligible to become magicians, regardless of Color.

For some reason, a memory came back to him: Yamyar leaping up in the air while shouting "BYE BYE" before they left. *No, I've not wasted my efforts training people like him.*

Confident, Aaro walked away without saying a thing.

The Color Ceremony—Part One
~Jaremon~

Black, from darkness fades away.
Upturn your weary eye.
Shadows will not kiss you now.
There's Color in the sky.

　　　　　—Mage Palacious is-a Star, from the poem *The Puller's Dyemoon*

The Island of the Red Tower was renowned for its grand, resplendent architecture, but as far as Jaremon was concerned, not a single building on the whole island could compare with the stadium.

It was a massive, mathematically perfect stone structure, oval in shape, and all the way around ringed by thick, polished pillars that conveyed so much strength that they appeared to hold up the sky. On the inside, row upon row of elevated seating faced down to the center arena, where the Color Ceremony would take place.

It was an exciting and celebratory place for every mage and magician; this was where they stood when Color was found in them. But for every youth, entering the arena was like stepping into battle. Those filled with pride entered confidently with straight backs and heads held high. Those full of dread cowered as they slinked under the arches. This was a place of foreboding; for better or worse, it was where each one of their lives would change forever.

But there's little reason to fear now. She got four gold chips. Jaremon smiled. He was pleased to see Kalaya's confidence blossom as she went through the day and earned the chips necessary to ensure her success. *Now all we have to do is wait and see what Color she is.* His mind cycled through all the possible variants. *She could be Blue, Cyan, or Yellow. Violet would be a surprise. Or maybe Green, like me?* Then, in an instant, his smile disappeared as an image of her getting Red flashed before his eyes.

No, she can't be Red! That would be disastrous; it would put an immediate end to their relationship. Even though he didn't believe in the Color gods, it simply wasn't wise for Green mages to grow close to Red mages. It was said that, from the dawn of O'Ceea, the god of Red and the god of Green were great enemies. *If Kalaya were Red, we'd always be fighting. I'd certainly have to end things between us.*

But after making a quick calculation in his head, he calmed down. *There is only a two point three percent chance of her having Red.* With odds like that, he didn't need to worry.

"Make sure you nap if you have a chance," Kathy, Kalaya's mom, said to her before they separated. "You've had a very long day."

"There won't be any time to nap," Kalaya said.

"I know. But just try, okay?" her mother insisted.

Kalaya gave Jaremon a pleading look.

"She'll be fine, Mistress Kathy," Jaremon reassured her. "They have couches and stuff in the waiting area and pako pods to chew."

"Good. Make sure you use them."

"Yes, Mom." Kalaya looked over her shoulder at the stadium and tilted her body toward it. "I'd better get in there."

"Hey—before you go, whatever happens, just remember . . ." Jaremon stepped forward and said, ". . . don't touch your face."

Kalaya raised her eyebrows at him. "Don't touch my face?"

"Yeah. Girls who touch their face during the Ceremony rarely get Colors."

"Right. Good advice, thanks. I'll make sure not to do that," Kalaya said. It was clear that she thought he was being ridiculous.

"I'm serious. The research on this is quite solid," Jaremon reiterated.

"But I got four gold chips. Isn't that enough?"

"It should be, but you still need to be extra careful."

"I never realized you were so superstitious."

"I'm not superstitious." He could tell from the bemused look on her face that she didn't believe him. "Look, people who are superstitious still believe in the Color gods, and I don't. Superstitious people believe the gods control who gets a Color and who doesn't. I don't believe anything like that. Everything I'm telling you is based on empirical evidence. There are a lot of educated people who've collected some powerful statistics backing up the dangers of face touching."

Before she could respond, a loud whistle sounded from deep within the stadium.

"You'd better go. I'll see you after," Jaremon said, and Kalaya turned and followed the crowd inside. *This is my last chance. What else does she need to know? I'm forgetting something.* "Oh, and don't fiddle with your hair either. Actually, just keep your hands down at your sides."

"Okay," she said, giving him a nod of agreement. Then, just before she disappeared from view, she shot Jaremon a voice projection. "Thanks for believing in me today. I couldn't have done it without you."

This is going to work out great. "You have what it takes. Just remember what I said and you'll be fine."

"Right. See you after." She disappeared inside.

✳   ✳   ✳

"My poor girl, she must be so nervous. I nearly passed out twice while I stood on the stage waiting for my name to be called," Kathy said to Jaremon as they made their way through the aisles to find her husband, Cale, and her younger daughter, Aliva.

"Yeah, a lot of kids are nervous when they enter the arena," Jaremon agreed.

"A lot? Isn't everyone?"

"Oh no. Twenty-eight percent report no fear at all. I, personally, wasn't concerned when I was up there," Jaremon said right before they joined Kalaya's father and sister. "Hello, Master Cale, your wife and I are here. These are great seats, by the way. Thanks for saving them for us."

"Jaremon! Welcome, join us," Cale said.

The stadium was filled with seats that surrounded the oval stage where the Ceremony would take place. There was really no reason to come early, as the best spots in the stadium were divided into sections, one for each island that had children standing before the puller that night. But Kathy had insisted that Aliva take Cale to save them spots as soon as he had finished his duties for the day, "just in case" there was no room.

Jaremon disliked the arranged seating. He thought the Color Ceremony should be an opportunity for those from the various islands to interact with one another, but instead it was an event at which people from the same island stuck together. For his island, the Island of the Golden Vale, it was even worse; people sat together based on clan. *They say this is supposed to help us build clan support,* he thought to himself as he looked around, *but I'm sure all it does is create more rivalry.*

"How did my girl do today?" Cale asked.

"Excellent. She got four gold chips."

A big smile spread across Cale's face. "She is very talented." But Jaremon detected signs of worry creasing the corners of Cale's eyes when he added, "I wish I could have been there."

"It's okay, she understands," Jaremon said. "You have an important job."

"Do you need anything, dear? Some water, perhaps?" Kathy asked.

"My bottle is still half full of pako juice!" Cale said, and he wiggled a flask in the air.

"When is it going to start?" Aliva asked.

"Soon," Jaremon said as he pulled out a package of dried seaweed and offered it to the others.

On the floor of the stadium was an enormous stage. This was where the Ceremony would take place. At the center there was a tall pedestal to which the children, one by one, would be called forward. They would have to walk up a set of stairs and stand at the top. There—before everyone—that night's puller would begin the ancient practice of examining them to see if they had a Color inside.

"Weren't you even a little nervous?" Kathy asked, breaking Jaremon out of his thoughts. "You must have been nervous."

"Nervous of what?"

"Being a void pull."

"Oh no. I knew my odds of that were low, and I was careful to keep all of the best practices," he replied as he chewed on his piece of seaweed.

"I'm really grateful Kalaya has you in her life."

"Oh, absolutely, Mistress Kathy!" The voice of Olan from behind them caused the hair on Jaremon's neck to rise. "Kalaya is a gem, and Jaremon is the perfect guy for her."

Great. Olan is-a Twig sat down directly behind them. *What does he want?*

"Everything okay, Jaremon?" Cale asked.

"All is well," Jaremon reassured him, then glanced over his shoulder at Olan. "Hey, this is the Cloud section."

"Is it?" Olan said. "Yet, here you are, and you're not a Cloud."

"I'm here to support Kalaya," Jaremon said.

"What a coincidence. Me too. I hear she did quite well in her testing today." Olan leaned forward and appeared genuinely happy.

"Yes, she did. Four gold chips!" Kathy said.

"Wow. That's really impressive. She must get her skill, as well as her looks, from you." Olan grinned.

His words made Aliva snicker, but Kathy seemed to be flattered. She said, "Oh, no, no. I can't do much with projections. Just the odd flavor enhancement now and again. Everyone knows she gets everything from her father's side of the family."

"Mmm." Cale nodded solemnly.

For some reason, the sharp, slicing motions of the Crimson in Olan's collar irritated Jaremon more than usual tonight. He began to feel the same way he had right before he'd punched Olan last night. He knew that, as a Green mage, he shouldn't have any problem with Crimson mages; Crimson was a separate Color from Red and, technically, should not be in conflict with his Green. But the more he was around Olan, the more agitated Jaremon became. He was starting to feel that Crimson was essentially just a darker shade of Red.

"Why aren't you sitting with your family?" Jaremon asked. "I'm sure your brothers miss you."

Olan shrugged. "I wanted to be able to stand alongside all the people who love Kalaya, so we'll all be cheering and celebrating together when she gets her Color. She deserves all the support she can get—she's trained so very hard."

"What a kind thing to say," Kathy said. "I'm sure Kalaya would love the support of another mage. You're absolutely welcome to stand with us."

"I'm honored. Thank you." Olan beamed.

Hmm. He's up to something.

Sure enough, as he continued to suck up to Kalaya's family, Olan projected in Jaremon's ear, "Will you still love her if she has no Color?"

Oh! So that's it. He wants to get under my skin. Too bad for him. It won't work.

"Har har!" Olan projected the sound of his nasty laugh into Jaremon's ear. "I can't wait to see the look on your face when Kalaya is exposed—officially—as a slugneck."

I can't stand Crimson mages. Please, Kalaya, don't be Red or Crimson.

Despite looking away, Jaremon couldn't stop feeling the intense emotion that Olan's collar stirred up in him, and his thoughts were filled with all sorts of insults that he could project back. *No, he isn't worth your time.* He closed his eyes and tried to imagine a string of pleasant Colors coming out of Kalaya: Indigo, Blue, Cyan . . . But for some reason, all he could see was Olan's dragon swooping down and taking Kalaya's wallaroo away from him.

✳   ✳   ✳

"When's it going to start?" Aliva whined. "This is taking so long."

"The opening ceremonies should begin soon," Jaremon said.

It was now the top of the Violet watch. Most people had taken their seats and were talking amongst themselves as they waited.

"All that boring stuff they do at the beginning is so drench," Aliva continued to complain. "It always takes forever."

"The opening ceremonies are crucial," Jaremon explained.

Aliva shook her head. "No. They're drench. It should just start with the pulling."

"Patience, patience," Cale said kindly. "We've all been waiting for this moment. Now, if I'm not mistaken, I believe Igar has just arrived. It should begin shortly."

Jaremon looked down at the floor of the stadium and saw that, as Cale said, the famous magician Igar is-a Moon had appeared and was approaching the stage.

Igar was a bald, Red-Cyan magician with a matching bi-colored goatee that split into two long braids of hair. Although he was very short—four feet at most—he stood with an air of confidence that belonged to one who'd spent many years inside the gates of the Magician's Workshop.

"Masters and Mistresses, Mages and Magicians, allow me introduce myself." Igar projected his voice out so that everyone could hear him clearly, no matter how far away they were. "I am Igar is-a Moon, magician of the Second Magnitude, and your host for this evening. Tonight is a monumental night for many of the children from our divine region."

The crowd broke out into loud applause.

"Color is a gift. It is not earned. Yet, every year, Color is found among us. We will discover it again tonight and celebrate those who possess it, and mourn with those who don't, all while recognizing that, no matter what happens, we all will be forever changed."

Igar spread out his arms as he spoke. "Now, without further delay, bring out our future!" He waved his arms in the air to keep the audience clapping as the trapdoors of the stadium floor burst open and one hundred and twenty-four youths from the Penta-Islands emerged.

As they stepped out and into the light of the stadium, they were led up another set of stairs. They then filed out onto the stage, where they were positioned in a giant circle around the looming pedestal in the center.

"A bit fewer than average this year," Olan's snide voice projected into Jaremon's ear again. "I'm not nearly as good at statistics as you. Does fewer mean Kalaya's odds go up or down?"

Neither, you brainbust. But Jaremon redid his calculations based on the actual numbers, just in case. And—for some reason he didn't understand—the new odds did indicate that her chances had gone down a little. But he was confident the difference was trivial and it wouldn't cause any issues.

"Do you see her?" Cale asked. "How does she look?"

Jaremon scanned the faces of the children as they marched out until, at last, he spotted Kalaya, squished between two kids he didn't know.

And she was touching her face. *Kalaya, come on!*

He watched helplessly as Kalaya rubbed her nose and brushed a strand of hair out of her eyes. Jaremon wanted nothing more than to project a warning to her, but that was forbidden, and no one—not even Olan—would dare interact with those on stage. *I can't believe she did that.*

"What's wrong? Something happened." Cale somehow knew.

Don't say anything. You could make it worse by pointing it out. "Nothing. She came out and almost tripped, but she's fine."

"She did?" Aliva asked. "Where is she?"

Jaremon pointed her out and tried not to let her foolishness put a foul taste in his mouth despite his fears that she just dropped her odds by thirty to forty percent—at least! *But it could turn. Everything now depends on when they call her out.*

After all the kids were gathered on the stage and lined up around the pedestal, the stadium grew quiet. This was the part of the Ceremony when Igar was supposed to announce the arrival of the puller. But instead, he stood completely still, almost as if he were frozen in time.

What's happening? Something's happening. Jaremon felt uneasy and searched his memory for any instances when this kind of thing had happened before. He didn't like unpredictable things. And then he heard it: the deep, sweeping strings of twin violins scratching out the most iconic tune in all the islands. *It's the "Song of the Damned."*

Jaremon knew what this meant and was one of the first to stand. Almost as soon as he was on his feet, he was followed by everyone else in the stadium. The bright white mask of Devos Rektor flashed right in front of Jaremon's eyes. In that moment, thousands of Devos Rektors appeared in the stadium, one for each person. It was brief but terrifying, and Jaremon felt his heart leap and his throat constrict at the unexpected sight of it.

Then another trapdoor on the stage opened, and—as Jaremon expected—Greydyn, the Master Magician, rose up through it. Everyone started clapping and cheering, and he waved and smiled back at them. *After his recent mistakes, it seems the Master Magician has regained a lot of favor by teasing the return of Devos Rektor in the recent Glimmerings. That was a smart move for the Workshop. Everyone loves the Lord of Chaos.*

Greydyn—who almost certainly wore a body mod face projection that kept his skin looking smooth and young—stood confidently before them with a vitality that made it difficult to discern his true age. This was one of the biggest mysteries about him, but based on the number of Grand Projections he'd been involved with, and how long he'd been the head of the Workshop, Jaremon had calculated that he must be somewhere between sixty-two and sixty-five.

"It's so wonderful to see you all!" Greydyn cried out over the sound of the loud, steady cheering.

"What a surprise!" Igar exclaimed. "I had no idea you were coming to honor us with your presence!"

The words sounded honest, yet Jaremon suspected it was a scripted line.

"The pleasure is mine. It's not often I get to spend time with so many of the wonderful people from Region 2," Greydyn answered.

"TELL US ABOUT DEVOS!" someone from the Bone clan screamed, causing a ripple of "tell us, tell us!" chants from those nearby.

How classless. Leave it to the Bones to shout at the Master Magician.

"So how are you doing? You look absolutely wonderful," Igar said, ignoring the chants.

"I feel wonderful, too! But, no, no. Tonight's not about me. It's about them," the Master Magician said. He rotated his body to face the boys and girls who were patiently waiting for the Ceremony to begin. "I'm here to celebrate all those who are about to become young men and women. They're the only reason we're here."

Several of the kids shook with excitement. Without a doubt, this was the closest they'd ever been to the Master Magician.

"I'm overjoyed to see so many eager young faces—faces of those who love projections as much as I do. Each of you has a story to tell. Wouldn't it be terrific if there were time to tell them all? Unfortunately, we face limitations living on islands. There are only two-hundred and eighty-eight spots in the Workshop after all—but, oh how I would love it if there were room enough for all of you to join me.

"I realize, though, that not all of you will receive a Color tonight. Not long ago, I stood where you now stand. Green was found in me, and my fate was sealed. But I tell you, even if I didn't have a Color, I would have kept laughing and playing. So, if a Color isn't pulled from you tonight, please promise me this: don't walk away from projecting."

That's nice and true—in theory. But I certainly don't believe he would be so optimistic if he didn't have Green, or some other Color.

"Projections are for everyone," the Master Magician continued. "Some of you may have heard the line 'Color, no Color, nothing will keep me from laughing and playing.' Those are the words I want you all to hear and understand. I hope our upcoming Grand Projection will help us all to stop and think about Color in a different way."

The crowd was silent, and Greydyn wrung his hands together like he was concerned. *I sure hope he wasn't expecting people to applaud for that.* It was clear he had said something wrong, and he needed to come up with something to win back the crowd—fast.

The Master Magician raised his hands and the white mask of Devos Rektor appeared above him. "Think of Devos. Think of how much pain and suffering he and his army rained down upon the Old World. His waters rose and caused what was once a united kingdom to break apart. Now we live scattered across the islands.

"But do you remember what stopped the Flood? Do you remember what brought Devos down? The magicians and mages were not enough. It took the combined work of all people—yes, every single person, Color, no Color—to shatter the storm cloud he had cast above all O'Ceea. So please understand, no matter the outcome for you tonight, we in the Workshop stand united with all of you."

What a strange speech. Jaremon wasn't sure what to make of it. No one from the Workshop had ever said anything like that before. From the silence of the crowd, Jaremon was sure he wasn't the only one left confused.

"Well!" Igar bounced out in front of the Master Magician with a big smile. "You sure said it. Now, everyone! Before you take your seats and we commence the Ceremony, don't you think—while we have the Master Magician here—we should do something to encourage him to give us just one more little Glimmering? What else can we expect from this year's Grand Projection? Come on everyone, if that's something you really want, Let! Me! Hear! You! Screeeeeam!"

As soon as Igar said the words, the crowd started to clap and cheer again. Greydyn appeared to sigh, then raised his hands and motioned for the crowd to be silent. "Well, I wouldn't be a very good Master Magician if I spoiled a story by giving something away, now would I?"

The statement made Olan snort with laughter.

"But I will say this much." Greydyn spun his hands above his head and projections of dark violet and indigo storm clouds appeared above the stadium. "We at the Workshop have long waited for the right moment to reveal the origins of Devos." He stretched his arms out and wriggled his fingers, and large drops of projected rain started to fall.

"There are many ancient myths about the Flood. People throughout history have longed to know where all the rain that filled the Old World came from." He flung his arms down and a huge torrent of projected water fell. Jaremon felt the sensation of the deluge pelting him. He felt wet but remained perfectly dry. "If it is really true that the Lord of Chaos found a way to make his projected rain real, how did he come to possess this magical talent?"

The crowd twittered with excitement. Some jumped up and down, others stomped, and most clapped. The sound of chanting rumbled across the stadium. "Devos! Chaos! Devos! Chaos! Ka-Ka-Chaos! Ka-Ka-Chaos!"

This is going to be the best Grand Projection ever, Jaremon thought as the storm clouds dissolved. *I can't wait to see how they explain the way Devos made real rain.*

The only other person in history who was widely believed to have turned projections into real things was Tav. Jaremon, like most, believed Tav was a real, historical person. But, as he lived so long ago, it was impossible to know anything about him. For example, did he really claim to be the creator of all life, as some asserted? Who could know? And, if Tav really had found a way to live forever inside of a projection, why hadn't anyone else done so since?

Jaremon knew many people worshiped Tav as a god, but he couldn't. He liked a lot of the stories people told about Tav, just as he enjoyed the ones about Devos. However, the facts he knew to be true about O'Ceea proved that the things people claimed Tav had said and done were nothing more than made-up fantasies.

The Master Magician stepped down and took a seat in the VIP section in the front row of the stadium.

"See, Aliva. That wasn't so drench, was it?" Jaremon asked.

"I guess not," Aliva admitted. "I still think they should've started with the pulling, though."

Olan leaned forward and said, "The puller should come out next."

"I hope it's not the same one from last year," Aliva said. "Remember how long it took for him just to climb up the stairs?"

"Aliva," her mother chided. "You're being insensitive. The pullers are all very old. It's probably really difficult for them to climb up all that way."

"Sorry," Aliva apologized.

But she's right. This part of the Ceremony is always really long and tedious.

A few moments later, a human form—Jaremon could not tell if it was male or female—emerged from a trapdoor in the stadium floor. Like all pullers, this one was wrapped tightly in what appeared to be nine strips of Color-infused fabric. The Dy'Mageio claimed that they were, in fact, true ribbons of Color, the same as those that were pulled out of mages. But Jaremon couldn't believe that. They were certainly fantastic, though. These magical bandages gave off dazzling, bright, beautiful light that swirled across every surface of the puller's body—that is, every surface except the white, shapeless emptiness in the spot where a face should have been.

Pullers were faceless. This was the way Dy'Mageio showed their devotion to the gods. Whenever Jaremon saw one, he found himself wondering, *Why would someone ever want to throw away their face and hide behind some empty mask?* Jaremon had long been interested in Dy'Mageio customs and history, and he found himself scrutinizing this puller's every move.

The mysterious figure made a complete circle around the stage and passed in front of every single child who stood ready to be examined. Following behind the puller were four other faceless forms. *Acolytes. Two men and two women*, Jaremon determined, though it was hard to be sure, as all Dy'Mageio wore identical plain white clothes and head coverings. He knew these four were acolytes, though, because of the limited number of Colors that eddied and billowed around them. Unlike pullers, acolytes had not yet earned the right to display all Nine Colors. The one closest to the puller was likely a woman, based on her figure. She had five Colors loosely wrapping her—Crimson, Red, Yellow, Orange, and Green—whereas the man next to her had only Yellow, Orange, and Blue.

"They're so creepy," Aliva said quietly. "I don't understand why anyone would want to join that guild."

"The Dy'Mageio aren't a guild," Jaremon told her. "People don't really join it. It's more like they become it. You have to give up everything to become one of them."

"Who'd ever choose to do that?"

"Not many people do," Jaremon said. "Most of them were taken to the Island of the First Watch as babies and dedicated to the Dy'Mageio."

"Don't forget all the people who are summoned," Olan said in a creepy voice.

"What? You can be summoned?" Aliva's voice quivered.

"Not exactly," Jaremon said as he shot an annoyed look at Olan. "Every once in a while, a commoner will wake to see a Color swirling around them. If that person goes to the Island of the First Watch, they can either lose their face and become Dy'Mageio, or ask a puller to put that Color into their collar."

"Wait. Do you mean there's another way to get a Color?"

"Well, no, it's not really the same thing. But . . . yes, some people have become mages that way."

"Whoa. That's mega," Aliva said.

"It's a very rare occurrence, though. They say a commoner is more likely to be struck by lightning twice than to have a Color appear on its own like that."

"It's way more common than that," Olan said.

"No it isn't. I've studied Mage Rouwand, and everyone knows he's the undisputed authority on the subject."

"Wow," Aliva said with a look of deep admiration. "I guess Kalaya's right about you. You really do know your stuff."

Jaremon knew a lot about Dy'Mageio from his studies on Color, and he had concluded that they were little more than an outdated sect of lunatics. They considered themselves disciples of the Color gods. Dy'Mageio did not contain their Colors in a collar as mages and magicians did. Their Colors ran free over them and marked them, like dye. Through intense worship and complete devotion, Dy'Mageio actually believed they could obtain all Nine Colors from these imaginary spiritual creatures.

But their Colors aren't like ours. How many people have had more than three pulled? Jaremon knew there were very few; each additional Color a person received was an order of magnitude more rare. *They can't be real Colors. Their beliefs are just a foolish relic from a time when people were ruled by superstitions. I'm glad I was born in an age when most people see through all that and understand so much more about what Color really is.* Jaremon, like most modern people, could not understand the appeal that becoming Dy'Mageio still had for some people. *Who would want to spend their entire life on some worthless rocky island saying prayers and devoting themselves to a bunch of non-existent gods just to get a bunch of imitation Colors that they don't use for anything?*

But he couldn't completely write them off. Certain aspects of modern life were still affected by the Dy'Mageio. *Like this moment. All these people are praising the puller, even though most of them would consider the person absolutely brainbust for still believing that the Color gods exist.*

"Argh," Aliva groaned. "Look at how slowly he's moving. I'm going to die of old age before Kalaya's name is called." Her mother gave her a stern look, and Aliva cleared her throat and added, "Uh, I mean . . . woo hoo! I love this part. It's so fascinating. Go, puller, go!"

As the puller ascended the stairs that led up to the top of the pedestal and the four acolytes stood guard at the base of it, the audience began to cry out, "Color, Color, find within us Color!" This was a fragment of an ancient chant that people had once recited, hoping the gods would find favor on them and bestow their child with a Color. Because of tradition, this part was still chanted today, even though few still believed in the gods.

Jaremon began to speak the full chant softly under his breath. He had it memorized in the ancient language. *But only because of its historical significance, not because I actually believe saying it will have any influence on Kalaya's odds of receiving a Color.*

As he was whispering the chant, something about this puller captured his attention. *Is it? Could it be?* He focused his eyes. *Yes! That's the Magician Puller!* He was sure of it.

There were a number of pullers, but only one Magician Puller. Jaremon didn't know the man's actual name—he wasn't sure if anyone did—but he knew that this man was a long-standing magician of the Third Magnitude and was therefore one of the most important people in all the islands. Jaremon had watched a chronicler's archive of him while conducting a study on the current Third Magnitudes, so he recognized him now by the way he walked. All Dy'Mageio moved around with their head down in a kind of humble stoop, but Jaremon noticed that the Magician Puller held his head up, as if he was looking straight forward. Jaremon doubted anyone else would know this, however, so he happily shared the information with Kalaya's family.

"Wow," said Kathy with a look of shock. "The Magician Puller himself!"

"Come on," Olan groaned. "You can't possibly know that. Every puller looks the same."

"I pay attention to details, Olan," Jaremon said with a scowl. "You should try it. It might help your scores."

"So is this puller better than the others?" Kathy asked enthusiastically.

"Oh, certainly. He's one of the Eight."

"Is this good or bad news for Kalaya?" Aliva asked.

"Very good news," said Jaremon.

"Oh." Aliva sounded disappointed. "Well, at least the puller's finally at the top."

Now that the Magician Puller had arrived at the top of the pedestal, he raised the ancient Staff of Light in the air with both hands, and the nine Colors that had until then been wrapped tightly around his body began to unfurl. Nine strands of light, contained in something like frayed strips of cloth, spun up toward the tip of the staff and then pressed together, forming a tight ball. After all his Colors were collected, the puller threw his arms open, and the Colors shot straight up into the sky above the stadium, where they compressed in on themselves and formed a rainbow-colored moon.

The crowd broke out with shouts of joyful adulation and resumed chanting, "Color, Color, find within us Color!"

"Isn't his dyemoon magnificent?" Kathy said. "It's so bright, Cale, it feels like day has returned."

I don't know why people always say that. It made no sense to him. *It's not that much brighter now.* While it had the appearance of the enigma that presided over the Island of the First Watch, it wasn't anything like it. *People should really go and see the real dyemoon for themselves so they don't get drawn in by emulations like this.*

"Color, Color, find within us Color!"

It was finally time to start.

The Color Ceremony—Part Two
~Jaremon~

Most people assume the word 'mage' originated from Dy'Mageio, and, though there's no hard evidence for it, it is an intellectually sound conclusion. Though Dy'Mageio ways may seem bizarre to modern O'Ceea, the islands would not be floating anywhere as high as they are today without them.

—Mage Rouwand is-a Stump, *Insights from the Insightful*

Igar, the announcer, stood in front of the young people and called out the first name. A short, nervous-looking sixteen-year-old boy stepped forward, collected a black collar from an acolyte, and carefully ascended the pedestal.

Poor guy, Jaremon thought. *Going first must be awful. This kid's got no chance.*

No one knew exactly when they would be called to stand before the Puller. There was no prepared order. As the children stood in their ring around the pedestal and waited for their names to be spoken, the magicians in charge of the Ceremony were determining which child to send forth next.

While many people searched for clues to help them predict what the magicians would decide, and there were countless theories on the subject, Jaremon was confident that he had figured out the correct pattern for the Ceremony.

"How long until Kalaya goes?" Aliva asked.

"Since there will be so many void pulls, they have to mix it up to keep the crowd interested. They start off with the least likely, then throw in a few sure things to keep us from getting bored—or upset," Jaremon whispered. "They could use her as one of the sure things, but based on how well she did today, I'm quite sure she won't be called until closer to the end. They save the best, and most exciting, for last."

"Sure do," Olan interjected. "Jaremon, you were one of the very last ones in your year, right? I can't remember."

"No," he answered. "I was one of the sure things."

Much to his dismay, Jaremon had been one of the first to be called forward in his year. Because of the number of Twigs who had been there, he had come to believe that the magicians in charge must have confused him with one of his cousins—likely Geromen or Jaremoneth. But that was okay. He hadn't wanted to be one of the last three or four anyway. *There's way too much pressure on them.* But he did think it would have been nice to be one of the final ten. *Oh well. It doesn't matter. I'll get a higher score than any of my cousins. People will remember that.*

✳   ✳   ✳

The first child who was called forward produced no Color.
Neither did the second.
Or the third.
Even though it brought down the air of excitement each time a boy or girl came forward and no Color was pulled out, Jaremon breathed a little easier. *The more who don't have Colors, the higher the odds for Kalaya.*

He predicted the first Color would be pulled after seven, but it ended up being a surprise reveal when Red was found in the fourth kid.

Of course, it had to be Red to open the night. Jaremon frowned when the ribbon of ugly Color poured from the youth and spread out until it hovered like a giant, thin sheet just above the heads of everyone in the stadium. It lingered there—a canopy of Red stars—for a short moment before it dropped like a liquid, coating every person and object beneath it, like some kind of sticky paint. Jaremon hated the way the disgusting Color clung to him; worse, he hated how so many people were lured in by it, finding it 'enchanting' and 'enthralling.' *Reds are so self-absorbed. Wherever they go, they always try to smother all the other Colors.* Thankfully, it wasn't long before the Magician Puller reeled it back and everything returned to normal.

The next Color was found in the eighth kid, and then, to the audience's delight, back to back in the fourteenth and fifteenth. *Huh? There are way more Colors appearing in the beginning than expected.* Jaremon made some quick recalculations. "Sometimes they do this," he said to no one in particular.

"Do what?" Cale asked.

"Have lots of Color at the beginning. You know, to get everyone excited."

"Wow," Olan said. "It must be painful to be so enlightened. Look at you, you're shaking like a little leaf in a storm."

Jaremon ignored him. *I'm not shaking. I'm excited about Kalaya's future.*

One youth after another came forward. Some had Colors, but most didn't. Jaremon took great enjoyment in each Color that was revealed, and took note of that mage's face and the personality expressed in their ribbon for future reference in the Competitions. This was fun, but his favorite aspect of the Color Ceremony was the numbers. Jaremon ran the probabilities of Kalaya's success going up or down based on the outcome of each pull. Most people liked the different personal stories and drama, but Jaremon got excited about the real story the numbers foretold. Despite all this, one kid managed to grab his full attention.

When he first saw the skinny boy named Drungo is-a Ray stumble up the pedestal stairs and hold his black collar up in the air, Jaremon expected there would be nothing in him. But as the Magician Puller placed the staff on the young man's heart and pulled it back, a glimmer of dark Indigo could be seen.

Cheers from his clan went out, and the entire stadium watched in wondrous amazement as a glorious ribbon of Indigo was pulled out of his body. It spiraled up and away from the staff and shimmered in the air.

Most Indigo ribbons shot away, high into the sky, as soon as they were revealed, and the stars contained in the ribbon were almost never seen. All that was visible was the sparkle of the entire ribbon darting about the heavens, urgently doing some unfathomable work.

But it was a long time before Drungo's ribbon soared away; it hovered before him and then slowly moved around the stadium. Everyone in the audience could peer into the Indigo-tinged fire that was his ribbon. To Jaremon, it seemed to ripple like a stormy wave crashing against the rocks of a stony shore. He looked into Drungo's ribbon and marveled at the thousands of Indigo spirals and blinking lights that floated inside; they appeared like stars dancing together in one grand ballet, the very essence of a galaxy in motion. This Indigo galaxy was at once tangible and real while also feeling ethereal and forever out of reach, like the non-corporeal mist of fog in the dark of night. *Wow. This is a really exceptional moment. I've never perceived Indigo like this.*

Jaremon found there was something deeply moving about seeing a person's Color pulled. Even though he had never met this boy from the Ray clan, it felt like he was now peering deeply into the boy's very soul. It was as though, in that moment, he knew everything about Drungo, while at the same time he recognized that there was an endless universe within him that would require an eternity to explore.

And then it was gone. The swirling ribbon shot straight up, high above the stadium, as Indigo was prone to do, and rocketed back and forth like hundreds of stars shooting in every direction.

The look of pleased confidence on the boy's face reminded Jaremon of how excited he had been when Green was pulled from him. It was an experience that made him feel entirely vulnerable and exposed, while at the same time utterly loved and known.

"Look at that!" Igar is-a Moon hollered. "Congratulations to Drungo is-a Ray, O'Ceea's newest Indigo mage! I guess there will be no more rowing for you!"

Drungo now held up the thick band of cloth with confidence. This would be his collar. He would wear it for the rest of his life. It would be infused with Indigo and mark him as a mage: someone worthy to compete for a place in the Magician's Workshop.

The Magician Puller twirled his staff in the air and reeled the ribbon out of the depths of the sky and back down to the pedestal. In just a few heartbeats, he had the Indigo ribbon twisted up into a concentrated ball of light at the end of the staff. He then touched the staff to the black collar that Drungo held in his outstretched hands. The Indigo light went into the cloth, transforming the ordinary black fabric into the precious object everyone in the islands desired: a Color collar.

Drungo wasted no time clasping the collar around his neck. As soon as it was secure, he turned to his right, tightened his hand into a fist, and plunged his elbow down while shouting out his own name, "Drungo!" Then he did it again. Spinning to his left, he made another fist, plunged his elbow down, and called out even louder, "Drungo!"

It was a ridiculous-looking move, but judging by all the cheers and laughter, everyone in attendance loved it. *They're either celebrating with him or laughing at him.* Jaremon suspected it was the latter.

Spurred on by all the attention, Drungo projected an indigo-tinted monkey in his hand. He held it high, then flipped it into the air and toward the audience. He did this over and over until dozens of projected monkeys were scurrying around the stadium.

Finally, the Magician Puller had had enough. He ushered Drungo towards the steps of the pedestal and off the stage.

✳   ✳   ✳

It took a little longer than average before the next Color was drawn. It came from the forty-sixth child, a girl, quiet and shy. The Color was Cyan. As the Magician Puller spread it out, it seemed to glisten and gleam with a soothing, delicate beauty like that of a peaceful sea. It was very much unlike the wild, turbulent feel of Drungo's Color.

Jaremon loved how every one of the Nine Colors came out differently and not only reflected the qualities that made up that Color, but also served as a unique reflection of the distinct individual it came from. This girl, he observed, had a measure of grace that was very different from what he'd observed in most Cyan mages. As her Cyan sea rippled above him, he was moved in a way he couldn't quite identify. It gave him the sense that she was very present and alive, yet at the same time veiled and alone. *She's going to be a challenge to beat in the Competitions.*

All the citizens of her island were roaring in celebration. Jaremon felt genuinely happy as he watched her clasp the collar around her neck, bow to the audience, and depart the stage. *Cyan was right for her.*

After her came a long, dry stretch of void pulls. One by one, a kid would step forward, no Color would be found, and the kid would leave with a black collar. It was a cascade of devastation. While many descended the pedestal and got off the stage—and out of sight—before exploding with emotions, most didn't. Some cried right on the spot. A few went into immediate shock and stumbled around, not knowing where to go. Two even went so far as to fall down on their knees and beg the Magician Puller to try again. Such outbursts caused a miserable sensation to swirl around inside Jaremon, and he was thankful that it never lasted long. Following every void pull there was always a new child—a new hope—who would climb to the top of the pedestal and replace the one who came before.

After ten void pulls, the crowd grew uneasy and began to chant, "Color, Color, find within us Color!"

I can't believe so many people still hold onto that old superstition. He knew that some people believed that Color would one day disappear from the islands if the gods were not continually worshiped. The feeling grew worse, and the chanting louder, as five more children came and went. *Fifteen is far too many voids in a row. We need a Color now, before all this pressure causes someone to have a nervous breakdown.* Jaremon knew how people were prone to worry at times like this. *It will turn around. Color always regresses toward the mean.* It was then that Igar called the name he'd been waiting for.

"Up next is"—he paused for dramatic effect—"Kalaya is-a Cloud!" Everyone in her section jumped to their feet.

Okay. Good. They consider Kalaya to be one of the sure things needed to turn everything around. She's number sixty-two. That's a good number. It isn't as good as making it to the end, but it's nice to know the magicians see the potential in her, too.

"Here we go." Jaremon smiled at Kathy, Cale, and Aliva. *All right. Please, something nice like Cyan or Yellow.*

"She'll break the negative streak, right Jaremon? That's how it works, right?" Olan said out loud, while privately projecting into

Jaremon's ear, "Or she'll crash and burn in front of the Master Magician."

Jaremon leaned forward. *Come on, Kalaya, you can do this.*

The girl—at the very moment of becoming a young woman—took a deep breath and planted her feet firmly in front of the Magician Puller. Jaremon could tell from the way her fingers twitched that she was nervous.

Don't play with your hair. She fiddled with the black collar in her hands, but kept her arms down. *Good. You can do it.*

"Kalaya did quite well for herself today, receiving a grand total of twelve chips: six bronze, two silver, and four gold. This great achievement will grant her access to the first privilege level, which I must say is quite incredible for a sixteen-year-old! At this pace, it won't be many years before we'll see a guild pin on her collar," Igar announced. "As a Cloud, she comes from a rich heritage. The last member of her immediate family to get a Color—her grandmother, Agatha was-a Cloud—was a Yellow-Orange magician of the Second Magnitude and served the people of O'Ceea in the Workshop for over twenty-five years. Will Kalaya be the next?"

Several members of the Cloud clan started to chant her name. "Ka-lay-a. Ka-lay-a. Ka-lay-a."

She raised the black collar high up in the air and squeezed her eyes shut. The Magician Puller raised the Staff of Light and placed it squarely on her heart.

The crowd was silent with anticipation; it was time to see another Color.

Jaremon held his breath and focused all his attention on Kalaya's face.

You've got this.

The Magician Puller pulled his staff back . . .

. . . and no Color was attached.

Void

~Jaremon~

Solid, patient, and grounded, Green mages excel in matters of teamwork and support. They can be very focused and intelligent, often becoming masters in their chosen field of study. When healthy, they grow strong and nurture those around them. However, unhealthy Green mages, like my ex-husband, are known to be greedy, arrogant, dismissive, controlling, and competitive and—like nasty little trolls—horde resources for themselves.

—Mage Kylee is-a Silk, *Color Me Curious: What Your Color Says About You!*

Jaremon shifted his eyes away from her. *I can't believe it.* Disappointment flooded over him as the Magician Puller lowered his staff and turned his faceless head away.

"Oh dear," her mother said as she turned her face away as well.

Everyone around let out a collective sigh of defeat as they sat down.

"That was . . . unexpected," Aliva said under her breath.

As he looked back at the young woman still standing at the top of the pedestal, Jaremon saw that all the color had drained from her face. It was hard to watch as she lowered her arms, looked down at the black collar—void—in her fragile hands, and fastened it around her neck. It had a checkered pattern, indicating she was at the first privilege level. This was the reward for her high chip count—but Jaremon knew she would find no joy in that.

He turned his focus to the white stone pillars of the stadium. *It would have been beautiful to see them light up for her in the Competitions.*

"That throttlewog!" Olan exclaimed with utter outrage the moment the Magician Puller turned away. "How is this possible? Didn't they see her chips!?"

For once in his life, Jaremon actually agreed with Olan. It wasn't fair. *She deserved this more than anyone else.* Her clan was due for a Color. Her family was one of the few good ones left on their island. *She worked so hard for it.* He looked around. *The whole region must be feeling her pain right now.*

To her credit, she didn't make a scene. Devoid of emotion, she stepped down the stairs of the pedestal, off the stage, and decended through the floor to the exit.

"Drench me," Olan said and leaned back in his seat. "I thought for sure . . ."

Her time had come . . . and gone. She was searched and found void. Why did this have to happen to us?

"Take me to her," her father said abruptly.

"No, no. It'll be too hard for you. I'll go." And without giving her family a chance to protest, Jaremon left his seat and slid away through the aisle. *She's going to want to talk to me.* He'd always known there was a chance of this happening, but he had not adequately rehearsed the words he knew he should actually say.

✳   ✳   ✳

Jaremon descended into the vast labyrinth of rooms and hallways that lay below the floor of the stadium. This monument was not just for the Color Ceremony; it was also used for the

Intra-Regional Competitions, and every other year it was used for one of the O'Ceea Championship Games. The space underneath the stadium was dark; those who traveled down here were expected to project their own light. It was a disorienting place, and—for someone like . . . her—it probably felt dreadful. *She must be confused, alone—with no idea what to do, or where to turn.* Or, at least, that was how he imagined she was feeling.

He, however, knew this space well. He had spent a lot of time here during his past two seasons in the Competitions. He remembered how he had lit up these halls after a glorious victory, and how he preferred to walk through them in darkness after a humiliating defeat. Jaremon was perfectly capable of lighting up the halls as he searched. Instead, he opted to remain in the darkness, projecting only enough faint light to keep from stumbling.

He walked a long distance before he heard, "Jaremon? Is that you?" Her voice came to him like an arrow through his heart. She was still far away. He hesitated. He wanted to go to her, but everything was different now. He wasn't sure he was ready to see her just yet. He knew he should go and comfort her, but something—some agonizing feeling deep in the pit of his stomach—kept him from moving.

"Jaremon, I hear you. Please keep calling so I can find you," she shouted.

What? I haven't made a sound.

"Yes, I'm coming your way," she said again. "Dad, is that you? Are you here, too?"

What's going on? Who's talking to her?

"Kalaya is-a Cloud," a powerful voice called out.

Who said that?

"Master Magician?" she gasped. "What are you doing here? Did I . . . did I do something wrong?"

"No, Kalaya. Not at all," the Master Magician said.

What's he doing here? Jaremon's curiosity about this startling situation unfroze him. He needed to know what was going on, so he crept toward the sound of their voices. *Could the Master Magician really have left in the middle of the Ceremony? That's unheard of.* The Ceremony would certainly continue without him, but his absence was bound to create a stir of controversy.

"I have come to tell you in person how deeply sorry I am for what just happened," the Master Magician said. "It's painful when someone doesn't receive a Color. I truly hate it and have long wished for the islands to be different."

"Really? Um . . . thank you," she replied.

Why is he talking to her?

"I saw your giant blue wallaroo earlier today."

"You did?" she asked. Jaremon knew that tone. It was the way she spoke when she felt embarrassed.

"Don't be ashamed. I absolutely loved it."

He did?

"You did?" She sounded as stunned as Jaremon felt.

"Yes, and I believe your grandmother would have especially loved it."

"My grandmother? Uh . . . how would you know . . . I mean . . . did you know her?"

"Of course. Agatha and I worked together in the Workshop. She and I were close friends."

"I never knew that," she said. "Um . . . I mean . . . I'm sorry. I'm confused. Are you really the Master Magician?"

"Yes, I am. I hope it's all right that I came here."

"Certainly, it's an honor."

"It's my honor. I know how much Agatha would have wanted to be the one standing here. I'm certain she would have clapped with joy to see your wallaroo. You deserved the gold chip you received for it."

"But . . . why would she have liked it?" she asked tentatively. "It was blue."

"She would have loved it because it was blue. Isn't that why you made it that color?"

"No. I was trying to make it look real, like the ones you made in *The Roo and the Rower*."

"Yours looked pretty real to me," the Master Magician said. "We have no idea what color wallaroos really were. All we know about them is from a few bones in a museum."

See! That's exactly what I said.

"For all we know, they could have been blue," the Master Magician continued. "Maybe they don't exist today because they were blue and yellow and thus heartlessly exterminated in some ancient purge."

There was a long pause before she spoke. "Did my grandma like the color blue?"

"Did she?" He laughed and then paused before he replied. "Don't you know?"

"What?"

"She made things blue—all the time. Certainly you knew that about her?"

That's interesting. So it's some family thing. Jaremon hadn't considered this as a possible source of her problem. He crept closer, wanting to get a look at the two of them. But as he got near, he realized their voices were actually coming from below him. *They must be on a lower level than I am.* He made his way to a stairway, and when he took a couple steps down it, he saw—far down the hall—the Master Magician and Kalaya surrounded by a warm, inviting glow of yellow light.

"No, I didn't know that. I actually don't know as much about my grandma as I would like," Kalaya admitted. Then she paused before saying, "I'm glad she wasn't here to see me today."

"No, no. Don't say that," the Master Magician insisted. "She understood that the nature of Color is a great and confusing mystery. She was the one who told me 'Color, no Color, nothing would have kept me from laughing and playing.' I didn't believe her at the time. I couldn't believe that anyone could keep on laughing and playing after receiving such a devastating blow. I know I wouldn't have been able to. But Agatha was different. It would have been true for her. I hope it will be true for you."

After a long pause, Kalaya said, "I'll try, but . . . I'll never be a magician."

"No, you won't. That is, unless the islands change their beliefs about Color. And—let me tell you a secret—I believe they will, certainly in your lifetime. You and your blue wallaroo would be a great asset in the Workshop."

What!? Jaremon couldn't believe what he had just heard. *Could the Master Magician be colorblind? Maybe there's something to those rumors about him being sympathetic to Nu:Kinrei. He did grow up in Region 6.* The very thought that this might be true changed the way Jaremon viewed him. *Maybe he shouldn't be allowed to be the Master Magician after all.*

"Goodbye, Mistress Kalaya—forgive me, I must return to the Ceremony. May you find joy in the wonder of all the blue creatures you project," he said, and then he turned and left her behind in the dark.

*   *   *

Jaremon remained on the stairs for a long time. *What did the Master Magician mean by all that?* None of it made any sense to him. But nothing was really making sense at all tonight. *It doesn't matter. I have to talk with her—now. It will only get harder the longer I wait.*

He took a deep breath, gathered his thoughts, and then said, "Ula-Thaow." A little glowing ball that looked something like a moon materialized in the air. The projection illuminated the halls and hovered in front of him as he made his way down the steps.

As he came down to the lower level, he could see her more clearly, leaning against a wall a few feet away. *All right. Be gentle.* He stepped toward her and called out in a soft voice, "Hey."

He could see her red, puffy eyes turn toward him. He did not meet her gaze. Instead, he lowered his eyes to her collar—her black, Colorless collar. The light of his moon reflected off of the black cloth in an ominous way, and he felt his throat constrict.

"Jaremon!" Kalaya's lower lip quivered when she saw the moon he'd made.

She needs to cry. I can help her with that. He pushed the little moon toward her, until it hovered above her face. After looking up at it, Kalaya dropped to her knees and broke down crying.

"You're safe with me. Let it out. Let everything out," Jaremon said, holding back all the things he wanted to say. Tears, he had found, seemed to help people process things, and even though the act of crying did not come naturally to him, he had an innate ability to create projections with a certain kind of Glory that somehow helped others weep. *There is value in this,* he had decided long ago, so he embraced the skill, even though he didn't understand it. It was something that would make him unique—and improve his scores.

Kalaya cried and cried, until she was finally still. She looked up at him and asked, "Did you bring my dad? Is he here?"

"No, he's up with your mom, back in the stadium."

"Oh," she said. She paused for a moment before starting to cry again.

He sat down next to her.

"I'm sorry, Jaremon. I touched my face," she whimpered. "When I came up on stage, I touched my face."

"All that's in the past now. You have to let go of it."

"But I messed up. Right?"

Yeah, you did. "There's a lot of pressure when you're on stage."

"It was so humiliating." She was breathing fast. "You don't understand what that feels like. Everyone was watching me. My clan, my parents, the island . . . you. Everyone." She paused to try to catch her breath. "Everyone thought I was going to get a Color. And then this happened."

"The odds were in your favor."

She pressed the palm of her hand into the side of her face, and under her breath she said, "I don't want to hear about your idiotic odds anymore."

Okay. She's angry. I need to do this now before things get worse. "We should probably talk about what all this means for us," Jaremon said into the silence.

He could see Kalaya's body tense. "Wait, what? What do you mean?"

"It's going to be really difficult now. We won't be able to see much of each other anymore. I'll be living at my uncle's training camp for the next half year, and you'll be at home. Then there'll be the Competitions. I'll be pouring all my focus into—"

"Are you saying . . . wait, what are you saying?" Kalaya asked as she stood up and wiped her eyes with the back of her hand.

He stood up after her and said, "Well, I've been giving it some thought, and it seems that—due to these unforeseen circumstances—it would be the wisest choice for both of us if we—"

"Wait! Are you saying we should break up?"

Kalaya, let me speak, I'm trying to make this easier for you. "I don't want to, but it just makes sense. Long-distance relationships between mages and commoners never really work."

"That's not true. There are lots of Grand Projections in which relationships like that work out just fine—like *Washed Away*. That's one of your favorites."

"Grand Projections aren't real. You know that."

"Your mom is a mage and your dad is Colorless—it's worked out for them! Right?"

She had to bring that up. He took a step away from her and said, "That's different!" Then, regaining his composure, he stepped back toward her, looked into her eyes, and said, "Kalaya, I want to compete in the O'Ceea Championship Games. My parents never did."

"Is competing really that important to you?"

"You know it is."

"Is it the most important thing in all the islands?"

"Well, I wouldn't go that far," Jaremon said.

"No, it is. That's how you feel. And you know what? It's fine. You're . . . you're right. You're right about this," she said firmly.

Good. She's going to be fine. This is the best decision for both of us. "You know how my uncle always says a competitor can't let anything hold him back."

"Sure, of course. He's right." She took some deep breaths before continuing. "You will be gone all the time . . . relationships like that are really hard."

Jaremon nodded. *This is going more easily than I expected.* "I'm glad we're in agreement here. This really isn't easy for me."

She turned her eyes away from him and looked up at his projected moon. "You really are a very talented mage."

That's nice of her to say. "I think I have a shot of getting into the Championships this year."

"I think you do, too," she said. She wiped the last of her tears from her face and with confidence said, "No, I'm certain you'll get to the Championship Games. This is your year. You shouldn't let anything hold you back from making your . . . simulitcrums."

"Simulacrums," Jaremon corrected.

"Right. Those," she mumbled.

She's going to let me go without a fight. Jaremon felt a weight lift from him. "You can come see me compete. I'd like that."

"Hey, you know what—I'm done," she spoke with urgency. "I don't want to be underneath this stadium anymore."

"Oh, okay, sure," Jaremon hesitated. "Here, follow me."

"No," she said. "That's okay. I'll find my own way out."

"Really? Are you sure?"

"Yeah. I want to go find my dad."

"Oh. Yeah, that's a good idea. You go. I'll see you later."

She turned away, climbed up the stairs, and left Jaremon and his moon below and behind her.

Thoughts raged through his mind.

That could have been a lot worse . . . it was for the best . . . both of us will be better off . . . we'll be able to find people more suited for us . . . at least I'll be able to focus all my time on training.

I'll miss holding her hand.

I'll miss her.

As the voices took over his mind, the moon Jaremon had projected went out. And there, below ground, deep within the catacomb-like vaults under the stadium, he realized he was alone in the dark.

The Color Ceremony—Part Three
~Kai~

I'd be! Ly-ing! If I! Said I
Un-der-stood everything I say!
Yet, people line up, just to hear every word.
Sometimes—when I feel buh-buh-bad!
Then I just re-mind my-self! I'm famous!
I'm faaa-mous! I'm faaaaaa-mous.
People care about everything I say!
Even if—it's nonsense, na-na-nonsense.

> —Opinionator Gary is-a Heart, as performed in the musical
> *Oops! I Probably Shouldn't Have Said That, But Did*

Kai is-a Shield smiled as he watched Drungo is-a Ray celebrate his newfound Indigo Color by flipping projected monkeys into the crowd.

"Drungo!" He shouted his name while thrusting his elbow down to the ground and posing like a champion. It looked ridiculous, but Kai loved every bit of it.

He clearly didn't expect a Color. Judging by the quality of his projected clothes, it was clear his family was very poor. Those in the Ray clan, from the Island of the Swinging Vines, were known to be ship rowers, not magicians. *It's likely that no one in his entire clan expected him to have a Color, and now, here he stands: an Indigo mage.* Kai hoped things would go well for him.

After Drungo had flipped his last monkey and struck his final pose, the cheers and laughter of the crowd died down and Kai could hear Snap's dad shout out at the top of his lungs, "I LOVE YOU, FREAKY INDIGO DRUNGO!"

His voice rang out loud and clear, much to the amusement of Talia, who stood next to Kai. She did her best to stifle a laugh.

"But Dad, flipping monkeys is your thing," Kai could just barely hear Snap say to Limmick.

"Nonsense. There never can be too many monkeys!" he bellowed.

Kai was happy they were here. Limmick had chosen to come with his entire family so that he could stand in support of Kai, disregarding what others from their island might think. Limmick had made it clear how disgusted he was by the way things had gone at the elders' meeting the day before and wanted to make a point by being here tonight. "Kai should be supported, not condemned," he'd said after the meeting had ended.

And here I am. By the time the Ceremony is over, I'll be free! Kai turned his head ever so slightly toward Talia.

"Why are you so happy?" Talia whispered when she noticed his smile.

"Everything's going to work out tonight. I can feel it."

Kai and Talia stood with what he thought must be somewhere between a hundred and a hundred and fifty other children. They were all gathered around the giant white pedestal in the center of the stadium. As Kai looked around this ring of kids, he could see that every single one of them was terrified.

Well, almost all of them. There was one very tall, imposing boy who stood with a measure of strength and confidence rarely seen during the Color Ceremony. And stranger still, he managed to maintain that confidence even while standing before thousands of people dressed in nothing but threadbare. *Who's that guy?*

"How is it possible for you not to be nervous?" Talia asked.

"Hey, I've survived King King, the prohibition, and that awful clan meeting. This is nothing."

Talia looked at him in disbelief. "You're certain you don't have a Color. That's why you're so happy."

"Well, if that Ray kid had one, I'm certainly void."

"Why? That makes absolutely no sense."

"Exactly!" Kai said with a sideways smile.

Talia shook her head and tried to maintain a look of graceful composure. "You're crazy, Kai, you know that, right?"

"It's trying to make sense of Color that makes people brainbust. But you don't need to worry. You have a two hundred percent chance of having one, according to the odds."

Despite the risks, she kicked Kai's foot.

See, we can still have fun, even with everyone in the entire region staring at us. Kai wanted to say a lot more, but with everything going on around them, communication wasn't easy. This last exchange spanned the time it took for several kids to be pulled, because they dared to speak only when the sounds of cheering and clapping were sure to drown them out.

He didn't expect to be comfortable here in the spotlight with the tremendous number of eyes peering down on him. But with Talia at his side and his hand fire safely hidden inside his clenched fist, it wasn't so bad. In fact, he kind of liked it. *Look at us. We're standing on a stage in the middle of the stadium. For years we've come and watched other kids doing this, and now it's us. Isn't it incredible?* Kai wanted to say this out loud, but he remained quiet when he heard the next words out of Igar is-a Moon's mouth.

"Weston is-a Wave!"

What! Weston's next? Kai saw his friend twitch. Weston had hoped his name wouldn't be called until late in the evening. Everyone knew there were more Colors drawn from the kids called at the end. The magicians in charge of the Ceremony always saved the most talented, entertaining, famous, and controversial children for the end. This was a show, after all. They had to keep people in their seats until the very last pull.

Kai knew he'd be the absolute last kid standing on the stage.

Everyone wanted to see this controversial child stand before the puller. He'd heard that people who otherwise had no reason to come to this Ceremony were here just to see him—even people from other regions. And if the size of the crowd was any indication, the rumors were true.

Okay everyone, it's time to focus your attention on Weston. His childhood friend had the ability to fill projections with significant Power. For this reason alone, it seemed inevitable that he had a Color in him. When Kai and his friends had discussed their theories, Talia said she was certain Weston would be Red because of his 'all-in' nature. Although Kai—deep down—held on to the hope that all of his friends would remain common, he knew how much Weston desired to become a mage. If it were to happen, he was sure Weston would be Yellow, owing to his cheerful optimism. Snap had no theory and told them, "Guessing is for bloomers." When they'd asked Luge, he didn't want to guess, but eventually he picked Red and Yellow, so as not to choose sides. Weston, of course, just wanted a Color—any Color.

When Weston was called, members of the Wave clan stood in support of him. This was the accepted practice for their island. It was unusual for anyone from another clan to stand with someone; even close friends didn't break this unspoken custom.

"Here we go, moment of truth," Kai whispered to Talia.

When Weston arrived at the top of the pedestal, he raised his collar high. The puller held the Staff of Light in front of him and then lowered it to the boy's chest. "This is your life, come what may," the puller's voice rang out.

Talia whispered under her breath, "Please, let there be something."

The staff was pulled back from his chest.

Kai stared intently for any shimmer of Color. But, to the shock and dismay of every Wave, there was nothing to be seen.

A void pull? Kai was as stunned as Weston looked. Disappointment crashed over him. *No way! That's not fair.* His feelings surprised him: he realized that he didn't want his friend to remain common after all. *Ah, bud! I'm so sorry. I was wrong. You would have been such a great mage.*

Weston put on his black collar in sullen silence. His clan sighed in defeat and sat back down. Weston's father dropped his head into his hands. Everyone looked miserable. But the worst part was the blank expression that now shrouded Weston's face. Kai had never seen his friend look so wooden and lifeless. It was devastating, and Kai felt like his own heart was about to break.

He suddenly felt self-conscious about the fire in his hand and looked down to make sure it was hidden. It wasn't. The flame had grown bigger and was now showing through the cracks of his clenched fingers. He quickly pushed his hand flat against his leg so that the flame would disappear into his upper thigh and not be noticeable. He glanced at Talia. Like his, her face was pained. But there was something more. Creases of worry formed around the corners of her eyes.

She's thinking that if Weston didn't have a Color in him, she can't possibly have one in her. "Don't worry Tal, you'll do just fine."

"What?" Talia looked a bit lost as she took a moment to process his words. "No, Kai, I'm not thinking about myself. I'm concerned about Weston. You know how he gets when things don't work out."

She was right; Weston had all his hopes set on becoming a mage and had no other aspirations for his life. *What will he do now?*

"You're so focused on not wanting a Color," Talia whispered as Weston hobbled down the steps of the pedestal and through the trapdoor on the stage, "you can't see what being found void does to others."

Kai thought about what she said, but before he could respond, Igar announced the next name.

"Talia is-a Leaf!"

What?! Right after Weston? He wasn't expecting Talia to get called for a long time. No one was. She had the chips and the reputation to be one of the last ones of the night. A lot of murmuring and a few cries of surprise and dispute came from the people of their island as they tried to grasp what this meant.

Talia stepped forward without saying a word to Kai or looking back to anyone in the crowd. She seemed unaware of the commotion around her. To those who didn't know her well, it appeared that she walked with confidence and possessed no doubt. But Kai—who believed he knew her better than anyone— saw fear in her.

And that panicked him. *She doesn't think she has a Color. First Weston, then her. She's resigned herself to it.*

"Look at that," Igar, the announcer, said. "It's been a long time since the entirety of the Island of the Four Kings has stood up in unity for one child."

Indeed. Every single Leaf, Wave, Stone, and Shield were on their feet. *Unbelievable! Everyone's hopes really are all on her. If a Color doesn't come out now, the island won't know how to deal with it.*

Igar continued, "Oh, forgive me! I was just informed this is actually the first time all four clans have ever stood for one child. As we all know, the Island of the Four Kings has gone through a bit of a rough patch over the last eight years. Could this be the Ceremony it all turns around for them?

"Oh, and on top of all this, Talia is a D. Leaf, a branch of the Leaf clan that hasn't produced a Color. Ever. Is that really true?" He paused for a moment. "I'm told it is. Wow! This really is a mind-shattering moment. Could this be the evening that changes the course of history for this family?"

Every single eye was on her as she ascended the pedestal. *You're going to do it, Tal. I know it.*

When Talia was elevated for all to see, she gripped her black collar and pressed it against her stomach. The puller bowed to her, lifted the Staff of Light high into the air, lowered it in front Talia's heart, and then gently pressed it against her.

"This is your life, come what may."

Please, please, please. He knew now that he was desperate for her to have a Color. *I've been such a bloomer. You deserve a Color, Tal, more than anyone.* He'd always wanted that for her, he just hadn't seen it until now.

The stadium was silent.

The puller strained.

Kai could hardly breathe.

The puller pulled the staff back, and . . .

. . . Cyan burst forth.

She did it. She did it!

Ignoring etiquette, Kai jumped up in the air and shouted out loud, "Talia did it!"

The crystalline ribbon of sea-green light pulled from Talia was the most beautiful form of Cyan Kai had ever seen. It flowed out from her and cascaded upward to create what looked to be a canopy of water above the heads of those who filled the stadium.

Kai was entranced by the beautiful patterns of reflected light that shimmered above them. They calmed him, just as Talia had calmed him numerous times before. *Is her light calming others now?* He looked around at the kids on the stage, and sure enough, several of the upturned faces looked more relaxed than they had moments before. *You did it. You did it!*

The Cyan sea was made up of countless stars; this universe inside of her Color was ordered and well-balanced; the spiraling constellations orbited one another with the reliability of a ticking clock whose many unseen gears moved together in perfect harmony. Cyan sometimes came out stormy, like a sea no experienced sailor would dare navigate. But not Talia's.

The people from their island filled the stadium with the roar of their grateful cheers and applause. For the first time—possibly in his entire life—Kai felt proud to be from his island. *They all stood together for Talia, and they all received this Color—her gift.*

He grinned from ear to ear when Talia knelt down, held up her collar, and humbly waited for the puller to reel back her Color. *A Cyan mage. It's so perfect.* Kai didn't have to see her face to know there were tears swelling in her eyes; he could feel them.

He knew Talia didn't have grand desires for fame or fortune, like many who longed for a Color. Her desire had always been simple and pure: she wanted nothing more than to make the islands a better place by sharing her gifts with others. And because of this, he felt a giant weight lift from his soul. There wasn't a single person in all O'Ceea who deserved a Color more than she did. *And the people of our island finally have what they've been longing for. They couldn't have found anyone better to bring about our long-desired restoration. Yes, yes, yes. Everything's going to be better now.*

It was then that Kai caught sight of his grandmother's serious stare. Talia's Cyan hadn't moved her. Her eyes bore into her grandson, and the weight of responsibility crashed over him again. All the soothing effects of Talia's Cyan disappeared. Jade is-a Shield still expected Kai to produce a Color. He ripped his eyes away from her.

He felt people looking at him, judging his every move, trying to catch a glimpse of his unconscious projection—his disability, as some called it—that had once again flared up. *No! This is Talia's moment. Stop focusing on me.*

A surge of anger hit Kai as the puller reeled in Talia's Cyan light and placed it into her collar. *No, don't take it away. Her Color needs to be out, flowing over all of us, not locked up inside some piece of fabric.*

Kai watched as Talia descended from the pedestal and went down through a trapdoor in the stadium floor. He wanted nothing more than to grab her as she passed by him and give her a big hug, but he knew he couldn't. After she disappeared, he felt truly alone on the stage, despite the fact that Luge was still with him.

Kai struggled to focus as child after child was called forward. They climbed up and down the stairs. Time passed. It was as if he'd flown out into the deep Indigo of space. He floated there, as if looking for some planet with a sign of life that he could move to and escape from the painful expectations his grandmother had placed on him. *She'll never be satisfied until she has someone in the Workshop. And who else is left but me? Sorry, Grandmother. I'm not going to go down that path.*

He barely noticed the murmuring of the crowd when the Master Magician left his seat in the VIP section, and he didn't notice at all when Greydyn returned.

Kai remained in this state for a half nightmark. One by one, others were called, until fewer than fifty kids remained on the stage. Then the announcer called a familiar name.

"Luge is-a Stone."

Hearing his friend's name shook Kai from his daze. *I bet he'll be glad when all this is finished.*

The Stone clan rose to their feet. Luge took a black collar from an acolyte, stepped up the pedestal, and stood before the puller like a healthy patient being examined by a doctor. The staff touched his chest. It was pulled back. And . . .

No Color was attached.

Luge took a deep breath and beamed; all was well with him. No Color made sense to him. He was now free to continue on with his life, building things with his hands, as he had expected.

When Luge came down, he walked out of his way to pass by Kai and whisper, "Come back to us, bud. You don't need to hide. It'll all be over soon."

He's right. I'm acting ridiculous. Everything is going to work out. There's no way a Color is going to be found in me. My grandmother will be upset about not having a magician in the family, but when I'm found void, she'll have to get over it. Talia is a Cyan mage now. She'll be able to give the island what they want. He took a deep breath and faced the section where his grandmother sat. But he did not look at her. Instead, he focused on the woman to her left. His mother was already looking at him, and as soon as she saw him turn to her, a giant smile came to her face. *Color, no Color. It won't make a difference to Mom.* Kai relaxed and his own smile returned. *It'll all be over soon.*

The Color Ceremony—Part Four
~Kai~

There isn't a person alive in all the islands who would deny that children feel a sickening pain in the moments when they are waiting to stand before a puller. And why wouldn't they? They are about to be given one of three names that will brand them for all time: Color mage, commoner, or cursed.

—Magician Elden is-a Bone, *Meet the Magicians*, on his inspiration for the character Narlo

The number of children left on stage shrank until there were only three remaining: a girl from the Island of the Maple Valley, the guy dressed in nothing but threadbare, and Kai. They stood next to one another in a little clump, but they didn't speak or even look at each other. The girl was almost certainly going to be called next.

Kai had heard of her before. She was Trista is-a Rose, a famous legacy whose grandfather was a current magician of the Third Magnitude. She came from an ultra-elite household, but her family did not expect her to match the success of those who came before her. She was free to become whoever she wanted. At least, that's what people said. But based on the number of chips Igar reported she had earned that day, it appeared she was talented and driven. Moreover, she wanted to be a magician; Kai could see that desire in her eyes.

But who was this boy dressed in threadbare? *Why has he been held off until the end?* He was almost certainly being used as filler. The goal was always to have a lot of Color found at the end of the Ceremony. But not too much. It was considered good entertainment to have a few void pulls dispersed throughout the final ten. *The magicians must not expect anything from this poor boy.*

Sure enough, Trista was called next, and when the puller placed the Staff of Light on her chest . . .

Orange exploded out of her.

Kai liked Orange. He found it was always able to lift his mood. Orange captivated. It delighted. It burst out of a person with zest. Trista's galaxy of oddly shaped Orange stars skipped, twirled, and danced in the ribbon as it flew and explored the space around them. The stars soared up and then down and spun wildly in circles. Unrestrained for a time, the ribbon of Color was free to move about and revel in the unexpected.

"Magnificent!" the boy in threadbare said as he shifted his attention from one playful cluster of stars to another. Kai watched with amazement as the Orange ribbon unexpectedly swooped over to the boy and spun around him until he was wrapped tightly in something like a cocoon of starlight. *Whoa! Magnificent is right.*

Orange resisted being reeled back in, so it took great effort for the puller to unravel the boy and draw the ribbon back to the staff. But it was not long before he was able to lock it into Trista's collar. *This puller is skilled.*

Once the girl had the now-Orange collar clasped around her neck, Kai leaned over and asked the boy, "What was that like?"

"Incredible. Better than anything I've experienced in a Grand Projection," the boy said as he intently watched Trista skip down the stairs.

Igar, eager to keep the attention of the audience, boomed out, "We've saved what must be the best story of compassion until now. Standing in nothing but his threadbare is Kaso, an orphan from Region 3. At great personal cost, this Blank traveled all the way here in order to be pulled. But when he went to register, he discovered the rules had changed, and he would not be able to participate tonight without a sponsor. Dressed up as the Crimson Blade with a bunch of poozers, he was sorely tempted to cheat. But he chose the higher path. One by one, he asked every mage he met to sponsor him—not realizing what he was asking." Igar laughed. "I bet some of you mages out there remember him.

"Well, I'd like you all to know he found a sponsor. There is still a flicker of compassion in the islands—that, or utter foolishness. Perhaps it was both, for it was Aaro is-a Tree—whom everyone knows to be a compassionate fool—who chose to sponsor him. He knew nothing about the boy. He didn't know if he could even earn a single chip. When Aaro was asked why he did it, he said he just had a sense that it was what Tav wanted him to do."

Huh. That's a good story. Kai looked out and saw only two people standing for Kaso: a young boy and an older man. *That must be the compassionate fool.*

"Was he right? There's only one way to know. Young Kaso is-a Tree, step forward and let Aaro and all the islands see what the Staff of Light reveals."

Wow, and I thought I had a lot of pressure on me. This is a whole other kind of incredible. Why does the most popular entertainment always require someone to be crushed under such impossible expectations?

Kai wanted to say something to Kaso as he stepped forward, but he was without words. It didn't seem to matter, though. Kaso didn't appear to need anything from him, or from anyone else. He strode up the stairs of the pedestal with a strength of presence that made him appear unshakable.

The puller positioned himself in front of this orphan as he had done for every other child, but then he did something unexpected. Kai hadn't heard the puller say anything personal to any of the other kids who had stood before him, but when Kaso met him—this boy with the size and presence of a man—he paused and said in a voice just loud enough for Kai to hear, "I look forward to getting to know you, warm one."

Kaso jolted. He appeared to be taken by surprise at that and stood with his hands firmly at his sides.

"This is your life, come what may," the puller said.

He held the staff on Kaso far longer than he had on anyone else. There was tension in the puller's arms, as if there was some kind of struggle. It seemed to Kai that the puller was searching longer and trying harder than usual. *Either that, or he's just creating more drama and suspense for the audience. There's always a lot of that at the end.*

Finally, the puller pulled back on the staff. Kaso looked down at the space between it and his body. Kai saw nothing there. But the puller kept a tight grip on the staff, and—acting like something was attached to it—he continued pulling back with great force.

Is there something there? The staff began to jerk about. *Yes. Is it invisible?* Then, all at once, there was a flicker. Kai peered intently up at the pedestal and saw what looked like thin wisps of translucent ribbon spiral out and around Kaso. At first, the wisps did not materialize as a Color at all. They were dark and blacker than a night lit by the thinnest sliver of the moon—but then there was a faint burst of light. *A Violet flash!*

The ribbon began to shimmer, just enough to be seen. Kaso's Color spiraled around him and the pedestal like a slow-spinning tornado of glistening Violet light, then gradually became brighter as the ribbon spread out. The crowd could see it now, and Kai heard people draw in their breaths and say things like: "In an orphan?" "That's one to keep an eye on," and "Wow, he's a real life Chipper!"

It was common for Violet ribbons to spiral around the person they came from and not go out very far, but Kaso's ribbon behaved differently. It twirled around the pedestal in a much wider arc than normal, allowing Kai to reach out his hand and place his fingers into the ribbon itself. Inside the dark Color, the stars were shrouded and difficult to see, but Kai knew that they were there; he could sense them—these tiny blinking suns.

As the ribbon flowed around his fingers, it acted like a liquid, so Kai made a cup with his hands in an attempt to capture some of it. It formed a little pool in his palms, and to his surprise, he immediately felt the stars radiate out heat, like a wood stove. When he peered into the pool of Kaso's ribbon, he noticed that one star was flitting about in his hand fire, almost like it was dancing. *I project fire, but he projects actual heat! Who is this Kaso?*

Kai knew this was a rare moment. Few had experienced a Violet ribbon like this. Something about the way it warmed him made it irresistible. *Are all Violet stars warm like this?* He doubted it. Violet revealed. Violet exposed. Violet was majestic. It contained glimmers of things to come. But he'd never heard it described as warm.

"Unbelievable! This unknown, foreign-born orphan is a Violet mage! But more than that—he's of the illustrious Deep Dark variety of Violet!" the announcer shouted.

Please be quiet, Kai thought. *You're ruining the moment.* But it was too late; the Violet stars left him, and the warmth was gone.

"It appears this act of compassion has paid off for Aaro is-a Tree. Maybe Tav wanted Aaro to remember what it's like to have someone in the O'Ceea Championship Games who's actually eligible for the Magician's Workshop," the announcer said with a chuckle.

The puller easily reeled in this Color. He placed it into Kaso's collar, and the young man left the stage.

Kai was now the only one remaining.

*   *   *

After this there will be no more expectations. In just a moment, I'll finally be free. Igar went on and on as he summarized the exciting events of the evening, took care of the final bits of business, and set the stage for the final pull.

"What a night-night-night! I guarantee you the events we have witnessed here will be re-enacted for countless generations to come. But we are not yet finished!"

This is it.

"Kai is-a Shield, step forward and make your ascent."

Kai took a deep breath, grabbed the final black collar from an acolyte, and hurried up the pedestal. He started out excited, but as he climbed the stairs he felt his legs begin to weaken. It was far more intimidating up here than he expected. *Just relax. It'll all be over soon.*

"Kai and his family of S. Shields need no introduction. His father, Flint was-a Shield, stood before his own generation in this very stadium when Violet was discovered within. But, before him came Malroy is-a Shield. Orange exploded out of him and filled the former glorious stadium that had crowned this hill.

"Two generations of only-born male mages have preceded Kai. Could he, an only-born male himself, become the third? Moments like this arise only a few times. All of you who have sailed across the sea to experience this for yourselves, get ready! This is the time! This is a moment that may very well be history in the making!"

Please stop talking.

All the Shields in the stadium were on their feet. And they

were not alone: five others stood for Kai. There was Snap and her dad, Limmick. *Wow, look at all the glares they're getting.* Then there was one very old man in a section set aside for those from orange regions. Kai did not recognize him at first, but then he realized it was Magpie, the friend of Forecastle is-a Wave, who had often stopped to teach him a few tricks with projections whenever he had run into him. *Why is he standing for me?*

In addition to these three, there were two men in the VIP section also standing. Kai felt his heart jolt when he saw them. The men were positioned on either side of the Master Magician, one to his right and the other to his left. *It can't be.*

But it was. Kiranik and Daganok, the two wealthy twins from Region 6, were standing for him—and shouting.

"You special, Kai!"

"You make history special!"

Kai nearly stumbled on the last step when he heard them. *What's going on? They're friends with the Master Magician? And they're risking their reputation by standing for me?* He didn't understand it, but he had something more important to focus on. He now stood directly in front of the puller.

Dy'Mageo look even creepier up close. Faceless and blank, it was impossible to read any expression. Kai couldn't get any sense of who the person standing before him really was.

"I welcome you, Kai," the puller said to him by voice projection. "I can't imagine the pressure you are under. I'll do my best to make this as pleasant as possible."

Kai hadn't expected to get a voice projection. *I wonder if he does that with every kid?* But then he recalled that the puller had spoken out loud to Kaso. *Maybe he's just having extra compassion on me?*

Igar was still announcing. "Mage Malroy took the Orange that was found within him and used it in innovative ways to train a generation of mages, many of whom advanced as far as the Workshop and continue to serve us today. I've had the great honor to call most of them personal friends, and I can tell you that they all hold Mage Malroy in the highest regard. Today, we will see if any of that talent has been passed down to his grandson.

"But wait. I'm getting a message. Well, how about that! The omens do appear to be in Kai's favor. Orange was just revealed in Trista and Violet in Kaso. That mirrors Malroy's Orange and Flint's Violet . . ."

That hadn't occurred to Kai until Igar mentioned it. *Just a stupid coincidence.* But it seemed he was the only one who felt that way; the entire audience started twittering amongst themselves, and he heard several gasps of surprise.

". . . This has to be one of the most exciting Color Ceremonies I've ever experienced. Could the Color gods still be around, looking down upon us and sending a sign? Ha ha. Whatever you want to believe, leave it to the S. Shields to once again capture the attention of the islands. They've made their mark on history again and again, both positive and negative . . ."

Did he really have to mention that?

". . . Will they make history again today? Puller, place the Staff of Light."

The puller nodded and Kai raised his black collar up in the air. The Staff of Light was lowered toward Kai's heart, and he heard the ominous words, "This is your life, come what may."

When the staff touched Kai, it sent a rustling through him. Something like a hand reached inside him and began rapidly flipping through the pages of his soul. He winced, but the puller did not move. They both remained frozen in place.

Nothing changed until Kai felt a wave of pressure. It did not cause him to move, but it seemed to make the puller stumble back half a step. When the puller recovered, he shuffled closer to

Kai and sent another voice projection to him: "I remember when your father stood in this exact spot. I also remember his time in the Workshop. He was a valuable asset. He was a good man— don't let anyone convince you otherwise. You have such a rich heritage. Now it's your turn to continue it."

The voice projection shook Kai to the depths of his soul, and he felt the invisible hand tearing through him. Then it stopped. Kai's eyes widened.

It had found something. *No! Please, no!*

When the staff was pulled back, something like a dam broke inside him, and Kai began sobbing. A bright Blue ribbon—like the afternoon sky—gushed out of him and filled the air with a series of churning Blue galaxies.

The Blue came out of Kai in a concentrated ribbon, but as it traveled away from him it seemed to vanish, lost in the stadium, like a small object disappearing in a vast expanse of sky. But it was only an illusion. The constellations of stars and galaxies contained in the ribbon spread out and filled the air, then shone again, blinking their Blue light on and off like fireflies.

Usually everyone saw a Color ribbon at the same time, viewing it together—but Blue ribbons were different. They were known to appear in front of individuals, giving that person a short, deep encounter with the unique collection of stars before them. Then the ribbon would disappear, only to show up some- where else a moment later. In this way, Kai's Blue ribbon bloomed in and out of existence all through the stadium.

Blue went everywhere and could appear in front of anyone, but it had a tendency to be more active around the people who cared about and knew the person from which it came. Thus, Kai's Blue concentrated around the people who were standing for him, his mother in particular. It also formed something like a cloud around Snap.

He knew Snap was fond of Blue. He'd seen the look of wonder on her face when she'd seen others experience it like this at prior Ceremonies. "It's the best Color," she always said.

Kai couldn't see any beauty in it, though. He felt that his lifetime of sorrow was on display for all O'Ceea to see. *Blue. Blue. Blue,* he kept repeating in his head. He lost control of himself and didn't care that his hand fell open, exposing the flame within for the entire stadium to see. Except, for some reason, the fire was no longer there. He barely noticed.

The Shields shouted in exultation. He heard some cry, "We're back!" and others, "We've done it!" as if they had had some role to play in this happening.

From Kiranik and Daganok, he thought he heard, "Yes! You next Master Magician. You Kai. We believe for you!"

What? Did they really just say that? No, they're standing right next to the actual Master Magician.

"Unbelievable!" Igar thundered. "We're witnessing a moment of history right now! The gods have found reason to bless the S. Shields with three generations of Color!"

Not bless. Curse. The third generation is cursed.

"Don't be mistaken, the children here today will be telling their grandchildren about this very night. What a spectacular celebration of Color we have all witnessed! Thank you to all the parents who raised this beautiful generation of children. And I want to give my personal thanks to the Master Magician, who chose to spend his precious time celebrating with us—but wait!" The announcer paused. "What's this?"

The staff started to wiggle in the puller's hands, and he reeled back on it again. *Oh, please. Isn't Blue enough?* Kai felt something snap inside his chest. *I don't need a second Color,* he thought as a golden ribbon of Yellow tore out of him.

The ribbon was wrapped tightly around itself like a ball. As soon as it left Kai, it shot straight up into the sky and formed a single giant Yellow star that shone like the sun. Everyone in the audience was captivated.

The Blue ribbon continued to blink on and off around the stadium, but no one was paying any attention to it anymore. All eyes went up, waiting for what they knew was about to happen.

Every time Yellow was pulled, it would—after hovering in the sky for a moment—burst and throw down narrow ribbons of golden flame. Each one went directly to a person, enveloping them in its light. People loved this and always cried out for it to shine on them. A Yellow magic's ribbon never broke into very many rays—a handful to a dozen at most—so being struck by one was a sign of tremendous luck. Uncountable stars rotated around the person, and for a brief moment they felt like the most beloved person in all of the universe.

"Unbelievable! Young Kai has a second Color. The Yellow of dawn!"

All around him was celebration, but Kai was full of anguish. He was the first to grasp what Yellow meant. *Oh no. No! No! No! Not Yellow.* Kai reached out his hands and tried to dissolve it like a bad projection, but it was no use.

It can't be. I can't be. Kai watched in horror as five sunbeam-like ribbons of Yellow turned downward and wrapped five people—none of whom he knew—in thousands of his stars. Unlike Blue, which seemed to know whom to appear to, Yellow fell on people at random.

But whenever they appeared together, their age-old conflict began.

The sheer brightness of Yellow extinguished the light of Blue, which struggled to remain visible, then blinked out of existence.

But it wasn't really gone. Kai's Blue reappeared and turned to its advantage. While Yellow was focused and blinding in its intensity, Blue was expansive. It spread to the concentrated spot of Yellow, surrounded it, and labored to extinguish it like water on a flame.

But Kai's Yellow was not easily doused. It fought back by shining even brighter and managed to retain one small, radiant star: a flicker of Yellow in a pool of Blue. Then—just as it seemed like Yellow was about to be overcome—the single star exploded with a giant, blinding burst. Yellow's rays ripped through the Blue, then Yellow shot away to some other place, where it waited.

When Blue reappeared, as it always did, Yellow shot to it and burst it apart.

This happened over and over. An endless battle in the sky, the flood of Blue and the blinding Yellow raging against each other.

It was impossible to look at the glorious Yellow and the delicate, vanishing and reappearing Blue at the same time. Those who tried to take in both at once often described it as feeling like their heart was splitting—which was exactly what was happening inside Kai as he watched the battle of his two Colors rage around the audience.

The Shield clan went deathly silent, while the rest of the stadium erupted with a mixture of cheers, jeers, and ridicule. Many of the kids who'd left the stage were now flowing out of the trapdoors in the stadium floor, desperate to see what all the commotion was about.

"Could this Ceremony get any more entertaining?" Igar was jubilant. "Witness the eternal incompatibility of Blue and Yellow. Their conflict rages on today, just as it did in the days before the Flood. This is a night none of us will ever forget."

I'm a Blue-Yellow mage? Kai's brain felt thick and heavy. *I've got Conflicting Colors?* He looked down at his hand and saw that, sure enough, the fire was back and raging worse than ever.

The puller battled to subdue the Blue and Yellow ribbons and bring them back to the staff. It was like trying to force together two magnets with the same polarity; they refused to be near each other.

After a great struggle, the puller was able to retrieve both Colors. Despite their resistance, he managed to lock them away into Kai's collar—where their battle would continue for the rest of his life. This moment, which Kai had believed would be his liberation, had just become a life-sentence.

It was now time for him to fasten the collar around his neck, but he couldn't do it. *It's going to strangle me forever!* His eyes went out of focus and he felt his strength drain away. Kai is-a Shield—the boy who had just become a young man—slumped down to his knees. Gulping for breath, he cried for help: "Täv, rescue me."

The Consequence

~Kaso~

My trainer was a Violet mage, and believe me when I say there's a reason our team was so successful. Serious and focused, Violet mages are often thought to be the wisest and most observant of the Nine Colors. They're balanced, strong, and insightful. These types are able to see things with pinpoint accuracy. I can't stress enough how magnificent they are. If everyone in O'Ceea were like my trainer, we'd certainly be living in paradise.

—Mage Kylee is-a Silk, *Color Me Curious: What Your Color Says About You!*

Kaso entered the stadium as a boy with a single chip and barely a sponsor. He emerged a Violet mage.

It was now well into third nightmark, when most people were usually asleep—though that certainly wasn't true tonight. A thick crowd was flooding out of the stadium, surrounding Kaso on every side. They were all strangers, yet every person who addressed him used his first name and acted as if they were old friends.

"Congratulations, Kaso," one stranger said. "I knew you would do it."

We've never met before.

"That was the most pristine Violet I've ever witnessed," an older lady said, "and I've attended a lot of Ceremonies."

"Thank you, Mistress. Was there warmth . . ." Kaso wanted to ask the woman how his Color had made her feel, but she turned and left before he could finish speaking.

"You're going to go far, young mage," another stranger said. "But let me give you a little piece of advice: when you find yourself on top of the islands, make sure you don't forget your roots. They're what raised you up so high!"

Uh—okay. Thanks?

"You held yourself with dignity and honor up there, Kaso," another Violet mage said. "Good job. You made us proud."

Proud? No one trusted me earlier today, and now everyone loves me?

He was uncomfortable with how everyone looked at him so differently now that he had a Color. It was like he'd instantly become a celebrity. Countless people offered to house and feed him, including a wealthy looking man who claimed to have a large yacht that he'd use to sail Kaso anywhere he wanted to go in O'Ceea. Then there were the tailors: they all begged him to come to their studios, where they would project a proper set of clothes on him at no charge—as long as he told people where he had received the outfit.

It wasn't long before he found himself completely surrounded by a cluster of trainers. They wouldn't leave him alone and pleaded with him to join their teams. Even a representative of Nosy's asked if he would allow them to create a new item for their menu: an aromatic baked fish plate called Kaso, the Orph-Found.

Kaso knew exactly what they were doing, and he politely turned down every single person.

Becoming a mage changed things. He'd seen it happen before: not often—orphans didn't usually interact with mages—but often enough. One of the things that made him angry was how he and all the kids in his orphanage never knew whether the next delivery of food would arrive before the last one ran out, while mages, and children of mages, never had to worry about a single thing. The gap between mage and commoner was wrong. Most mages, it seemed, believed they were a better kind of person than commoners were. *And now I'm one of them.*

He'd never considered this aspect of getting a Color before. While many orphans dreamed of becoming a mage for all the perks and pleasures, Kaso was driven only by a desire to enter the Workshop so that he could use his abilities to bring warmth back to Grand Projections. He feared that if somebody didn't do this—and do it soon—the Workshop would fracture and break apart even more than it already had. His focus was bringing back the joy that projections created in people. And, in his resolve to do everything in his power to prevent anything bad from happening to the Workshop, he'd missed the obvious: it would require him to become a mage.

As he was thinking about this, he realized that he hadn't seen Coby since the beginning of the Ceremony. *Why am I still standing here? None of these people are my friends.*

He'd had a taste of celebrity, and he felt it was more than enough for a lifetime. So he wordlessly broke through the crowd and searched for his brother. He needed to find Coby and Aaro, get out of this place, and return home to Auntie and his real friends at the orphanage. *And if Aaro doesn't keep his promise and take me home, I'll just find that man who offered to sail me anywhere I wanted. At least that's one good thing about all this attention. I have options now.*

Being a head taller than the crowd enabled Kaso to look around with ease. But the people flooding out of the stadium were numerous, and he realized that finding his brother might be more difficult than he'd originally anticipated. *Where are they?*

As he searched, he felt a subtle tug on his sleeve. At first he thought it might be Coby, but when he spun around, he was met by the face of an old, hunched-over hag of a woman. Although she was clearly an actual person, something about the way her skin reflected the light of the sky lanterns made Kaso think she wasn't real.

"If you're wanting to break free of all those trappings of celebrity, you best be following me," the woman said.

"Who are you?" Kaso asked skeptically. Something about her green eyes looked strangely familiar, though he couldn't quite figure it out.

"Come. Come," the woman cackled. "Follow me. Just over here." She pulled Kaso with unusual strength, but it wasn't enough to move him. "Just one moment!" she insisted. "I need to speak words with you—away from prying eyes and ears."

All right, she seems harmless enough. "What is it that you need?" Kaso asked as he followed her into a nearby alley.

She looked up at him and a wild grin split her face. "I just wanted to say . . . it's high time for all us rainbow-colored people to get squigglin', wouldn't you agree?"

Of course. I should have seen this coming. Kaso stared at the woman and recognized the eyes shining back at him. Although this poozer was a master of changing costumes and faces, he couldn't seem to disguise his eyes.

"Quint."

"At your service, Big Brother." Quint bowed. "No need for me to be tipsy-toeing around like this anymore, is there?" He lowered his hand in front of his face and the old hag was transformed into Migo the Marauder, the barbarian warlord he'd poozed around as earlier in the day.

Quint continued, "Actually—perhaps it wouldn't be prudent to present this pompous poof." He raised his hand back up in front of his face and the barbarian transformed into an ordinary young man with light blonde hair and a scruffy goatee. It was roughly the same face he'd shown when Kaso first met him, back in Region 3, only he didn't have a goatee before, and his hair was longer then.

"That's better," Kaso said. "You haven't looked like yourself since I first met you."

"Ha ha! Oh, my newly minted mage—I'm sorry to say, but I doubt anyone knows what Quint really looks like," he smirked. "Why bother to limit yourself to only one face when there are so many to choose from?" He lowered his hand back down and was instantly the old hag again.

Although Kaso was impressed with how quickly Quint was able to change looks, it disturbed him to think that he might never know what this young man actually looked like.

"Here, have a poisoned banana," Quint the hag said, holding out a single yellow banana. "You must be famished after standing up there for such a knee-shakingly long time."

"A banana? Is this some kind of joke, Quint? What happened to the others, anyway? Is Treau okay?"

"Just eat the poisoned banana. It'll make you feel better. Trust me."

"Quint, this is serious." Kaso leaned away from him. "I saw all of you get caught cheating. There are significant punishments for that. It was irresponsible and dangerous and almost ruined my chances at getting this Color collar. It's not wise for me to spend time with you."

As Kaso moved to leave, Quint slipped in front of him and pointed to the banana. "Come, come, my Violet victor. Just one tiny bite. It's poisoned, so a nibble is all you'll need."

"Quint!"

"Oh, all right. I'll peel it for you." Quint wiggled his fingers over the banana and the peel started to unravel like a flower blooming.

"Stop it. I'm not some stupid monkey."

"Ding! Ding! Ding! We have a winner!"

"What are you talking about?"

"Must I go on and on explaining such expository explanations for every little thing? I thought Violet meant you had insightful insight." Quint sighed. "I'm an old hag. I've offered you some poisoned fruit. You eat it. You go crazy. That's how the story goes, right?"

He's the one who's gone crazy. I really need to find Coby and get off this island.

"It's the banana, isn't it?" Quint frowned at it. "That must be what's confusing you. You were probably expecting a mango." The banana in his hand changed into a mango. "Or maybe grapefruit?" The mango turned into a handful of grapes.

Kaso raised an eyebrow. "Those are grapes."

"Indeed. Grapes are fruit, are they not?"

"Quint!" Kaso was exasperated. "I'll give you one last chance to explain what you're talking about."

"That's fair and just. Okay, listen to my words and listen true. You see all those people out there? You saw how they treated you after your Violet was pulled, right? You're good. You're set. There's no wiggle of doubt that you'll soon trade up your mage for magician."

"Yeah. I want to become a magician."

"Boom! And you will be. Now, enter the old hag and the banana." Quint held up a banana and waved it in Kaso's face. "The Workshop will fling wide its doors. You'll stroll inside, swear your vows, and—un-happily ever after—be projecting bananas for King King the rest of your life."

So that's how he thinks it works, hmm? "I'll do a lot more than that."

"Indubitably, yes, of course. Mangos and grapefruits and monsters and explosions that feel hot—oh, I don't doubt you'll be doing a lot of those. Won't it be wonderful? Just like a banana to a starving monkey. But—oh no!—the banana's poisoned. And sure enough, you'll eat it—starving monkeys always do. You'll die. But don't worry. You'll rise up again and find yourself transformed and transfigured into a glorified and oh-so-glorious deathwalking slave."

Kaso had heard enough. "Quint, thank you for all you've done to help me. I do think there is some part of you that actually does care, but it's time for me to say goodbye. I wish you the best in your travels."

He left the old hag behind in the alley, but he didn't get far before he heard the familiar voice again. "I'm offering you freedom, Big Brother!"

Kaso ignored it and scanned the crowd for Aaro and Coby, but he still couldn't seem to find them.

"We'll conjure truly grand projections, you and I," Quint projected his words to Kaso. "Grander than the grandest of them all."

"What about Treau, Bankfort, and Forcemore?" Kaso asked the question out loud. "Are you offering them freedom, too?"

"It's unthinkable to think any other thoughts." Quint's answer dropped straight into his ear.

Kaso stopped, turned, and found himself face to face with the old hag. "And how do you plan to manage that? Aren't all of you going to be punished?"

"What is punishment but an opportunity for growth?" Quint spoke out loud. "I, for one, welcome it with wide open arms. Punishment builds character, strong moral fortitude, and—I hear—it's really good for your teeth, too."

There they are. Finally! Without saying another word to Quint, Kaso brushed through the crowd and toward his little brother, who was standing with Aaro next to a fountain that shot up Colors in the style of the Crystal Lake.

Kaso expected Quint would continue to follow him, but the Yellow mage lagged behind and only called after him, "O'Ceeya later then, Big Brother. Our paths will cross again! We're brothers, honest and true, you and I. Sparks of the highest order!"

Quint then went silent and—with a wave of his hand—became just another face in the crowd.

*   *   *

"Slow down! I want to look at it," Coby insisted.

They wasted no time at the fountain after they reconnected; Kaso was eager to get going. He moved swiftly through the town with his little brother and sponsor, Aaro is-a Tree.

"Please?" Coby asked again.

Kaso let out a sigh and stopped in front of what looked to be a popular restaurant. He squatted down to let his little brother get a look at the band of Color around his neck.

"There's hardly any Violet in it at all." Coby sounded worried as he examined the collar. "I thought Violet mages had a lot of Color in their collars. Is it enough to get into the Workshop?"

"I hope so."

"Is it, Uncle Aaro?"

Uncle? Coby, you know you need to keep your distance.

"Yes, it is," Aaro said. "But please, I've already asked you not to call me Uncle."

Good. I can't let Coby be hurt by another man he cares about.

"Yes, Mage Aaro. But Auntie isn't our real aunt and she lets us call her Auntie."

"Excuse me, young mage." The maître d' of the restaurant stepped in front of Kaso. "I'd like to offer you a table at our humble establishment."

"No thank you, Master," Kaso replied in a polite but firm tone.

"It's no trouble. In fact, it would be my great honor. We have a master chef in our kitchen—Violet, just like you. You must come and try a dish."

Kaso shook his head and stood back up. He was taller than the man and hoped his height might help enforce his refusal. "I'm afraid I must decline."

But the maître d' was insistent and continued to press Kaso about coming inside. It was a real struggle to break away without causing a scene. *Apparently 'no' doesn't mean the same thing here that it does in Region 3,* Kaso thought after they were moving through the city again.

"So—Mage Kaso—is there anything else you want to see or do before we leave?" Aaro asked.

It's weird hearing my name said like that. "I'm ready to go now," he replied.

"This is your moment. I don't want to rush you."

"No, I've had enough of people acting like they care about me when all they really want is to get something from me."

"Wow!" Aaro nodded his approval. "It didn't take you long to figure that out. I'm impressed."

"It seems pretty obvious. That man just wanted me to bring in business. He would have kicked me out of his restaurant if I'd walked in without this Color around my neck."

"Quite true," Aaro agreed. "So then, let's go down to the docks. Once we're there, I'll speak with Mage Malroy about detouring his boat so we can take you two back to your Auntie, if that's still what you desire."

"It is," Kaso said. "You're still willing to take us all the way home?" Although Aaro had promised he would, part of Kaso wondered if his new Violet collar had changed Aaro's mind.

"Yes, of course. I have over a week before my team officially begins training. Plus, I'm looking forward to seeing your island's twin falls. Coby's told me all about them."

"Thank you," Kaso said. "Have you done what you've come here for? Back on the boat, Mage Malroy said you two were on a dangerous quest. I don't want to make you leave early just because I'm ready to go."

Aaro smiled at him and said, "It's okay. I believe we've both accomplished what we came here for. Malroy's already back at the boat getting it ready."

"But Kaso," Coby said, "do we have to go back to Auntie? I mean, right away?"

"Yes, Coby."

"I don't want to—I want to stay with Mage Aaro longer."

Kaso looked suspiciously at his sponsor. *What have you been promising my little brother?*

"Coby, we've talked about this," Aaro said. "Kaso isn't just your older brother. He's the person whom Täv has given the responsibility to take care of you. You need to follow him, not me."

Hmm. Does he really believe that?

"But you must be one of the best trainers in all the islands," Coby stressed. "I just know you are, and Kaso needs someone to train him."

"Coby, do you trust your brother?" Aaro asked.

"Of course! I just think you're the best person he's ever going to find to train him. He needs a trainer to get into the Workshop!"

"Well, if you trust him, then you should trust his decision," Aaro said.

"Plus," Kaso added, "Mage Aaro hasn't offered to train me."

"But I'm sure he would. Wouldn't you, Mage Aaro?"

"Don't worry, Coby." Kaso spoke before Aaro could say anything. "I'll be able to—" Kaso stopped speaking when he felt something tickle the inside of his ear. He shook his head back and forth.

"You pick up a stray?" Aaro asked.

Kaso nodded. He seemed to have walked through someone's voice projection. It happened occasionally when someone didn't design a message to self-dissolve or if their aim was poor. Whatever this message was, it didn't make a lot of sense; the words he heard were garbled, and no matter how hard he tried, he couldn't seem to shake or extinguish it.

Then the voice became crystal clear. "Warning. Detour. Access to the dock has been diverted. Please turn around and use the South Gate."

Aaro and Coby heard the message, too, as did the people around them. But while the others began turning immediately, Aaro kept moving north.

"Shouldn't we turn, too?" Kaso asked.

"Have you ever known an IP message to sound like that?" Aaro asked over his shoulder.

Kaso shrugged. "I can't say. I've not heard many IP messages before."

"Why would we take the South Gate to get to the docks on the north side of the island? I think someone's playing a game," Aaro said.

Trusting that his sponsor knew what he was doing, Kaso followed after Aaro down the path.

When they eventually reached the North Gate a few moments later, they saw something that shook Kaso to his core: Treau's body was slumped in an iron cage that hung from the highest point of the gate. As they moved closer, they heard the words, "This is what happens to those who cheat!" projected over and over in a loop.

Oh no. I knew something bad was going to happen.

"Treau?" Kaso took an apprehensive step toward the gate. The poozer was unmoving, and for a brief moment, Kaso thought he might actually be dead.

"Hey, Kaso." Treau opened his eyes and peered down at them.

Kaso felt a wave of relief when he heard him speak. "What's going on?"

"I see you found yourself a sponsor. And you're Violet. I'm glad."

"What happened?"

"The IP put me up here on display to demonstrate what happens to poor Blanks who aspire for more."

Kaso could hardly believe what he was seeing. "But, Quint said—"

"You can tell Quint I wish his ancestors had drowned in the Flood." Treau spit out the words like milk turned sour. "He should be in here with me."

Kaso stood back and listened as Treau told the story of what happened. After the old tester froze him and the others, the IP arrived and arrested them all. But because Quint's security projections on the globe were such high quality, the IP could not prove it was a forgery. While there was a record of a Treau is-a Wave in the registry, none of the officials who worked in the registration tent recalled making the entry, and no one from any of the branches of the Wave clan claimed to know him. The IP deduced that he had somehow made a forgery in the registry and had stolen the globe. But they had no idea how this happened.

Without proof that Bankfort and Forcemore were involved, the IP merely escorted them to their ship and told them that if they ever set foot on the island again they would be arrested and locked up. Quint and Treau were charged with possession of stolen globes and creating a false identity, but Quint somehow managed to escape. Treau had not seen what had happened to Quint because they'd been taken to separate rooms to be interrogated. Treau was found guilty and locked up in the cage. Tomorrow, he would be taken by the IIRP to the Island of the Howling Jackals. There he would receive a prohibition and jail sentence that could be as long as half a year, depending on what the judge decided. After that, he would be escorted back to his home.

"But you don't have a home," Kaso said. "Where will you go?"

"Who knows. I've survived this long."

"You could join us at our orphanage," Coby exclaimed. "Auntie would take you in! I know she would."

"Thanks, Coby, but I'm never going back to an orphanage. Ever."

Kaso struggled to know what to say; the story bothered him on a deep level. He didn't know whether he should address the fact that if Treau's name was in the registry, then his name must also have been forged. He would have been listed as Kaso is-a Wave. *I wonder if the IP found it? But maybe they didn't know to look for it because I dissolved the projection of me in the globe.* Quint clearly was the one behind this; Kaso hadn't committed any crime. But still, he didn't know what to say. The best he could come up with was, "I just can't help but feel like I should have done more to warn you."

"No, I wasn't listening. I chose to cheat, and I got what I deserved. I'm glad you're not in here with me. Quint, on the other hand . . ." Treau clenched his fists. "If you see him again, tell him that when I get out, he can expect a lot more than punches."

Kaso hated seeing Treau stew in his anger and bitterness. He cast a warm blanket and draped it around Treau's shoulders. "It's going to be a long night. I hope this helps you rest."

As soon as the warmth touched his skin, Treau let out a sigh of relief and the tension in his body started to ease. "Thanks,

Kaso," Treau said as he huddled with the blanket. "You're a good guy. I knew Color was in you. Go find yourself the best trainer you can to prepare you for life on this drenched planet, compete for as many years as it takes you to win, and do everything in your power to make sure you never have to rely on anyone ever again."

The Choice

~Kaso~

There's really no one quite like Aaro is-a Tree. He's gone a bit crunchy for Tav, sure, but he's a brill-ee-ent trainer! There's not a dibbly-dabbly dollop of doubt in my mind that he would have reached Tier One long ago if he hadn't decided to permit commoners on his team. Some say that makes him a moldbrain, but I don't know any moldbrains who have such talent.

—Trainer Mage Rumingo is-a Spark, *Things Trainers Say (When They Think No One Is Listening)*

As soon as they'd left Treau and resumed walking down the path to the docks, Coby ran ahead of Kaso and turned to face him.

"See, even Treau thinks you should go train with Mage Aaro."

"He didn't say that," Kaso answered quietly.

"He did too! He said to get the best trainer. That's Mage Aaro."

"I'm honored that you think so highly of me," Aaro said. "But the best trainer is that man standing on the dock." Aaro pointed ahead to a man about his same age. "Unfortunately, he doesn't train people these days."

When they arrived at the boat, Aaro officially introduced them to Mage Malroy. He looked utterly different than the old man Kaso had first seen from Quint's ship. Instead of being frail, skinny, and stooped over, Malroy was straight-backed, broad shouldered, and energetic. *I guess this is what he's really like.* Kaso didn't comment on it. He couldn't shake the image of Treau swinging helplessly up in the cage.

Treau is right, he thought as they boarded the boat. *I really should have a trainer. Which means I'll need to find a team.*

He suspected joining a team wouldn't be hard—especially if the way people had treated him tonight was any indication. He'd only just become a Violet mage and he'd already had a number of offers. *There'll be plenty of others too, when word of my ability spreads.*

Even though it was now fourth nightmark, Malroy had prepared the boat to depart and was now untying the dock lines. He seemed rushed, eager to leave. *I'm glad I'm not the only one who wants to get out of here as quickly as possible.*

"You know you don't have to take us, right?" Aaro said to Malroy. "What happened tonight was significant. He might need some support."

"The actual moon might be hidden, but we can still see some stars," Malroy said as he pointed up to the sky. "I think I'll sail by their light tonight and forego my sky lanterns."

"I'm not talking about sailing at night," Aaro said.

"I know what you're talking about, and I'm saying it's a good time to set sail."

"We can take a ferry to Region 3," Aaro said.

"No, I haven't set off on a good long journey for ages," Malroy insisted. "I'm looking forward to it."

"All right, all right. I get it. I won't try to knock you out of your state of denial."

Kaso didn't understand what they were talking about, but he said, "Thank you, Mage Malroy. I do not take your kindness for granted."

Malroy responded with a bow and said, "It's my pleasure."

They settled themselves on the cutter and it was soon out on the water.

Coby is too trusting. Kaso looked out across the water. It was very dark, and he could hardly see a thing. *I can't just join up with anyone. Most men can't be relied on. We'll get back home and take it slow. I was too rash in making my decision about Quint.* He thought of Treau in the cage. *Look where following him could have landed us. But I didn't know of any other choices then. He did get us here like he promised. But I have a lot more options now.*

"You'd make a good sailor," Malroy said to Kaso.

"What? I don't know the first thing about the sea, or ships."

"All that's easy to learn," he said. "The real trick is securing something you already appear to have: faith."

Kaso glanced over his shoulder at the man. "I think you've got me wrong. I do live in a Tavite orphanage, but I'm not that religious."

Malroy laughed again. "I don't mean that kind of faith. Here you are, out on the ocean in the black of night. You have no idea who I am and you haven't known Aaro much longer. Your life is completely in our hands, yet you haven't shown the slightest sign of fear. But, lest I'm assuming something, let me ask you. Are you afraid, at all?"

Kaso hadn't really considered it. "No, I guess not. Not about sailing at least."

"Ah, and why is that?"

"I guess because I have a sense you know what you're doing—it's your boat. I know you're going to be careful with it, so I don't need to worry."

"I thought this boy was an orphan," Malroy said to Aaro. He then asked Kaso, "Who taught you such good sense?"

"My orphanage auntie," Kaso replied.

Malroy gave Aaro a curious look and asked, "Auntie, hmm? Does she run the orphanage alone, or is there an uncle, too?"

Kaso explained that Auntie was not married and ran the orphanage all by herself. Malroy responded by asking, "So how old is this auntie of yours?"

"Really, really old," Coby said. "Almost as old as you and Mage Aaro."

"Perfect. Aaro likes really, really old women."

Malroy started to joke about how Aaro had never managed to find a woman to settle down with; Aaro joked about how Malroy had to wear a disguise so that he didn't have to interact with his wife. *It's nice to see old men who are able to be so lighthearted about such serious things.*

"Kaso, as much as I'd like Aaro to meet your really old auntie, are you certain you want to go back?" Malroy asked. "Let me be clear. I'm not trying to change your decision about going home. I just want you to know, you'll be hard-pressed to find a better trainer than Aaro."

"See!" Coby exclaimed. "Everyone's saying the same thing, Kaso. Why don't you believe it?"

"I don't doubt he's a good trainer. It's just that . . . we're foreigners here. Our place is at home. I should find a team there."

"And Mage Aaro hasn't offered to train you. I know, I know. You're just making excuses," Coby grumbled. "You always do that when you're scared."

Be quiet, Coby. "I'm not scared. Mage Malroy just said so."

"You are scared!"

Kaso stared down at his little brother. "Of what? What am I scared of?"

"I don't know, but I know you're scared. Just like when you run away and hide deep down in the ocean. I hate when you do that! If seabreath were real, you'd never come out. You'd go far away and not come back—like Dad." Coby started to cry.

"I'd never do that. You know it."

Coby looked up with questioning, tear-filled eyes. He was still sobbing, but he managed to say, "I just want you to get into the Workshop. Then Dad will know where we are, and he'll finally come and get us."

He's not looking for us, Coby! Can't you see that? Kaso didn't have the heart to say this out loud. "Things will start getting better now, Coby—trust me."

They sailed in silence until Aaro offered to take Coby down below and put him to bed. When he returned a little later, Kaso was ready to speak.

"I apologize for my little brother. Coby doesn't understand that our father is never going to be a part of our lives again."

"I sensed a deep hurt in him," Aaro said. "He formed a connection to me very fast—too fast. That's why I don't want him to call me Uncle."

"I appreciate that."

"And Kaso," Aaro said, "I think you know I'd be willing to train you."

"Yes, I know that. Coby was right. It was only an excuse."

"I respect your decision to go home. But know that you are a pleasure to be with and you'll be a great addition to whatever team you choose. I will warn you, though, there are a lot of teams and trainers in the islands that I hope you never run across, let alone join."

Kaso nodded. "I just want to take things slow. A lot's happened today."

"That's wise."

The two watched as the clouds finally broke and the full moon appeared above the horizon. Although he already felt confident that everything would be fine, the added light of the moon gave Kaso an extra measure of comfort.

"Kaso, there's something I've learned in my time as a trainer that I think might help you make a wise decision when you do select one. But I don't want to share it unless you're interested."

"I'm interested."

"All right. It's pretty simple. Look for a trainer, not a father." Aaro waited for Kaso to respond, but he didn't. "Do you understand what I'm saying?"

"No, not really."

"I've found that many young men and women who seek training are—deep down—looking for a father. They don't know it, at least not consciously. But I sense it. They look to me to guide them in ways that only a father can. But I can't. I can only be a trainer for them. I can teach them all I know about projections, but I can't give them whatever their actual father failed to provide."

When Kaso didn't say anything, Aaro continued. "I'm going to take you back to your home. But if at any point you want to train with me, you're welcome to join my team. If you do, know that I'll be your trainer—and only your trainer. I'll never be able to replace your true father. This will be so even if you keep my clan name and remain Kaso is-a Tree."

"I know." Kaso sighed. It was encouraging to hear Aaro say these things. "Do you think . . . Can you help me get into the Workshop?"

"Certainly. Though you should know I have many unorthodox views about the Workshop. Namely, I don't believe getting there should be a student's focus."

"Isn't that the whole point of training?"

"No, not for me. I believe that people—all people—were made to project. Projections were meant to be a part of ordinary, everyday life —just like everyone should breathe and eat and smile and cry and form close relationships with people who love them and all of the other things people do."

"Okay, but that sounds like something every trainer would want," Kaso said. "If everyone were making projections all the time, there would be a lot more work for trainers, right?"

"You're very shrewd, Kaso," Malroy said.

Aaro nodded and said, "You would think that would be true—and it should be—but most trainers believe the opposite. They don't want to train everyone. They only want to train mages, and then only mages that they think will be successful and help their team win. I don't care a whole lot about winning or losing. I want my students to improve in their ability to make projections because I believe that this will help them find what everyone's truly looking for in life."

Does that mean he doesn't only train mages? "What is it that everyone's looking for?"

"It's a secret," Aaro laughed. "I can't tell you everything all at once, now can I?"

"Are you being serious?"

"No. What I think everyone's looking for is life—real life."

"I don't understand."

Malroy cut into the conversation. "This old, wise senior trainer and fool of a friend is saying that the thing that everyone is looking for in life is life. Brilliant, huh?"

That makes no sense. "Uh, I . . ."

"You can tell him it sounds stupid," Malroy said. "I do that all the time and he still invites me to his New Beginnings Day celebration—though, on this point, I do agree with him."

Can I really say what I think? "Uh, then I guess I should say I think it seems like a meaningless answer and thus kind of stupid."

"Thank you," Aaro said. He sounded sincere. "I appreciate it when people are honest."

The light of the full moon reflected gloriously on the water, and Kaso felt strangely at peace. He sat with this feeling for a long time, staring out across the sea, until a memory of Quint jostled up a fear. Curious to know what these two men would think, he asked, "Will I become a slave if I enter the Workshop?"

"That's a strange question," Aaro said. "What's made you anxious about that?"

"Someone said I'd be stuck projecting bananas for King King the rest of my life if I made it in there."

Malroy and Aaro chuckled. "That's funny. But, no, I doubt that would be true," Aaro said. "The Workshop is an extraordinary place, where people get to work on amazing projections—there is good reason they call them Grand. However, if you got in based on your skill, I suspect you would find yourself spending most of your time adding heat to explosions. They've been eager to find a someone to do that ever since Magician Melphia retired."

Quint was right. Kaso was quiet and thought on this.

Aaro saw the concern on Kaso's face and asked, "What's bothering you?"

"Am I making a mistake?" Kaso asked. "I mean, maybe it isn't a good idea for me to try for the Workshop. What do you think?"

"I don't know you well enough to answer that. But I can tell you the Workshop isn't for everyone. Unfortunately, living and working there has the ability to change a person for the worse, though I suppose that could be said about any profession. I don't know if most of the bad things that happen there can be blamed on the Workshop itself. That being said . . ." Aaro paused.

"Aaro believes it's important for a person to be prepared," Malroy broke in.

"That's one way to describe it," Aaro said.

That seems wise. So I will need to look for someone who can train me in more ways than just making projections.

"As a trainer, it's my job to prepare people," Aaro continued after gathering his thoughts. "And while not many of my students from Cloudy Peaks have been allowed to join it, I do think the Workshop can be a good place for certain people, as long as they are ready for what they will experience there."

"Hey, Kaso." Malroy leaned against the railing. "I have a much less optimistic view of the Workshop than Aaro does. I believe it can and will kick you to the ground, even if you're ready for it. I don't think you should try to get in there, at least not at your age. But you'll be better served listening to Aaro on this. I'm a bit of a pessimist on these sorts of things."

"A bit?" Aaro said with a smile. "You're right about one thing, though. I do agree there's a lot of evidence that all manner of harm does come to those who aren't prepared."

All that happened today made it clear that I'm not prepared. I'm not prepared at all. And that means we can't go back to the orphanage.

"All right, you've convinced me. Coby's right. I need you to be my trainer."

"I haven't been trying to convince you."

"I understand, but you're right. I want to go to the Workshop, and I know I'll need the right help to be ready for it. So I'd like you to train me."

"You need to understand what sort of team you would be joining, and what my motivations are as a trainer," Aaro said. He then went on to explain his convictions at length.

✳ ✳ ✳

Whoa, he really is a different kind of trainer. No wonder that short announcer said all those demeaning things about him during the Ceremony. Kaso pondered Aaro's words for some time before he asked, "So are there any mages on your team at all, or will I be the only one?"

"Yes, there are other mages, of course," Aaro replied. "I train people, regardless of what their collar says about them."

I wonder what mages think of training with commoners. "Well, I certainly don't understand why you would train people who have no chance of earning a spot in the Workshop, but I suppose I shouldn't care—as long as I will be eligible."

"You will be. It is an official team, fully accredited by the Workshop."

"Okay," Kaso said. "I agree to join your team then."

"You'll have to keep the name Kaso is-a Tree as long as you are in Region 2."

"That's fine. It's better than being a Blank."

Aaro stared at him intently. "I'm not adopting you, Kaso. You have to remember that."

"I know."

"And if at any point you want to return home, all you need to do is tell me."

"I will."

Malroy burst out laughing. "Well, all right. I guess we'd better change course. To our home among the Cloudy Peaks. I guess Aaro's date with your wonderful auntie must await another day."

"Hold on," Aaro said. "There is one last decision to be made. What about Coby? I haven't sponsored him."

"I'm capable of caring for my brother," Kaso stated.

"I'm certain you are, but you aren't nineteen—legally you both are under the authority of your official guardian—your auntie."

"Yes. But she released me, and she put Coby into my care before we left the orphanage. I can take care of him," Kaso explained.

This did not seem to be enough for Aaro, however. The trainer insisted he would move forward only with Auntie's approval and blessing. After some discussion, they came to the decision that Kaso and Coby would both return with Aaro to the Island of the Cloudy Peaks to meet the other members of the team and to get a taste of what life there would be like. They would send a message to Auntie asking for her temporary approval, and then they would go in person to ask for her blessing at a later time.

Aaro turned his eyes on Kaso and said with excitement in his voice, "I have a feeling this is going to be a good year for our team. I look forward to introducing you to the others."

Kaso bowed respectfully and then turned to gaze up at the moon peeking through the clouds. Although he'd just made one of the biggest decisions of his life, he didn't feel the least bit nervous.

This is good. This is right. I'm a young man now, and I'm about to prepare for my future.

The Butterfly Girl

~Talia~

Never shall Green and Red be mixed,
Nor Blue and Yellow be.
It is a curse! It is! It is!
Do not be found in me!

—Children's counting-out rhyme

A solitary cyan butterfly with yellow wings fluttered outside the open doorway of Kai's house. Talia knew she could make it fly inside if she wanted to—and she really, really wanted to—but that would almost certainly alert Mistress Jade of her presence.

Come on, Kai, look outside. It was late in the evening, and Talia was crouched low inside a bush. She didn't dare move or risk getting any closer for fear of triggering the Cyan Spa advertisement that was on the roof. Talia hated the way that projected woman looked—*she's far too beautiful to be real*—and the way she lazed next to her ridiculous looking, projection-perfect boyfriend. Now that Talia was a Cyan mage, she was offended. *The way these two announce how wonderful it is to be somewhere other than home gives Cyan a bad name.*

Talia spotted Kai through the doorway, lying on the floor and languishing in the middle of the room. *He's not acting at all like the great and marvelous Yellow-necked Kai I know he is. Maybe this is an expression of his Blue side?* Blues, she'd observed, were moody, melancholy, and prone to brood over their problems. And Kai had problems, more now than ever. *All this must be tearing him apart.* She wanted to prove to him that they were still friends and that everything was going to be all right.

It made sense to Talia that Kai had Conflicting Colors. He'd always seemed to have two incompatible natures. She knew and loved the exuberant, fun-loving, bright-as-the-sun boy she'd spent unending watches with. However, she had thought that the other side of him—the one he tried to keep to himself—was just a result of all his misfortune.

But Colors don't lie. Still, it doesn't mean he should be banished. I hope he doesn't believe everything that people are saying about him. She wanted nothing more than to go out and do something fun with him tonight. *Everything's been so serious!* So she waited, hoping for just a single glance outside. *Come on, just turn your head.*

Kai was unmoving.

This isn't working. The Violet watch had already ended and it was nearing the second nightmark. *I guess I'm going to have to try something else.* She had practiced a new kind of a projection during her eighteen-day prohibition, and this would be the perfect time to use it—if she could pull it off.

The prohibition she'd received for her involvement with making King King was intended to stop Talia from making projections, but it did the opposite. Unable to see reality as it really was, and unable to feel anything with her hands and fingers, she'd spent her time focused on other forms of feeling, like emotions.

Emotions fell under the category of Glory, and they were a hotly debated subject across the islands. It was generally understood that projections could stimulate the five senses, but they couldn't carry any specific emotion. Talia had been taught that there were no 'feeling' projections; no one could create a happy projection or cast an angry sensation. But for as long as she could remember, she had been able to make projections that triggered real emotional responses in others.

Uncle Lemmet, her mother's brother, was the head trainer for their island, and he had talked to her at length about the many schools of thought regarding Glory. Thus she knew about the various techniques employed by trainers to teach students how to set off emotions in others. For Talia, it always began with identifying the emotion she wanted to evoke and then feeling it herself while she created a visual projection. She had what her uncle called an inborn affinity for empathy. No one had taught her this. She just did it, naturally.

But during her prohibition, she couldn't create a visual projection—so she had started practicing ways to convey feelings through the other four senses. She began with well-known ways to add Glory to projections.

Music was an easy way to trigger emotions, but Talia had always been tone-deaf. So she turned to words, which—if done right—could also evoke emotional responses. After working at it, she found she was able to scare her mother merely by creating a projected whisper of the word spider. All she had to do was imagine the creepy eight legs of a spider crawling up her neck, over her ear lobe, and into her ear canal. The frightening emotions this stirred up in her somehow was carried inside her whisper projection and gave her mother the same feeling.

Everyone knew smell and taste projections could stir up strong emotional reactions, so Talia spent a lot of effort on them. This was risky, however. The smell and taste of pumpkin pie created the feeling of delightful anticipation in her, but when she projected it for her father—who hated pumpkin pie—his reaction was disgust. The responses she got varied from person to person; it all depended on how that person felt about pumpkin pie. She spent a good portion of her prohibition focused on these two senses, but they never seemed to achieve her objective.

So Talia turned her efforts to touch. The feeling of scratching the scalp created a calming emotion in her mother. The feeling of pressure against a precise spot on both sides of the neck reduced built-up tension in her father. A finger poke to the lower back caused her older sister to sit up and pay attention. While these techniques were well known, what Talia discovered next was not.

She decided to try experimenting with applying projected pressure to spots beneath a person's skin. Could people feel things inside them? That's where emotions come from. She knew it was possible, though difficult, to create a projection that could pass right through a person. Why not stop the projection partway through? The result was something she called internal butterflies.

She'd experimented on herself and the other members of her family, and sure enough, she found a way for her internal butterflies to evoke emotions, just as her visual projections could. This turned out to be the easy part.

The great difficulty was control. Because these butterflies were invisible, she had no idea where they were most of the time. Controlling them also required a measure of blindsight, a technique that only the most talented mages had ever mastered.

An internal butterfly needed to travel to a specific place inside someone. If it went somewhere else, it would—at best—do nothing, and—at worst—create an unintended emotional reaction.

Just last week she had tried to convey the joyous feeling of her eighth birthday party when making an internal butterfly. But when she attempted to place it underneath her sister's left rib, hoping it would cause her to giggle, it missed and landed underneath her knee cap, where it caused her to twitch and kick their father.

Without extreme control, Talia figured there was no point to any of this. As a result, she had decided the idea was impractical, and in certain circumstances could be dangerous, and she gave up on experimenting. But right now, she needed something to get Kai's attention. It would have been easy in normal circumstances. All she would have to do is send a voice projection over to him. *But that's not an option tonight. His mother or grandmother might accidently hear it if I miss.*

She knew she could try and poke him, but that didn't appeal to her right now. *No.* Her mind was made up. It would be much more fun to challenge herself and try to send Kai an internal butterfly.

Talia focused all her energy on an emotion she hoped would resonate with Kai, and then she cast the internal butterfly out several times. She tried her best to aim the invisible projection at Kai, but it was small and she kept missing. *These things are impossible to position.*

Her eighth attempt finally worked—but it went into Kai's mother.

"Wow." Declarious could be heard through the open window. "I just got the most peculiar feeling. Quite tremendous, actually."

Oops.

"You did?" Kai asked.

"Yes. I don't know exactly how to describe it. I wish I could." She pondered for a moment before saying, "It kind of felt like a hug."

That's amazing. She totally understood it.

Now that Talia knew where she had accidently placed the invisible butterfly, she easily directed it over to Kai. "Oh! I feel something too!" he exclaimed, and he sat up.

Okay bud, now look out the window.

"What do you mean?" his grandmother said. "I don't feel anything. Why do you two feel something I don't?"

"I don't know, Mother Jade," Declarious said. "It's the strangest thing. I feel as though a close friend has come to visit me."

"Yeah, that's the same thing I feel." Kai, now quite alert, began to look around the room. He noticed the cyan butterfly with yellow wings that Talia had projected for him earlier. His eyes lit up. "I'm feeling much better, Mom. I'm going to go outside for a walk."

"I'm so glad, dear. This feeling is such a wonderful gift from Täv. Please do everything you can to try to hold onto it," Declarious said.

"Hmm. Just make sure to stay away from people, Kai," Jade warned. "Everyone on this island only wants harm to come to our family. There is no one you can trust—especially that Cyan girl. Do not forget the elders' rules."

Why does she dislike me so much? Talia didn't understand.

"I know, Grandmother."

"It is going to be hard, but you will just have to accept that you will not be able to have a relationship with her ever again. Not unless you get into the Workshop, of course."

"That's not true, Mother Jade," Declarious said. "The elders are just overreacting. They'll come to see reason in time."

"You were not born on this island, my dear. You do not know how they can be. And you do not know the Leaf clan like I do. Trust me. If Kai wants to be with that Cyan girl, the only way is for him to become a magician."

She's right about my clan. Talia sighed. *I don't understand how Mistress Jade can be right about so much and yet be so wrong on the most important things in life,* Talia thought as she slipped out of the bush and headed deep into the forest, pulling the cyan butterfly behind her like a kite.

Kai exited his home and followed after it, as she knew he would.

"We look forward to seeing you at the Cyan Spa," the advertisement couple called after Kai as he left his house, "where the mistakes of the past can be washed away!"

Talia, running ahead of Kai, led him away from Brightside and through the forest to a small clearing. This was a significant place for them: the spot they had first met, eight years earlier.

"I knew you'd be the D. Leaf who'd break the streak," Kai said as he stepped into the clearing.

"You did, huh?" She stood a little straighter when she said, "My collar looks pretty good, doesn't it? My dad thinks so, at least."

"Yeah, it does. I'm really happy for you."

As Kai stood there, illuminated by the pale moonlight, Talia caught sight of the Blue and Yellow collar clasped snugly around his neck. This was the first time she'd seen him in person since the Ceremony. *He looks different. Changed, but it's not just because he's a young man now.* Talia hesitated, then said, "You're not disappointed? Even a little bit? I know how much you were looking forward to all of the buds being common."

"Oh, yeah. I'm really sorry about that. I was wrong . . . I realized it when Weston was void. I felt so horrible for him. Do you forgive me?"

"For being a total pruner to Weston?"

"Ha, no . . . I already asked his forgiveness. I'm asking yours . . . I was really wrong to want all of you to be found void. I never quite understood just how much pressure you were under, you know, with no one in your family ever getting a Color and all."

"Yeah. Well, I forgive you—you moldbrain," Talia said with a huge smile.

Kai didn't smile back. "Thanks. I really am sorry for how I treated you."

"Hey, that's in the past," Talia said. "Being a mage is pretty mega, right?"

"Yeah, I guess."

He just turned deep Blue. Talia was hoping they would be able to have fun together tonight. Now that they were mages, they were no longer prohibited from making projections outside a playground. "What's wrong?"

"I'm just sad."

"Why?"

"Isn't it normal to feel sad when saying goodbye?"

Talia's breath caught in her chest for a moment. Here, in the dark of the forest, the little finger of fire in Kai's hand looked more real than ever. "Goodbye?" Talia asked. "You're not going anywhere, are you?"

"You know what the elders decided."

"I know," Talia said glumly. "But you'll still be here—on the same island as me—right?"

"Sure, but we'll have to keep separate. Me leaving might actually be the best thing for everyone."

"Kai, what are you talking about? No one wants you to leave," Talia said. Kai gave her a look that froze her heart. *Could my clan be behind this?* "What happened, Kai? Who wants you to leave? The elders can't banish you for having Conflicting Colors, can they? All the islands in Region 2 voted against that kind of action long ago. Right?"

"It's not the elders," Kai said. "It's the entire Shield clan."

He can't be serious. "But . . . but . . . I don't understand. Your own clan is banishing you?"

Kai laughed. "No, but there are other ways of eliminating problems—or in my case, Conflicted problems." Kai sat down and leaned against one of the big mango trees. He beckoned her to join him, but Talia was feeling too stirred up to sit.

"Kai, I'm sorry, but none of this is making any sense. I think I'm missing something—maybe my family didn't tell me everything."

"Tell me what you do know."

"All right." Talia crossed her arms and started to pace. "When you had Conflicting Colors pulled from you, it confirmed what a lot of people wanted to believe: that you and your family are a danger to the island. So it was decided that you would not be allowed to train at the island's camp, nor be part of the island's team."

"Correct. I cannot train, participate, compete, or interact with any of you in any way."

"Wait—you can't interact with any of us? I thought it was just me," Talia said.

"Nope. The entire team, the trainers, support staff, the cooks—everyone."

"Is that legal?"

"Apparently so. Poison has to be locked away in a safe place." Kai shrugged, and then he stared down at the flame in his hand.

I really hope no one actually said that to him. "Oh, Kai. I'm so sorry. You know there are still a lot of people who don't see you that way."

"Yeah. But I also know you can't go against the will of the island, and you, Mage Talia is-a Leaf, must do right by your clan. We're breaking the rules by even talking right now. But I figure that's okay because we're saying goodbye."

Oh no, he's dissolving into Blue. No, stop it, Kai. Stop. "I don't care what my clan says," she said, and then added, "You know I don't see you the way they do."

From the crinkle in his forehead and the way he tightened his lips, she could tell that he wasn't sure what she thought of him anymore.

The Butterflies

~Talia~

True friendship rests together with no need for words.
—Lucas, *Life of Rice*

"Kai, you're still my closest friend—that hasn't changed," Talia told him. "You are not poisonous to me—or anyone else."

"But—"

"Don't interrupt me. You're not poisonous. You're the remedy. Everyone appears to have missed this, but it's so obvious. The team needs you."

"They'll do fine," Kai said.

"No, they won't. Look, everyone is placing all their expectations on me now. Me. Alone. Weston was void and you were Conflicted. The only other ones from our class to have Color were Eddy and Koygen, and as much as everyone likes them, no one expects them to get very far."

"There are others on the team already who might—"

"No. Gravis flared out. Melaine has peaked. And I just heard Rylee's moving to another island to find a better team." Talia let out a loud sigh.

"There's Sten. He made it into the Championships once."

"Three years ago, and despite working super hard, he hasn't been able to get back since," Talia said. "Look, my only point is that I'm the island's only real hope for a magician now."

"Aren't you humble," Kai said with a smile.

"No, I'm actually terrified."

"Why? It's true. You're amazing. I have no doubt you'll make it all the way."

"Kai, the only reason I've gotten this far is because of your help. There's no way in all the islands that I should be as talented as I am—without your training, that is."

Kai frowned. "Talia—I haven't trained you."

"Come on, what else should I call what you do?" Talia turned her eyes away and looked up at the stars. "You can't leave. Eventually, the elders will wake up and realize how much the island needs you. How much I need you."

Kai hesitated, then said, "Well, the Shield clan has had enough of my family. If we were projections, they would have dissolved our entire branch long ago."

"Well, thank the gods you're real."

"Uh-huh. Let's thank them. After all, they're the ones who gave me these Conflicting Colors." Kai pointed to his Color collar with his hand containing the fire.

"Stop it. You don't believe in the Color gods."

"Neither do you—you brought them up." Kai smiled.

"It's an expression, Kai. I was expressing thanks that you're real! I'm thankful to whoever or whatever is out there that made you real. Thank you, Tav! Thank you, Color gods! Thank you, Lord of Chaos! Thank you whoever you are!"

"Okay, I get it," Kai said. "You can stop."

"No, Kai, you don't get it. You're real. You can't allow yourself to be extinguished like some annoying orphaned voice projection."

"You calling me annoying?"

"Annoying, aggravating, exasperating, and infuriating."

"That's a lot of –ings." Kai laughed. "But seriously, Tal, the

Shields had a meeting this morning. It's over. They said the Color Ceremony was the last disgrace they would endure."

"But they can't kick your family off the island. That's not legal."

"No, but they'll make our lives miserable until we leave by our own free will."

Talia felt her pulse quicken. "You can't just let them snuff you out like that."

"Tal, I don't want to spend the rest of my life trying to be Yellow and cheerful around people who want me to be Blue and disappear."

"But you don't have to disappear. You can train and compete as an independent. You're the only person on this island who actually has a shot of becoming a magician. Once you get into the Workshop, no one will care about your Colors, and you'll be treated with the respect you deserve."

"You sound exactly like my grandmother."

Gross. "Come on, Kai, it wouldn't be so bad to become a magician."

"But look at the price people have to pay to get there. No! Look at the price my family has paid trying to get someone there."

What do I say to that? "Come on. Nothing bad will happen to you. I won't let it."

"Oh yeah. Do you have that much Power?"

"Of course not. Our adventures with King King proved I have no Power," Talia said. "But you're good. You should at least try to find a way to train. Surely, there's some trainer out there who will take you in."

"With what money? I'd need a Tier One or Two trainer to have any hope of getting through the Competitions on my own."

Talia thought about that for a moment. "What about those tourists from Region 6? They had to be some of the richest people in the islands."

"I'm pretty sure that's true. Did you see them at the Ceremony? They were sitting next to the Master Magician."

"Really? I didn't notice. Wow! Did they give your grandmother enough money to hire someone—even for a short time?"

Kai laughed and laughed. "They didn't give us any money at all."

What? But tourists always make a donation after visiting Kai's family—even if it's just a small one. "Seriously? Nothing? Your grandmother must have been furious."

"That's one way to put it. But they did give her something, some little trinket. My grandmother said they intended it for me: 'Very valuable for Kai Master,' 'Keep forever. Precious good.'" Kai did a flawless impersonation of them.

"A trinket?"

"Yeah. Grandmother was furious over the whole thing. She may have thrown it into the ocean for all I know. I never saw it."

"Huh." Talia couldn't help but wonder what it was.

Kai got that solemn look in his eyes again. "Why me, Tal? I was the only kid up there praying not to get a Color, and then I got these two."

"I can't imagine what your grandmother's reaction was. I know how she is with Conflicting Colors."

"I think she's still in shock about it. I don't think it's really sunk in yet." Kai stopped and looked away for a moment before saying, "I wish I could separate them, wrap them up into two boxes, and give one to Weston and the other to Snap. Weston could be Yellow, yeah? Snap would be happy with Blue, right?"

"Kai—you can't, so stop thinking like that. You're the one who's in shock. But I know you. In a few weeks, you'll turn this to your advantage. You're the Yellow mage. You know you are, and Yellows love to be the center of attention. People are going to be traveling from all over the islands to come experience your projections. You'll be spectacular."

"Yippee," Kai said with mock enthusiasm.

"You'll love it." Talia laughed.

"Actually, I've been meaning to tell you, it's a little-known fact that Cyans are the egomaniacs of the rainbow. Which is great, because the truth is that it's going to be you—and not me—who's going to be the one drawing the biggest crowds. Your father will have a long line of men at your door asking for your hand."

"Oh, yes, definitely. Look at me—I'm the hot Cyan-tress who makes every male swoon."

"I'm glad you've finally come to see how beautiful you are." *Did he really just say that to me?* "Come on, Kai, stop it."

"I'm serious. People are going to flock to see you."

"Only if I score high numbers. No one's going to be coming for my looks."

"Yeah, good point. I've been meaning to suggest you get some body mods—"

Talia gave him a solid, physical shove. "Pruner."

"Hey, what about no touchy-touchy?"

Is he referring to that time on the beach when he picked me up and spun me around? The feelings from that moment came back to her. She tried to drown the fluttering feeling by saying, "Kai! Stop it."

"Stop what?"

"Come on, Kai." *You know I'm sensitive about not being beautiful. You do know that, don't you?*

"Talia, you have to understand something. Without body mods, your natural looks only intimidate other women. I only said that for their sake."

She picked up a handful of dirt and leaves and threw them in his face. "Nice try, bud."

"At least I found a way to change the subject." Kai smiled. He then got a funny look in his eyes, paused, and said, "I'm glad you came to get me. This really is the best place anywhere for two loser mages to hang out. Don't you agree?"

It certainly is. She sat down next to Kai. They were silent for a long time, but that was okay. She felt comfortable here, like this, next to him. And as she thought about all the butterflies she'd made with him in this spot over the years, she unconsciously projected one. It was Cyan in color and fluttered out of her hand, sparkling like a jewel.

"Nice," Kai said. "See? What would the islands be without Cyan?"

"They'd be nothing without Yellow and Blue," Talia said, and a flood of yellow and blue butterflies poured out of her and lit up the darkness. "See how beautiful those two Colors are together?"

Kai's eyes went wide. Yellow butterflies with blue wings and blue butterflies with yellow wings danced together in the air. It was spectacular. *Despite being Conflicting Colors, they really are breathtaking.*

Kai and Talia both lay back in the grass and allowed themselves to become lost in the moment. The butterflies that filled the sky weaved in and out amongst one another to form a glowing canopy of light that enveloped them. Night was gone. They were now under what appeared to be a bright blue sky filled with dozens of fluttering, yellow suns.

Time stood still as they gazed at this canopy of floating butterflies that covered them. Talia's heart stirred with longing. It was a strong, powerful emotion. *Did I put that feeling into them?* She hadn't intended to. *Maybe Kai is influencing my projections again.*

She turned her face away from the butterflies and whispered to him, "Do you know how it works?"

"How what works?" Kai whispered back.

"Your ability. How you're able to make other people's projections better."

Kai teased, "Oh? Is that what I do?"

"Stop it. You know I couldn't do all this on my own. That's why I'm so afraid of you leaving."

Kai was silent for a moment, then said, "I have no clue how it works."

"Oh." Talia hesitated. "You want to hear something crazy?"

"What?"

"I'm terrified that my abilities are going to fade if we're not training together, on the same team."

"Yeah, they probably will," Kai said casually.

Talia's heart skipped a beat. *No. No! Don't say that, even as a joke.* "Really?"

"Of course not. I just wanted to fragdaggle you."

"Kai! You just gave me a panic attack. Don't joke about stuff like that."

"All right, all right. I just don't think you need to worry about it. You're talented all on your own," Kai insisted.

"But you don't really know what will happen, do you?" *Please tell me it won't happen.*

"Talia, I can't imagine anything you've learned will go away. It wasn't like I did everything for you. All I've ever done is just boost you."

"Boost?"

"That's what I've been calling it," Kai explained. "Like lifting up a small child."

Wow. "Thanks a lot." *He thinks I'm a little kid.*

"You know what I mean."

"No, actually I don't. Am I going to fall on my face when you're not there to boost me anymore?"

"Absolutely," Kai said and then started to cackle. "It's all part of my nefarious plans. Mwa ha ha!"

Now that I want to be serious, he's decided to go all Yellow? "Come on, Kai—will I?"

"I have no idea. But don't worry. No matter how far the Shield clan pushes me away, I'll always be there to help you in the Competitions, even if it's from the sidelines."

"Yeah, because that sounds mega legal," she said.

"Since when is it illegal to cheer on your friends? But—" Kai suddenly became very serious. "I really don't want what happened to my dad to happen to you."

Oh no. Don't go there, Kai. "What do you mean?"

Kai took a deep breath and forced himself to smile. "You know what? Nothing's going to happen to you. I'm sorry. I shouldn't have brought it up."

Talia glanced up and saw that the blue and yellow butterflies were starting to fade. She thought about recharging them, but decided to let them go.

"So, what else do you want to talk about?" Kai continued. "How about the plight of all those malnourished child rowers in Region 5? Or the enormous income gap between those with Color and those without? We could have a lively discussion about some incurable disease, like schmezits or crimson plague. Any of those ought to totally and utterly ruin the moment."

Talia forced a laugh to indicate that she understood Kai was trying to make a joke, even though she didn't find any of it funny.

The two were quiet as they watched the butterflies flicker out of existence one by one, until only a single butterfly remained. As Talia stared intently at this last butterfly that flitted around them, she noticed it wasn't flickering at all. *Huh. At least one of them had some Power in it. Maybe my ability with Power is growing. That would be nice.* Talia turned her eyes from the butterfly and looked back at Kai. "I'm really going to miss you."

The Easy Route

~Talia~

As a Blue mage, I can say with confidence that Blue is the most dependable and unshakable of Colors. We Blues are visionaries, artists, and dreamers. As blue fills the sky and the sea, Blues fill O'Ceea with beauty and joy. This is why Blue has such conflict with Yellow. Try to imagine the sun existing someplace other than the sky. Yellow is dependent upon Blue. Yet, Yellows believe they are higher than the sky that holds them up. With no firm basis in reality, Yellow mages often act irritatingly cheerful, attempting to charm others. They'd say they're only trying to make the islands a brighter place, but if you ask me, they're nothing but attention hogs.

—Mage Kylee is-a Silk, *Color Me Curious: What Your Color Says About You!*

What if I lose him forever? It was a terrible thought, and although it was warm outside, Talia shivered. She desperately wished she could find a way to persuade the elders to change their ruling. *They need to understand how valuable Kai is.*

But deep in her gut, she knew it would never work. The stigma against Kai and his Conflicting Colors was too strong on their island. "I just wish there were some way we could train together. Things won't be the same without you."

"Excellent. My nefarious plan has worked."

What plan? And what's with him and that word? "You know,

for something to be nefarious, it has to be evil," Talia informed him.

"Really? Is that what nefarious means? That's so drench."

Talia couldn't help but smile when she saw the dumb look on his face.

"Yes!" Kai pointed at her. "I finally got you to smile—for real!"

Talia's smile broadened, and she said, "The Workshop would really benefit by having you. The recent Grand Projections seem to be missing fun. They're not playful anymore."

"Exactly. Bring in the idiot. Kai the Great Goo Bomb, the boy who made Grand Projections stupid again."

"Ha. That really would be great."

Kai rolled onto his side and stared right at Talia. "Can I tell you something weird?"

"Can I say no?"

"Of course not."

"Then, please, tell me. I'm dying to know," Talia said.

"Sometimes I wonder if the islands have gone insane. I mean, what if everything is backward? Grand Projections are grand and all, but you know, I'd rather be running around here making our terrible Little Projections. I'd trade it all—the Workshop and all its glories—to keep what I already have."

"Isn't that what you've been telling the buds all along?"

"Yeah, I guess," Kai said. "But, I just can't picture mages or magicians running around carefree, delighting in stupid Little Projections the way we do. Everyone in the islands thinks getting into the Workshop is the highest goal in life—but it seems like it ruins something inside people. I don't know. I sometimes feel like I'm the only person born who doesn't think becoming a magician is the absolute best thing in the universe."

Here he goes again. Back to Blue. "Don't be so dramatic. You're not the only person. Luge thinks that way, and isn't what you're saying exactly what Tav taught—I mean, wasn't the prohibition that killed him given because he refused to join the original Workshop?"

"Well, not exactly. There weren't any magicians or workshops way back then. And his prohibition was given because he refused to—" Kai opened his eyes wide, as if an idea had just exploded inside him.

"What?"

"You know what? You're kind of right. If Tav had lived in a time when there was a Workshop, I think he probably would have refused to join it. I've never seen it that way."

"As always," Talia said cheerfully, "you should thank me for illuminating you on what you already believe."

"Yup, like I've always suspected: you're the true follower of Tav and I'm some heathen skeptic."

"I didn't say I believed it," Talia defended. "I personally believe someone would need to have mold for a brain to reject a position in the Workshop."

"Thanks."

"Come on, Kai, you really are a moldbrain—but not for that reason. Stop closing your eyes to the obvious."

"What, sorry, I no hear you, you speak louder?" Kai laughed and started to make goofy faces. "Yes, you speak more louder. Me sorry. Moldbrain make me very deaf . . . and blind."

Ignoring him, Talia said, "You want to get into the Workshop—even more than I do."

"Oh, wow. Hey, you're right. I must have forgotten."

"Stop trying to hide—I know you. Look, the Workshop is more complicated—and more painful—for you than probably anyone else in all the islands. I understand what the pressure to become a magician has done to your family. Especially your dad. Obviously, you're terrified of what pursuing it will do to you. And you're right to feel this way. But running away from it isn't the answer."

"Can we talk about child rowers now or something—anything—more cheerful than this?"

Talia stared at him.

"What? I'm not running away," Kai exclaimed. "Look, I'm just sitting here. No running, see. Sitting."

Talia kept staring right at him.

"I just want us to keep playing and making projections together," Kai continued. "You, me, Snap, Weston, Luge. That's all I ever wanted."

"We're mages now. Nothing will be the way it used to be, and even if it were, it wouldn't fix the problem."

"And what will? Training and competing for years, just for a chance to get into the Workshop? Come on, Talia, that's not the answer either!" The fire in Kai's hand leapt up.

Whoa. There it is.

Kai looked away. "I'm sorry, Tal. I shouldn't get angry at you."

"It's fine. You need to get your anger out. I can handle it." Talia tried to look directly into Kai's eyes, but he wouldn't let her. *He can't face it.* "Come on. Just get angry. Let it out."

Even though he was sitting still, she could tell that every muscle in his body was tense. "Aw, all right. You win. Let's get this over with," Kai grumbled. "A part of me—probably a big part—wants to be a magician. And yet the very thought of it makes me want to throw up. No—it's actually much worse than that—I hate that I want it!"

"Why? It's a good thing."

"No, it isn't! Not for me. Not for my family. I only want it because it's what I'm expected to do. Grow up, become a mage, and then devote everything to becoming a magician. Then everything will be okay." Kai rubbed his fingers up and down the side of his face. "But it won't be okay. I hate that everyone, for my entire life, has been telling me I need to be something—something that makes me want to—" Kai stopped himself from saying more.

Come on, Kai, tell me what it makes you want to do.

"Aaagh!" His face went red. "Why can't people just let me be! Talia, please . . . just let me be."

Colors don't lie. He really is Conflicted.

Kai took a few deep breaths and started to relax. "Tal, I really don't want to get angry at you. I just want the pain to stop."

"Go on. Keep talking. This is good."

"Why did I have to be the one with Conflicting Colors? I didn't want to disgrace anyone at the Ceremony. I wasn't trying to cause any problems when we made our King King. I didn't do anything to tarnish our island's reputation. I was just a little kid when my dad . . . when everything happened. Why does everyone have to take everything out on me? Talia, honestly. Why?"

"I don't know. You're right. It's not your fault. You're not the problem."

That seemed to surprise him. "Really? Do you really mean that?"

"Of course. You should be angry," Talia said. "What's happened to you isn't right."

Kai's eyes darted back and forth. It seemed like he was having a difficult time concentrating.

"Kai, it's true. You're not the problem."

In the silence that followed, Talia thought about all the expectations that were now placed on her. *They created the problem—why do they keep expecting kids like us to fix it for them?*

Kai finally broke the silence. "I just want to be able to make projections with others and laugh and play with them."

"We're adults now," Talia said.

"Yeah, I know. But why does the Color Ceremony always seem to mark the moment when childhood relationships break apart? Isn't it even more important for adults to stick together than for kids? I mean, you just told me how you're afraid you'll fail without me there to boost you. But you know—I need you, too. We need each other. And you and I need Weston, Luge, and Snap. And they need us," Kai said. "Talia, I'm scared."

Ah, that's what this has been about. He's as scared as I am.

"I know I'll fail without all of you—you especially," he continued. "But the elders' decision, my clan, my grand-mother . . . everyone seems to be doing everything they can to keep us apart."

"It's not like I'm leaving the island," Talia said. "We'll still be able to see each other."

"From afar—you training on the far side of the island and me all the way over here—woo hoo! Plus, we'd need to always be hiding, sneaking, deceiving. Like now! Is that how you want to live? I don't want my life to become like that, and especially not with you."

He's got a point. "I agree—it's no way to live. But what other choice do we have?"

"I can leave."

"That's not the answer!" Talia exclaimed. "You just said we need each other."

"Well, then that only leaves us with one option."

"Yeah. One of us needs to become a magician," Talia said. "I know—I've been thinking about it, too. That's the only way we'll ever be free to do whatever we really want."

"No, Tal," Kai said. "Not just one of us. Me. I have to become the magician. You can too, of course. But if I'm not a magician, nothing's going to change."

"That's not true."

"Yes it is. You know this island. Unless I bring honor back to my family and clan, the rest of the island is never going to let me come near you—they won't now that you're a mage, and it'll only be worse once you're a magician."

He's right. He's absolutely right. "But if I become a magician, I'll have influence with the elders," Talia suggested.

"Tal, you know I'm right. A magician—even one of the Second Magnitude like you're going to become—can't be with someone who's Conflicted."

"'With'? Did you just say 'with'?" Talia stood up.

"Uh, yeah." Kai looked uneasy.

"What do you mean by 'with'?" she asked as she hovered over him.

"Uh— this is bad, right?" Kai got up and stepped away from her. "There's no way I'm going to be able get out of this one, huh?"

"Nope. Come on, tell me what you mean." Talia followed him.

"Uh, like hanging out with?" Kai said. He started to run.

"Ooooooh, that kind of 'with,' is it?" Talia shouted as she raced after him. "You only meant the 'we're just friends' kind of 'with,' did you?"

They ran, weaving in and out of the trees.

"You're taking this the wrong way."

"What way do you want me to take it?" She dodged to the right. "This way?" Then she dodged to the left. "Or this other way?"

"Um, neither."

They kept running around until they found themselves standing on either side of a large tree. Kai asked, "Are you upset?"

He doesn't have a clue. "No, no. Everything's just great, bud. I just want to be 'with' you right now," she said as she leapt around the tree and grabbed him. He tried to get away, and in the process, they both tripped and fell to the ground.

They burst out in nervous laughter as they jumped back up and faced each other.

"This is what you meant by 'with,' right?" Talia leapt forward in an attempt to pin him down.

"No, I was thinking a little bit more like this." Kai dodged out of the way and shot a burst of projected water at her. It hit her on the side and burst like a water balloon, but instead of the water being clear, it was a dark bright orange color that exploded over her and then disappeared.

He would throw Orange at me right now.

As he scrambled away, she threw a balloon of her own. This one burst royal violet and splattered all over Kai.

They threw bursts of colored water, chased, and attempted to tackle each other until all the tension in them faded away. Unable to continue, they collapsed on the ground near one another. Talia was keenly aware that their hands were close—closer than they'd ever been—but not touching.

Please don't let this be the end. Kai's right, I wish moments like this could go on forever. But the islands just don't work that way. There has to be a better reality—somewhere. Talia was still uncertain about the future, but she felt slightly more confident now.

After a long while, Kai broke the silence. "We've taken heat all our lives over our friendship, and it hasn't torn us apart yet. What could a few Colors do to stop us?"

"A lot. We're adults now—we have collars—and people don't give as much grace to adults as they do to kids."

"'We'll stand our ground, we'll ascend the peaks!'" Kai laughed as he quoted a famous line spoken by Narlo, one of her favorite characters from a Grand Projection.

"'May the world be flooded again!'" Talia finished the quote. *Why don't things ever work out like they do in stories?*

"It won't be so bad. Especially if we decide to go the easy route," Kai said.

Talia rolled over to face him and leaned her head on her hand. "What's the easy route?"

"It's an easy four-step plan. One: I go away and train really hard. Two: I destroy everyone's projections in this year's Intra-Regional Competitions. Three: I get into the Championship Games and pour out everything I've got to earn a top score. Four: I humbly submit myself to the Workshop and am welcomed in as their newest magician. And, zango! We're together again."

Talia laughed. "Oh, right. Easy."

"Yup. No problem. I'm crazy Kai. I've got a hand full of fire and Conflicting Colors around my neck. As a Blue-Yellow mage, nothing's impossible for me."

"Except living in reality."

"Overrated. We live in a world of projections; anything is possible. Even serious Cyan magicians like you know that."

"Uh, Cyan mage," Talia corrected. "I'm not a magician."

"Not yet, but you will be. Both of us will. Remember, we're going the easy route."

"Of course."

"But," Kai added, "since you're so much more talented than I am, you'll almost certainly beat me to the Workshop. Don't worry, though—I'll catch up soon enough."

"I certainly hope so."

"So let's make a plan—right now—that you'll meet me at the door and give me a tour of the place once I finally break in there. Deal?"

"Deal," Talia said. *We're never going to be free to be friends again, are we?* There was a long pause. *I'm going to really miss you, Kai.*

Kai kept his eyes fixed on the solitary blue and yellow butterfly that still flitted around the forest. "Thanks for keeping that one around this whole time. It's helped."

"It's nice, isn't it? I think it's one of the most realistic ones I've ever made. I'm going to have a hard time dissolving it when we go."

"So don't."

Talia stared at him. *You know the rules, Kai. Remember what happened when we broke them by leaving King King undissolved?*

"It's just an innocent little butterfly, Tal—what harm could it do? It'll be way out here in the middle of nowhere. No one will ever see it. And without anyone to recharge it, it'll go out on its own soon enough."

"Yeah, I guess you're right. At least Weston isn't here to soak it with more Power than we can handle," she joked. As she said this, another joke came to her. "Hey, if you really are as nefarious as people say—and your family has had enough influence to destroy our entire island—it really ought to be easy for you to become one of the two eighty-eight, right?"

Kai didn't laugh, or say anything. *Oh no. That was a mean thing to say.*

But he turned his eyes to hers and said, "Talia! That's it! You're absolutely right."

Is he being serious? "I am?" she asked.

"Yup. I'm vile, foul, and odious."

"What? No, you're not. That's crazy."

"No, seriously. I repent!" Kai looked up and shouted to the sky. "I shall turn from my nefarious, island-destroying ways and forevermore use all my talent for good." He turned back to Talia and said in a quieter voice, "And then it will be really easy to get everything every decent, straight-and-narrow soul could ever want. I'll just walk up to the Workshop, take a step inside, and instantly become a magician. Everything will end happily ever after. That's how it works, right?"

You almost got me there, Kai. "Yup, that sounds about right," she said.

"Hurrah! That's it. That's the plan!"

Wait. She looked deeply into his eyes. *I think he might mean it. Could Kai is-a Shield really want to get into the Workshop?* "You're serious, aren't you," Talia said.

"Of course. I'm going to become a magician. It's the only life for someone like me."

"For real. You're not joking?"

"No, honestly," Kai said. "I'm honestly being serious."

"But who's going to train you?"

"I'll figure that out."

"It's settled then?"

"Yup, settled!"

"No problems?"

"No problems—only happily ever after!" Kai said.

If only real life worked that way.

The Red Rider

~Weston~

*If you haven't ever be doubt'n that we commoners aren't just as
invaluable as them magician, you better go experience fer yerselves
them Curse'ed Epics. It's a grandy. It'll prove ya that it's only when
them magician, and mages, and commoners all get together—
together!—that we get ta be shatterin' them stormy clouds that
rascally Devos Rektor keeps on makin'. We'll get him! You'll see.*
—Mistress Delia is-a Wasp, *Commoners Worth Quoting.*

"Hello? Mistress Jade? I have a voice delivery for you,"
Weston called as he knocked on the door of the Shield home.

"Weston?" Kai answered from inside.

The whole way to Kai's house, Weston had been looking
forward to showing off his new bike and the red rider uniform he
now wore. When the door creaked open and he saw his friend, he
placed his hands behind his back and stood at attention.

"Good morning, young mage, is Mistress Jade at home?" he
asked in a commanding voice.

"What are you talking about, Weston?" Kai asked with an
amused look.

"Is your grandmother here?"

"She's next door," Kai said as he glanced down at the intricately
carved black lacquered box in Weston's hand. "What are you doing?
Is this a game?"

"A game? No, of course not. I'm here on official business: delivering a voice projection. Your grandmother's been spending a lot of time—and gryns—at the communication tower, trying to find you a trainer."

"Yeah, I know." Kai smiled. "But I mean, is this your job?"

"You'd budder believe it!"

Kai stared back at him with a blank expression. "You didn't really just say that, did you?"

"Yeah, bud. You'd budder believe I did," Weston said again with a wink.

"Okay, you really have to stop saying that."

"No way. It's my new favorite expression. It works in all kinds of situations. 'Mom, can you pass the budder?' or 'I heard you're sick, I hope you start feeling budder,' or—"

"Or 'you'd budder stop saying that or I'm going to punch you.'" Kai raised his fist.

Ha! He used it. It's catching on already. "You can try, but my real fist is so much budder than your silly projection punches."

Kai sighed and covered his face with both his hands. "Okay, enough. What are you doing here? For real."

"I'm working—or, at least, I'm supposed to be." Weston laughed. "Full time, too. I'm making this my career."

"Career? I don't understand. Delivering messages isn't a career. It's a job for kids to teach them responsibility and give them a little spending money."

"Sure, I mean, that's how most people see it." Weston leaned casually against the door frame. "I did this back when I was eight, but I totally loved it. I earned more gryns that one year than I ever did working for my family sewing threadbare—and that was when I was little and too scared to climb all the way up to the top of the tower."

"But . . ." Kai seemed to be at a loss for words.

Weston understood Kai's confusion; up until now, no adults, or even young adults, rode around delivering voice messages. People saw it strictly as a part-time job for children. Whenever they had some spare time, kids would ride their bikes over to the base of the communication tower and wait for a voice message from another island to come in so that they could deliver it.

"But," Kai continued to stammer, "you earned three gold chips in Power and you only went to three testing booths—that's unbelievable! Think of how many more chips you'll earn when you have enough money to pay for more tests. It ought to be really easy for you to reach the third privilege level.

"You could do all sorts of things then," Kai went on. "You should see if the Island Patrol will hire you. They're always looking for people who have enough Power to clean up illegal projections. You'd do a really great job, just like you did after Gropher and the others trashed those twins' yacht at the Glimmering."

"Are you kidding? I don't want to be a garbage man."

"They're called sanitation custodians. And it's a good job."

"Oh, don't get me wrong, I have a lot of respect for them and the valuable public service they perform for us all," Weston said. "It's just not the life for me. It's really important to be passionate about one's job—like I am about being a red rider."

"But," Kai said with a frown, "Weston, there are lots of other jobs available for someone with your credentials. You ought to be able to get a better-paying job than this."

"Oh, I'll be earning plenty of gryns, you just wait and see," Weston said. While it was technically true that the pay wasn't great, this didn't bother him; he'd figured out the trick to making a fortune as a red rider. *And the best part is, no one else has thought of it yet!*

"I don't understand how you can earn enough to live. It's only, what, four gryns per delivery?"

"It's called tips, buddy boy. They're the secret to great wealth, after all. A lot of people don't realize how many fortunes throughout history have been made though tips," Weston said with a big grin on his face. "The key to big tips is making sure people feel validated and cared for. It's easy work and unlocks untold wealth. What could be budder? So, take this package right now so I can get going to my next delivery."

"Oh, right." Kai took the box that held the voice projection and rummaged around the house for some coins. When he came back, he placed five gryns into Weston's outstretched hand.

"Wait, this is only . . . five gryns?" Weston said after he counted the payment. "Come on, Kai, I'm not going to be able to survive with a one gryn tip."

Kai smiled. "That's my point. Who can afford to tip very much? You know how poor we are."

"Yeah, well, you wouldn't know it by how many messages your grandmother has been sending out the last three days. And she's been offering to pay a whole lot to get you a Tier One trainer."

"That is none of your business, Young Master Weston!" Jade's voice boomed from behind him. "Your place is to deliver messages—not listen to them."

Oh great, she heard me. Weston tensed. Although Kai was one of his best friends, Mistress Jade scared him. "Yes, Mistress. Kai has your message. I need to be going."

"Wait one moment. I want to listen to it first. I will most likely need to send a response," Jade said as she went into the house and picked up the box.

Weston watched as she unfastened the clasp, opened the lid, and lifted a spongy yellow cube from the box. She held the cube up to her ear while she paced around the room. Although he knew he shouldn't, Weston strained to hear the message that the voice cube held.

Sadly, because she turned her back to him, all he could make out was, "Unfortunately . . . for a Conflicted . . . can't charge less than . . . ten weeks payment in advance."

Jade, visibly upset, swiped her hand over the cube to erase the message. "Here, take this back. I do not want it cluttering up our home." She handed Weston the box. "And give me back one gryn. You are to receive only four. Tipping just serves to corrupt young hearts and minds toward laziness."

Weston reluctantly gave back his measly tip. He took the box from her, slipped it into his satchel, and left without a word. *Unbelievable! Who does that!? I wonder if Mistress Jade sat on a monkey when she was a kid. I really hope Kai can find a trainer and get out of here, soon.*

✳   ✳   ✳

Weston spent the rest of the morning riding messages around the island.

"Whoa, a response already?" Treena is-a Stone blinked several times in surprise. She was a prominent Orange-Yellow magician of the First Magnitude. She lived on the Island of the Magician's Workshop most of the year, but whenever she had a break, she came back to her home in Little Hills, the best neighborhood on this island. "It's not even been a full watch since I sent the last message."

"I'm glad you're satisfied with my performance," Weston stated. Before this job, he'd never interacted with any of the island's celebrities. *And now I'm hand-delivering one a private message. How mega is my life?*

"Yes, I'm very impressed. I've always believed such valuable work shouldn't be left to children," Treena said as she took the box, opened the lid, and grabbed the spongy cube. As she listened to the message, a look of pleasure crossed her face. After the message finished, she swiped the cube clean, reached into her purse, and pulled out ten gryns.

Ka-clink! This is what it's all about!

"Oh, Magician Treena, it's only four gryns for a delivery," Weston reminded her.

"The rest is a tip," Treena said absently as she stepped away from the door and spoke a new voice projection into the cube. She listened to it and was satisfied, so she placed it in the box, closed the lid, and returned the box to Weston, along with enough gryns for the sending fee. "Get this to Rieta as quickly as you can and there will be another good tip in it for you."

"You got it!" Weston spun on his heel and turned back to the tower. *Oh, buds alive! Ten gryns and a promise for more! Easy money.* Weston couldn't stop smiling. *And I thought my life was going to be so drench without a Color.*

Weston wasted no time as he peddled out of town, through the forest, and up the hill that led to the communication tower. He made good progress as he rode up the worn path, but he slowed when he came across Kai's mother, Declarious, who was riding a bit slower up ahead of him.

"Hey there!" he called.

"Weston! How nice to see you." Declarious smiled as he rode up next to her. "Kai told me you'd become a red rider, but I thought he was only kidding."

"Isn't it great? I get paid just to bike around the island. It's a dream job, really. I get lots of exercise, perform a community service, and get paid pretty well. I just earned a ten gryn tip on my last delivery."

"Wow, that sure was generous." Declarious sounded surprised. "But didn't you earn a lot of high chips during your testing? I know you have a great ability with Power."

"Oh, sure, back when I used to make projections. But none of that really worked out." Weston pointed to the solid black of his collar. "Kids can't place all their hope into becoming a mage—that's just not realistic, is it?"

"No. No. You're right—it's not wise to get your expectations up. But there are still plenty of good jobs for someone with your talent."

"Well, it's a tough job market out there, especially for a young void pull like myself. I could be a ship rower or sew threadbare like my family, but that's never really been my thing. My mom says I should be grateful for any job, really."

"That's true. Times have been pretty tough since people stopped coming to our island for training. But I think that might provide an opportunity for someone like you. I know many families who've found it terribly difficult to afford to have their family icons recharged. There's no law saying that job can be done only by a member of HiSSAnClaP."

She doesn't understand how much money someone like me can earn off tips. "I really appreciate your advice, Mistress Declarious. But because I'm not a mage—and I'd be working outside of the guild—I doubt many people would risk hiring me."

"Oh, no. I know a couple dozen people who'd be thrilled to pay someone with your talent."

Mistress Declarious is so considerate wanting to help me, but she just doesn't understand basic economics. "Outside the guild, I'd have to charge less than half the going rate for the work." *Businesses can't survive charging only half.*

"That's true, but half would still earn you fifty to a hundred gryns for each icon you recharged. That's got to be more than you earn in an entire day delivering messages."

"Oh, you'd be surprised how much one can make. I can do about fifteen messages a day—it'll be more, once training season starts. And tips aren't taxable—you can't forget to take taxes into consideration when it comes to these kinds of things." Weston loved this part of his plan. *Tax-free means a lot more gryns for my family at the end of the day.*

"I think you'd easily be able to do half that many icon recharges a day, and more if you were willing to travel a little. I really think you ought to consider it."

"Okay, I will," he replied casually. "Although, if I did recharges, there would be insurance premiums to pay. People expect professionals to be insured these days—mistakes do happen after all. And as everyone knows, insurance isn't cheap."

"Weston," Declarious said with a sigh, "you've been a dear friend to Kai. I just want the best for you. I know not getting a Color can be devastating, and that you might be scared to do something with projections, but I do hope you find a way to use your talent, even without a Color. As both our families know, it's really tough to survive on less than two hundred and fifty gryns a day."

"Oh, trust me. I plan on making a lot more than that. Just look at Talia's family! None of them have ever had a Color, but they've worked hard and are pretty wealthy now. So you don't have to worry about me. I'm devoted! I'll work as long and as hard as necessary to make my new career a success."

"Yes, but Talia's family built their business up over many generations, slowly buying and building property."

"Which is exactly why I need to start now!" Weston said with a big smile. *That recharging idea would be perfect for Kai though—if he doesn't get into the Workshop, of course. Then again, I don't know if too many people would trust someone who has Conflicting Colors with their family icons. That collar is really going to hold him back.*

As they rode up the last of the steep hill, the forest started to thin, and Weston was able to catch glimpses of the communication tower through the trees.

It was a huge stone structure that had been constructed on the highest point of the island. Rising higher than anything else around, it provided an unobstructed line-of-sight view to each of the towers on the neighboring islands.

Every civilized island had at least one communication tower. It was the primary means of long-distance communication in the islands and was how people sent messages to far-off loved ones, conducted inter-island business, and broadcasted news-worthy events. It was a truly incredible system, and even though he was only a red rider, Weston felt privileged to be a part of it.

"Mistress Declarious?" Weston asked. "Do you think they'll ever reopen the second communication tower?"

"Oh, I don't know. The island used to send out a lot more messages. I suppose if the economy rebounds there'd be enough demand for it. But it's pretty run down now. They'd have to repair it, or more likely build an entirely new one."

That would be so cake. Maybe Luge's family would be hired to do that. Weston had always been fascinated by the towers. They rose up so high in the sky. *Maybe that's why I liked Luge's treehouse so much. It was kind of like a tower. I wonder when he's going to show it to the other buds.*

The towers were not only the means by which the islands communicated; they also functioned as the Timekeeper's Perch. Through the nine watches of the day, a mage known as the timekeeper was perched at the very top of the tower. Today, the timekeeper was Carlay is-a Stone, a gorgeous Blue mage in her late twenties. Weston knew she was way out of his reach—and much too old for him—but he always felt his pulse quicken at the thought of her curly, fire-orange hair and deep cyan eyes.

While on duty, Carlay stayed in a perch at the top of the tower and projected a number of colored beacons up into the sky that indicated the time of day. Timekeepers were responsible for keeping track of the watches by cycling through the Nine Colors, starting right before sunrise with the Crimson watch and finishing after sundown with the Violet watch.

When Weston and Declarious arrived, there were two Yellow beams of light shining into the sky, indicating that it was the middle of the Yellow watch.

Most people in O'Ceea had long since rejected the Color gods as real deities, but the tradition of naming each watch after one of the Colors was an ancient one, and thus it still held. This bothered some people, but not Weston. *Learning all about the Color gods in history class was so interesting.* He'd always been fascinated by stories of people who unexpectedly found a Color wrapped around them. It was such a rare thing and no one really understood why it happened. *It'd be monkey-flipping mega to be summoned to the Island of the First Watch.*

"You bike up this hill several times a day?" Declarious asked. They were close to the base of the tower. The hill got steeper in this spot, and although biking up it was no big deal for Weston, it looked like Kai's mom was getting tired.

"Yup. I guess this hill is one reason that it's mostly kids who do this kind of work. It can be quite tiring," Weston said as he got to the top, leapt off his bike, and leaned it against a tree.

"You must really love your job," Declarious observed as she got off her bike. She placed her hand on the side of the tower to stop and catch her breath. "It's amazing that Mother Jade's been making so many trips here lately."

"Yeah. She's wildly determined," Weston said with a laugh.

"That's one way to put it."

The stone steps at the base of the tower were wide, but as Weston and Declarious ascended, they were careful to hold the railing. The steps grew steeper and narrower toward the top, and one misstep could mean a nasty tumble. It would have been a terrifying climb for anyone afraid of heights. In fact, many people had to hire someone to climb the stairs for them. A few weeks ago, Weston would have really struggled with this. But after spending a few nights sleeping up in Luge's treehouse and flying out of it countless times, his fear was completely gone.

When they reached about halfway up, Declarious stopped and asked, "You're not afraid of the stairs anymore, are you?" She'd been with Kai and Weston in this very spot many years earlier when Weston had a panic attack and she'd had to carry him down. It was the main reason he'd originally quit doing this kind of work when he was a kid.

"Nope!" Weston looked to her with a gigantic smile. "It's like you said. I really love my job."

At last they climbed the final step and arrived in the spacious area at the top of the tower. The round, vaulted ceiling was supported by four pillars, one in each corner. In the center was a circular opening through which the timekeeper's beams of color traveled up into the sky. A wobbly construction of ladder-like scaffolding led up to the Timekeeper's Perch near the hole, where Carlay is-a Stone sat on a swing and kept track of time.

"Hey, Carlay," Weston called up, "I have something I want to give you." He pulled a small bag out of his pocket and grabbed the ladder to start climbing up.

"Hold, dearest Youthful Master. I'll descend to you. We can't risk your young-tastic self plunging to its premature doom." Carlay scrambled down a few rungs of the rickety scaffolding with the expertise of an acrobat before leaping down and landing beside him with grace.

What a mega way to live. "Take a look." Weston handed her the bag. "I know you like these."

Carlay opened the bag to find a handful of pako pods. As soon as she saw them, her eyes popped. She pulled the bag up to her face and inhaled deeply. "These smell extraordinary!"

"Yeah, I just got them a couple days ago. They're from the Island of the Red Tower."

Carlay started to shake and quiver with excitement. Weston didn't know anyone who cared about pako pods more than she did. "I'm absolutely, positively, mega-gobbly in love with Red Tower pako! But each one costs more gryns than a basket of Limmick's fresh-cut cod! Are you sure you don't want them for yourself?"

"Nah, they aren't really my thing. I only bought them so I could chew on 'em while training—and during the Competitions. But, since that won't be happening, I thought you should have them."

"Well, I offer you the greatest of thanks, Youthful Master. I don't know of a single timekeeper who would turn down pako. The pod I have in my mouth is getting decrepitly old, so I'll gladly take these from your generous hands," Carlay said as she took the bag and climbed up a post that led to her perch.

While Weston was talking with Carlay, Declarious had lined up behind the other two people who were waiting to send out a message.

The head tower mage, an older woman named Rieta is-a Leaf—who was from a different branch of the Leaf clan than Talia—was speaking with one rather worried looking woman about the best way to compose a message.

"You figure out what you want to say yet?" Rieta asked without masking her impatience.

"Yes." The woman cleared her throat. "Dearest Mother, I . . . hope all is well and that Father is doing better."

Rieta raised her eyebrows. "You sure you want to waste gryns on well wishes?"

The woman pressed her lips together and said, "No. I guess not. Okay, how about—Dearest Mother, I thank you for your generous offer to host us at your new home on the Island of the Oak Falls, but work has been very pressing and I cannot get away now. I do so look forward to seeing you in six weeks for Family Day and the Festival of Trees. Please give my best to Father. I love you. Marian."

"If you say 'I' and 'You,' you're wasting half a gryn. 'Love' is more than enough."

"Ah—all right, sure."

That felt like it was about sixty words. I could never remember all that. Weston loved seeing the tower mage work. Each island's tower was operated by a mage who possessed a unique set of skills. A tower mage needed a great memory, the Power to send voice projections a great distance, the ability to juggle the numerous messages flowing in and out of the tower at any time, high ethics, and discretion. Weston thought it must have been nearly impossible to find someone with all these qualities. *Now there's a job that pays well. Too bad it's another mage-only thing.*

"That's sixty-seven words, plus an additional eight gryn inter-regional surcharge for relay costs to Region 4, bringing your total up to twenty-four and three-quarter gryns."

That was sixty-seven words? I thought for sure it was closer to sixty. Wow, it's a good thing Rieta's so good at this.

The woman reached into her purse and handed over the requested amount. "My goodness. The cost of having a family. Let me know if she even bothers to respond." She made her way over to the stairs.

"Yes, yes. I'll send a rider as soon as I hear anything," Rieta replied. She then faced a tower to the west, raised her hands high in the air, then thrust them out over the water while whispering the message under her breath. Weston felt a sensation like a sudden blast of wind brush against his skin. It seemed to swirl around him before it shot out and away.

"Tell me," Rieta said to Weston after she'd finished sending the message, "how did she look?"

"Huh? Who? That woman just now?"

"No! I could see with my own two eyes that Marian was frustrated. I'm talking about Treena—the magician you just delivered a cube to! How did she look?"

"Oh! Uh, happy, I guess," Weston held out the message box he was carrying. "She gave me this response for you to send back."

"Yes, no wonder. I'd send a response back right quick too if I got a message such as that," Rieta snickered. Just as she was about to say something more, she held her finger up at him and a vacant expression came over her face. She stared intently off into the distance for a long moment.

A message is coming in. This place is so mega!

"Uh-oh," Rieta said as she took a foam cube from the big pile next to her. Holding it up in one hand, she started to wave the fingers of her other hand at it, projecting into it the message she had just received. When she was finished, she placed the foam cube into a black box, latched the lid, and tied a projected seal over it that ensured no one would tamper with it until it got to its intended recipient. Then she set it onto a table next to her. "Heathron isn't going to be happy about this."

"Heathron is-a Stone?" Weston asked.

"Who else? His daughter's husband—that Green-Blue magician from the Island of the Swinging Vines, the one who projected all those fat warrior hippos in the Championship Games two years back. His scores are dropping. He may not be able to keep his place in the Workshop if he doesn't turn things around before this year's culling."

I remember that guy. He was hilarious. "Oh, that's too bad."

"Indeed. Poor Heathron," Rieta went on. "He really doesn't need news like that today. He's already got so much going on—what with his in-laws visiting and all."

"Do you want me to deliver the message?" Weston asked.

"No, that's okay. Heathron really shouldn't hear this devastating news right now. We'll wait a few days to deliver it. I have another message waiting for you to carry, but you just catch your breath for now."

Weston shrugged. "I don't need to rest. I'd like to go now."

Rieta raised her eyebrows. "You know, you might just be the best rider I've ever had. But I won't risk you burning yourself out in your first week. Take a short break, and then you can deliver it."

The man who was next in line cleared his throat impatiently and said, "Rieta. Last I heard, discretion was a requirement for employment here."

"Yeah, yeah. I didn't say what the score was," she growled. "You have a message to send or did you just want to stand there and eavesdrop while I conduct business with my employee?"

Declarious waited patiently while the man, a worker from Nosy's, submitted a long string of financial information to the company's corporate headquarters in the cluster of islands formerly known as Region 6. *Huh, I didn't know Nosy's was from there.*

When he finally left, it was just Rieta, Weston, and Declarious at the top of the tower—and Carlay chewing pako up in her perch. Declarious rubbed her hands on her dress and looked around as if she were taking in the view from the top of the tower. From here, they could easily see the other Penta-Islands.

"I'd like to send a message to the Island of the Cloudy Peaks."

"Ooohh, really? That island's got a sixteen gryn surcharge," Rieta said.

"It does? I didn't know that. But it's in our region—"

"Who's it going to, dear?"

"It's just a general message," Declarious said.

"There are no general messages unless you're a licensed reporter. I must have a specific recipient or I can't send anything."

Declarious stammered a bit, and Rieta tapped her foot impatiently. "Come on, dear, I'm a busy woman."

I've never seen Kai's mom like this before. Something's got her really worked up.

"It's to Malroy is-a Shield," she said at last.

Oh no. This is going to get ugly.

"Malroy, is it." Rieta eyed her suspiciously. "He was such a good man. It was such a shame when we all found out he was rock-chewin' crazy. Jade seems to have caught the disease now, too, hasn't she? She's been up here nonstop the past two days, right Weston?"

"Yes, Mage Rieta."

"Good thing her body's still in good shape, otherwise I'd be concerned about someone her age making it up all these stairs—Green forbid—without falling down. I don't need a scandal like that on my watch.

"Anywho," Rieta continued, "you know I can't send a message to someone who's been banished from the island."

"You know perfectly well that Malroy wasn't banished," Declarious corrected.

Oh buds alive. This is not good. "Can I go deliver that message now?"

"Why, I think that would be an excellent idea. Do you mind helping dear Declarious down as you go?"

Declarious stared at Rieta. "I'm not leaving until you send my message."

"I'm so sorry, but I don't make the rules, you know."

"But Malroy was never banished," Declarious insisted.

"Yeah, yeah," Rieta said impatiently. "He left before the IP could sentence him. Same thing."

"No, it's not. That means it's not illegal to send him a message."

Rieta let out a long and loud sigh and said, "All right, dear. But first things first. Here, Weston, you can go now and deliver this to—"

"Actually, Weston, could you stay behind for a moment? Just while I send the message."

Rieta raised an eyebrow. "This is a rather urgent message. Weston shouldn't wait a moment longer than he already has."

"It won't take long," Declarious said. "My message is very short."

Weston shrugged. "Why, sure, Mistress Declarious, you know I'd do anything to help you and Kai."

"Oh, don't we all know that," Rieta said. "All right. But by sending a message to Cloudy Peaks, you'll incur a surcharge."

"I understand. I want you to send this: 'Malroy, it's time. Implement Plan 2C. Declarious.'"

"Plan 2C? What are you talking about?" Rieta asked. "Are you trying to sound like a spy in some Grand Projection?" Declarious remained silent. "All right, it's your gryns. Eight words—"

"Hold on. It's only seven," Declarious corrected.

"2C is two words, so it's eight."

"All right, fine. I'll pay two gryns," Declarious said.

"Plus your surcharges, dear—which brings your total to twenty-two, if you please."

Whoa! The surcharges to that island are crazy high!

"What? Explain to me how that's twenty-two gryns."

Rieta let out a sigh. "Eight words cost four, plus relay fees, and the surcharge—you agreed to that, remember?"

"You're charging me four gryns to send an eight word message to Malroy? That's twice the going rate! And how can you in good conscience charge a sixteen gryn surcharge for Cloudy Peaks?"

"You're forgetting the relay fees, dear."

Declarious shook her head. "It's only two gryns per relay—and my message only needs one. Eight divided by four is two, plus two, minus twenty-two, is minus eighteen—that's how much you're overcharging me."

"I'm impressed with your math, dear."

Wow, she rattled off all those numbers like nothing. She really is super good at math.

"You know how poor we are," Declarious said as she dug around in her coin purse.

"Yes, Jade has made that abundantly clear every day for the last eight years. But somehow, she's managed to spend a tremendous number of gryns up here the last few days attempting to get Kai a trainer. I'm beginning to wonder if you're all as poor as you let on."

Rieta accepted the gryns from Declarious and then started to sort through them. "I'll send the message momentarily. Best of luck to you. Goodbye."

"I'm going to wait," Declarious said. "I'll just stand on the landing below. Please let me know immediately when you get a response."

Rieta rolled her eyes. "Nothing would please me more, dear."

✳   ✳   ✳

Weston spent the rest of the Yellow and Green watches biking messages around the island. The first four times he came back to the tower, he found Declarious still there, waiting patiently.

"What's Plan 2C?" he asked her. He was dying to know, but Declarious wouldn't tell him anything. *Maybe Kai and his family really are spies, working for some mysterious, mega-wealthy elders. Or maybe they're double agents wanting to start a rival Workshop. The Shields do have all kinds of strange people coming to visit them.*

He went home for the Cyan watch, took a nap, then ate a quick Blue lunch with his family. It was the middle of the Blue watch by the time he got back to the tower. Declarious was gone, and Rieta was pacing aggressively.

"Did Malroy send a message back?" Weston asked her.

"It's not ethical to share with third parties anything regarding the messages that are sent, received, or retransmitted upon this tower."

Wow, what's gotten into her?

She sat down on a bench—which was unusual, as she normally did her work standing up—and said she was feeling a bit tired and might close the tower early today.

She gave Weston three cubes, and he went out on the deliveries. When he returned at the top of the Indigo watch, he found Kai there, standing in front of Rieta with a message box in his hand and a look of frustration on his face.

". . . I don't understand. I have a collar. How can I be considered underage?"

"No underage minor can send a message without prior approval from their legal parent, sponsor, or licensed trainer," Rieta stated.

"Hey, bud, what's going on?" Weston asked as he walked over to them.

"The tower mage isn't allowing me to send a reply to a message without my grandmother or mother present."

"Really? But you're a mage."

"Oh, he certainly is, isn't he?" Rieta scoffed. "But he's asking to send a message to an individual who is unauthorized to receive communication from minors on an island known for not having the highest levels of security. I don't make the rules, but I must follow them for everyone's safety. All you have to do is go home, get your mother, and come back. That won't take you too long now, will it?"

"But I'm not a minor."

"All right," Rieta said. "You're a young man, but a young man is still a measure less than a man. All you need to do is go get one of your elders."

Sometimes I think people make up rules just to torment Kai and his family. I hope he can find somewhere else to live where people aren't so mean to him.

"But . . . I'll never make it back before Violet watch," Kai said when he saw one of the three beams of light disappear, marking the middle of the Indigo watch.

"You'd better hurry, then."

"Come on, bud, we can do it," Weston said.

Kai reluctantly turned away from Rieta and the two friends descended the tower steps as quickly as they could.

"Sorry about that. She's been in a foul mood all day," Weston explained.

"Seems like it. You don't have to come with me, though. Don't you need to work?"

"Nah, it's okay. I've been going all day, and I work however many watches I want. It's another one of the many benefits I get with this job," said Weston. Then, once he was sure Rieta couldn't hear them anymore, he whispered, "So, your mom was up here and said something about Plan 2C. Do you have any idea what that is? I've been dying to know all day."

"Hmm. Are you sure you want to know?"

"Of course I do!"

"All right, but you have to keep it secret."

"I promise."

"I need more than that. This is serious stuff," Kai insisted.

Hot mildew! I bet he is a spy after all! "I promise to keep it secret, and if I don't, you can make another King King demon and boil me alive with fireballs."

Kai laughed. "Okay, okay. The plan means I'm going to see my grandfather. You get it? '2C' equals 'to see,' like with your eyes."

Weston stopped and stared back at Kai. "Really? Is it really that stupid, or are you just being a Kai with me?"

"I can't be anything other than a Kai with you."

"Ah, bud. Come on! Tell me what it really means. I need to know."

"I'll tell you later," Kai said when they got to the bottom of the steps. "I need to go get my mom so I can jump through the tower mage's little controlling hoops. I need to send a message to my grandfather before Violet watch."

"No, wait," Weston said, and he pointed up at the top of the tower. The two beams of Indigo light Carlay projected into the sky began to flicker, indicating the communication tower was no longer open to send or receive messages. "Wow. She really meant it when she said she was going to close up early."

"Unbelievable," Kai said as they heard Rieta coming down the stairs.

Weston scratched the back of his head and said, "That's so weird. I wonder why she would tell you to go back and get your mom if she wasn't going to be here?"

"Do you really need me to explain that to you?"

Ooh, yeah. She's probably just messing with him.

"But," Kai continued, "I still need to get a message to my grandfather." Kai pulled Weston into the bushes. He then projected green shrubbery over both of them in what Weston assumed to be an effort to blend them into the trees.

"Great. Thanks, Kai—I'm still on duty," Weston said with a frown.

"It's a red shirt and black pants. I can reproject that in my sleep."

"Well, I guess you could try. But there's certain regulations for the uniform. It has to be the right shade of red, and—"

Kai placed his hand over Weston's mouth. "Shhhhh. We don't want her to hear us."

Gross. I can't believe he just did that.

They waited until Rieta appeared at the base of the tower, then watched in silence as she stepped onto the path and headed down the hill. When she was long gone and there was no way she could hear them, they came out of hiding.

"Uh, bud, what are you doing?" Weston asked as Kai started to climb back up the tower.

"Going up to take in the view. It's supposedly very romantic at sunset."

"What? No really, what's going on?"

"I'm going to send a message to my grandfather."

He can't be serious. "Oh, no. This is going to be King King all over again." Weston's palms started to get sweaty. "Kai, I really hated my prohibition. I don't want that to ever happen to me again."

"It's not illegal for a mage to use an unattended communication tower to send an urgent message. You don't need to do anything. I'll send it on my own. I just need you to tell me how to do it."

"I don't think this constitutes an urgent message."

"It's urgent for me. Come on." Kai resumed climbing the stairs. "Who'll care?"

"Uh—lots of people. The nightmarkers for one, and they could arrive at any moment. Then we'll have to have those evil little drops put into our eyes again," Weston whined as he followed

Kai. "You know, Budski, the more you keep doing stuff like this, the more I'm coming to believe what people say about you."

"Good." Kai smiled. "It's about time you realize how nefarious I am. Talia would be proud of you."

"Nefari-what?"

"Nefarious. It means I have malevolent intent."

"Malev-a-who?" *I'm starting to think Kai just makes up words.*

"It means I'm a dastardly evil villain who wants to harm others."

"That's not true. You just want to send a message to your grandfather because Mage Rieta wouldn't let you."

"Exactly. Nefarious."

Weston shook his head. "Oh budder."

The Message

~Weston~

Full of a zest for life, Orange mages are silly and playful. They are considered the pleasure-seeking portion of the rainbow, and let me tell you—I know that first hand. They love to be happy, sometimes to a fault. To avoid pain, they may laugh in situations that would cause others to despair. Oranges shine fun into O'Ceca.

—Mage Kylee is-a Silk, *Color Me Curious: What Your Color Says About You!*

When Weston and Kai were halfway to the top of the tower, Weston leaned against the railing and stretched his legs. He really did love his job, but all this up and down was making him sore. *Aw, man. My legs are going to turn into tree trunks if I keep this up. I guess I can always get body mods to make them appear more normal.*

"All right," Weston said. "If I'm going to help you, I need to know everything. What's Plan 2C? For real."

Kai cleared his throat. "Okay. A long time ago, when my grandfather left the island, he and my mother came up with a variety of plans to get us all back together again. I guess they've been trying for years to work something out. In all the Plan 1s—Plan 1A, 1B, 1C, and so on—my grandfather would be allowed to come back to the island and live with us here.

"The Plan 2s were the plans where we would leave this island and go to live with my grandfather on Cloudy Peaks, where he's been living for the past eight years. In Plan 2A, all three of us—my grandmother, mother, and I—would go and live with him. In Plan 2B, just my mother and I go. Plan 2C is the one where just I go and live with him."

Wow. They've really worked hard planning this stuff out.

"So, that's all it means," Kai said. "I'm going to leave and live with my grandfather."

Weston was disappointed. "And here I thought you were spies or something mega like that."

"Nope. Just regular people."

"So why do you have to send a message? Wasn't your mom's enough?"

"I guess Grandfather's worried that my grandmother is manipulating us in some way—you know how she can be sometimes—so he just wanted me to send him back a message saying I'm agreeing to go. Basically, that I'm okay with Plan 2C."

"Are you? I mean, I know he's your grandfather and all, but isn't he—"

"Unsafe, crazy, a problem, dangerous, or otherwise nefarious?"

"Uh . . . yeah, I guess. But I was just going to say: isn't he a stranger? I mean, you don't really know him, right?"

Kai got a distant look in his eyes, then resumed climbing the tower. "I do remember him. I actually have a lot of memories from when I was little."

"So is he going to train you?"

"I guess. He was once considered one of the greatest trainers in the islands," Kai said with a shrug. "I could do a lot worse."

That's true. Unless he really is crazy. "Are you okay going with him? Like you said, lots of people think he's . . . you know—lost it."

"My mom says he hasn't. But I'm still pretty nervous. I don't really know what to think. I just know I'm ready to get off this island, and I'll go anywhere if it means I can train and compete. This seems like the only way." Kai paused and furrowed his brow as if he was angry about something. "I am concerned about one thing, though. If he really does love me and wants all of us to get back together—like my mom says—why didn't he at least show up at the Color Ceremony? I understand he's not allowed to come back here, and my grandmother would have had a fit if he'd tried to get in contact with me. But there's no reason he couldn't have been there to stand for me."

Weston looked at the Blue and Yellow embedded in his friend's collar—those Conflicting Colors—and wondered if Kai got it worse than he did when he was found void. *That was a really drench night for both of us. The drenchest of drench.* He couldn't imagine there was any worse feeling than what he felt when the puller found no Color in him.

His thoughts took him back to the Color Ceremony, when he stood before the entire region—vulnerable and exposed. After that horrible moment, he thought his whole future was over. He thought for sure he was doomed to be a poor tailor, just like the rest of his family. But then things changed; he figured out he could make a killing as a red rider. Everything had started to look up.

But what does Kai have? An unquenchable fire in his hand and two Colors that will battle for the rest of his life? He's always tried to hide the fire by clenching his fist in public, but everyone knows it's there. How can he handle Conflicting Colors on top of that?

"My mom said there had to be a good reason he wasn't there for me. She insisted that the Malroy she knew would have been there if he'd been able. But I don't know." As Kai continued to talk, the tension in his brow started to fade, and he smiled again. "She knew him well, so I guess it's smart for me to trust her, right?"

"Yeah, your mom always seems to want good things for others. She was even talking to me earlier, trying to help me out. She had a lot of nice things to say."

"Good. You should listen to her. You can do so much more than ride messages around."

"Yeah, yeah. But right now, we should focus on sending your message so we can get down from here. I'm really nervous we'll get caught."

Kai stopped and positioned himself in front of Weston. "Okay, let's hurry and do it. How does it work?"

"You don't know?" Weston asked. Kai shrugged his shoulders, so Weston explained. "Well, it's pretty simple. You tell the tower mage your message, and he or she formulates a voice projection and sends it to a nearby tower. Depending on what island you want it to go to, the message is relayed from tower to tower until it gets to where you want—"

"No, I understand that part," Kai interrupted. "I don't understand what a tower mage actually does. Does the message have to hit the mage in the other tower?"

How do I explain this in simple terms? "Sort of. The tower mage has to have enough Power to get it all the way there. But they don't actually aim at the other mage. The goal is to hit the pillar of light coming from the other timekeeper, so they aim high up. That way, they can project the message out with a fairly big cone."

"Huh. I always thought tower mages needed to have unbelievable precision to hit such a small spot so far away."

"Nope. They do need a lot of precision, but not nearly as much as they'd like you to think. It all happens way up in the sky, which is good, because it keeps people on the ground from accidently hearing the messages."

"So then how does the message get down to the tower?"

"Ah, bud, come on, tower mages are trained to catch messages. The timekeepers have a big part to play in it. But this is complicated stuff. It took Carlay half a day to explain it to me." *And what a glorious day that was.* "Oh!" Weston felt a streak of panic rush through him. "The timekeeper!"

"What?"

"Carlay's still up there."

"So what? We're not doing anything illegal. Maybe she'll help us," Kai said as he set off up the rest of the stairs.

I sure hope that pako I brought her earlier will keep her from getting upset with us. Weston shivered. Getting yelled at by Rieta would be bad enough, but he didn't think he could handle looking bad in front of Carlay.

*   *   *

"Mage Timekeeper," Kai called up to the perch as they climbed up the final steps of the tower. "As there is currently no tower mage, do we have your permission to send an urgent message?"

"Hello there, Junior Mage! I'm happy to inform you that my permission is not needed. If there's an urgent message to be delivered, and you have enough Power to do it, then send away!"

"Great! Thanks!" Kai replied, and then he said to Weston, "See, we're fine."

As long as this qualifies as urgent.

"But," Carlay added, "for Weston's sake, just make sure Mage Rieta doesn't find out he was involved."

"Ah, bud, she's right," Weston said. He looked around nervously. "I'm not fine with this. Mage Rieta is my boss, after all. Carlay's seen me here with you."

"Don't trouble your youthful heart, Youthful Master. I won't tell."

214 ᐧ *The Magician's Workshop*

"See, you're fine," Kai said. "So what do I need to do?"

Even with Carlay's affirmation, Weston was sure they were about to do something that would put his new job in jeopardy. *And then what would I have?* But he knew this was important to Kai, so he said, "Just aim for the Indigo pillar of light coming from the Island of the Silver Thorn. And, oh, before you send the actual message, you have to tell them where it's coming from, and that it's a relay, and what island it's going to, and who it's for."

"So, what am I supposed to say, exactly?" Kai asked.

"I don't actually know that part. Mage Rieta doesn't really say any of that stuff out loud," Weston said. "It probably doesn't really matter, as long as you tell them where you want it to go."

"I will, but—what if I don't have enough Power to get it to the first tower on my own? Can I create the message and then the two of us add our Power together to send it there?"

"No!" Weston's palms started to sweat. Then he projected to Kai, "Bud, you're getting me more and more into this."

"You know my Power is just average," Kai projected back. "Just this one thing. Then we'll leave."

"Fine, if it gets us out of here, then I'll help," Weston projected. "But don't do or say anything that will cause Carlay to know I'm helping you."

"You know—wait a moment," Kai now spoke out loud. "I want to listen to the message my grandfather sent one more time before I send a response."

Weston threw his head back and clasped his hands around the back of his neck. "Ah, bud! Come on. Mage Rieta may come back, and if she does, I'm totally going to get busted. We've been up here way too long."

"No, it's great. You should hear it. It's really funny." Kai opened up the message box he had been carrying around with him all this time and took out the yellow foam cube. Weston motioned for them both to crouch down, so they squatted low and listened to Malroy's voice.

"Dearest Declarious. Ha! I've forgotten how much I used to enjoy saying that. Plan 2C is it? That was always one of my least favorites, but at least it's a step in the right direction. I pray Täv may eventually bring us all together some day. I'm frustrated—as I'm sure you are—that everything's taken so much longer, and been more painful, than we had hoped. You've carried the entire burden. Please know how thankful I am for everything. So I will plan to meet you tomorrow at the top of the Blue watch, at the prearranged meeting spot.

"But, as this is Plan 2C, I'd like Kai to send me a message. I need to know he understands the choice he's making and that this is his wish. If at all possible, can you have him send something back today so I can make the proper arrangements as soon as possible? I'll wait at our tower until the Violet watch for his reply.

"And if Rieta is still the tower mage: hello 'dear.' I trust you and Randell are healthy. It will be lovely to hear a good report that you've treated my family well in these communications. I haven't forgotten all the good times we had in the training camp. I hope you haven't either. I have made this message as long as is practical, fully knowing that even you can't charge Declarious a single glyn—not even a surcharge—for receiving such a message, even one as intolerably long as this. How long is it now, anyway? I should try and make it two hundred and eighty-eight—wouldn't that be funny? I do wish you well, and I hope you've enjoyed this delightful message."

Whoa, I bet this is why Rieta was so upset at Kai and wanted to leave early. Malroy really likes to push buttons. No wonder he has the reputation he does.

"Isn't that great?" Kai said. "When I heard that, I felt a lot better about going with him."

"Phenomenal!" A faint laugh came from the Timekeeper's Perch. "I've dearly missed hearing Malroy's voice."

"Really?" Weston asked. "So, he's not crazy?"

"Drench the thought!" Carlay exclaimed. "No! Mage Malroy is wonderful and inspiring. The island hasn't been the same since he left. I've always wished he'd stayed to stand trial. I'm certain he would have been found innocent.

"Kai, if you manage to find a way for him to train you, I advise you to listen to him—do everything he tells you to," Carlay continued. "He was my trainer and taught me everything I know. I wouldn't be up here without him."

"Thanks. That's good to hear." Kai held up the voice cube. "I think I'm going to keep this message a little longer." He put the cube away. "All right, let's do this."

Weston watched as his friend stood up and started waving his hands in a circular motion. "This is a message from the Island of the Four Kings. And, um, it's a relay, going to the Island of the Cloudy Peaks, for, um, Malroy is-a Shield. Uh, hi grandfather, this is Kai—your grandson on the Island of the Four Kings. We got your message and, um, yes, I would like you to, um, train me. Uh, I guess that's all you need to know. It's my choice and—"

Buds alive, Kai. "Wait, hold on," Weston interrupted. "That isn't going to work."

"Why? Is my message too long?"

"Of course it's too long. You're probably over seventy words already. Plus, you're saying 'um' and 'uh' all the time."

"I am?"

"Yeah, but those aren't the only problems," Weston said. "I just realized, you're sending a message that has to be relayed."

"Yeah? What's the problem with that?"

He's so clueless. Good thing I'm here to help. He'd get so busted if he tried this on his own. "Our tower's flickering, which means if you tell them it's from here, they'll know it's an emergency message."

"It is."

"No, it's not. When they realize it's a personal message, they—at the very least—won't relay it. Worse, they will probably tell Mage Rieta about it tomorrow, and then I'll be busted and maybe lose my job. Sorry, bud—we can't do this. You can just come back in the morning."

"Mage Timekeeper?" Kai called up.

"Sorrowfully, I must affirm that the youthful master is right."

Kai sighed and lowered his eyes, but he made no move toward the stairs. Instead, he raised his hand and stroked his chin while humming quietly to himself. Then he looked straight at Weston with a glimmer in his eyes that Weston knew all too well.

"Oh no," Weston groaned. "What are you planning to do now?"

Kai looked off into the distance. "Where's the Island of the Cloudy Peaks? Can we see its symbol from here?"

"Oh sure, it's way over there." Weston pointed to the northeast, where the far-off symbol of two golden mountain peaks shimmered in the sky. "It's that one, past Silver Thorn, on the left. You see it?"

"Yeah. Do you think we can hit it from here?"

"What?" Weston exclaimed. "No way. I don't think even Mage Rieta could project something that far. That's why island relays exist."

"Let's try. Grandfather said he's waiting there until the Violet watch. There's still one beam of Indigo in the sky." Kai looked up. "Mage Timekeeper, how much time is left?"

"Not long," she said. "The sun is very close to the horizon."

"Okay, we need to do this now."

No, bud. We should go. "Can't you just come back tomorrow? I'm sure he'll understand."

"But it's worth a shot, right? It won't get us into any trouble. The worst that could happen is that it doesn't make it and is lost at sea."

Weston looked around nervously. There didn't seem to be anyone around. "I guess, but there's no way it's going to make it that far. So why bother?"

"Oh, come on." Weston heard Kai's projected voice in his ear. "Imagine how great it'll be if it does. You're all Power. You'll score silver or gold in every Power category there is. You're amazing! Come on, just try."

"Me?" Weston projected back to his friend as he stared out at the Indigo light in the distance. "I don't know. I doubt it will work."

"It will. Trust me. I can help you. You create the message, and I'll boost you as you cast it out. I bet it'll have enough Power to get there then."

This is crazy. Absolutely crazy. "All right, but only if you promise we'll go down—right after we try."

"I promise."

Weston cracked his neck left and then right, planted his feet, and focused all his attention on the light. *Carlay would think we're such weeds if she knew we were trying this.*

Kai leaned forward and projected, "Do you want me to repeat my message without all the 'umming'?"

"No, I got the idea." Weston cleared his throat, then thought, *This is a message for Malroy is-a Shield from Kai is-a Shield on the Island of the Four Kings. 'Hi grandfather, this is Kai. We got your message, and yes, I would like you to train me.'*

Weston tried to look like he wasn't sending a message, while at the same time lifting up his hands and thrusting out his fingers in the direction of the distant island. *I really, really, hope Carlay isn't watching.*

Weston felt the projection go out of him—but without the whirling, windy sensation he felt whenever Rieta sent hers. *Either I did it wrong, or she's adding that windy feeling for show. Probably for show,* Weston realized.

"Did it go?" Kai projected.

"I think so," Weston projected back. As the message was invisible, there was no way to tell if it had traveled far enough or not. "Can we go now?"

"Let's just do it one more time. Just in case your aim was off."

"Bud, it's too far. It's time to go." Weston groaned the words out loud before projecting, "Come on, you promised."

"Okay, okay," Kai said. After giving one last look at the island in the distance, he made a move toward the stairs while saying out loud, "Thanks, Mage Timekeeper."

But she did not respond. *Uh oh, that's not good.*

As soon as they started their descent, the sun set. Indigo light faded away from the tower, and three beams of Violet light shot up into the darkening sky. *Hopefully she didn't respond because she was concentrating on the time change. That must take a lot of focus. Maybe she wasn't paying any attention to us when I was sending the message.*

As soon as they were halfway down, Weston felt the tension in his shoulders start to release. But it wasn't until they were back on their bikes, heading down the hill and through the thick of the forest, that he was completely at ease.

"You know, that was kinda fun," Weston said at last, breaking the silence.

"I know. It was so great!" Kai grinned. "You sent that thing soooooo far."

"I hope so. But I doubt it got all the way there."

"No, it did. I could tell," Kai insisted.

"Uh-huh, right. I didn't jump, or fling out my arms, or anything. It couldn't have gone far."

"No, really. It's hard to describe. When I assist someone like I just did, I get a sense of the other person's projection—almost like it's my own. I could feel how much Power it had. You really have a lot of talent—I hope you know that."

Sure, I know. But that doesn't really mean anything now, does it? "I have a lot of Power but a striking lack of Color," Weston said.

"So what? You don't need to be a mage to do everything."

"Yeah, your mom said the same thing. I've been thinking a lot about it all day."

"That's great," Kai said, but then his smile faded. "I've been worried about you since the Ceremony. You've seemed to be making . . . oh, I don't know how to say it . . . poor decisions."

"Yeah, I know. I was really devastated, but I think I'm all over it now." Weston glanced back up at the tower. "It all clicked when I was standing up there with you and Mage Rieta—when she was talking about you being a young man and thus not really a man yet. Right then I realized something about this job. I did fourteen deliveries today. But that's only because I was biking at a casual pace, went home to nap during the Cyan watch, and took a few breaks to eat. The position is called 'red rider,' but maybe 'rider' is the wrong word. It's too casual—riding is what little kids do. But I'm not a kid anymore. I need to be going fast and really working."

Weston suddenly shouted, "I got it!" and skidded to a stop.

Kai had to turn and brake hard to avoid hitting him. "Bud, what are you doing? Is everything okay?"

"I figured it out! I'm not going to be a red rider anymore."

"What? Really? That's great!" Kai looked relieved. "I'm glad you finally saw how foolish you've been acting."

Weston, caught up in the moment, leapt off his bike and proclaimed, "From now on I'll be known as the Red Racer!"

Kai was quiet for a moment. Then he said, "Weston, are you all right?"

This is the best plan I've ever had! "We're young adults now, Kai. We need to start acting like it. I bet I can do twenty-five to thirty deliveries a day if I acted like the spectacular Red Racer! People would certainly pay me extra tips if they knew they would get their messages faster."

"What? You've had a long day. Did you get enough to drink?"

"I'm fine," Weston said. "No, wait. I'm not fine. My uniform. I need you to reproject it."

"Oh, sure," Kai said, and in a flash Weston was again dressed as a red rider.

"Now, we need to change it in some way—to let everyone know they're not dealing with a common red rider anymore but someone special: the Red Racer!"

"What?"

"You're saying 'what' an awful lot, Kai. Come on, don't you get it? I need to be dressed like the Red Racer."

"Who's the Red Racer? Is he someone in a Grand Projection I haven't seen?"

"No, bud. I just thought this up. The Red Racer is me! Isn't it absolutely brilliant? Now, I need you to project something onto my clothes that will tell everyone I'm fast—mega fast."

"I can project a little hat in the shape of a flying fish. Flying fish are mega fast."

"Come on, Kai, this is my career. This is serious stuff!" Weston said.

He thought for a moment. "Hey, how about you cover my body with big, bold lightning bolts?"

*   *   *

"You really kissed the rainbow with these!" Weston said as he spun around trying to look at all the big, bold lightning bolts that covered his body. He and Kai were parking their bikes just inside the entrance to Brightside. "Now I'm certain I'll earn a fistful of lykes by the end of the year."

Kai smiled and said, "I'm going to miss you, bud. I'm going to really, really miss you."

"Ah, I will too. But, with all the coins I'll be earning—and my flexible schedule—I'll be able to come visit you all the time."

"That would be great."

They were about to turn and walk away from each other when Weston said, "Hey, tell your mom thanks for the inspiration. I don't think this would have been possible without her encouraging me to set my sights higher."

Kai looked at Weston like he was crazy. "I don't think that's the message she wanted to get across to you. I think she was encouraging you to use your projection skills."

"Nah, she just wanted to make sure I would be able to earn over two hundred and fifty gryns a day. And if I can do twenty-five to thirty deliveries, that shouldn't be any problem at all. Remember, tips make a huge difference. They're really the secret to this whole thing. I bet you didn't know that tips can't be taxed—that makes around a forty percent difference at the end of each day."

"Forty percent?" Kai looked skeptical.

"Yeah, bud! Actually, I bet it's even more." Weston went on and on about all the great benefits that come from tax-free money. *Kai's a good friend. I'm going to miss him, Conflicting Colors and everything. I hope he finds someplace where people will accept him as he is.*

"See you tomorrow?" Weston asked.

"Sure. And keep your eye out for a response to that message we sent. I know you got it there."

"Uh-huh, yeah. If something actually comes in, I'll come straight over—for free." Weston laughed.

They parted ways, but before they got too far apart, Kai called out, "Hey, bud! What teacher did you have for math in school? Was it Master Strumbolla?"

"Nah, I never took math. You know all us H. Waves are makers of threadbare. My family taught me all the math I'll ever need to know measuring out fabric and cutting stuff. Why?"

"Oh, just wondering. You might want to take a class sometime. Knowing a bit more math might help you out."

"Nah, I'm fine. Actually, I'm pretty happy I didn't waste any of my childhood learning that stuff. The Red Racer doesn't need anything more than basic addition and subtraction to serve the islands!"

"No, I guess he doesn't."

The Parade of Colors
~Kalaya~

*There are some whose faulty logic has led them to the erroneous
conclusion that making distinctions between those with Color and
those without is an archaic practice with roots in the barbaric and
ritualistic past and thus should be abandoned. These people call
themselves 'colorblind.' Though they are generally quite harmless,
I find it particularly troubling to know that there are still those
on O'Ceea who cannot see reality, and actually believe that Color
doesn't matter.*

—Mage Rouwand is-a Stump, *Insights from the Insightful*

Kalaya felt strange as she stood on the sidelines and watched
the Parade of Colors. Seeing all the grinning, happy people
waving brightly colored flags was disheartening and somehow
made the black collar tied around her neck feel extra tight and
itchy. She had planned to stay home and in bed, but Dad wanted
to be here and needed her help. So, here she was, once again
observing the parade she'd always dreamed she'd one day march
in.

"What's happening now, Kay?" Dad asked.

"The jugglers just passed, and the clan flag bearers are dancing in front of us now," Kalaya explained.

"Are the magicians there, leading all the mages?"

"Yes, they're coming up next."

"Mmm. Can you see how the mages decided to dress this year?" Dad asked.

"Uh, they're still pretty far away." *Wow, look at all of them.* She winced as she saw the first signs of the great multitude of mages flowing down the street toward them. She could only see the first few, but there seemed to be so many more than she remembered. *Our island must have over four hundred and fifty mages now.*

"It looks like they're wearing armor," she said when they got closer. "They sort of look like the holy warriors from *To the Depths and Beyond.* Oh. And they're wearing capes that match the Colors of their collars."

"Warriors, eh? I hope they look better than they did last year." Dad chuckled. "Remember, they were wearing those crazy-looking hats? Tell me again how you described them."

The memory would usually have made her smile, but today Kalaya just felt dull amusement. "Like a pointy pickle."

"Ha! That's right." Dad burst out laughing, and the sound of it almost helped her feel better.

At least now—without a Color—I'll get to spend more time with Dad again.

Kalaya stared out at the crowds that lined the street. The entire population of the Island of the Golden Vale had gathered to watch as all the magicians and mages from their island marched in the annual festival. The parade began with the eldest mages and progressed down in age to the youngest. Everyone with Color was here to be celebrated. At the very end of the procession, the newest mages would strut down the street to wild cheers and applause.

People always wondered the same thing as they sized up each of the brand-new mages: would any of them have what it took to be the next magician for their island? The theorizing about each person's chances resulted in a betting pool, with predictions made about who would get into the Workshop. People loved to speculate on this island. They even placed bets before the Ceremony on the kids who they thought would have Colors. But Kalaya didn't want to think about that. *I'm sure many people lost a lot of gryns—maybe even some lykes—betting on me.*

This was an average year for the Island of the Golden Vale, with a total of nine new mages: four Bones, two Twigs, two Staffs, and even a Silk. *But no Clouds.* Although her mom and dad assured her that it wasn't her fault, and that she had done nothing to be ashamed of, Kalaya couldn't help feeling like she'd let her entire clan down. Every single Cloud had expected her to get a Color. *Even Jaremon believed I was a sure thing, and he's rarely wrong.*

Kalaya was jerked out of her depressive thoughts by Alfonzo is-a Bone, a famous, retired Yellow magician of the Second Magnitude. Alfonzo was a little older than her parents and was well-known for his bright optimism and charismatic personality. Today, his hair was bone-white and matched the whiteness of his teeth, which he flashed at the crowd as he gave them his iconic grin. As he passed her, Kalaya was struck in the mouth by the taste of sweet lemon pie.

"W-w-hoa," she stammered. Her mouth started to water as the delicious taste dissolved into it.

"What is it? Did I miss something good?" Dad asked.

All of the children around them jumped up and down with hyper enthusiasm as they held their mouths open, hoping to receive another sweet burst.

"Didn't you feel it?" Kalaya asked. "Magician Alfonzo is throwing flavor projections into the crowd."

"Really? Aw." Dad frowned. "Too bad. I love those. Do you think you could try to reproject the one you just got for me?"

"Um." Kalaya shuffled her feet. She hadn't made a projection since the checkered black collar was placed around her neck. "Maybe if you wait, one will find its way to you?"

"Good idea!" He opened his mouth, stuck his tongue out, and pointed to it.

Oh great, Dad. You look just like a little kid. While Kalaya felt some measure of embarrassment from this, it also encouraged her. *If he's okay looking like a fool in front of everyone, why do I care so much?*

His silly gesture caught the attention of one elderly Blue mage—a former teacher of her dad's—who laughed and flicked something at him. Her dad closed his mouth and let out a contented sigh. "You know," he said after taking a moment to enjoy the flavor, "your grandma was the one who started doing that."

"Doing what? Projecting taste into the crowd?"

"Mmm. Most magicians and mages in her era just marched by as if they were better than everyone else. But not her. Mum thought the whole thing was ridiculous. She decided that if she had to march, she'd at least pass out some joy. She was especially good at finding people in the crowd who were sad. She would project sweet flavors at them to try to cheer them up."

I wish she were here today. Her dad's story caused her to think about what Master Magician Greydyn had said about her grandma. *There's so much I don't know about her.*

The more Kalaya thought about this, the more she wondered why her dad had never told her about how her grandma's projections had come out blue. *He knew I was struggling to change the color of my wallaroo.* "Hey, Dad—" Kalaya was about to ask him, but she stopped when she heard her mom's voice.

"There you two are!"

Kalaya glanced over her shoulder and saw her mom and sister.

"Aw!" Aliva whined as she joined them. "I knew we'd be late. How much did we miss?"

"Just the opening acts, the magicians, and the first few mages," Kalaya answered as a cluster of acrobatic clowns tumbled past. They were Colorless, just like her, but they were allowed to make public projections and march in the parade with the mages because they'd reached the third and highest privilege level, as indicated by the star pattern printed on their black collars. *It must have taken them years to get to that level, and they're choosing to be clowns?*

The clowns suddenly launched a swarm of projected bunnies into the crowd. As soon as one of the bunnies touched someone, both the person and the bunny were overcome with fits of laughter, and the two would roll around on the ground together. Kalaya was thankful that none found her.

"Oh wow!" Aliva gasped. "Mom, look at all the colorful capes on the mages!"

"I see!" her mother replied cheerfully. "Isn't it wonderful?"

"Yeah. So mega! Way better than those dumb hats from last year," Aliva said. She then asked Kalaya, "Are you sad you're not marching with them?"

"Of course I am."

"Yeah, me too," Aliva said as she looked up with a squint that caused a crinkle to form around her left eye. "I thought you'd be a mage for sure."

Great. Even my little sister sees me differently now.

"Ali, you know not everyone gets a Color," their dad spoke up, "and that's perfectly fine. Look at your mother and me. We're Colorless and couldn't be happier."

"I guess so," Aliva shrugged.

"Don't listen to your father, my poor darling. He's just trying to make Kay-Kay feel better," their mother cooed. "I understand how much you want to have a Color. So, remember, if you work really hard and improve your skills, maybe you'll be able to march in the parade one day yourself."

"That would be so perfect," Aliva said.

Oh yeah, how absolutely wonderful. Kalaya stared blankly at the parade as it continued to slog along. *I could always just cut myself off from the magic.* The dark thought struck suddenly and sent a frightening chill through her. *Yikes. Where did that come from? That's so . . . No. I couldn't do that. Dad would be destroyed.*

Kalaya quickly distracted herself from that train of thought by focusing on three mages in their mid-thirties. They faced the crowd, pressed their fingers together, and projected the sound of trumpets.

BA-DA-BA-DA-BA-DE-DA-DOOO!

"What a sound! That has to be the Three Red Mages!" Her dad laughed again.

They blasted out their happy, carefree tune. But the song struck Kalaya as being nothing more than obnoxious noise. "Yup," Kalaya confirmed, "there's no mistaking them." *Dad once told me about an island he visited where those with Color trained alongside commoners. Maybe I should go there. I wonder what Jaremon would think if he saw me facing off against him in the Competitions?* The thought amused her, but only briefly. Any thoughts about her ex-boyfriend made her deeply sad.

"Your breathing changed," her dad observed. "What's wrong?"

I love how he always knows when I'm sad. "I'm just thinking about Color."

"Ah, yes. There's a lot of that around us right now. It must be blinding."

If only I were blind and didn't have to see it.

The middle-aged mages had passed, and the long stretch of those in their twenties and younger started strolling by. Unlike the older mages, who looked more contented with their place in life and seemed happy to just be in the parade, the younger ones strutted with confidence. Kalaya figured this was because they still believed they had a shot at getting into the Workshop.

"Hey, Dad? Now that Mom's here, is it okay if I go home?" Kalaya asked.

"What?" her mom asked. "Aren't you having a good time?"

Of course I'm not. What could I possibly enjoy about this? Kalaya avoided the question and said, "I don't really need to be here anymore."

Her mom said, "I'd rather you stay. The whole island is here, after all."

But—

"I also think it might be valuable for you to stay," her dad said. "Don't worry. I'll be here with you when he passes by."

Kalaya worked her mouth back and forth and let out a long sigh. She knew it wouldn't be long before the one person she did not want to see would appear.

And, sure enough, barely a moment passed before she saw him.

"You're breathing faster, Kay. I assume that means you've spotted Jaremon," her father observed. "Does he see us?"

Kalaya tried to swallow, but for some reason couldn't. "No, I don't—I don't think he does." *I don't think he's even looking.*

Her mom sighed and said, "What a shame you two are done now. He was such a sweet boy. It'll be really hard for you to find someone like that again."

Thanks for the reminder.

It was not hard to spot her ex-boyfriend's team. The young Twigs—every single one of them—had projected wild, brightly colored hairstyles onto their heads. The hair on the young women sparkled in the sunlight and floated out above their shoulders and around their heads as if they were angelic beings. The young men, on the other hand, had styled their hair to resemble various elements: blue icicles, blades of grass, wisps of fire, jagged rocks, swirling storm clouds.

Kalaya presumed they had done this in an effort to look different from everyone else. *But you're all mages. You already stand out. You should be satisfied with everything you already have. Why do you need more attention?*

It should not have come as a surprise to Kalaya, but Jaremon was no exception to this. He wore green hair that twirled up over his head. It looked wrong on him and made Kalaya think of the top of a palm tree. She knew he'd been growing out his natural light brown hair for several weeks. But real hair got in the way of the wild and crazy styles that were popular on their island, so most young men and women shaved it off and spent a lot of gryns to have stylists project the latest hair fashions onto their heads.

His uncle must have made him do that. The Jaremon I know wouldn't see any value in those kinds of hairstyles. Even though she thought he looked ridiculous, Kalaya felt her breath become short and constrained as she watched him go by. *Here, Jaremon. I'm over here.* The heart of the young woman without a Color ached as her Green mage kept his eyes locked straight ahead. *Why won't he look at me? He has to know I'm here.*

Jaremon never once turned his head to face the crowd. He kept his arms stiffly at his sides and walked with determination, as if he were a soldier going to war and not a mage being celebrated. *I wonder if he's ignoring me, or if looking straight ahead is another stupid superstition of his.*

To her surprise, it was the Crimson mage, Olan—with icy-blue hair shaped like frozen lightning bolts—who turned and made eye contact with her. *Ugh, why did he have to look? Oh well. At least I won't have to experience his projections ripping mine to shreds anymore. Looks like he was right about me all along.* She crossed her arms and braced herself for the inevitable projected insult.

But, when she looked at him, she saw something strange. She wasn't sure how to read it—this was unlike any expression she'd ever seen on his face before. He wasn't snide, mocking, and cruel, nor was he proud, arrogant, and smug. His lips were pressed tightly together, and his eyes seemed troubled and confused. *Could he actually be sad that I'm void? This has to be some sort of prank.*

She heard a faint squeaking noise and turned her head to the left. There, hopping around on her shoulder, was a tiny blue wallaroo. *Did I unconsciously project that? Oh no, am I going crazy?* She looked back at Olan. He raised his eyebrows, pointed at the wallaroo, and smiled—as if he actually cared about her.

Did he project this on me? Is this some kind of mind game? Honestly! Does he think he can do whatever he wants just because he has a Color and I don't?! The memory of her wallaroo being ripped apart by his dragon, coupled with the disgusting kiss sensation he'd projected on her cheek, caused her to flush with a mixture of embarrassment and anger. *I need to get out of here.* "Dad," Kalaya started to speak.

But before she could say anything more, her dad turned his face to her and said, "I know. Let's go."

Relief washed over her as she took his arm and started to lead him out of the crowd.

"Where are you going?" her mom asked.

"Out," Dad responded.

"What's that supposed to mean? We're already out!"

"See you back at home, Mom," Kalaya replied without looking back as she fled the parade. As soon as they were away from the noise and commotion, she breathed easier. She could also now hear the squeaking sound of the wallaroo, which was still bouncing around on her shoulder.

"What's that funny little noise?" Dad asked. "It sounds cheerful."

"No. It's nothing. Just a worthless stray projection," Kalaya said as she aggressively waved her hand over the wallaroo. To her surprise, it dissolved quite easily. *Huh. That's weird. I thought for sure Olan would have tried to make that stick on me for as long as possible.*

Kalaya turned and tried to lead her dad down the street toward their home, but he stopped and shook his head. "Not that way, Kay."

"Why not? I thought we were going home."

"No," her dad said in tone that was suddenly grave and serious. "There's somewhere else I want to take you."

41

The Garden of Heroes
~Kalaya~

One of the best quilts I've ever worked on now resides with Agatha was-a Cloud. What a woman and what a project! Her life had many secrets. It was truly a pleasure to chronicle her story and capture its essence in each of those uniquely designed squares. I must say, it was no easy feat to hide so many things in plain sight.
—Narralogist Mage Yance is-a Nook, *A Narralogist's Narrative*

I wonder why Dad brought me here? He came to visit Grandma last week, and Mom just said this morning that the new HiSSAnClaP caretaker was doing a good job with her.

Kalaya felt confused as her dad led her through the Garden of Heroes, but she didn't really mind. She had always loved coming here and couldn't imagine that there was a more peaceful place anywhere on O'Ceea.

The garden was nestled at the top of a grassy hill that was covered with projections of bright, glowing sunglit. These vibrant yellow wildflowers were shaped like little stars. They had once covered the nearby valley so that it looked like a river of light, and this was the reason the island had been named 'Golden Vale.' People said real sunglit warmed everything it touched, and travelers used to come from all over to pick it. The last actual flower had been picked over a hundred years ago, but locals kept projecting these precious flowers all over the island.

This hill was on a high point of land next to the sea, and from here Kalaya had a clear view of the surf and many neighboring islands. People came here, to the Garden of Heroes, because it was calming, quiet, and proven to be a wonderful place to refocus and get some perspective on life.

It was also a graveyard.

At least a hundred intricately designed stone pavilions and shrines were built on this hill. Each one was unique and was filled with projections that served as a memorial to the departed. These were refreshed on a regular basis, and family members and loved ones visited to keep the memories of their ancestors alive. But unlike in the graveyards for commoners, the IP were on constant patrol here. In the Garden of Heroes were memorials to every magician and famous mage who had ever come from this island, and they needed to be protected from damage, decay, and vandalism.

"You want to spend some time with Grandma?" Kalaya asked as she ran her fingers through the illusions of sunglit.

"Mmm." Her dad gave an agreeable grunt.

The two walked arm in arm down the path that led to her grandma's shrine. Because Agatha was-a Cloud had been a magician of the Second Magnitude, she'd been given a large plot of land overlooking the ocean that had a view of the Magician's Workshop—far off and to the west. She now dwelled in, and presided over, a circular obsidian shrine the size of a house that had been constructed in her memory. It had a high, vaulted ceiling held up by twelve marble pillars that glinted Yellow and Orange.

The shrines for magicians of the Second Magnitude were larger than the white-pillared pavilions given to those of the First Magnitude and smaller than the golden, tower-like temples built for those of the Third Magnitude. Magicians who rose to the Third Magnitude were rare on this island, so there were very few structures like that, and though the entire garden was guarded by the IP, these temples had private, live-in guards.

It was foolish of me to hope I would have a memorial here one day, Kalaya thought as she looked around at the monumental structures that surrounded them.

"You remind me a lot of her, you know." Her dad's voice pulled her out of her morose thoughts.

"I do?"

"Yes. She was driven and determined, and when she had a goal fixed in her mind, nothing could stop her from achieving it."

That was true of Grandma, but I'm not like that. As Kalaya looked up at her grandma's shrine, she was struck by the way this woman would be remembered for all time. *Without a Color, what can I ever hope to achieve that's worthy of being remembered? Even if I work hard and eventually obtain the third privilege level, I'll never be a mage—I'll never go to the Workshop.* "No, I'm not like her," Kalaya said. "She had a Color and was able to work on Grand Projections."

"She was, but I suspect that even if she hadn't had a Color, she would still have found a way to bless the islands with her projections."

"But how? You have to be a magician to contribute to a Grand Projection."

"Of course. But she loved projecting for others and bringing them joy. She wouldn't have let a lack of Color stop her."

As they ascended the stone steps that led to the pavilion, Kalaya's heart beat a little faster. *I wonder if she'll have a reaction if I tell her that I didn't get a Color?* She tensed and stopped right outside the open archway that led to the center of the circular shrine. "I'll wait outside so you can talk with Grandma alone."

"I wish I could, but Mum isn't really here, is she?" Dad sighed. "Projections of the dead—even the best, like your grandma's—are only wisps of smoke compared to the actual person. But come, follow me inside. This visit is for you, Kay."

It is? "I don't understand."

"Mmm." Her father stepped into the darkness of the shrine. Kalaya hesitated, then reluctantly followed. *This is strange. Usually he asks me to wait outside when he visits Grandma.*

It took a few moments for her eyes to adjust, but as they did, she heard the relaxing sound of crashing waves echoing through the chamber. It was her grandma's favorite sound, and she had insisted that it play continually in her shrine.

Kalaya felt like she was entering a museum whenever she came here. The entire shrine was decorated with various artifacts and projections from some of Agatha's most famous works. It was an impressive collection, and she had admired it from the time she was a young child. It was one of the things that had given Kalaya so much desire to become a magician. *Grandma really was amazing.*

This was the first time she'd been here since the Color Ceremony. Curious to see if there was any evidence pointing to what the Master Magician had told her, Kalaya scanned the collection of projections she knew so well for anything that was unnaturally blue. But, as she suspected, there was nothing out of the ordinary.

I bet he was just saying all that to make me feel better. But, then again, why would someone as great as the Master Magician even care about me at all, let alone have a reason to lie to me about something like that? Feeling just as confused as before, Kalaya joined her dad at the center of the room, where her grandma, Agatha, sat in an enormous oak rocking chair that looked somewhat like a throne for a queen.

Most people had a young or middle-aged version of themselves projected in their shrines. But not Agatha. Her projection represented the fifty-year-old version of herself, from several years before she died. "It took me all these years to gain a teaspoon of wisdom," she'd once said. "I'm not going to have some young imprint of me passing out advice after I'm gone. No one should have listened to anything I said when I was young."

Her grandma's eyes were closed when they approached, and she appeared to be in a deep and peaceful sleep. When Kalaya was a little girl, she'd always felt bad about waking her. She fixed her eyes on the long, luxurious quilt that was wrapped around her grandma.

Kalaya loved looking at this quilt. Each square displayed a different moving image that replayed some significant memory from her grandma's life. If she reached out and touched a particular square, she could hear, smell, taste, and feel some sensations from that moment. There were many squares to experience, and she knew them all. But the one that always captivated her the most was the moment that Yellow and Orange were pulled out of her grandma. This was a sequence Kalaya had reached out and touched over and over as a child, but this time, it was painful to even look at it. She focused on three other squares.

The first was the moment Agatha entered the Workshop and bowed her head to the Master Magician. The second showed her spinning in the beautiful dress she wore on the day she got married. The third showed her holding her newborn son in her arms. Kalaya lingered on this square for a long time. *Dad was so cute and tiny back then. Look how much Grandma loved him. She didn't even seem upset or disappointed about his condition.*

It was then that Kalaya noticed that many of the squares imprinted on the quilt were slightly blue in color. After examining the quilt more closely, she realized that this was only true of the most precious memories of Grandma's life—like the one of her infant son. *That can't be a coincidence.*

Strangely, the square dedicated to the Color Ceremony wasn't tinged blue. *That must be a mistake.*

Dad took Kalaya's hand and squeezed it gently. She knew this was his way of telling her that it was time to speak. So, taking a deep breath, she faced the projection and said, "Hi Grandma."

As soon as Kalaya spoke, her grandma's eyes popped open, and she replied the way she always did: "Grandma? Oh my. I always wanted to be a grandmother."

"And you were," Dad replied. "A good one, too. You would hold Kalaya for watches without end."

Her grandma flickered in and out of existence and then was suddenly up and on her feet, reciting her welcome speech. "Welcome to my shrine! Hope it's not too messy, though there's not much I can do about that now, is there? If you don't know who I am, ask me, and I'll tell you everything. If we've met before, forgive me, and let me say, 'Welcome back, it's so nice to see you again!' Now, whoever you are, relax. You can talk to me about anything. I've got nothing but time—you know."

Kalaya loved seeing her grandma's eyes. They were just like hers: light brown with golden flecks sprinkled throughout. Kalaya had first discovered the flecks in her own eyes when she was six, and she'd immediately felt self-conscious, thinking they were a defect. But when she told her dad, he said, "They're bits of stardust, projected there by Tav when you were born, so that every time I looked into your eyes, I would remember how much of a miracle you are."

"But Dad," she would tell him, "you can't look into my eyes."

"Not like your mother can, but I do see them—in my own way. They shine out to me in the golden outlook you have on life. This stardusted nature of yours, like all the rest of you, is a wonder."

Kalaya had always remembered this. Years later, she asked him another question about it. "Was I really a miracle? Was it difficult for you and Mom to get pregnant or something?"

"No, there was nothing out of the ordinary."

"Then . . . why do you always say I'm a miracle?"

"Because you are. Every life is a miracle, and you're the miracle Tav gave to me."

Kalaya smiled at the memory and took a deep breath, releasing the tension inside her. She looked into her grandma's eyes. *Stardust. I wonder where you are now—the real you, not this similitude.*

Similitude? The word triggered something in her. *That's not the right word. What is it? Simulitcrums? No, that's not right either.* The tension flooded back, along with a memory. *Jaremon loved the flecks in my eyes.* He'd often told her that since her grandma had the same gold in her eyes, it was a clear sign that she'd get a Color. *He was wrong!* "Dad, what are we doing here?"

"I wanted you to hear something for yourself," he answered, then turned his attention to the projection. "Hello. Please tell us who you are."

"Well, before I do that, I'd like to know who you are."

"I'm Cale is-a Cloud, your son."

"Nice to meet you. I'm Agatha is-a Cloud, though if I'm here, I guess the term 'was-a Cloud' would be more accurate. But that feels like a bit of a morbid way to introduce oneself, don't you think?" Her grandma laughed.

Although this was not the first time Kalaya had heard her grandma say that, it still brought a little smile to her face.

"Okay, on to the boring stuff. My mother, Hellen was-a Staff, married my father, Henrick was-a Cloud, and so I was born in the line of the P. Clouds. I myself stayed a Cloud by marrying into the L. Clouds at the oh-so-wise age of twenty-one. Ask me if you want more details on that scandalous whirlwind of a marriage." Grandma laughed. "Let's see . . . you're here because I was a magician, I presume. So let's talk about that. I received a Yellow-Orange collar when I was sixteen—what a surprise that was, by the way! Didn't see it coming. I then competed for nine interminable years before finally getting a score high enough to permit me to enter the famed Magician's Workshop. What a day! I was a faithful little servant as a magician of the First Magnitude for seventeen years. Then, when I rose to the Second Magnitude, I was finally able to relax. Those years were the best of my life. But times like that can last only so long. Eventually, I was 'displaced'—as they so tactfully called it in my day—and not too long after, some people came along and built me this fancy structure and told me it would be my 'forever home.' Eternity is nice, by the way."

None of this was new information, but Kalaya couldn't help feeling like she was missing something. She and her dad stepped away from her grandma so they could talk without triggering any responses.

"Impressive history, right, Kay?"

"Yeah, but—Dad, I already know Grandma's story."

"Mmm. I wanted you to hear it again, first, before you tell her about what happened at the Ceremony."

"What!?" Kalaya felt her heart leap into her throat. "I don't want to do that." *Please don't make me. Please, please, please!*

"Kay, trust me. I think you'll be surprised."

The thought of talking with her grandma about what happened at the Color Ceremony made her want to leave. "Why? Do you think she'll have a response? What if it's negative?"

"Knowing Mum, she'll have made sure there was a response. Go on, Kay. Tell her what happened. You'll be fine."

Kalaya swallowed and took a nervous step toward her grandma. "Um. Grandma, I—" Kalaya struggled to communicate what had happened in a way her grandma would understand. "I've finally grown old enough to stand before a puller at the Color Ceremony . . ."

"The Color Ceremony?" her grandma interrupted. "I went to that when I was sixteen. Received two Colors—can you believe it? What a surprise that was."

Ugh. She's going to be disappointed. I know it. "Well—in my case—it didn't exactly go so well."

Her grandma blinked several times and flickered in and out of existence before saying, "I'm so sorry, but I'm not sure I understand that question. Can you say it differently?"

Kalaya swallowed nervously. "There was . . . no Color found in me."

Her grandma blinked several more times and flickered again. "I'm so sorry, but I'm not sure I understand that question. Can you say it differently?"

Kalaya looked at her dad. "I'm clattering her. I don't think this is a good idea."

"It's all right. You just need to tell her what's really troubling you. I know it's hard, Kay, but you have to say the words," her dad encouraged her.

Kalaya twirled her hair around her fingers and looked down at her toes. "Grandma. I found out that—I mean, uh—what I'm trying to say is . . . I was a void pull." She cringed as she waited to see disappointment come over her grandma's face.

But it didn't happen.

Grandma shrugged her shoulders and said, "Void pull? What an ugly term. I'm sorry. I'm sure that was disappointing. But don't be sad. You're not alone. The puller couldn't find a Color in my son, either. He was devastated—said he let me down. 'Nonsense,' I said. It didn't stop me from loving him, or him from making projections. He's quite talented, my son. You hear those ocean sounds? He made those for me." Her grandma raised her head up, listened to the sound, and let out a contented sigh.

I can't believe she's not disappointed in me.

Kalaya stared at her grandma with wonder. This was just a projection and not a real person, but even so, Kalaya recognized something genuine that she'd never noticed before. Grandma Agatha didn't judge her. She didn't appear to judge anyone.

"So stop calling yourself a void pull and go on with your life. Laugh. Dance. Love. And don't ever stop making projections— they enable us to meld our story into the Grand Story."

Wow. I guess the Master Magician was right about her philosophy. "But how can I do any of that without a Color?"

"There's something mysterious and wonderful about Color— that you can be sure of," her grandma answered. "But having one—or two or three—does not make a person any better than another, and it certainly doesn't make any difference at all when projecting. Believe me. I'm old, so that means I know things."

While Kalaya stood there considering all she'd just heard, her dad cleared his throat and asked, "Do you think it's important to have a Color?"

Agatha shrugged her shoulders. "There's something mysterious and wonderful about Color—that you can be sure of. But having one—or two or three—does not make a person any better than another, and it certainly doesn't make any difference at all when projecting. Believe me. I'm old, so that means I know things."

"Does a person need a Color to be good at making projections?" he asked.

"There's something mysterious and wonderful about Color— that you can be sure of. But having one—or two or three—does not make a person any better than another, and it certainly doesn't make any difference at all when projecting. Believe me. I'm old, so that means I know things."

"Okay, Dad, stop. I get it." Kalaya stepped away and faced him. "But she can't really mean that, can she? I mean—look at her life! She got where she did because of Color. She had two."

"Tell us about your two Colors, Mum."

"That's right, I had two Colors: Yellow and Orange. What a surprise that was. Didn't make my life any better, though. Ask me what I think about Color and I'll tell you."

She's serious. She really doesn't think Color matters. Kalaya couldn't believe what she was hearing. "But you made it into the Workshop!"

"The Workshop is a wonderful place, but it shouldn't be the only place people make projections. I would have kept on making them even if I'd never made it in--and for a long time, it didn't look like I would. It took me nine interminable years of training and competing to get a score high enough to break into that joint," Agatha said with a laugh.

It was strange. Kalaya had come here innumerable times, but she'd never asked about any of this before.

"Kay, I want you to understand something." Her father's voice became very serious. "Because of my condition, I was assumed to be a void pull from birth. You know this. There were two things my teachers felt I needed to understand: the importance of Color, and how tragic it was that I would never have one of my own. But Mum was different. The very words you just heard are the same ones she spoke to me over and over. Having a Color doesn't make one person better than another."

"But . . . even if Grandma is right, no one else in all of O'Ceea thinks that way. Mages and commoners aren't the same." *Commoners have never been able to contribute to a Grand Projection.*

"It's true that mages have a lot more freedom and options than others. But limitations aren't so bad. I don't know how many people actually understand what limitations truly are. To me they appear to be things that limit you."

"Ha ha. Funny, Dad."

He smiled back as he said, "But they start to look different when you see them up close. I've come to understand that limitations have the potential to liberate you."

Kalaya raised her eyebrows. "Um—that doesn't make any sense. Limitations are bad things."

"But do they have to be? Here, I want to show you something. Look at me. Look deep into my eyes. Are you doing it?"

"Yes, Dad. I'm looking into your eyes."

"Good. Now, while you can see me, I've never been able to look at you. I've never been able to see my precious daughter. But tell me, who in all the islands knows you the best?"

"You do," Kalaya said. "No one else comes close."

"Exactly. I've had to learn how to see people in other ways. My limitation has forced me to make a choice. Will I become a blind man, or will I choose—somehow—to see? I chose to see, and guess what? In my own way, I can! Somehow, a man with these"—he pointed at his two sightless eyes—"can perceive."

"You're right—you do it all the time. It's amazing. Like earlier, at the parade, you knew the exact moment I saw Jaremon."

Her dad nodded. "Yet when people find out that I can't see, they think it's so terrible. But it's given me something I doubt I would've ever had if I had normal sight. It's one of the greatest gifts I've ever received.

"What's that?"

"The understanding that life is so much bigger than I could have ever imagined. That may not sound very valuable, but trust me—it is. Let me give you an example. Because of how I was born, I'll never be able to see Color. When I meet someone, I can't look at their collar to see if that person is above or below me. As a result, I'm one of the few people in all the islands who doesn't care about it.

"Most people have a small, narrow view of life that says a person's Color, status, and rank is everything. But from what I've seen, Color isn't the thing that determines whether someone's life is going to be good or bad. I was once assigned to a murder case involving a mage who was rolling in lykes, and let me tell you, his life was truly miserable. Yet I've also encountered numerous commoners who love life and embrace it with open arms."

Like you do.

"Your value was taken from you at the Color Ceremony, Kay." The emotion in her father's voice made his words come out thick and raspy. "But that's because you let it happen. You let them name you 'worthless.' But you aren't. You never were before, and you aren't now."

Her father reached out his hand to find her as he spoke. Kalaya stepped in front of him and let him place his hand on her face. It was warm, soft, and comforting.

"Take encouragement from what the Master Magician said to you. Listen to the message my mum left. And listen to what I'm about to say. You are Kalaya is-a Cloud—my precious daughter—and you and Aliva are the most valuable things in my life. 'Color' is nothing but a meaningless word to me."

His words filled her eyes with tears that streaked down her cheeks and ran onto his hands.

"And, Kalaya, you don't need one for me to love you," he finished.

She fell into his arms and he held her tightly as she sobbed. She didn't care about all the stupid customs that held people back from touching, because in the arms of her father, she felt safe and loved. *I have the best dad in all the islands.*

When she eventually stopped crying and pulled out of his embrace, she saw that his blank, empty eyes had also filled with tears. "Thank you," Kalaya sniffled. "That means a lot to me."

"Good. It better," he said as he cleared his throat and wiped his face with the sleeve of his shirt. "Plus, you don't have a choice. I'm your father. Daughters have to listen to their fathers."

That made Kalaya laugh. Even though she still felt deeply sad, it was good to laugh again.

They said nothing for a long, long time. It was one of those tranquil, untroubled moments when everything seemed right in the islands.

She was still smiling when she thought of something else to ask her grandma. "So what now? What can someone without a Color do for work?" She knew what she was about to hear; she'd heard her grandma's passionate speech about work many times before.

"Work?" her grandma said in a way that felt different than the times Kalaya had heard it before. For some reason, it felt honest, real, and personal now. "Find the people you love. Make projections for them that inspire them to grow and bloom. Sing songs to them that fill them with emotions. Build them a house or a boat. Cook them a meal. Stitch their threadbare. The possibilities are endless! Love others, bless them—live your life as life was meant to be lived! If you do this, you'll be free to do most anything you can imagine."

Kalaya pressed her lips together and asked, "Even if the projections I care about the most come out blue?" The words slipped out of her mouth before she had a chance to think.

"Blue is lovely, but I was Yellow and Orange."

Huh. She had a response for that? Kalaya stepped away and asked her dad, "Did Grandma ever tell you that her projections came out blue, like some of mine do?"

"No. I've never heard anything like that before."

"I didn't tell you about this, but Master Magician Greydyn told me that she couldn't control color."

"Really?" Dad said. "I suppose he would know. But if it's true, Mum kept it a secret."

"Is it all right with you if I spend some time trying to find out if she put something about it into her icon?"

"Of course," Dad said enthusiastically. "Now you've got me curious."

So she began. "Grandma, some of the things I project come out blue. Someone told me that some of your projections also came out blue. Is that true?"

"Who did you hear that from?" Grandma asked.

"Um, Greydyn, the Master Magician."

"Oh, he's a marvelous person. Grey and I were good friends."

"But Grandma, were your projections really blue?"

"Who did you hear that from?"

"Greydyn is-a Ring."

"Oh, he's a marvelous person. Grey and I were good friends."

Why does she keep calling him Grey? Something about it seemed odd, so Kalaya decided to try a different approach. "Someone told me your projections came out blue. Is that true?"

"Who did you hear that from?"

"Grey, your good friend."

Her grandma tilted her head and blinked several times. "Ah, well then! You've found out about my little secret, have you? Congratulations—I worked hard at hiding that," her grandma said with a wink. "Things I made often came out blue when they weren't supposed to. It was really quite embarrassing, to tell the truth. Did you know that during all those interminable years when I was in the Intra-Regional Competitions, I only projected naturally blue things to try to cover it up? Blueberries, blue fabric, blue birds, you name it. If it was blue, I projected it.

"But that all changed a few years after I got to the Workshop. Grey discovered my secret. He was a young man then, and different from the others. He taught me to love my projections—no matter whether I could control the color or not. It was something I wished I'd known when I was a young girl. I might have saved myself a lot of headaches and anxiety—and probably would have been a better competitor, too!" Her grandma laughed. "Of course, whenever I made anything official for the Workshop, someone had to correct the color, but that didn't matter. Grey was a good man and never shamed me. He was a true blessing, sent to me from Täv. If I could say anything to him now, it would be 'thank you.'"

When her grandma finished speaking, Kalaya realized that her dad's mouth was hanging open. "Unbelievable," he said. "I thought I'd heard everything Mum put into this projection."

Kalaya reached out and placed her hand on his shoulder. *She didn't even tell Dad. Being a magician and having a problem like that must have been terrifying. No wonder she kept it a secret.*

"You should show her," her dad said after a moment. "You should make the wallaroo."

"Huh? Here?"

"Yeah. Pretend your grandma is more than a projection and show her how you make things blue, too."

Kalaya hesitated. "I don't know . . ."

"Come on, get to it. You've already decided you want to. I can tell—I can see it in the way you're scrunching your lips together.

"What? You saw that?"

"Your breathing changed again. You always do that when you're scrunching up your lips and preparing to make a projection," Dad said with a silly grin.

Kalaya ran her fingers through her hair and let out an exasperated sigh so loud that he was sure to hear it. "Yeah, yeah. Okay, Dad, whatever you say." She tried to sound annoyed, but the smile that crossed her face made her voice light.

"That's my girl."

"Young woman, you mean," Kalaya corrected.

"You're right. My daughter has become a young woman. I like the sound of that."

Kalaya pivoted her body to the side and shut her eyes. She then focused all her energy on creating a picture of a wallaroo in her mind, and once again, the ancient creature materialized in front of her.

And, as it had every time she'd made it before, it came out bright blue.

The only difference this time was that it didn't bother her. Her dad couldn't see it, and her grandma wasn't real. There wasn't a single person around to judge her for it. Because of that, she was able to see something different in it—something that she'd missed in all her efforts to make it perfect. It was a striking shade of blue, and she saw it as beautiful and precious, like a sapphire in the sun. Kalaya soaked in the Glory of it. *It may be even more stunning than sunlit.*

And, all on its own, the wallaroo started to dance with the smooth and realistic flow of true motion. It bounced left and right and spun with joy as Kalaya had always dreamed it would.

"Did you do it?" her dad asked.

"Yeah, I did," Kalaya spoke quietly.

"How does it look?"

"You know what?" Kalaya paused and tried to find the right words to describe how she felt. "I . . . I actually like it!"

The Secret Plan

~Jade~

There is no truer and more faithful friend than Jade is-a Shield. Despite her poverty, she holds herself with an elegance most magicians only dream of possessing. As children, we were inseparable—until she set her eye, and heart, on Malroy, that is. The love between them was the envy of us all. You could tell from the way that Mulroy looked at Jade that nothing could ever tear him from her. And, despite the tragedy that's befallen them recently, I still believe this is true. I'm confident they'll come out the other side of their separation stronger than before.

—Mistress Waddlebee is-a Stone, "Eye Opening Interviews and Outlooks," *The Weekly Word*

Jade is-a Shield was completely and utterly exhausted. The sun had not yet risen—it wasn't even the end of the Crimson watch—but all she wanted to do was lie down. She reclined in her favorite chair and wrapped a warm shawl around her. It had been a long week of running around, trying—unsuccessfully—to get others to do what she wanted.

"Kai, go and fetch my messages from the communication tower. There ought to be several there for me. I have a good feeling about today. I had trainers Aybert and Billbore both convinced you would be a valuable asset for their teams. I have them bidding against each other for you."

Kai didn't move; he was too busy casting a projection of some silly little thing in the corner of their living room.

"Go on, go," Jade insisted. "I want to know what they have to say."

"Grandmother, we don't have to go to the tower to fetch messages," Kai replied without looking up. "I told you, Weston agreed to deliver anything that arrived for us."

"You know we cannot afford the messenger service. We no longer live in Little Hills, now do we? So, go on."

Kai sighed. "Weston is my friend. He agreed to do it for free."

"Nothing is free, Kai. Anyone who offers something for free expects something later. I do not want to be beholden to any Wave. Do you know I once accepted a fruitcake from Weston's grandmother, Marma is-a Wave? She said it was free, but not even a week later, I received a message from her. She expected me to attend her daughter's wedding."

"That's called an invitation, Grandmother."

"Oh sure, that is what she called it, too. But I knew the truth. She just wanted another wedding gift. She did not care at all about us. I don't even like fruitcake! But of course, I went and paid her back with a gift. We should have been even, but it did not stop there. I suffered through one wedding after another— you know how many children those Waves have. That was the most expensive 'free' fruitcake I ever received. Thankfully, the scandal with your father put an end to all that nonsense. At least our tragedy produced one good thing. Now, stop being lazy and go."

Kai still didn't move. "Don't worry. Weston will come if anything arrives for us."

"If?" Jade scoffed. "I am certain there are at least three messages waiting for me to reply to. Weston will take too long. He takes too many naps, just like his father."

"Mother Jade," Declarious called from kitchen, "I'm sure Kai will be happy to go out and check for you, once he's finished his projection."

What a family I have. I bet Waddlebee doesn't encounter such stubborn resistance whenever she makes a request. "Projections are never finished," Jade reminded them. "I once dated a mage who spent over a year on one single projection. In ten years of training, he never made it past Intra-Regionals. I am sure glad I saw through him. I cannot imagine a life worse than the one we have now, but I am certain it would have been infinitely more dreadful if I had stuck with that throttlewog. Kai? Kai! You are not listening to me."

Her grandson did not look up. "Projections are never finished. I got it."

That boy's planning something. He's never been so focused practicing before. What is it that he's making now. A ship? Jade's stomach alerted her to her hunger. She took her tray and laid it on her lap. She then diverted her stream of instructions away from Kai and to his mother. "Declarious, it is nearly the top of the Red watch, and—"

Before Jade could finish, Declarious exited the kitchen carrying a plate with toast and two eggs cooked precisely the way Jade liked them.

"I have your breakfast right here." Declarious gently placed the plate on Jade's tray.

"Oh. Good." The smell of the fresh eggs wafted into her nose and she relaxed a bit. "Did you add the—"

"Taste of salted bacon? Yes, mother dear. I also projected your favorite raspberry jam on the toast."

"Well," Jade said and adjusted the tray on her lap. "Good then." *Declarious is far more gracious than normal this morning. Something's brewing.* As she happily ate her breakfast, she puzzled over what it could be. *I'll have to press them on this when I'm finished eating. There's no sense letting a warm meal go cold.*

The Cyan spa advertisement went off outside. This was followed by a firm series of knocks on the front door that rattled the walls of their poorly constructed home and gave Jade quite a shock. Kai jumped up from the floor and darted across the room. "Weston!" he exclaimed as he flung the door open.

"Hey, Budski!"

So, the boy came after all. I sure hope he doesn't expect a tip for this. We need every coin we can get if we're going to find Kai an appropriate trainer. "Weston, good to see you so early this morning. Did you sleep well?" Jade asked, but she did not wait for a response. "Kai told me of your kind offer to bring our messages for free. I wish we could provide you a tip, but I am afraid—what with Kai's training to worry about—we simply must be prudent and conserve our limited resources."

"I understand," Weston said, smiling politely. "Hopefully that won't be a problem much longer."

Hmm. I wonder what he means by that? Jade looked up at Weston for the first time. He wore the red shirt of a red rider, but . . . *Why's he covered with all those ridiculous lightning bolts?* "Well? Are you just going to stand there? Bring my message over to me. I would expect someone wrapped in lightning to be far faster than this."

"I'm sorry, Mistress Jade," Weston said, "but this message is for Kai."

Kai? Who does he know outside this island?

Kai took the black lacquered box from Weston's hand, glanced back at his grandmother, read the look on her face, and said, "Don't worry, Grandmother. It's just from my girlfriend."

Everyone stared at him.

"Girlfriend?" Jade exclaimed. "You do not have time for all that nonsense."

"I'm a young man now, Grandmother. And a highly desirable one now that I have two Colors. You know how it is. You had a boyfriend or two when you were my age—didn't you?"

Declarious covered her face with her hand and tried to hold back a laugh.

"But Kai . . ." Weston looked confused. "It's from your—"

"I know who it's from," Kai jumped in before Weston could say anything more. "Let me take it outside. I know how distasteful you find these matters of romance."

What kind of scheme is he working? There's only one girl he's interested in, and she's from this island. "Wait—tell me where you are going!" Jade shouted after them. As Kai and Weston ran out the door, she jumped up out of her chair.

The two boys climbed onto their bikes and rode down the path that led into the forest. Jade didn't have a bike but prided herself on being surprisingly fast for her age. She chased after them on foot. "Hang on, Weston is-a Wave! What about the messages for me?"

"I'm sorry, Mistress Jade," Weston called back without slowing, "but there were no messages for you. I have to go."

She tried her best to keep up, but the boys easily got away.

Jade was completely out of breath when she returned home, but she put on a determined face and said quite forcefully to Declarious, "Tell me what is going on."

"You'll have to wait until Kai comes back and ask him," Declarious replied as she gathered up the morning dishes and placed them in the washbasin.

They are all up to something. What could it be? "Do you know who that message was really from?"

"I believe I do, yes."

"Well?" Jade placed her hands on her hips and waited.

"Kai has made a decision, but it's for him to tell you, not me."

Well! He speaks to his mother but not to me? What's happened to the respect young people once had for their elders? Jade felt frustrated beyond measure, but she knew that Declarious was stubborn and true to her word. She wouldn't give any more information. *I guess I'll just have to go and pay Rieta another visit.*

✳   ✳   ✳

When Jade arrived at the top of the communication tower, she found Rieta brooding, her arms crossed and her brow furrowed. *Hmm. She must have overheard some bad news again.* "Good morning, Rieta darling," Jade said as she climbed the last stair. "I have a very pressing question . . ."

"No, there are still no responses. I already told you that if I get anything, one of my riders will bring it straight over."

Wow. She's in an exceptionally bad mood today. "No, no, it is not about that. My grandson, Kai, received a mysterious message this morning, and as I am his grandmother and legal guardian, I expect you can tell me who it was from."

As soon as she finished speaking, Rieta stood a little taller and said, "You don't know?"

"I am afraid not. Kai had a pressing matter to attend to and unfortunately had to run off soon after it came in."

"I see," Rieta said, and she paused to consider. "Well, as you know, it's illegal for me to share any personal information that I receive as a part of my work here."

"Of course," Jade agreed. "I would never ask for specifics. All I am wondering is who would send a minor a message? My grandson does not know anyone from any other island."

"He knows at least one person," Rieta corrected.

"Yes, evidently he does." Jade frowned. "Please, darling. Soothe an old woman's fears and give me something."

"I just did. It's someone he knows," Rieta reiterated. "From another island. Someone you all know."

Oh dear. I bet it's someone from Declarious's clan. Jade sighed. "Family?"

Rieta nodded.

"A trainer?" Jade asked.

"At one time."

Looks like I was right to be afraid Declarious would go off and try to help. There's no doubt she has a kind, sweet family, but there's not a talented one among them. Those Silks think they can train, but who have they gotten into the Workshop? Jade thought. *Let's see. Two of her relatives are retired trainers. But which one would she contact?* Jade puzzled over this before asking, "What level of trainer?"

"Tier One," Rieta whispered.

Really? Neither of them was anywhere near that good. What former Tier One trainer could Declarious possibly know? Jade's mind raced as she tried to solve this riddle. *Someone we all know. Family. Former Tier One. Kai didn't want me to know who it was.* She searched her mind for every Tier One trainer she knew. *Who could it be?*

All at once, it hit her. *Oh no!* Jade let out a groan. "You are not talking about Malroy, are you?"

Rieta pressed her lips together and gave a casual shrug. "Mmmm. I can't say," she said in a way that told Jade she was right.

I can't believe they're talking to him behind my back. Could they have convinced him to come and take Kai? No, no, no. This will utterly destroy his chances of getting into the Workshop. "How could you let them contact him? You know what he did to my son!"

Rieta looked offended and projected to Jade, "Of course I know. I did everything possible to prevent Kai's message from going out. But that didn't seem to stop him now did it?"

Something has Rieta really upset. Serves her right. I know she always liked Malroy better than me. "Oh dear, what happened?" Jade asked.

"I can't prove anything," Rieta said with a scowl. "But he somehow found a way to send a message to Malroy without me. I closed up the tower early—for personal reasons—but when I returned this morning, I received a response from Malroy. A response to a message that I did not send!"

"Impossible," Jade said. "If you closed up early, no one would have transmitted his message. And Kai does not have enough Power to project that far."

"You think I don't know that? If this were easy, I'd be out of work!"

Incredible. If it's true . . . His talent grows every day. This is just another reason I cannot let Malroy taint him, too.

"Our faithful timekeeper said he came up here last night to send an emergency message. Right, Carlay?" Rieta called up to the perch above them.

"Indeed he did," said Carlay. "But do not fault the junior mage. It was a terrible emergency! There were vicious hell-beasts chasing him! Blood was everywhere, and the flood waters were rising. Kai had to be rescued! But nary a soul was here to assist him in his dire time of need. The message had to get out—by any means possible."

Cheeky girl. She liked Malroy, too. I remember when she was his student.

"You hear that, Jade? That grandson of yours is nothing but trouble," Rieta grumbled. "He influences people. See how he's found a way to convince a noble timekeeper to lie and protect him? Maybe it's for the best that Malroy's coming to take him away. Good riddance, I say."

Jade narrowed her eyes. "Take him away?"

"Of course. What did you think they were talking about?"

So, he thinks he can come and take my Kai? There's still time to stop this. Jade's mind started racing and she blurted out, "I need to send a message to Malroy canceling everything."

"Too late. He sent his response from the Island of the Silver Thorn, so he can't be far."

What? He's already left? "You cannot mean to tell me that he is coming here? He knows it is illegal for him to return."

"He said the wind's been in his favor and they're to meet at some 'prearranged meeting spot'—the fool didn't say where. Hoping to avoid unwanted attention, I'd say."

Just like Malroy, sneaking around. I knew he hadn't changed. How long have they planned this?

She figured this prearranged meeting spot had to be at Forecastle's property. Forecastle is-a Wave owned a private dock on his large isolated parcel of forested land, where he and his uncountable, ridiculously named children made their living building boats. He and Malroy had always been close, but she hadn't realized they'd stayed in contact all these years. *I bet Malroy will be wearing some ridiculous projection masking his real identity. If he were born common today, I'm sure he'd run off and join some band of worthless, clanless poozers.* Jade normally did an excellent job of hiding her displeasure, but not now. She was fuming with anger as she said, "How long until he arrives?"

"Sometime in the Yellow watch, he estimated."

"What? That is little more than a watch away!" Jade looked up at the timekeeper perched above her and saw two beams of Red in the sky.

Carlay called down, "It'll be one beam soon."

Jade reached for the railing to steady herself. *Do they expect to ship Kai off behind my back so fast? What have I done to deserve such ingratitude?* "I . . . I need to go."

"Yes, do," Rieta agreed. "But remember—you didn't hear anything from me."

Jade felt as if someone had just struck her across the head, and her mind swirled with thoughts. *Malroy. Coming back to take Kai. Without my permission. Impossible. I won't let it happen.* "Wait." Jade stopped at the top of the steps. "Hand me a cube and call a rider. Anyone but Weston. I want to send a message to someone on the island, and it needs to be discrete."

When Rieta heard the message, a smile crossed her face. For the first time that morning, she looked pleased.

*   *   *

"Kai? Are you here?" Jade called as she pushed open the door to their home. She'd done the unthinkable and hired a rickshaw to get her back quickly, but even that wasn't fast enough. It was the top of the Orange watch. *But where are they?* There was still time. *Did they leave without saying goodbye? They wouldn't do that, would they?*

"Grandmother? We're in here," she heard Kai call.

Jade moved swiftly through the house and pulled aside the curtain that separated the living room from the space in the back where they all slept. Kai and Declarious sat on his bed. Next to them was a small, brown satchel that she knew must contain the few physical possessions Kai actually cared about.

"Grandmother, I have something to tell you," her grandson said. "It's good news—so don't be nervous. I found a trainer. A really good one."

Stay calm. Pretend you know nothing. "That is lovely, dear. But I am afraid we will not be able to afford a good trainer."

"I know, but this one's agreed to train me for free."

"Then he or she simply will not be good enough to take you all the way to the Workshop," Jade said. "Remember what I told you: everything has a cost. Good trainers never give away their services. Even though we are poor now, we cannot settle for less than the best. Your future is too important to risk on just anyone." *Pay attention to that last bit, Kai. I only want what's best for you.*

"This isn't just anyone, Mother Jade," Declarious said.

No, you're right. This is the man who caused my son—your husband!—so much anxiety that he resorted to cheating just to please him. As much as Jade wanted to say it, she knew that she had to keep quiet and play nice for her plan to work. "Wonderful. How about we wait until I finish my search. Then we will compare all of the trainers and choose the best one."

"Grandmother—you don't understand. I've already chosen this trainer. I'm leaving to go meet him right now."

He doesn't trust me to find him someone better. I wonder what Malroy told him? Jade felt her hand start to tremble. Her calm facade was starting to weaken.

"Mother Jade, be at peace," Declarious said. "It's going to be okay. I've given this decision my blessing. It's something I've long prayed would happen. I see the marks of Täv all over it. I don't believe there could be a better person to train Kai in all the islands."

How can she look me in the eye and say that? After everything we've been through on account of that man. "So you have made your decision, hmm? Do I not have a say in the matters of my own grandson?"

"Of course you do," Declarious said. "My hope was that you would be in agreement, once you saw how much this means to Kai."

Either I agree and they get their way, or I fight it and I'm made out to be the villain. What a choice I've been given. "Who is this wonderful miracle of a trainer?" she asked, curious if they would be bold enough to tell her the truth.

"Well . . ." Declarious hesitated. "Believe it or not, it's your husband, Father Malroy."

So they do care enough to be honest. At least that's something.

"I'm sorry we didn't tell you sooner, Grandmother," Kai said. "I just didn't want to upset you. I know how hard it is for you to talk about Grandfather."

"I see," Jade said quietly.

"I wish we had more time to talk about this," Kai said. "But the message grandfather sent said he had to come earlier than expected. He'll be here soon. I need to go meet him. Now."

When she said nothing in response, Kai reached out his arms, and Jade suddenly felt herself wrapped in a big hug projection that squeezed her tightly.

"I know you could stop this if you wanted," Kai continued, "but it means a lot to me. Grandfather can train me well and without cost. I promise I'll work hard and learn all I can. For a long time I didn't want to become a magician. But now—more than ever—I want to get into the Workshop. I think I may even want it more than you do."

That isn't possible. But something in the way Kai said this struck Jade. *He really does want it, though. He meant it the other night. He wants it apart from pleasing me. Not like Flint.* She pictured her son's face. *Flint never really wanted it for himself.* "Dear child, if you think you can just walk out of this house and leave me alone, you are sadly mistaken."

Kai's eyes grew wide with surprise. "But—"

"I am coming with you," Jade said firmly. "Time is wasting. If Malroy said he will be here soon, then we should not keep him waiting."

Kai exchanged a surprised look with his mother.

"You're not upset?" Declarious asked.

"Of course I am. This is a dangerous decision that will have repercussions for our family. But you have made your decision, and I would not dare be the one who stands in your way."

The relief was visible on Kai's face, and—before Jade could do anything to stop him—he ran over and gave her a real, full-bodied hug. "I love you, Grandmother."

As he wrapped his arms around her, Jade thought about what had changed in her grandson to make him suddenly want to be a magician so much that he'd be willing to leave their island and train with Malroy—of all people. *It's because of that Leaf girl. He was covered in pink about her the moment she projected those unnatural butterflies. I knew telling him he could never be with her unless he was a magician would have an impact. But I never expected it to work out this well.*

Jade felt a small measure of satisfaction knowing that he actually cared about becoming a magician now. *I just hope what happens next doesn't hurt that desire.*

The Return of Malroy
~Jade~

The Great Purges were, I submit to you, a most shameful blot on our rich O'Ceean history. With all respect to our ancestors, it is difficult to understand what could have motivated people to destroy all those unfortunate plants and animals endowed with Conflicting Colors. But now that florism and faunism have largely been snuffed out from the islands, we can begin to address the enormous burden those individuals with Conflicting Colors place upon our civilized society.

—Historian Mage Wesslemore is-a Trunk, *Historical Proofs and Horrible Goofs*

It was a struggle for Jade to appear positive as she awaited the imminent arrival of her husband. She was now at the Wave shipyards—located on the eastern end of the island and right next to the sea—and stood on the end of Forecastle's long dock with six others: Forecastle himself, Kai and Declarious, Snap, Luge, and Weston. *But no Talia. She was wise to stay away.*

Jade gave a disapproving look at her daughter-in-law as Kai moved around the dock and gave each one of his friends an actual, two-arms-wrapped-around-the-other-person physical hug. *See, Declarious? I told you not to coddle Kai so much when he was little. Hugging only leads to more hugging.*

Kai and his friends were talking nonstop, but Jade heard none of it. All of her attention was focused on Malroy's boat—which was now visible and getting closer rather quickly. A small smile tugged at the corners of her mouth as soon as she saw the sailboat. It seemed that during the time of their separation, her husband's interest in old vessels had only grown stronger. Malroy was approaching the dock sailing a small, single-masted cutter wrapped in complex projections that made it appear old and weather-worn. She remembered how he used to labor to achieve this sort of look while maintaining the traditional, sleek elegance of an ancient vessel. His fascination with this had never made sense to her. She found it unsettling to see a new, well-built sailboat so soaked with age.

The more Jade stared at Malroy's sailboat, the more she felt like she was peering back in time. *Pull yourself together.* She stood up straighter than usual, fluffed her hair, and wriggled her fingers at her face, projecting a bit of Glory onto her cheeks. *Malroy was always attracted to that.*

As the cutter came up to the dock, Jade was given her first look at Malroy in years. There were the obvious signs of aging—he'd gained a bit of weight, his windblown hair was now mostly white, and the intensity of his blue eyes had faded somewhat—but there was something else about him that seemed different, too. *He looks . . . happy . . . and full of that optimistic energy Orange mages radiate when they're young. I thought I'd never see that again. Not after Flint.*

Malroy grinned when he saw those waiting for him on the dock. Jade's eyes went straight to his mouth, just as they always had. *He still has that infernal smile.* He'd captured her heart with it years ago. Now she turned away. She wouldn't let him pull her back in with it again. She pretended to observe Forecastle's sons at work constructing a schooner back on the shore.

But she couldn't shake the feeling that there was something different in his face. Malroy looked older, but . . . *That's it!* All at once, she understood. *He's comfortable with how he looks. He isn't trying to hide his age with projections the way he used to.*

She turned back to look at him. *It's his face.* She stared at it and noticed something that was unlike the Malroy she once knew: the creases in his skin were soft and not nearly as hard as they'd once appeared.

The years of separation and oceans of animosity hadn't severed the connection between this married couple. Jade herself didn't understand the feelings that the sight of her husband stirred up in her. But if there was any hope of them reuniting, it lasted only a moment. As soon as he opened his mouth to speak, all her feelings of anger and betrayal came flooding back.

"Hello, m'lady." Malroy bowed his head to her after he finished securing the dock lines.

How dare you try to take my Kai away from me. "Malroy," she replied and politely bowed back.

"I must say, I'm surprised to see you're okay with this. I expected more . . . resistance."

"Yes, well, you were always the one with a flair for the dramatic. Me, all I have ever wanted was the best for Kai."

"I'm just glad to see that we're finally in agreement," Malroy said.

As soon as his boat was secure, Malroy stepped to the edge of the deck and addressed Forecastle. "So good to see you, my old friend. Thanks for letting us meet here."

"It is my pleasure," Forecastle said with a nod and slight bow.

"And now—the reason we're all here." Malroy turned and looked at Kai. "My dear grandson. It truly is good to see you with my own face," he said.

Kai glanced at his friends, who appeared to be in support of this treason. "Yeah," he agreed after a brief pause. "You look . . . just like I remember."

Malroy laughed.

Go ahead, laugh now. It'll all be over soon.

"Dearest Declarious, thank you for contacting me," Malroy said to their daughter-in-law. "Although this isn't ideal for any of us, I still have hope that Plan 1A will become a reality one day."

"As do I," Declarious agreed.

Oh, so they have more secret plans, do they? I wonder what 1A is code for?

"So, Kai. How do you feel?" Malroy asked.

"Um—good. Nervous," Kai answered.

"I imagine so. It's been quite a long time since you've seen me."

For a reason, too. Can't they see how he abandoned us?

"Yeah. It has." Kai shuffled his feet. Both he and Malroy looked like they weren't sure what to do next.

"Well—I suppose—" Malroy cleared his throat. "I suppose we should get going."

No. Not yet. Jade looked back to the forest, but there was no sign of what she'd been expecting. *He should have been here by now. What's taking him so long?*

Kai turned to his friends, waved goodbye to them, and then—after taking a deep breath—stepped aboard Malroy's boat.

No! She had to do something to stall them. "Malroy—it has been so long since you have seen your old friend. Why leave so soon? I am sure he would love to have you come up and have a proper visit. Am I right, Forecastle?"

The large shipbuilder said nothing and let Malroy respond. "It's probably best I stay where I am."

"Well, surely there is something you ought to say to him after all this time. He was such a close friend, after all."

"Um—okay. Well, Forecastle, anything you want to share about the last eight years here, in front of everyone, in this unusually awkward moment?"

Forecastle shook his head no. *Really? He has nothing to say?*

"All right then, I guess we'll head off," Malroy said with a shrug, but then—looking as though he'd just remembered something very important—he locked eyes on Forecastle. "No, wait. Actually, there is something I should communicate."

Jade now felt quite curious to know what Malroy had to say, but her husband had grown very still. *He's communicating by projection now, hmm? What have I done to deserve such secrecy? I'm certain Waddlebee's family has never treated her like this.*

Forecastle didn't speak words, but all of his muscles tensed up and it looked as though he was preparing to face something horrible—something with the power to tear him apart.

"Tsk tsk," Jade clucked her tongue in disapproval. "You know what they say about people who have projection conversations in front of others."

"Please, Jade!" Forecastle said abruptly. His brow was furrowed and he had a look of deep frustration. "This isn't about you."

"Of course," Jade said as calmly as she could. "But I believe you must agree this is a big moment for me and my family. Forgive me if I am lacking trust—I believe it is warranted. An awful lot of significant things have been taking place behind my back."

"Understandable," Forecastle said. "Our conversation now is private because it is solely about my son, Wheelhouse. I'd prefer not to discuss such matters with everyone."

This satisfied Jade. *The runaway thief? Yes, I'd want to keep a discussion about him secret, too.* She turned her attention back toward the shore.

While the two men continued their projected conversation, movement in the distance caught her eye. Jade breathed a sigh of relief when she spotted Captain Markus of the Island Patrol walking out of the forest, straight toward them. *About time. That was close.*

"Jade, what's going on?" Declarious asked as the captain approached. "Did you send for the IP?"

Jade did her best to look as confused as the others.

"Markus, my old friend." Malroy waved as the captain drew near. "Good to see you!"

Friend, hmm? They were never friends.

"Malroy is-a Shield. I must say, I didn't actually expect to find you here."

"Forgive me, Captain, but what are you doing here?" Forecastle positioned himself in front of Malroy. "This is a private meeting."

"I have just cause to enter your property," Captain Markus said. "I received an anonymous tip about some illegal activity, so I've come to investigate."

Weston's face turned to ash, and he and Kai exchanged nervous looks. *They must feel remorse about sending out that message last evening. I'm not surprised. Look at all the trouble it's caused. Guilt is the offspring of bad behavior, after all.*

"I didn't think we were breaking any laws, Captain," Weston blurted out. "Please, don't place another prohibition on me. I promise I won't make another projection ever again."

"You have nothing to worry about, Weston, and neither does Kai. I know about the message he sent out last night. As a mage, he has that right. And you broke no laws by merely standing next to him. I'm here about Malroy."

Malroy laughed. "I forgot how fast word travels on this island. Well, don't worry, old friend, I haven't broken any laws either."

Captain Markus observed him silently, then bent down and grabbed hold of the line that fastened his boat to the dock. "Are you sure? Seems like you've attached yourself here. And the terms of your banishment were clear: you agreed never to set foot on this island again."

"Well—I hate to correct the captain of the IP—but I was never officially banished, and the only vow I made was that I would never show my face on this island again. And I haven't. As for setting foot on it, you don't need to worry about that because my feet are firmly planted on this boat."

"It's true," Kai insisted. "Grandfather hasn't done anything wrong."

Captain Markus held up his hand, and Kai stopped speaking.

Good. Say no more, Kai. Watch Markus put an end to all this nonsense. "Markus, I am sorry you had to come out for this," Jade said. "It is a very unfortunate situation. They have made a plan for—"

Markus turned his eyes on Jade and made a clicking sound with his tongue, which she knew was a warning to keep quiet as well. "I've seen enough. It seems Rieta has been prying her nose into places it doesn't belong. Since you haven't stepped onto the island, Malroy, I see no problems here."

What?! Jade felt her pulse quicken.

"All right!" Snap exclaimed while Weston let out a sigh of relief.

No, no. This will not happen. I won't let it.

"I hope things go better for you on the Island of the Cloudy Peaks," Markus said to Kai.

"Thank you." Kai bowed respectfully.

"Stop!" The words burst out of Jade like hell-beasts from Helldoro. "You will not take my grandson away from me!"

Everyone turned and stared at her.

"Mother Jade," Declarious said as she reached out her hand. "What's wrong? We talked about this already. You agreed Kai could leave to go and train."

"I have changed my mind," Jade said firmly. "Malroy already took Flint away from me. I will not let him take my Kai and leave me utterly alone."

Malroy pressed his lips together in what was clearly an effort to keep from losing his temper.

Okay, are you going to respond or not? Are you still the same? Will you just ignore me and run away again?

Malroy looked to Forecastle—*probably for support*—but all the man did was nod. Apparently, her husband knew what this meant, and the tension on his face vanished.

"Dearest Declarious, it was lovely to see you again. It's been far too long. And Kai, I was really looking forward to spending a long time with you. It's a great sadness to me that we've not had the ability to get to know one another properly. Please understand, this is still my desire."

"Wait. What's going on?" Kai asked.

"I'm sorry, Kai," Malroy continued. "I'm not going to go against your grandmother's wishes. If she doesn't want you to leave, I'm afraid you'll need to stay."

Would you look at that? Maybe he has some sense in him after all.

"But—" Kai looked like he'd just been punched. "I don't want to stay. I want to go and train to be a magician. As soon as I heard you were coming, I finally felt like I actually had a chance."

Malroy remained silent. Everyone else on the dock was visibly uncomfortable. *They should have known this was never going to work.*

"Kai, maybe we should go," Snap said.

"No, please don't. Please—tell him how much I want to go with him," Kai said, but silence was the only answer he got. "Oh, come on, buds. Tell him how everyone on this island treats me."

"Not everyone," Forecastle said. "I know it appears that the citizens of this island are against you—and while that is certainly true of many people, there are those here who believe in you."

"Thanks, Master Forecastle," Kai said. "You and your family have always supported me. I'll never forget how you stood in my defense at the elders' meeting."

Forecastle nodded.

Yes, that was kind of him. But one just act does not entitle him to a lifetime of goodwill.

Kai turned to his grandmother. "Please, let me go. I want to train. Grandfather is a good trainer, better than anyone else! I want to get into the Workshop. You want me to get into the Workshop. If I go, we'll both get what we want."

If you go with him, you'll never make it past the first round of the Competitions. "I am sorry, Kai, but you are not leaving with him. It is my responsibility to keep you safe."

Kai clenched his teeth together. "What if we stay here? He can move back home. We'll be a family again."

Kai, you clearly don't understand anything, do you? Jade gave her grandson a look that made him shudder.

"Okay. How about if he moves back to the island?" Kai suggested. "I'll live at home, and he can live somewhere else."

"Impossible," Captain Markus stated. "Malroy surrendered all rights and privileges as a member of this island the day he left."

"I know, but . . . uh, Mom? I want to train with him. What should I do?" Kai clenched his fist. His knuckles were starting to turn white and wisps of his hand fire were flickering up through the cracks in his fingers. It looked as if it were trying to consume him.

Relax, Kai. Forget this notion and allow me to make everything better.

"Um, Kai," Luge said as he stared at his friend's fire. "I really think we should go."

"No, please stay," Kai said. "I don't want to be alone."

He doesn't want to be alone, hmm? Now he knows how I feel.

Declarious raised her hands up to her face and let out a defeated sigh. Her skin was now glowing bright yellow, an unconscious projection of her own that Jade knew meant she was under tremendous stress. *How embarrassing. At least it proves to everyone that Kai gets his unconscious projections from her side of the family and not mine.*

"Kai," Declarious said firmly, "you have your collar now. You're a young man, with more freedom to make your own choices."

Maybe so. "But Kai cannot go against the will of his elders, now can he, Markus?" Jade asked.

The captain shook his head.

"But his elders are in disagreement," Declarious said after a brief pause. "Mother Jade, you want Kai to remain with you on the island, correct?"

What's she plotting now? "I believe that much is obvious, dear."

"And Father Malroy, I know what you want, but can you please say it so Kai will know, too."

Malroy looked at Kai and said, "I want our family to be together."

Really? Does he think he can fool anyone with that? "Our family—what is left of it—has been together. We decided the proper arrangement a long time ago. It has worked out for us for all these years. There is no reason to change it now."

"Master Forecastle, Captain Markus," Declarious said, "can you bear witness and affirm that Father Malroy and Mother Jade are in disagreement, and thus the decision for Kai's care must fall to the next generation?"

"I affirm it," Forecastle said without hesitation.

"Yes. That much is clear," Markus agreed.

Declarious then asked, "And do I have the support of either one of my elders?"

Jade suddenly felt nervous. "Declarious, you know I love you like a daughter—I always have and I always will—but I cannot give you my support. I trust you will understand. I know what is best for Kai."

"Malroy?" Forecastle turned to his friend.

What will you do, Malroy? Will you go against my will?

Kai's grandfather was silent. It took several long moments before he finally looked up and met Jade's cold stare. "I'm sorry, Jade. But . . . I grant Declarious my support."

Really! Anger surged through Jade. "Only because it gives you what you want!" she snapped. *They all planned this—they planned to turn my grandson against me. Look. Look at Kai's hand fire. See what all this turmoil is doing to him. Look, it just leapt up twice as high.*

"So now, with the support of one of my elders," Declarious said, turning to face Kai, "it is my responsibility to determine where my son will go. Kai, I know what you have wanted. Has anything changed?"

"No."

"Then it's my decision for Kai to be trained by Malroy is-a Shield."

It's over. He'll never get into the Workshop now. The only training he will get is the kind that leads him to despise me. What did I ever do to deserve such a life?

"While he undergoes training, he will be under the care of Father Malroy," Declarious continued. "But when the training season is over and Kai is no longer participating in the Competitions, he shall return home to live with me and Mother Jade."

"I am one witness," Forecastle said.

"It shall be as you say," Captain Markus agreed.

"But . . ." Kai stared at his mother. "Isn't there any way you can come, too? You could do Plan 2B, right?"

"No, I'm afraid not. Your grandmother needs my support. She can't be left alone."

"That is honorable of you, Declarious," Forecastle said. "I believe Täv would desire this."

I hate it when people use Tav's name like a weapon. They only speak that way so no one can disagree with them.

"That is your decision?" Malroy asked.

I'll be quiet. I shouldn't be—for Kai's sake—but at least I know my place.

"Yes, it is decided," Declarious said.

"All right, let's be off," Malroy said, and immediately he began to untie his boat. He was about to push it away from the dock—*Malroy can't wait to get away from me, can he?*—when Kai jumped off the sailboat, ran to his grandmother, and gave her a physical hug.

"I know this hard for you. But it's what I want," Kai said. "I hope you understand. I love you, Grandmother."

Whoever decided hugging was an appropriate way to say goodbye was a real throttlewog. Jade scrunched up her nose and gave him a light pat on the back, just to show that she wasn't angry with him.

Kai released her and then gave his mother a hug as well. "Thanks, Mom. For everything."

"I love you, Son. Don't forget what I taught you about projections," Declarious said as she ran her fingers through his hair.

"I won't. And Grandmother, don't worry," Kai said as he turned and climbed back into the boat. "I'll devote all my time to training. You'll get your wish. Someone in the family will be in the Workshop again."

"Yes, dear. That would be wonderful," Jade said, putting on her charming face. "Remember, you are always welcome to come home."

"Buds, thank you for staying. I know it was awkward, but hey—now you have a great story to tell Talia." Kai laughed his infectious laugh, and they understood that he really thought everything was going to be okay.

"Oh yeah," Snap agreed, "she's going to love this."

"I think she'll be happy she wasn't here," Luge said.

"The Red Racer—for one—is glad he came to see you off." Weston paused and then said, "Thanks for being a good friend."

Dear, I sure hope someone doesn't start crying. Jade turned and watched Malroy intently as he reached for the dock and—with a wink and a wave—shoved the boat away. *Don't you dare harm him, too.* She tried to communicate the message with her eyes, but Malroy didn't meet her gaze.

"Oh, and please come and see me at the Competitions!" Kai shouted to his friends. "I'll try to give you all a good show."

"You'd budder!" Weston exclaimed. This was followed by an annoyed grunt from Snap and then a projection shove so unexpected that it caused him to lose his balance and fall into the water.

"Yes!" Snap pumped her arm. "Payback!"

Kai and Malroy burst out laughing as they watched a soaking wet Weston struggle to pull himself back up onto the dock.

But Jade found no humor in any of it. She watched silently as the cutter sailed off,
leaving her
alone
on a dock
full of others.

She walked away, determined not to look back. Their family was once again broken, and just as before, it was all Malroy's fault.

She had done everything to prevent this from happening. And failed. Now, standing apart, she felt the weight of it. *I lost Flint, and now I'm losing Kai.* The thought was distressing. Despite her resolve not to glance back—she turned to take one last look at her grandson.

Kai and Malroy had not gone far. They were watching something fluttering in the air in front of them, something yellow—and blue! *Something unnatural.* Jade held the traditional Tavite belief that Tav was the one who had projected O'Ceea into existence, long before he had walked among them as a human. However, she also held the non-Tavite belief that Tav had refused to create anything with Conflicting Colors.

Her grandson gazed at whatever this twisted, unnatural thing was. He looked like a wonderstruck child. Jade squinted to focus on it. *A yellow and blue butterfly? She's making them again!* Jade spun around and scanned the shoreline. *Where are you hiding, Talia is-a Leaf? I know you're here—yellow and blue butterflies don't exist in nature.* She didn't see any sign of the girl and figured she must be hiding in the forest. *Nothing was tainted until vot began corrupting the islands. Perhaps O'Ceea needs another Great Purge. It's been far too long since the last one.*

Luge yelped, "Look, Talia's here!"

Kai shouted back, "Tell her thank you. For this. And for coming. It was the best send-off I could have ever wanted. Oh, and tell her I'll be waiting for her at the end of the easy route!"

It won't be so easy for you now—now that you're leaving me. Jade considered what motivated young men. *He'll miss that girl. That will be enough to bring him back.*

The butterfly turned from following Kai and flitted its way back to shore, gliding just above the surface of the water. But instead of continuing toward shore, as Jade expected, the butterfly soared up and headed straight for her.

What's this about? It landed on her arm. Instinctively, she waved it off and away, but it immediately fluttered back to her.

Jade stood still and watched as it landed on the back of her hand. The little footsteps it made on her skin felt realistic. *Very lifelike.* Instead of dissolving it right away, she decided to examine it more closely. It moved quite naturally: the lines on its wings were precise, and its antennae moved with fluidity. *It has tremendous Kingdom and Glory—despite being such an obvious abomination.*

She looked out at Kai, but the cutter was now far away and she could no longer easily see him. *You'd better get trained fast, or that girl's going to beat you into the Workshop—and then her family will be the ones living in our mansion.*

Okay, time to go. She shook her left hand and thwacked her fingers at the butterfly to dissolve it, but nothing happened. *What's the matter? I surely have more Power than this little thing.* She threw out her hand, bending her wrist with great force while snapping her fingers. Still nothing happened. She tried once more, this time swinging her hand right at it as if to slap it.

But instead of passing through—as it should have—her hand struck the butterfly and knocked it to the ground. Jade was taken aback. *What's going on?* She bent over and looked at the butterfly, which was twitching helplessly on the ground. She reached out and touched its wing. It was solid. *What? Could it be real?*

She picked it up and held it in her hand. She watched its blue and yellow wings flap two final times before it stopped moving.

It wasn't a projection at all. She poked at it. *It was real.*

A rainstorm of guilt and shame flooded over her, and she struggled to catch her breath. As she looked down at the dead butterfly in her hand, images of her son's face flashed before her. Her heart flooded with so much agony that she felt as though it were going to burst. *Malroy. Flint. Kai. What have I done?* Here was a piece of the story that she had refused to look at for so long. It wasn't much, but it was enough to show her that she was guilty. She was a villain. She was the villain.

No. That's not true. She pushed everything away—all the memories, all the feelings, all the guilt—and staggered further away from the others in an emotional daze. Just like one of the ancient refugees of the Old World, fleeing Devos Rektor's torrential rain, she wondered if she had the strength to hold back the rising water that threatened to drown her in chaos.

The Private Ceremony

~Layauna~

There are always 288 magicians employed in the Workshop. Of these, 200 are magicians of the First Magnitude, 80 are of the Second Magnitude, and the top 8—those of the Third Magnitude— are the ones who have risen highest among all magicians. It is a rare and precious person who can make it that far.
—Magician Philean is-a Moss, *Meet the Magicians*

Layauna is-a Bolt stood in front of the faceless man who'd been introduced to her as 'the Magician Puller.' In his ancient, veiny hands was an even more ancient-looking staff. As soon as she laid eyes on it, she knew that she was looking at the legendary Staff of Light. She wasn't sure if the man or the staff scared her more.

They were not standing up on some glorious, vaulted pedestal, nor were they in a giant stadium or auditorium. No crowd had gathered here. There were no cheering members from her clan, nor was there a Festival of Stars for her to participate in. They were out on her grandfather's balcony. The only people in attendance were Grandfather Eyan, the Magician Puller, and two silent, faceless acolytes.

This was nothing like an ordinary Color Ceremony, but she had been assured by her grandfather that it was authentic in every way that mattered. *This is the actual Magician Puller. He's holding the actual Staff of Light. He's about to point it at my heart and see if any Color actually exists inside me.* Layauna could hardly breathe. *This is the moment.* She'd both anticipated and dreaded it for as long as she could remember. What happened right now—or didn't happen—would change everything.

They'd risen early, during the last nightmark, to prepare for this event. So much had to be done for this, Layauna's own personal Color Ceremony. But as Grandfather had so many servants, she really didn't need to do a thing except wait. So she stood, waiting, and watched three beams of Crimson shoot up into the sky. The first watch of the day had begun. *Ugh. That Color . . .* She turned away from it and shivered. The sun had not yet risen, and the air was still quite chilly. She was thankful for this, however, because it made her fitful shivering appear to be caused by the cold and not by her uncontrollable emotions.

"My sweet granddaughter," Grandfather Eyan said, "you have trained long and hard and have finally arrived at this moment. I am certain a Color will be found in you today."

"But, what if . . ." Layauna couldn't bring herself to say the words. *What if there's nothing and I'm void?*

"We've discussed this, Dearling," he said, as if reading her mind. "I've been around Color my entire life. I know how to recognize it in someone. Your trainers have told us over and over how exceptionally talented you are."

"But—lots of talented people are Colorless."

"My granddaughter is not going to be common."

"Mom was, though. Why do you think I'll be any different?" Layauna asked reluctantly. She'd been afraid to bring this up before but could no longer resist. *He must have felt the same way about Mom when she was sixteen.*

"It's normal for Color to skip a generation." Her grandfather sighed. "You know that. Now, please, don't worry. I have full confidence in you."

Somehow, that made her feel worse. "I just don't want to disappoint you."

"How could you do that, Dearling?"

Easy. By not having a Color. Layauna couldn't bring herself to say it; she turned her eyes away. *I wonder if he remembers what it's like? He must have been nervous when he was assayed.* It was hard to imagine her grandfather in this position. As a magician of the Third Magnitude, he had achieved a great deal in his career. *He was never at risk of being common.*

Because he had spent many years as one of the Eight, Grandfather Eyan was more elite than most magicians alive today. In fact—though he had been retired for quite some time now—many still considered him to be one of the Eight. He was without a doubt one of the most influential men in all the islands, and his great wealth and power reflected this.

Layauna didn't know how vast her grandfather's fortune was, but she believed it must be substantial. She sometimes imagined he had secret vaults hidden throughout the mansion, filled with shining, platinum whispers. After all, he owned homes throughout the islands and had two yachts to transport him between them. Dozens of servants attended to his every whim. Any object he desired, he owned. His name was attached to several of the most popular Grand Projections of the last generation. This reputation gave him access to anywhere he wanted to go and anyone he wanted to meet. And if he wanted something done, it was so. Layauna knew from experience that he lacked nothing and was used to having his will satisfied.

But today, despite his great influence, he would be completely powerless to affect the outcome of the Ceremony; the weight of humiliation lay completely on her shoulders. The fear of disappointing him grew stronger with every heartbeat.

Ever since she had left her mother and brother, Layauna had lived under the care and protection of Grandfather Eyan.

Most of these past three years had been spent training. She ate, slept, lived, dreamed, and breathed on that horrible island with the dome. There, she was instructed by an entire team of trainers and assistants. She knew it wasn't normal. Most teams had one trainer for ten to fifteen students. Layauna had a dozen all to herself. And very few kids were trained before it was proven that they had a Color.

The dome was awful, but thankfully, she didn't have to spend all her time there. Sometimes she was allowed a break to come to this place—to her grandfather's mansion, on the Island of the Summer Breeze. It almost made her time enduring the dome worthwhile.

According to Grandfather's personal narrologist, this island once had an overabundance of potatoes growing on it and had been inhabited entirely by potato farmers. It was known as the Island of the Potato Patches for many, many years, until the day the Workshop bought it. They relocated the farmers, uprooted the potatoes, and renamed it the Island of the Summer Breeze. Now it was covered with private mansions instead of potatoes. It was no longer a place for work; magicians came here to retire and live out their days in peace and privacy.

Every time she stayed here, Layauna found herself intimidated by the size of her grandfather's mansion estate. It wasn't just one building, but nine—one for each watch of the day, her grandfather joked—connected to one another by breezeways that crisscrossed the immaculate grounds. But after a night or two, she'd grow accustomed to it and soon couldn't imagine herself living anywhere else.

She liked to stroll among all the buildings; to zigzag through the gardens filled with flowers from every season; to swim in any one of the three swimming pools; to sit next to the pond and watch the large orange fish and exotic green ducks; or to lie down at the base of the tall, golden spire and marvel at how it seemed to puncture the heavens. The estate had a small amphitheatre, four kitchens, dozens of rarely occupied bedrooms, and countless other rooms, all filled with marvelous, largely unused luxuries. It was celestial.

The mansion estate was situated on a point of land that jutted out into the ocean. As a result, nearly every room had an ocean view. Layauna loved to open her window and feel the sea breeze on her face and hear the sound of waves rolling in and out, day and night. She wandered the trails that meandered along the bluffs and down to the private cove and beach, which she thought had to be one of the most beautiful spots in all the islands.

Recently, her grandfather had decided to bring in real white sand to cover the rocks, instead of using projections. Real sand! It was unheard of. The white sand was absolutely stunning when contrasted against the blue sea and the dark marbled earth tones of the cliffs that surrounded the bay. Whenever Layauna imagined herself getting married, she pictured the ceremony taking place right there, on the sand.

It wasn't until she walked along the beach for the first time that she understood why Grandfather Eyan had decided to bring in real sand. It was smooth, and walking on it was almost like gliding over silk. The sand was so immaculately clean that it made a faint squeaking sound each time she took a step. Layauna knew no greater joy than walking barefoot on the fine powder-like substance under the light of the moon.

Back in the mansion, there were servants for everything: cooking, cleaning, washing, carrying, organizing, sailing, healing, entertaining. If anyone in the family ever wanted to experience a Grand Projection, they had only to ask. Within a day, a troupe of the very best reprojectors would gather at her grandfather's

288   *The Magician's Workshop*

amphitheatre, where they would reproject the splendor of a Grand
Projection.

Layauna and Sorgan had experienced a number of Grand
Projections here when they were little, but—if the servants were
being truthful—the amphitheatre had gone unused for many
years. Grandfather Eyan always seemed to ignore it. This struck
Layauna as rather strange. Her grandfather had dedicated his life
to projections, and yet they appeared to play such a small part in
his life now.

When she had first left home with him on that rainy day so
many years ago—*I was such a naive young girl back then*—she fool-
ishly anticipated spending a lot of time here at his mansion. She'd
looked forward to walking along the garden paths and relaxing
by the pool, watching Grand Projections in his amphitheatre,
being waited on by servants, and eating all the marvelous food
she could handle. Sadly, visits to her grandfather's estate were
always far too short. Most of her time had been spent training on
the island with the dome.

Strangely, this also seemed true for her grandfather, who didn't
spend much time at his estate either. *Why even bother having a
place so big if you're never there?* He was always busy, sailing all
over O'Ceea, doing some kind of work she did not understand. *I
thought people were supposed to stop working once they retired. What
under the Colors could be so important for Grandfather to spend so
much effort on when he has all these luxuries to enjoy?* Of course, she
didn't dare ask him about that kind of thing; she'd learned in her
time with him that he wasn't a man to be questioned lightly.

"All right, Rollen," Grandfather Eyan said to the Magician
Puller, his voice shaking Layauna out of her thoughts. "Are you
ready?"

"Yes, Eyan," the Magician Puller replied. "Everything is in
order. Let the Ceremony begin."

Layauna looked over at the Magician Puller. He was dressed in white, and she realized that all of the Colors that had been wrapped around him were gone. She looked up and saw his dyemoon hanging above them. *When did he make that?* She had been looking forward to seeing his Colors unfurl and shoot up into the sky. *I must have disappeared into my thoughts again.* This was something her trainers had noticed her starting to do more recently.

Layauna's breath caught in her throat as she realized what was about to happen, and she felt the sudden urge to gag. *Just relax. Relax.* She tried to steady her breathing, just as one of her trainers had taught her to do. *Think about cheerful things. Butterflies. White sand. Blue water. Grandfather's food.*

Another trainer had stressed the importance of keeping her spirits up when the Staff of Light touched her, so she tried to make her thoughts positive. *Everything is going to work out. I have a Color. Everyone believes I do. I have to. I'm a Bolt now.*

Three other trainers had drilled into her the importance of believing in herself and not letting fear in. But as soon as the Magician Puller placed the Staff of Light directly in front of her heart, Layauna's mind went blank and fear came rushing back.

She darted her eyes away from him and over to her grandfather, hoping to find strength in his eyes. But they were shut. She noticed his lips moving slowly and silently, almost as if he were saying something. *Could he be praying?* Layauna had never spoken to him much about religion before and wasn't sure what he really believed. She'd never seen him do anything like this. *If he's praying, who's he praying to? The Color gods? Tav?* She couldn't picture him praying to either.

Then it hit her. For the first time in the three years that she'd been under his protection, she realized how important this must be for him. *There'd better be a Color in me.*

The puller pressed the staff against her.

"This is your life, come what may," he said.

His grip tensed on the staff—everything was happening so fast!

Layauna saw through squinted eyes that there was tension in the muscles of his arms.

He found something?

Maybe he found something!

He pulled the staff away. Slowly. Ever so slowly. And . . .

. . . there was no Color to be seen.

✳   ✳   ✳

I'm a void pull! Layauna lowered her head and shut her eyes. She couldn't bring herself to see her grandfather's face. *What's he going to do with me now? Everything he's spent—all my years of training—everything he's done . . . And the party! Oh no! He's going to lose face in front of all the most powerful people in the islands. All because of me!*

"Layauna," her grandfather called to her, but she just squeezed her eyes tighter.

I can't look. He's going to have the same expression that Father did . . . right before he left.

"Layauna. Dearling. It's all right. I'm not angry with you. Please open your eyes."

If she could have sealed her eyelids closed forever, she would have. But she knew that wasn't possible, so she reluctantly opened them and looked up.

The expression on her grandfather's face was grave, but it lacked the anger that she had expected to see. "It's all right, Layauna. This sort of thing happens."

"But . . . your party. So many important people are coming."

"Don't worry about that."

He can't really mean it. Can he? She felt like she was in a dream. A horrifying dream. "But I'm—void! You had so many plans for me when I . . . when I . . . became a . . . a magician."

"No, Dearling, you're not void."

"But—"

"These private Color Ceremonies need to be conducted a little differently than the big events," he explained. "In a big stadium, with the crowd cheering and all the adrenaline and emotions flowing through you, Color comes out more easily. Sometimes, in these quiet, private Ceremonies, the staff needs to be placed onto the child another time to compensate for this difference."

"Really? So I might still have a Color inside me?"

"Of course, Dearling. Do you think I would have invited everyone to your celebration if there wouldn't be anything to celebrate? That would be rather silly, now, wouldn't it? Please, there's no reason to doubt. Let's just try it again. I'm sure it's just your nerves."

Of course it's my nerves. I've never had so much pressure on me in all of my life. It was an unbearable weight, but her grandfather's words gave her a measure of strength.

"Let's try again, Rollen."

"Are you absolutely certain you want to proceed? You understand the risks, right?"

The risks?

"Yes. I'm certain," Grandfather said. "There's nothing to worry about, Layauna. In a few moments you'll have your Color and all the hard work you've been doing all these years will be rewarded."

The Magician Puller lowered the Staff of Light and once again placed it on Layauna's heart. The pressure of it on her chest caused her to tense up. "This is your life, come what may," the puller repeated.

He held the staff on her longer this time, and Layauna felt more of the strange sensations it produced in her. It was like the staff had entered the very essence of her and was foraging around—looking for something. Last time, she felt this sensation only for a brief moment, in a small area, right underneath where the staff was placed. This time, the sensation spread into her entire chest cavity, before it—in one abrupt motion—thrust up into her right shoulder.

Once again, the muscles in the arms of the Magician Puller tensed, indicating there was something on the end of the staff.

He found something this time! Grandfather was right! Hope rushed through her, chasing away the worry that had filled her stomach.

But when the staff was pulled away, there was—again—no Color.

No! All the hope drained away, and all that was left was a disgusting smell, wet and musty, stuck in her nose. *Why can't I produce a Color like Grandfather expects?* The pain of this second void pull was worse than that of the first. *How could I let hope deceive me?*

"How about this," her grandfather said after a brief pause. "Forget everything that's happened so far. We're going to start the Ceremony off from the beginning. Let's all walk around and stretch a bit, then we'll begin, for real this time."

"Um—okay," Layauna replied meekly. *How can I forget being void?*

They did as he suggested. The puller drew his dyemoon back down beside him and stepped into it. The strips of color immediately unraveled, flew about him, and then cinched themselves tight around his body. In any other situation Layauna would have found this magical, but not right now. She left the balcony without saying a word and took a short walk through her favorite flower garden. When they all came back and got into position, Grandfather Eyan acted as if this were the first time she had faced the Magician Puller.

"My sweet granddaughter," he said, perfectly mimicking how he'd said it before, "you have trained long and hard and have finally arrived at this moment. I am certain a Color will be found in you today."

This time Layauna remained silent and did not give voice to her doubts. This seemed to please her grandfather, and a wide smile of approval lit up his face. "All right, Rollen, are you ready?"

"Yes, Eyan. Everything is in order. Let the Ceremony begin."

The puller held out his arms. His Nine Colors unfurled and went up into the sky, where they once again formed his dyemoon. Layauna, feeling a bit better, was happy she saw it this time. *It really is as remarkable as people say.* But the puller didn't give her any time to linger on his moon. In one quick motion he lowered the Staff of Light and pressed it against Layauna's heart. "This is your life, come what may."

The sensation went into her again—more frantic, this time—and journeyed through all the spaces around her heart. Then, in one sharp move that caused Layauna to jolt straight up, it shot down into her gut.

Again, the Magician Puller pulled with effort.

Again, when he pulled it away, there was no Color attached to the end of the staff.

And again, she was found utterly and completely void.

✳   ✳   ✳

After the third attempt, her grandfather thought it wise to change locations.

"Here's what we're going to do. Layauna, you go rest. Rollen, come with me." Grandfather Eyan gave the instructions, and—despite her inner protests and feelings of frustration—she obeyed.

How can he possibly expect me to rest? Layauna went to her bedroom and fell backward onto the fluffy comforter. As she started to sink into the soft bed, she stared up at the canopy of delicate lace fabric that draped down all around her. She couldn't imagine any Old World princess having a more luxurious place to rest. But right now, rest was completely impossible.

She squirmed around, unable to get comfortable on the bed. Even though a pleasant breeze blew in through the open window, she was considerably hot. Her mind raced wildly. She couldn't focus on anything other than feeling powerless, defenseless, and invaded. *And I have to go back! Why? Why can't it just stop?*

And that's when Blaze, her two-headed hell-dog, materialized right in front of her. When she saw him, she sat up and scrambled back against the headboard. He growled and bared his sharp teeth. The vibrations came from deep within his chest. He turned both heads and locked all four eyes on her.

Stay calm. Don't make any quick movements. The hell-dog stayed right where he was at the foot of her bed. He didn't move or do anything that indicated he would attack—other than growling and looking mean, but she was used to that. Layauna considered doing what the Master Magician had taught her: project some meat, or maybe the song her dad had sung to her. But as she stared back at those burning red eyes, she realized his anger wasn't directed at her.

But if he's not angry at me, what's he angry at? Then she smelled it again. That musty scent from earlier. And with it came a memory. She was little, and she had gone with her dad to visit her friend Mala, who had an actual dog. Layauna had loved playing with it. Later that day, as she and her dad were walking home in the rain, they met a man on the path who had another dog, which was soaking wet. This dog was mean, though, and when they got close, it started to growl. When they passed by, it leapt out and tried to attack Layauna.

It was a good thing Father was there. He had stepped between her and the dog and had kicked it until it went away. Her dad was badly bitten, but he said that was okay because it would have been much worse—even fatal!—if the dog had bitten her. He explained that he believed the vicious dog had tried to attack Layauna because her body held the scent of Mala's dog, the friendly one she'd been playing with earlier. These two dogs, he suggested, were probably enemies.

The memory was as clear as if it had happened that morning, even though she'd completely forgotten about it until now. *What if the same thing is happening with Blaze? Maybe I smell like something he really hates.*

The idea that Blaze wasn't angry at her brought her great comfort, and she felt all of her tension drain away. She noticed that Blaze also relaxed. He shut his mouth and lay down on the bed. Layauna thought about dissolving him, but she didn't have the strength. And he wasn't doing anything harmful anyway. *It's just a projection; projections can't . . . actually . . . hurt . . . people . . .*

She yawned and was soon fast asleep, dreaming about all of the delectable flavors her grandfather would project for their banquet meal that evening.

The dream lasted only a moment. All the delicious flavors faded away as she fell into a deep, hard sleep; the events of the morning had exhausted her. It took a servant loudly calling her name—while knocking on the door—to wake her.

As she rubbed the sleep out of her eyes, she saw that Blaze was still there, curled up, asleep on her bed. *I never thought I'd ever see him at peace like this.* The hell-dog wasn't nearly as scary when he was sleeping, but she was still afraid of him. She got up slowly and then quietly left the room, being careful not to startle him.

The servant said nothing as he led her to the tall, golden spire that stood at the far point of the estate. This structure looked out over the ocean and was the signature building—the monument people were bound to think of when speaking of Grandfather's illustrious property.

Layauna had never been allowed into the spire before, though she'd often been curious about what was at the top. *It must be more than just a good view,* she thought as she climbed the long flight of stone stairs. But when she reached the top floor, all she found was a large, vacant room.

Grandfather Eyan, the Magician Puller, and the two acolytes stood waiting for her side by side in the center of the room. They were surrounded and encapsulated by enormous, spotless windows that gave a clear view for miles in every direction. If the spire had been a lighthouse, this room would have contained the light.

"Isn't this is a much more inspiring place to reveal your Color, Dearling? I've had it cleared of my things so as to not obstruct your Color once it's pulled out. Here it will be free to shine out these windows for everyone to see."

No pressure, right? She took a deep breath and tried to clear her negative thoughts. *It's going to happen this time. It has to.*

She felt confident—or at least, as confident as she could when facing the very real possibility of another devastating rejection—and stood in front of the puller. After he created his dyemoon, he turned his blank, empty face toward her. She quivered, then held her breath as he placed the staff on her heart. "This is your life, come what may."

The now-familiar hunt for Color inside her began once again. This time, the jolt went through her neck and up into the back of her head, giving her an instant headache.

The Magician Puller drew his staff back slowly at first, and then gave a big tug. Layauna felt as if something inside her chest had snapped. It was a different feeling than the other times. *This can't be good.*

The puller sighed. Grandfather Eyan looked over at him, clearly irritated. "What happened?"

There was no reply.

"What happened? Did you lose it?"

"It broke free," the puller said at last.

"Then go back and get it," her grandfather said.

The Magician Puller placed the staff back on Layauna without any of the ceremony or formal words. In an instant, the sensation went straight back up into her head. He pulled more gently this time. Slowly and steadily, he tugged and tugged, determined to get it out of her. It felt like a thin, coiled rope was being drawn out. She could tell where it was: starting in her head, it moved down through her neck and into her chest. *Could this be it?*

He drew back the staff and she felt it come out—but there was nothing there. *Void. There's no doubt now. I'm void. How many times will I have to go through this before Grandfather accepts it?*

No one knew what to say after this. Even Grandfather Eyan—the great Yellow magician who had been so hopeful and positive—looked deflated. The room was silent for a long time, and everyone was uncertain what should be done next. A knock on the door brought them all back to reality.

"Go away. You know I'm not to be interrupted," her grandfather ordered.

The person knocked again.

"Go away!"

More knocking, and then a faint voice said something through the door. All Layauna could make out was "my apology" and "ruling elders."

"Marklemen, if that's you, come in."

Her grandfather's head of staff, Marklemen, pushed open the door and looked at them with wide eyes as he entered the room.

Whoa. Why did he come himself instead of sending a servant? Something important must be going on.

"My apologies, Magician Eyan, but—the ruling elders have just arrived."

"What!" Grandfather Eyan started to wobble. He twitched, and all the youth drained from his face. Moments before he had looked strong and healthy, but he now appeared twenty years older. "They're here, now?"

"Yes, they heard you were having a party and thought it would be—and I quote—'fun, yes, very good fun.'"

Grandfather stumbled over to the wall and stared out the window.

"What's happened?" Layauna asked. "Grandfather. Your face—it looks horrible."

"What? What's happened?"

"Magician Eyan, you . . . have lost your facial modifications," Marklemen answered.

Grandfather remained quiet for a short moment before righting himself. He stood up straight, cleared his throat, and said, "Thank you for alerting me. Go and tell them I will be right down." He then summoned the servant standing outside the door—the one who had brought Layauna to the tower—and said, "Find Agnes and have her meet me in the salon. I need to be redone. Go. Quickly."

Layauna kept her attention on her grandfather. *He hasn't regained control yet.* His right hand was trembling ever so slightly, and his forehead glinted with sweat. He was afraid—Layauna knew the look of fear—but she couldn't understand why. *Who are these ruling elders?* She'd never seen him react like this to anything. *Who can so easily strike terror in the heart of my grandfather?*

"Acolytes, go, both of you," the Magician Puller said. "This servant is feeling faint and is in need of sustenance." The two Dy'Mageio left at once.

After his attendants were gone, the puller asked Grandfather, "The ruling elders are actually here?" There was an unexpected measure of panic in his voice.

Could he be terrified, too? Although she knew better, Layauna had always felt that the pullers—all Dy'Mageio, in fact—weren't actually people. Now, after hearing fear in his voice, she wondered, *Maybe they really are individuals, just like us.*

Grandfather Eyan gave no response; his mind was somewhere else, and Layauna wondered if he had even heard the question.

"Eyan, what's going on? Are they really here?"

"Apparently." Her grandfather shook his head in what seemed to be an effort to clear the shock. Then his expression changed, and the fear in his eyes transformed into anger. "We need to finish this. Now!"

"I've done everything I'm capable of, Eyan. You know it's never a sure thing." He spoke in an ordinary voice. *He sounds like a common old man.*

"There are still places you haven't searched," Grandfather yelled. "Stop making excuses and search them!"

What's going on, Grandfather? She couldn't understand how he could bark commands at the Magician Puller like he would to one of his servants. She'd never heard of anyone who dared to treat Dy'Mageio like that.

"You know what they can do to you," Grandfather continued. "We don't have much time."

"You don't have to tell me that. I'm older than you are," the puller said.

"Well, then you'd better start acting like your life is on the line—because it is."

Grandfather. What are you saying? You're scaring me.

"All right, all right. I'll keep searching," the puller grumbled. "But you should have told me they were coming."

"I didn't know they were coming," her grandfather hissed through clenched teeth.

"They've been making an awful lot of unexpected appearances lately. I thought they were supposed to remain"—the Magician Puller paused—"discrete."

"Gather yourself. You know they've been taking a more active role ever since last year's fiasco."

"I don't like it, Eyan. I don't like it one bit. They were there, you know—in the elite box, on the first night of the Region 2 Color Ceremony—sitting on either side of Greydyn. I felt nauseous the entire night—what with them watching my every move." The Magician Puller couldn't stop talking now that he'd started. It was more than troubling to hear him grumble like this. "I felt them pressing down on me. It was like they wanted to drown me. It only lifted after I found Colors in those last two—and it's a good thing I did. A few weeks ago, they sent an ambassador—some aggravating poozer—to the Island of the First Watch, insisting that we find something in those two boys. I was made to lay in a golden visionarium so I could experience the horrors of what would happen to me if those boys were void. Things just keep getting worse, Eyan. How much longer do we have to submit to them?"

Who are these ruling elders? I didn't think anyone stood above Grandfather.

"Have you finished sniveling?" Grandfather asked with a tone of contempt. "I'm the one who has to go and greet them. They're probably already offended that I've taken this long." He turned to the door. "There is a Color in her. So figure out what's wrong and find it."

Layauna realized her limbs had gone numb. Her heart was racing. *What's going to happen to me now?*

The Longest Day

~Layauna~

Bobs: So, you're void again, huh, bud?
Toemer: Oh yeah. Apparently pullers get all fragdaggled when you dissolve their masks.
Bobs: Yeah, makes sense. Well, I'm void again, too.
Toemer: What? (Laughter) Bud! You're the most drenchous bloomer! (Loud laughter) No offense, bud.
Bobs: None taken. You know what really prunes my tree though? I guess you're not supposed to dissolve their robes. No one ever told me they don't wear any threadbare.
Toemer: (Laughter) There's always next year, bud.
Bobs: Yeah, I'm sure they'll have to find a Color in us. Someday.
—From the Grand Projection *Neckies and Nobodies*

Layauna felt anxious as she stood in the spire across from—and alone with—the Magician Puller. He didn't seem to even notice she was there. Her grandfather had left, and the faceless man just stood silently in the middle of the room, staring out at—what? *What's he doing?* Because he didn't have a face, she didn't have any idea how to interact with him. *How can I know what I'm supposed to do?* She understood for the first time how important faces were—and how creepy Dy'Mageio looked because they rejected them. *But Grandfather wouldn't leave me alone with this man if he thought I'd be unsafe.*

She wasn't sure if she should say something or remain silent.

He wasn't really a person she wanted to start a conversation with. He didn't even seem to be a person. But with the pressure mounting on both of them, she felt she had to say something. So she asked the only thing she could think: "Do I . . . I mean . . . do you believe there really is a Color inside me—somewhere—like Grandfather says?"

"I have no idea." He sounded annoyed, but Layauna found his blunt reply strangely comforting.

"Thank you for being honest with me."

"Don't thank me," he said with irritation. "Neither of us is going to be free to leave until I can find a way to convince the gods to produce a Color in you."

Convince the gods? Produce a Color?

Layauna wanted to understand what was really happening. She wanted to know why she was allowed to receive so many pulls. *This can't possibly be normal.* Now that she'd started, she wanted to ask so many questions, but she didn't dare speak any of them.

From what she understood, very few children stood before a puller in a private Ceremony like this. *I wonder . . . do they get multiple pulls, too?* By the way Grandfather was treating the Magician Puller, she figured not. *Why am I being given so many chances when most people get just one?*

She didn't like it, but she suspected she knew the answer. *It's because I'm the granddaughter of Eyan is-a Bolt.* Everywhere she went with her grandfather she saw how he received special treatment. She took a deep breath. *It's like he's a god to people.* But now he was demanding something no human—not even the Magician Puller—seemed to be able to give him. *Is it really possible to convince the gods to give someone a Color?*

Wait. Stop. This is crazy. There are no gods. Grandfather will just have to accept that I'm void.

The puller continued to stand in sullen silence. It seemed like he was doing absolutely nothing. *Is he praying or something?* After a number of moments, she decided to ask a question she didn't have an answer to. "What if there's nothing in me? Nothing's come out so far."

"That's not exactly true," the Magician Puller explained wearily. "No Color has come out, but every time I've cast the staff into you, it has hooked onto some expression."

"What do you mean?" Layauna asked. She had never heard this term before. "What's an expression?"

"The staff captures expressions. That's what it does. There are lots of them inside people, but the only ones that matter are the Nine Colors. All the others are vot."

Could that be true? I've never heard anything like this before. But I've never spoken with a Dy'Mageio before, either. "Is that what I've been feeling you pull out of me? Expressions?"

He nodded and said, "Most people describe it like a cord being pulled out of your soul—through your chest."

Layauna's eyes grew wide. "Yeah, that's exactly what it feels like." She paused to consider her next words before saying, "Are they really vot? Is there nothing good in them at all?"

The puller turned his creepy white blank face to her, and kept it there, unmoving, as if he was taking a good, long look at her. *Please stop. Or turn away. Please.*

"Do you want to know the truth—the real truth—about expressions?" he asked.

Uh, probably not, but . . . "Will it help?"

"It will, but only if you are willing to let me train you in how to please the gods. Maybe then they'll find you worthy of a Color."

Find me worthy? What does he mean by that? I'm a Bolt. And then the reality of her situation hit her. Here she was standing before the Magician Puller in her own private Color Ceremony. Yet, despite this grand honor, if she didn't produce a Color, she would be common. *I need to do everything possible,* she decided. So without hesitation she said, "I'm willing. I'll follow your instruction."

"Good. First, you must submit yourself and become a servant to the gods of Color."

Is he asking me to become Dy'Mageio? What's taking Grandfather so long?

He turned and faced the window for a few heartbeats before turning back to her. "Focus all your attention on the Nine Colors. Imagine each one of them. See them in your mind as clearly as you can. The goal is to push aside all of the other, Colorless expressions—just for this moment—in order to make space for the Color that is in you."

Layauna closed her eyes and concentrated. It had never been hard for her to imagine things, so it was not long before Colors were swirling through her mind. She hadn't been to an actual Color Ceremony for many years, but she had never forgotten the unique way each Color flowed into the air after it was pulled out of a person. She pictured Red falling and covering everything, Indigo shooting up into the heavens, and Violet wrapping around them. She marveled at the swirling stars and spinning galaxies moving within each of them.

"Good," the puller said. "Keep looking at all the stars."

Layauna opened her eyes. "How did you know I was imagining the stars?"

"I've spent my entire career watching children look at the stars that emerge from Color. Your grandfather is right. You have a Color in you. I saw it in the expression that was on your face just now."

The expression on my face?

"The expressions inside us shine out in the expressions that appear on our faces," he continued, as if reading her mind once again. "Haven't you ever wondered why mages of the same Color have so many similar physical traits that become more visible as they age?"

What's he talking about? "Uh, not really."

The Magician Puller sounded irritated. "All you need to know is that the Color gods are good and when one of them blesses someone, that person becomes more and more like them."

Does he really believe that? If so, that's disturbing. And if he's been trying to get me to fall in love with the Color gods or something, that didn't help at all.

"Now, next you need to sacrifice the other vot-filled expressions that are inside you."

Sacrifice?

The look on Layauna's face must have communicated her shock to the puller, who said, "Don't worry, I'm not asking you to do anything that will be harmful or painful. But you have an unusually high number of expressions inside you, and this is a problem. You need to get rid of as many of those as you can."

"But how? I don't even know what an expression really is."

"Not many people do. Some might think they're the same as the ribbons of Color, but they're not. I call them expressions because, like facial expressions, they reveal the things that exist inside of us. They are part of us—the broken, corruptible pieces of our selfish, lustful humanity—and, as such, we often find them precious. Dy'Mageio acolytes devote all their attention to catching and sacrificing them."

Grandfather, please come back soon. "I don't understand."

"This is in order to make room for Color, of course. If we desire to be holy we must be cleansed of them. It takes decades to become pure."

"Decades?" Layauna asked. "Then how can I do anything about it now?"

"There aren't any shortcuts, but there is one thing you can do that might help. I want you to close your eyes and look at the stars again."

She did.

"Which Color do you find yourself connecting to the most? Which seems the most pleasant to you?"

No one's ever asked me that before. There were so many Colors swirling through her mind. *How can I be expected to pick just one?* Even though they each had their own unique beauty, she decided she liked Green the most. She'd always believed that if her father had been a mage, he would have been Green, so that's what she picked.

"Now, I want you to sacrifice everything else except for Green. Take every big and little thing that is swirling around inside you, all your thoughts, all your feelings, all your desires, your dreams, your relationships, possessions, memories, everything. Take them and throw them away so that the only thing that remains—the only thing you care about and desire—is Green."

That's impossible. How could anyone do anything close to that? And why would they want to? He's asking me to sacrifice myself, my . . . face.

"Just picture Green," the puller said. "See it grow and spread into every part of you. Feel how alive, fresh, and newly born Green makes you. Nothing can stop it. It's flourishing, thriving, and covering over everything else inside you with life. Isn't it good? All of the gods are good. Why would you want to hold on to any other, worthless expressions? Throw them all away and make room for Green to grow."

Layauna tried to picture this. It felt like it would be no use, but then she got it. Green came alive for her. It lasted only a few heartbeats, but in this brief moment, everything else about her disappeared.

"Good. Good. You had it," the puller said. "She's ready. Let's try this again."

Shouldn't we wait for my grandfather to come back? She opened her eyes and was surprised to find Grandfather Eyan was already there, staring at the Magician Puller with a look of impatience.

They took their positions again, just as they had before.

Layauna felt better about this. *It's going to happen. I'm going to be a Green mage.*

But it didn't happen.

So they tried again.

And it didn't happen then either.

Nor did it the third time.

The Magician Puller went over everything with Layauna again. He instructed her to focus on Green. He described who Green was and how essential this god was for life and growth in the islands. Then he tried another time. Nothing.

He directed her to visualize the stars. Void pull.

He spoke encouraging words to her. Void pull.

He told her to stop touching her face. Void pull.

He commanded her to laugh. Void pull.

He went back and forth between saying one thing that fueled her pride and another that tore her down and made her want to cry. Void and void. He had her exercise until her heart rate was as high as she could get it. Void. He had her relax and bring her heart rate down. Void. He had her scream at the top of her lungs. Void. He had her curl up into a ball and imagine herself shrinking into nothingness. Void. Void. Void.

During this time, many memories came to her: brief flashes and fragments of things long forgotten. But the puller and her grandfather said these were of no value. All that mattered to them was Color.

Nothing worked. Several watches passed as the Magician Puller tried every trick, every strategy, every manipulation he knew. They were drained and battered. The puller leaned heavily on the staff; Layauna felt as if everything inside her had been ripped out. After all these pulls, she wondered, *How is there anything left in me?*

The acolytes came back several times, but the Magician Puller always had another task for them, so they were not present for the majority of the Ceremony. Grandfather Eyan also came and went throughout this time. There seemed to be a tremendous amount of work to be done with the ruling elders here, on top of all that was required to prepare the banquet. Projecting the right flavors onto the food was apparently time-consuming and delicate work. Layauna could see Grandfather was deeply torn between attending to her and to his preparations.

"Are you sure about Green?" her grandfather asked when he returned and found there was still no Color.

"I'm not sure about anything anymore." Layauna slumped to the ground. She'd never been so exhausted in all her life.

"Green is growth, harmony, and safety," the Magician Puller reminded wearily. "You said family—your family—is very important to you, and that Green makes you think about how everything is close together, like in a garden. You connect this to your desire to have a family."

Layauna nodded.

"Are you being honest?" Grandfather asked. "Are you being totally honest?"

Layauna nodded again. *Of course I am. I want this to be over with even more than you do.*

And that's when they heard it—the sound of laughter. It was faint at first, but unmistakable. Layauna couldn't help but be attracted to it. *I wish I were laughing—for real—right now.* She staggered to the window to search for the source. From her perch, high up in the spire, she scanned the entire estate without luck until—

There!

Directly below the spire, two men frolicked in and around her grandfather's wide, brightly tiled pool. They alternated between splashing each other and doing cannonballs into the water, and they appeared to be having a grand time.

Those must be some of Grandfather's friends—guests for the banquet. She longed to be set free from this tower and to be down there with them.

She was gradually able to make out the faint sound of their voices as they hooted and hollered back and forth. *What are they saying?* She scrunched up her face, trying to hear better, and managed to make out a few words: "You." "Man." "You." "Bud."

Then their voices grew louder. Soon she was able to make out exactly what they were saying. One started with "You, man." Then the second followed with "You, the bud!"

The two men repeated that same call and response several times.

"You, man."

"You, the bud!"

They laughed, splashed, climbed out of the pool, and jumped back in.

"You, man."

"You, the bud!"

"No. You, man!"

"No. You, big big bud!"

They didn't come any closer, but somehow their voices got louder and louder.

"Ha ha, you funny, Little Brother. I certain you biggest big big bud."

"I biggest bud. I too funny to go to meetings, must stay far away from First Watch."

"You come here to play instead."

"Yes, I come visit them here for big play for biggest big big bud."

When Layauna turned, she saw her grandfather was also looking out the window. His face had gone pale. *What's going on?* Layauna wondered.

"What are they doing?" the Magician Puller asked. "Eyan, tell me. What are they doing?"

Grandfather Eyan snapped out of his daze and responded, "Cannonballs, apparently."

"It's unnerving."

"You don't have to tell me."

Layauna didn't understand what could be so unsettling about two men playing in the pool. She liked that there would be a couple of adults at the banquet who were playful, who liked to have fun. She squinted and saw that neither one had a Color in his collar. *They're commoners. I bet they won't care that I'm also void.*

She liked them. But it was clear they were having a seriously negative effect on the two older men, who stepped away from the windows, and—to her dismay—redoubled their efforts to extract a Color from her.

*   *   *

After yet another failed attempt, Layauna—feeling worse about herself than she'd ever thought possible—became desperate enough to ask the thing she'd been thinking but knew wasn't wise to ask. "What if I just wear someone else's collar? Or take a Color from someone else and place it into mine?" She knew this was illegal—very, very illegal—*but isn't what they're doing to me now equally wrong?*

Asking this was a mistake. Her grandfather responded with utter disgust. Apparently, this was unthinkable. She received a lecture about the methods Dy'Mageio used to keep very careful track of every mage in O'Ceea. *But we have the Magician Puller here. Can't he do something?*

"Even if it were possible, Bolts aren't cheaters. If we were caught doing anything like that, it would destroy everything I've worked to achieve. Do you want the entire Bolt clan to lose face? How could you even consider asking something like that?"

All right. All right. Her face fell in shame. *I just want all this to stop.*

After a few more failed pulls, she noticed something peculiar about the funny voices from the two men in the pool, who were still calling back and forth. "You, man." "You, the bud!"

How can we hear them all the way up here—and through these windows? "Grandfather, are they—are those men projecting their voices up here for us to hear?"

"Yes," he answered as he paced around the room. He looked like he was in need of another makeover on his face.

"But why? I don't understand."

"It's not something for you to understand," the Magician Puller snapped. "Just focus on pleasing Green. This is your duty! If you just did it, everything would turn out fine."

His aggressive tone caused Layauna to step back in fear. *Is he blaming me for not having a Color? It's not like I can force myself to worship a god that I don't even believe exists!* The thought immediately triggered a feeling of anger, and she cried out without thinking, "What do you mean, my job? Isn't it your job to find Colors in people? I've been doing everything I can! I can't bear this anymore. You need to accept the truth. I'M VOID!"

"You'll stand for as many pulls as it takes to produce a Color!" the Magician Puller shouted back at her, and he abruptly placed the staff onto her heart. Once again, that awful thing started digging around inside her.

And then it found something. But it wasn't a Color—she somehow knew this. She closed her eyes as the puller pulled back on the staff. When this expression came out, she felt a burning sensation spread across the surface of her body.

Layauna closed her eyes. *Stop it!* She was seething. *Keep it under control. Keep yourself under control.* But then she heard the growling.

"Layauna," her grandfather said, sounding unhappy.

She opened her eyes and saw Blaze. The hell-dog stood facing them. *Oh no.* "Where did he come from?" The dog was looking back and forth between Layauna and her grandfather.

"It's nothing to be concerned about," the puller said. "It appeared after I pulled the staff away from you. Occasionally, unconscious projections can appear. Just ignore it." He began to lower the staff toward her again.

I'd like to see him try to ignore Blaze, she thought as she watched her hell-dog turn all four of his burning eyes on the Magician Puller. Both heads licked their lips and Blaze crouched down low. Layauna imagined that if the puller had a face, it would be filled with scorn and disdain.

Although she knew she should do something, she remained deathly still and quiet as the hell-dog stepped toward the man. One step. Two. Three. Blaze was right next to him. The puller tilted his head, and without warning, the beast lunged and tore into him.

The Magician Puller would have been devoured in an instant if Blaze had been a material being. But Layauna knew he was a projection, so she didn't expect it would affect the puller at all. Yet when the monster attacked, the man fell to the ground. It appeared that Blaze had knocked him over—but she knew he must have just been afraid and stumbled.

"Stop it!" the puller yelled while kicking and swatting at the hell-dog. He scrambled to get away, but Blaze wouldn't let him escape.

One of the hell-dog's heads sunk its teeth into the Magician Puller's face—or rather, the white projection that covered his face. The dog ripped the projected mask off the man, and exposed his true face.

"Get it off me! Get it away!" the Magician Puller screamed at the top of his lungs as Blaze lashed out with his claws.

Both Layauna and her grandfather thrust their hands forward and used all the Power they could muster to extinguish the beast. It started to work, but both of them were already exhausted; it took far longer than it should have for Blaze to be totally dissolved.

Then he was gone. It was over.

Layauna's heart raced. *What are they going to do to me now?*

The Magician Puller lay sprawled on the ground. Layauna looked at his face. Their eyes met. She quickly turned away, but in that short moment, she had seen the Magician Puller as he really was: a wrinkled old man with hollow eyes, sagging cheeks, a crooked nose, and lips so thin that they looked like one of the many creases on his face.

This well-weathered man remained on the floor for a long time, holding his arm tight to his body and rocking gently back and forth. He then dissolved the sleeve of his white shirt. There were three small, dark red indents on his skin.

What's going on? A projection couldn't have done that. Those must have been there before. But Layauna saw that the marks looked fresh. *He must have caused them with his own nails. There's no way that could be from Blaze.* The puller stared at the marks, and then his eyes shot up at her grandfather. "I can't do this anymore, Eyan. It's over."

Grandfather just stared back at him. He had been taking a long look at his face. *I wonder if he's ever seen it before.*

"What are you staring at?" the puller demanded.

Eyan lifted up his hand and a mirror appeared. "You seem to have lost something, my old friend. It's good to finally see you."

The puller's eyes went wide as he looked into the mirror. Then he whipped his eyes away.

"I think you should take a long look, Rollen," Grandfather Eyan said as he waved his hand in front of the puller, stretching out the mirror until it made an entire ring around him.

The Magician Puller was uncomfortably still as he looked at himself. "Am I really this old?"

"Yes, you are. You need a breakthrough to happen soon," Grandfather said. "Maybe Layauna will be able to help with that. Just look at the marks on your arm."

The puller shook his head and said, "No. I can't do this anymore. I'm too tired. I'm too old—I'm not going to make it."

"Nonsense. Stand up and find a Color in my granddaughter."

"It's over," the puller said as he stood up and dissolved the mirror. The white mask was back, and his face was no longer showing.

"No, it's not," Grandfather replied coolly.

"Stop! You just have to accept that she doesn't have anything of value to offer us. She's void. Maybe the gods have chosen to bless your younger grandchild instead."

"No, Rollen, she does have a Color. I know what it is. We've just seen it," Grandfather Eyan said, and he turned his eyes to Layauna. "You know what Color it is now—don't you?"

Yes. Layauna tried to swallow, but the emotion she felt stirring inside her made it difficult. *It's Crimson. I hate Crimson. I've always hated it. Crimson is the color of dried blood, the color of war, the color of hatred. Please, I don't want to be Crimson.*

"Go on. Say it," her grandfather insisted.

"Crimson," she breathed the word, then started to cry. "I'm Crimson."

"Of course you are, Dearling. See—I always knew you had a Color."

Why must it be this one?

There was a long silence. Layauna looked to her grandfather and had the sense that he was speaking to the Magician Puller via projections.

Finally, her grandfather spoke. "Rollen, are you ready?"

"Yes, Eyan. Everything is in order. Let the Ceremony begin."

The Magician Puller changed in an instant. *Wait, what's going on now?* Only a moment ago, he had been screaming on the floor like a terrified old man. Then he was filled with shame at the sight of his own face. Then he had refused to continue. But now, he once again felt like some distant and mysterious force of nature. *What did Grandfather say to him?*

Acting like this was the first time they had ever met—like nothing had just happened—he raised the staff, brought it down, and said, "This is your life, come what may."

As soon as the hard wood of the staff touched her, she felt invisible hands reach deep into her chest. They invaded every aspect of her very soul, digging aggressively for what the Magician Puller sought.

Layauna had come to hate this sensation; she ground her teeth together and waited for it to end. But as soon as she shut her eyes and tried to think of other things, a shot went straight into her heart and shocked her so much that it forced her eyes open.

The Magician Puller's muscles tensed, and her grandfather's eyes widened. She felt the ribbon—the thing she'd long hid—cling to the staff and burst out of her. The tower exploded with light.

Crimson light.

After he had pulled the ribbon out, the puller waved the staff back and forth in the air, and the Color twirled, swooped, and slashed around like a knife. Most Crimson ribbons had a few sections that were wider than others, but Layauna's was very narrow and thus appeared to be extra sharp. Inside the ribbon churned thousands of glowing constellations, spiraling galaxies, and sparks of burning light.

Grandfather's golden spire became a lighthouse at last. It ought to have been glorious, but Layauna didn't see it that way. She recoiled at the realization that this shade would now be bound around her neck for the rest of her life—for all to see. *I shouldn't be surprised. I'm filled with bloodthirsty monsters, after all.*

But—to her great surprise—the puller kept pulling. He took several steps back. The staff shook in his hands, and a deep, midnight-blue light entered the room. *Indigo? I have a second Color?* The deep Indigo ribbon unfurled from her and rippled straight up to the ceiling, where it shot back and forth as if eager to be free of her soul so it could begin toiling away at some vastly important work.

Layauna looked up as the two ribbons twirled through the room. The Indigo ribbon stayed as high up as possible, whereas the Crimson swooped and slashed in the air beneath it. She found the presence of Indigo deeply comforting. It was safe soaring up there, away from the unpredictable and cutting edge of Crimson. As she watched it, she felt as though she might perhaps be safe from the monsters in her life, if she worked hard enough. *And now that I have Color—two of them!—I can get into the Workshop and become a magician. Everything will get better then, just like Grandfather said.*

But the Magician Puller wasn't finished pulling; the staff continued to vibrate in his hands, and when he took yet another step back, there was a flash of Violet. This third ribbon glided out of Layauna with regal grace and began wrapping itself around her. Violet wasn't prone to shoot away like other Colors were, and hers stayed particularly close. She could easily see the starlight that now spiraled around her body like a vortex.

She'd heard rumors about how beautiful the stars were when seen up close, but rumors couldn't compare with what she now experienced. They didn't blur together; each star was distinct and completely unique. Each had a well-defined shape, a particular fire, and a specific feeling, as if it were alive. Each seemed like an individual—a character—rather than a nondescript particle of light.

Layauna turned her head and tried to take in all three of her Colors, all at once. She marveled at the spectacle that swirled around her. From inside her Violet cocoon, she saw the deep, dark Crimson ribbon swoop close to—but never pierce—both the Violet and Indigo. All three danced with their own rhythms, and the light of them made her think of a sea at night, glowing with brilliant waves of molten sapphire, amethyst, and garnet. It was a breathtaking sight. From the safety she now felt inside Violet, she stared right at the Crimson ribbon, and it no longer looked so horrible.

"Big happy!" a cry came from outside. "Three Color!"

"We celebration big," the echoing cry said. "Three Color. Very special!"

I'm a Three Color Mage. I'm a Three Color Mage! I have Color! An incredible surge of pride welled up in Layauna. *I'm not void!*

"Waahooooooooooooooooooooo!" she shouted at the top of her lungs.

The Ruling Elders

~Layauna~

Tav may have created the Old World, but we will create the new.
—Unknown source; recently found painted on communication
towers in all five regions. IIRP Investigation File 717CC4-211

Everything was a blur after the three Colors were pulled from her. Layauna watched with awe and wonder as the Magician Puller caught the Crimson, Indigo, and Violet ribbons with the end of his staff and sealed them into the black collar held by Grandfather Eyan.

When the Colors were contained, she turned her focus to her grandfather's face. It had regained the youthful appearance of health that she was used to seeing. *He must be really happy—his expression changed so fast.*

Grandfather congratulated her with a smile and a wink, and then he darted away to resume his work in the kitchen. The Magician Puller turned to follow after him without saying a single word to Layauna.

"I'm so sorry about my wicked projection," she called to him as he was leaving, but the puller did nothing to indicate that he heard her. "I hope you understand—I didn't mean you any harm. That monster just comes out of me sometimes when I get upset . . . I'm really sorry. I hope you can stay and enjoy the banquet. Do you know how incredible my grandfather's projections taste?"

The Magician Puller still said nothing—he just disappeared down the stairs. Layauna let out a long sigh. Then she smiled, realizing he was probably leaving and she wouldn't have to worry about seeing him at the banquet. She looked out the window and watched him walk away.

She had mixed feelings. A part of her was glad that Blaze had come out to defend her. *Still, I can't allow an attack like that to ever happen again. I'm a mage now. I must work harder to keep my monsters under control.*

She glanced back out the window and noticed that the puller was walking far out of his way to avoid the swimming pool where her grandfather's funny guests were still playing. She felt a sudden and strong urge to go down and meet them. *They were so excited about my Colors.* She ran down the stairs and over to the pool area, but by the time she got there, they were gone. *Oh well. I'll just have to wait until I see them at the party.*

Exhilarated over her discovered Colors, and not caring that she would get her threadbare soaked, she ran straight to the pool. She was so happy, she did a cannonball herself and squealed, "I the bud!" with a laugh.

It felt good and refreshing to be in the water, so she stayed in and swam, splashed, and dove. After playing in the pool for quite some time, she climbed out and sprawled on a reclining chair in the warm sun, soaking in the heat. For the first time, she could actually picture this being her life. *And what a life it would be.*

Layauna could have lingered there for several watches, laying in the sun and relaxing, but she was troubled by the memory of her grandfather's face when Marklemen came in and gave him the message about the ruling elders. *Who are they? And how could they be so powerful that they're able to strike terror into Grandfather?*

And the Magician Puller? I've never heard of Dy'Mageio being intimidated by anyone.

Layauna quickly decided that if these ruling elders were going to be at her party tonight, she needed to know more about them. She got up and immediately tracked down several servants she knew and trusted, trying to get some information. But all anyone would tell her was that the ruling elders were important—very rich and very powerful—and that all the servants had been given two strict orders: serve them in every way and leave them alone.

"So if you see them, keep your distance," one of the servants instructed her.

That's so odd. How can a servant be expected to serve while also keeping away? That makes no sense.

Her curiosity about the ruling elders grew stronger as the day passed, but it wasn't until the top of the Indigo watch that an idea came to her. *If they want privacy and space, I bet they'll be in Grandfather's Cyan bungalow.* She had reasoned a long time ago that if every building was named after a watch of the day, as Grandfather joked, then the bungalow would be named after Cyan. It was a building reserved for Grandfather Eyan's most special guests. *The ruling elders must certainly be there.*

Layauna snuck away from the mansion. The banquet celebration wasn't scheduled to start until the top of the Violet watch, so she knew she had plenty of time.

The bungalow was a small, stand-alone house built on the edge of a cliff overlooking the ocean. She had spent a lot of time there—it was one of her favorite places on the estate—and she knew it well. There was a small utility room around back that had a door to the outside. It made the perfect place for eavesdropping. She'd used it for this very purpose before, many years ago, to spy on her brother while they were playing Discover, Discern, Destroy.

This sure is a day for old, forgotten memories, Layauna thought as she slipped quietly through a hedge and crept up to the door of the utility room. Among the many unexpected flashes from her life that had come to her when she stood before the puller, one memory stood out: the moment her father sailed away from them. *The last time I saw him. That was so long ago.*

The memory had come to her after one of her void pulls, and it struck her hard. She could remember every little detail of that day—every detail except for the most important one. *My dad's face.* She couldn't picture it, which caused her to wonder. *Would I even recognize him if I saw him today? Tonight?*

She opened the door carefully and settled herself inside. Sure enough, she could easily hear voices coming from within the bungalow. Her heart raced as she listened to the conversation.

". . . don't see how any of this is serving our ultimate goal." *Grandfather's voice.* She'd recognize it anywhere. But for some reason, there was a strange warble to it. *He sounds upset.* She felt unsettled as she listened. She leaned in to see if she could tell who he was talking to.

"It be decided"—there was a faint pause before the statement was completed—"many years ago."

"I didn't decide it. None of the Eight did. How could they?"

"No, Master Greydyn agree—"

"You should say 'has agreed,'" Grandfather Eyan interrupted.

"Yes. Thank you. Master Greydyn has agreed."

"Of course he has—he's at the end of his career. What other choice does he have? But I do know he doesn't want his Devos Rektor epics—and his reputation—to be sucked down a whirlpool just so you can have an entire Grand Projection devoted exclusively to preaching the message of 'Color, no Color.' It's going to get destroyed by the Opinionators. Propaganda like that always does. How does that advance our goals?"

"Your granddaughter almost have no Color today." There was a short pause. "What happen if she have no Color?"

"She has three Colors; it just took a bit more effort to find them."

Yeah. That's an understatement.

"She one of the two eight eight, yes?" Another pause. "We have see her, she have Power, no?"

"It's 'we have seen her,'" Grandfather corrected. "And of course she has Power. I knew she was one of the elect three years ago."

"What happen if she have no Color today?" Pause. "How she allowed in Workshop?"

Why does he keep pausing before finishing his sentences? Whoever he was, he spoke in a very strange way. She had heard someone speak like this before. Where? . . . Of course, the two men in the pool. Why is Grandfather speaking to one of them in the bungalow? Maybe they're waiting for the ruling elders to arrive. Unless . . . Could those two be the ruling elders? It seemed unlikely. How could anyone be afraid of them? If they are the ruling elders, though, it would explain why Grandfather and the Magician Puller were so agitated in the spire. But, why? They were so playful and funny. She couldn't imagine any ruling elders acting that childishly.

"I know, I know," Grandfather said. "Society's old belief in the Color gods needs to change. Everyone needs an equal chance to get into the Workshop. I agree with you on that."

"Do you agree? Really?" Pause. "You mage-magician. You give up much if when everyone same-same."

"The islands can be flooded again for all I care. There will be tremendous social upheaval once the lies about Color are exposed—it doesn't matter! I just want the Workshop to achieve our objective—before I'm cut off!"

What's going on? What lies about Color? What's this thing he wants so much?

"We agree." The man paused yet again. "We float in same boat, yes?" Pause. "Ha ha. But this no time be so funny, Little Brother." Pause. "Yes. This serious meeting."

Little Brother? Up until now, she thought her grandfather had been talking with only one man. *If there are two brothers, and they sound exactly the same, then they must be the two from the pool. They looked an awful lot alike.*

"I'm not young like you." Her grandfather sounded strained. "Old men don't have the luxury of time. If I contribute anything to our efforts—other than being one of the elect—it's urgency. We don't have time for any of this, and the Workshop can't afford another fiasco like last year with King King."

"King King very popular in Region 6." He paused. "Give time. People come to grow on it."

"The expression is 'it will grow on people,' and no, it won't. It was an atrocity."

Yeah. It was the most drenchous Grand Projection ever.

"Ah, 'it will grow on people.' Yes, very good. A Green expression, yes? This language not mother tongue for us." Another pause. "Yes. We speak old language better—language of Old World. What everyone speak before Flood."

Layauna was starting to understand. Whenever there was a pause, one brother stopped talking and the other started. *What strange men.*

"Look." Grandfather sounded beyond frustrated. "I have many guests arriving."

"Yes, go. Party very special."

"Celebration for Layauna. She special."

"Hear me on this," he continued, as if they hadn't just spoken. "If you go ahead with your plans for this year's Devos Rektor Grand Projection, it will be a major disaster for the

Workshop, and an even bigger one for Greydyn. It will be the end of his career."

"The old ways have not found us every two eight eight elect."

"All person must be eligible."

Grandfather Eyan sighed. "Yes, fine, but how does another failed Grand Projection help us with that?"

"Ah. There be old, wise expression. 'Always thing must die . . .'"

"'. . . before better thing be born.'"

Silence followed and—even though Layauna was hiding in a different room—she could feel Grandfather's tension.

"What are you saying?" His voice was slow and grave.

"Old expression—"

"Yes, I know. I wrote that line," Grandfather barked at them.

"You write *Love Sinks*? It very true. 'Always thing must die.' Very quotable."

"Yes, very good line, that why we quote *Love Sinks*. 'Before better thing be born.' Very true."

"What are you talking about?" Grandfather Eyan growled. Layauna could tell he had lost his patience. "Are you trying to say you want the Workshop to die?"

What!? Layauna couldn't fathom this. *How could anyone want that?*

"You are one who say we must be urgency."

"Old way no longer fast enough."

"But . . . but . . ." Grandfather stammered, suddenly sounding confused.

"You don't care!" one of them commanded.

"You only care about our dream."

Layauna heard nothing for a long moment. It was so quiet, she felt she had to slow her breathing in case they could hear her through the wall.

"You're right," her grandfather said at last. "It is the only way."

What!? Grandfather, what are you saying!?

"You sacrifice everything for ultimate goal!"

"Yes, Eyan. Everything be sacrificed."

"Of course. Everything depends on it," Grandfather said. Something in his voice had changed. He sounded exhausted.

"Good. Now go—serve your delicacies."

"Welcome guests with gladness. Go now!"

Without another word, her grandfather left. Layauna heard the door open, then close; his footsteps faded away from her.

∗   ∗   ∗

Layauna didn't dare move. Her plan was to wait until the two elders left; if she tried to move now, they'd certainly hear her.

She waited a long time, but the two brothers did not speak. *I need to go—the servants are going to be searching for me!* She was starting to wonder if the men were actually still there when she heard something. One of them spoke. At least, it sounded like them, but the way they spoke was altogether different.

"Everything is coming together nicely, yes?"

"I cannot imagine it going any better."

"Do you have any more concerns with Eyan? He should be secure for a long time."

"I have no more concerns. After we broke in on him—there at the end—he fell back in line."

They're speaking without that strange accent. I thought they were foreigners. What's going on?

"And Layauna? I feel good about her."

"I have a good feeling as well. I like her."

They know about me and still like me?

"It sounded like she had to endure so much to find her Colors."

"It must have been brutal."

"I can't imagine. She must be very strong."

"Stronger than even Eyan knows."

Hearing them talk about her like this stirred up several contradictory feelings. Her heart swelled with pride, her gut churned with distrust, and a heavy, numb peacefulness flooded her mind.

"It proves our point, Little Brother. What if the Magician Puller could not manage to find her Colors?"

"She would not be allowed into the Magician's Workshop."

"Layauna could not be a magician. That would make her very sad."

"Would it make me very sad?"

"Yes, because the real Workshop would never reject her."

"Nu:Kinrei would accept her, Color, no Color."

What? Why would Nu:Kinrei care about me?

"This is why the rules must be changed."

"Yes, all who have talent must be trained."

"Layauna is incredibly talented. She could become one of the Eight."

"She may be one of the Eight one day. I'm certain."

Could I really become one of the Eight? The idea thrilled her. Over her three years of training, she had developed a strong desire to make her grandfather proud. *Becoming a Third Magnitude would certainly do that.*

"She is one of the elect?"

"She is. She will be one of the chosen. I'm certain."

I'll be one of the chosen. I'll be one of the Eight. Layauna felt herself relaxing. If she hadn't been crammed in a utility closet, it would have been easy to slip away into a blissful sleep.

"Ah, yes. We all need her to become great."

"We also need Kai to become great."

That's true. Kai needs to become great also.

"Do we?"

At this Layauna twitched. *Kai? Who's Kai?* She didn't know anyone with that name. *What was she thinking?*

"Kai is such a nice young man. Everything depends on him."

He sounds like such a nice young man.

"Kai really is such a delightful young man."

He really is such a delightful young man.

"He is going to be a powerful magician someday."

He certainly is.

"I hope Layauna can meet him."

"He is also one of the elect. Kai and Layauna would be perfect for each other."

Kai and I really would be perfect for each other.

"She know our voice now."

"She be our delight."

Layauna felt a wave of amusement. She could listen to these two voices forever. *They really are delightful.*

"Very good, Little Brother. You make big success."

"Yes, big cannonball."

"Ha ha! There you go. You very funny."

"Joke go very easy to me."

For some reason, the two ruling elders resumed the broken, foreign way of speaking that they had used when she first overheard them.

What strange, fun men. I can't wait to work with them.

"Now, come. It time we go."

"Yes, go. Our work here now done."

✳   ✳   ✳

Layauna sat in the utility room. She was unaware of how cramped her body had become. Her legs and arms were twisted in an unnatural position and her neck was kinked to the left. She didn't realize how uncomfortable she was until the sound of a door slamming woke her from her amused stupor.

What watch is it? How long have I been in here? She was about to climb out, but then she decided she should wait a bit in case they came back. She listened carefully. Once she was certain the two men had gone, she pushed open the door and left the bungalow.

As she walked back to the mansion, almost everything she had overheard slipped out of her mind. She tried to hang on to it, but the memory felt like water slipping through her fingers. The one thing that didn't fade was the thought of this mysterious young mage named Kai.

Who is this person who will be a powerful magician someday? Could he be as strong as I am? Layauna felt her cheeks start to burn. She had never had a boyfriend, and the thought of it both thrilled and alarmed her. *I have three Colors now, and tonight I'll get my collar and legally be a young woman. I wonder if that means Grandfather will let me go on dates.*

She thought about what having a boyfriend would be like and tried to imagine how Kai looked. She was in a good mood, not really paying attention to time anymore. But as soon as she got close to the mansion, a servant found her. Everyone was in a panic over her whereabouts; it was time for the banquet to begin.

The servants rushed around her and frantically made sure she was looking her best. A new dress was projected on her, she was made to smell like roses in bloom, and shimmers of Glory were woven into her long black hair. When they were satisfied with her appearance, the servants ushered her through one of the breezeways and straight to the banquet.

She stepped through the door. What she saw took her by complete and utter surprise.

The banquet hall was filled with people, and as soon as she appeared, projections of every size, shape, smell, sound, and variety exploded out of them. She had expected something like this. What she did not expect—at all!—was who the people were.

Her mom and brother stood beside the table of honor, and next to them were Layauna's two best friends. *Whoa! I haven't seen them in three years!*

And they weren't the only familiar faces. There were the Quake girls, whom she used to play with at the beach when they were all just little kids, as well some of her old neighbors, her favorite school teacher, all of her trainers, the captain of Grandfather's yacht—the one who always made her laugh—and, most unexpectedly, her childhood friend, Mala is-a Moss. Layauna had seen her only sporadically after Mala's mom remarried and they'd moved far away to a different region. *Oh wow! She's a mage now, too!* Layauna realized when she caught sight of the Red collar around her friend's neck. *Maybe we can spend more time together again!*

She saw a myriad of other faces she knew and loved. It was incredible! *And all of them are casting out their projections for me.* Layauna was overwhelmed by the wonder of it. For celebratory moments like this, all people—those with Color and those without—were free to make any projections they wanted, with no limits or laws to restrict their creativity. So her friends and family created their projections without fear, knowing there were security guards on hand who would be able to fix any problems that might come up.

She looked around the room in a daze. All these people were from her life. All these projections were for her. She'd expected this banquet to be for the people from her grandfather's social circle, but instead . . . *He did this all for me?*

Layauna looked at her grandfather, who stood in the center of the room, laughing heartily at the four golden birds that had landed on his arms and were singing to him. *Yes. He really did do all this for me.* A rush of love swelled inside her. *He wasn't stressing out all day to make sure he would look good in front of his friends. He worked so hard because he didn't want me to be embarrassed in front of mine.* The thought caused her heart to melt toward him. *All this time, he was worried for me! I have the best grandfather in all the islands!*

She released all of the tension that had been building up in her shoulders and soaked up all of the projected praise, which was being poured out for her. After all the years of horror and hard work, a reward had finally come.

Not a single worry pressed on her the entire evening. Her mother didn't expect anything from her, and Sorgan was actually fun to be around. And as much as she loved the gift of voice cubes she'd received back at Nosy's, it was far better to have her friends beside her, in person, to talk and laugh with.

Layauna couldn't believe her eyes when the food was brought out. It was a feast worthy of the Master Magician himself, and there wasn't a single piece of namra root to be found anywhere. She was amazed. Finally, she was able to experience all the spectacular flavors that had made her grandfather famous and—best of all—she could share them with the people she cared about the most. It was the celebration of a lifetime. Layauna reveled in the presence of her loved ones as she thought, *I'm going to receive my collar soon—I'll not be a child anymore. I'll be a young woman.*

After the guests had eaten so much that they could hardly move, her grandfather stood up and cleared his throat. Layauna knew what this meant, so she stood up, too, and moved to his side.

As was the tradition for those from Region 4, the banquet was capped by the presentation of the collar. One of the servants brought it over on a black velvet cushion, where it shone like a wild fire. Her grandfather picked it up, held it in the air for all to see, and said, "Few children have worked as diligently as my beautiful granddaughter to arrive at a moment like this. For three years, she has done everything she has been instructed to do. She has proven to be a most exceptional student. Here, in my hand, is the reward of her labor. Layauna, Dearling, my precious granddaughter, it is my great honor to be the one to present it to you—"

"Excuse me, Grandfather," Layauna said quickly, "Is it all right if I say something first?"

"Of course. This is your evening," Grandfather Evan said.

"What is it?"

"There's something I've been wanting to say to you, but I've been waiting for the right time." She was nervous, but she knew she had to say this. "A few years ago all of us—Mom, Sorgan, you, and I—were playing the story game. But the character I projected got out of control and bit the head off the character you projected. Do you remember that?"

Grandfather laughed and said, "I remember it like it was yesterday. That was the moment I knew you were someone to keep a close eye on."

"But . . . it was something I've felt really bad about—ever since it happened."

"That's all right, Dearling. It was just a game. They were merely projections."

"I know, but—I have to confess. I was angry . . . at you." It felt good to say this out loud. It felt right. "I'm not sure why I was angry. Maybe it was because I didn't feel like playing that game, but most likely it was because of that nasty namra root you insisted was so good for us to eat." When she said this, everyone laughed.

"I think my anger is what caused my projection to attack yours," she continued. "But I don't feel angry anymore, so I wanted to—in front of everyone I care about—officially apologize for what happened and tell you that you are the best grandfather in all the islands."

Grandfather did not say anything for a long moment. Layauna saw by the way his eyes started to tear up that he was overcome with emotion. "See—look at her," he finally said. "Admitting your mistakes in public takes courage. I've long known my granddaughter has what it takes to become a great magician, and here she is, proving it. Darling, you've done the right thing, and in doing so you have just moved one step closer to the Workshop."

Layauna breathed in deeply. "Thank you for not giving up on me," she said, thinking of how she had given up on herself by repeatedly calling herself void just a few watches ago.

"Of course. How could I give up on my own granddaughter?" He turned and addressed the crowd. "Hasn't she done an amazing job?"

Everyone shot out colorful streamers until the air was filled.

"I've only been able to get this far because you've believed in me," Layauna insisted.

"A grandfather can only do so much, but everything began to change when you finally embraced the tremendous legacy the Bolt clan offered to you."

She smiled. "Yes, well . . . someone once told me that 'great things happen after someone takes on a better name.'"

"You've always been a Bolt. And now, you are a young woman—it's time I present you with your collar."

The audience grew quiet. Her grandfather, the great magician, lifted the collar up in the air with both of his hands.

"I present to you all—Layauna is-a Bolt! O'Cea's newest Crimson-Indigo-Violet mage."

As he fastened her collar around her neck, her friends and family burst out with sounds of praise and filled the room with stars, projected in her three Colors.

"Now it's time to celebrate!" Grandfather shouted, and the room exploded with music. From that moment on, the party was a wild frenzy. All the tables and chairs were cleared away, and everyone started to dance and play amongst the cacophonic menagerie of projections that they cast into the space around them.

Layauna and her friends delighted in the freedom to make projections with one another, and the banquet hall burst with life. Vibrant balls of color shot across the room and splattered against every solid object that obstructed their path. Projections of bouncing fruit collided with glittering jewels that floated through the air. Silly-looking creatures and creatures acting silly roamed every part of the room. Pleasant sounds chimed together. Wonderful smells redolent of good memories filled the air. But best of all, Grandfather Eyan stayed for the entire celebration, casting the most delicious, mouth-watering tastes of chocolate banana pudding, fruit-flavored ice cream, and cookie-crumble-cake into the mouths of the crowd while dancing with joy as if he were a young man.

The celebration went on for the next two nightmarks with no sign of slowing. Layauna's excitement also seemed to know no end; she spun joyfully in the center of the room, dancing and laughing freely like never before, surrounded by all the people she loved most.

She had made it.

She had three Colors.

It was only a matter of time before she walked through the doors of the Magician's Workshop and took her place among the great.

END OF VOLUME TWO

The story of *The Magician's Workshop*
continues in Volume Three

Visit www.occea.com for notifications
about upcoming releases.

Oh and before you go—can we ask you for a favor?

Would you be kind enough to write a review? Your thoughts and feedback are most appreciated. They help the sales of the book and give us something most valuable: a connection to you, our readers. We wrote this for you to enjoy, and now that you've read all of Volume One and Two, we're eager to hear your thoughts. Thanks in advance. It means a lot to us.

—*J.R. Fehr and Christopher Hansen*

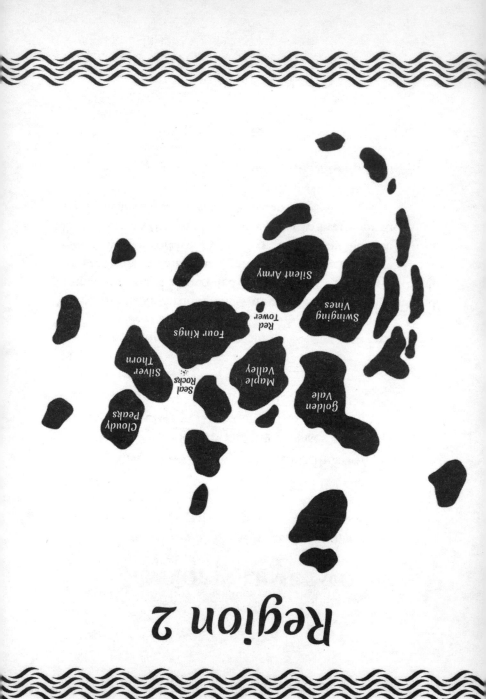

Silent Army

Swinging Vines

Red Tower

Four Kings

Silver Thorn

Seal Rocks

Maple Valley

Golden Vale

Cloudy Peaks

Region 2

Character Pronunciation Guide

Point of View Characters:

Layauna is-a Bolt (lay-ON-ah), Island of the Oak Falls
Aaro is-a Tree (ARE-oh), Island of the Cloudy Peaks
Jaremon is-a Twig (JARE-ah-mon), Island of the Golden Vale
Kai is-a Shield (KAI), Island of the Four Kings
Kaso is-a Blank (CASS-oh), Island of the Sunny Rock
Talia is-a Leaf (TAL-ee-ah), Island of the Four Kings
Weston is-a Wave (WEST-uhn), Island of the Four Kings
Kalaya is-a Cloud (kah-LAY-yah), Island of the Golden Vale
Jade is-a Shield (JADE), Island of the Four Kings

Other Characters:

Agatha was-a Cloud (AE-guh-thuh), Kalaya's grandmother
Bankfort is-a Blank (BANK-fort), a poozer
Cale is-a Cloud (Kael), Kalaya's father
Coby is-a Blank (CO-be), Kaso's younger brother
Carlay is-a Leaf (CAR-lay), a timekeeper
Daganok is-a Whoosh (DAH-gah-knock), Kiranik's twin
Declarious is-a Shield (de-CLAIRE-ee-ous), Kai's mother
Devos Rektor (DEH-vous WRECK-tore), the Lord of Chaos
Drungo is-a Ray (DRUHN-go), mighty happy
Eyan is-a Bolt (EE-yen), Layauna's grandfather.
Flint was-a Shield (FLINT), Kai's father
Forcemore is-a Blank (FORCE-more), a poozer.
Forecastle is-a Wave (FORE-castle), a ship builder
Greydyn is-a Ring (GREY-din), the Master Magician
Gunthor is-a Wheel (GUN-thor), a tester
Igar is-a Moon (EE-gar), the announcer
Kiranik is-a Whoosh (KEER-ah-nick), Daganok's twin
Luge is-a Stone (LUGE), a bud
Limmick is-a Wave (LIM-ick), Snap's father
Malroy is-a Shield (MAL-roy), Kai's grandfather

Markus is-a Shield (MAR-kuss), Captain of the Island Patrol
Olan is-a Twig (OH-lawn), Jaremon's rival
Quint is-a Blank (QUINT), a poozer
Rieta is-a Leaf (RYE-ee-tah), a tower mage
Rumingo is-a Spark (RUM-ing-go), a trainer
Snap is-a Wave (SNAP), a bud
Sorgan is-a Wind (SORE-gan), Layauna's brother
Treau is-a Blank (TRUE), a poozer
Waelyn is-a Wick (WAY-lyn), a tester

Christopher Hansen

Since he was a child, Chris's favorite Color has been Orange. He was attracted to its vividness, its excitement, and the zest of life that it awoke in him. For years he was fond of wearing bright orange shirts and britches. For a few short—and utterly terrific—months he had his hair dyed electric green. When he wore his orange clothes with his green hair, people said he looked like a skinny pumpkin. He thought this was a fab-u-lous description. There was even a season in his life when most of the food he ate was orange: cheddar cheese, cheese puffs, Cheetos, goldfish crackers, Cheez-its, and nachos. Eventually he began to eat healthier, and these days you can even see him eating a carrot now and again.

J.R. Fehr

J.R. Fehr has always liked Blue. But when he was a kid, he'd often hear people say that blue was their favorite. This bothered him. He thought it was drench for everyone to like the same color. Worse still, because there are so many shades of blue, it was difficult to know what anyone really meant by it. Dark? Light? Sky? Royal? Baby? This color, he found, was just too broad. But one day, while conducting research on the Nine Colors for *The Magician's Workshop*, he discovered Cyan. This was a shade of blue that he had never really noticed before. After identifying it, he became enamored with the peaceful feelings it awoke in him. He now sees this hidden Color everywhere. It glows in the ocean, flashes after sunset, dances in the Northern Lights, and sparkles in frozen waterfalls. Cyan, all along, was his favorite Color. He just didn't know how to see it before.